Jack Ryan, Jr., finds himself on the front lines
of cyber war and in the eye of a killer storm
in the latest novel in Tom Clancy's
*New York Times* bestselling series.

## TOM CLANCY POINT OF CONTACT

A former U.S. senator and defense contractor needs
someone to look over the books of Dalfan Technologies,
a Singapore company—quickly. He turns to Jack Ryan,
Jr., and Paul Brown, two employees of one of the best
financial analysis firms in the country, which also happens to be the cover for The Campus, a top secret American intelligence agency.

Brown has no idea that Jack works for The Campus.
Jack has no idea that the awkward accountant has been
tasked with uploading a cyberwarfare program into the
highly secure Dalfan Technologies mainframe on behalf
of the CIA. On the verge of mission success, Brown discovers a game within the game, and the people who now
want to kill him are as deadly as the cyclone bearing
down on the island nation. Together Ryan and Brown
race to escape both the dangerous storm and a team of
trained assassins in order to prevent a global catastrophe,
even at the cost of their own lives.

**PRAISE FOR *TOM CLANCY DUTY AND HONOR***

"A fun, fast read that is rich in Jack Ryan universe history."
—The Real Book Spy

*continued . . .*

# TITLES BY TOM CLANCY

## FICTION

TOM CLANCY

# POINT OF CONTACT

MIKE MADEN

BERKLEY
New York

BERKLEY
An imprint of Penguin Random House LLC
375 Hudson Street, New York, New York 10014

Copyright © 2017 by The Estate of Thomas L. Clancy, Jr.; Rubicon, Inc.; Jack Ryan
Enterprises, Ltd.; and Jack Ryan Limited Partnership
Penguin Random House supports copyright. Copyright fuels creativity, encourages
diverse voices, promotes free speech, and creates a vibrant culture. Thank you for buying
an authorized edition of this book and for complying with copyright laws by not
reproducing, scanning, or distributing any part of it in any form without permission.
You are supporting writers and allowing Penguin Random House to continue to
publish books for every reader.

BERKLEY is a registered trademark and the B colophon
is a trademark of Penguin Random House LLC.

ISBN: 9780451491473

G. P. Putnam's Sons hardcover edition / June 2017
Berkley premium edition / April 2018
Berkley export edition / April 2018

Printed in the United States of America
1   3   5   7   9   10   8   6   4   2

Cover photograph © Guan Jiangchi / Shutterstock
Cover design by Eric Fuentecilla

TOM CLANCY

# POINT OF
# CONTACT

# PRINCIPAL CHARACTERS

## UNITED STATES GOVERNMENT

*Jack Ryan:* President of the United States
*Scott Adler:* Secretary of state
*Mary Pat Foley:* Director of national intelligence
*Robert Burgess:* Secretary of defense
*Jay Canfield:* Director of the Central Intelligence Agency
*Arnold Van Damm:* President Ryan's chief of staff

## THE CAMPUS

*Gerry Hendley:* Director of The Campus and Hendley Associates
*John Clark:* Director of operations
*Domingo "Ding" Chavez:* Senior operations officer
*Dominic "Dom" Caruso:* Operations officer
*Jack Ryan, Jr.:* Operations officer / senior analyst
*Gavin Biery:* Director of information technology

*Adara Sherman:* Operations officer

*Bartosz "Midas" Jankowski:* Operations officer

## OTHER CHARACTERS

*Paul Brown:* Forensic accountant, Hendley Associates

*Weston Rhodes:* Ex–U.S. senator; board member, Marin Aerospace

*Dr. Gordon Fairchild:* Chief executive officer, Dalfan Technologies

*Lian Fairchild:* Head of security, Dalfan Technologies (Gordon Fairchild's daughter)

*Yong Fairchild:* Chief financial officer, Dalfan Technologies (Gordon Fairchild's son)

*Choi Ha-guk:* Chairman, Democratic People's Republic of Korea (DPRK)

*Ri Kwan-ju:* Deputy, General Administrative Services Directorate, DPRK

*Tervel Zvezdev:* Former member, Bulgarian Committee for State Security (CSS)

## THE NORTH SEA
## ALBUSKJELL OILFIELD, NORWAY
## LATITUDE 56° NORTH, LONGITUDE 3° EAST

Freeze or drown.

He wasn't sure which one would come first. It didn't really matter. Either way, Jack Ryan, Jr., knew he was going to die in the next two minutes.

The F470 Zodiac rubber raiding craft pounded through the chopping waves beneath a storm-shrouded moon. Jack clutched the safety ropes in both fists to keep from getting thrown overboard. So did Adara Sherman, seated in front of him. She was getting it worse than he was. Every bounce threw more spray in their faces. Jack's NVGs were spattered with ice. He couldn't risk wiping off the night-vision lenses while he was riding this bucking bronco. But a half-mile ahead he could still barely make out the oil rig, lights off, its hulking frame a black shadow above the surging sea. That was fine by Jack. The darkness shielded their approach.

Jack's teeth chattered and his mind clouded in the numbing cold. The freezing North Sea wind seemed to slice right through his five-millimeter wetsuit, and the stinging sleet felt like a broken beer bottle being dragged across his exposed skin.

Despite their misery, Bartosz "Midas" Jankowski gunned the engine full throttle, his goggled eyes fixed on his GPS. They were supposed to run quiet, but they got off late. At least the howling wind swept away most of the noise from the baffled fifty-five-horsepower outboard motor in back.

The high winds also meant a helicopter landing was out of the question, and fast-roping out of it—Jack's favorite new skill—even more so. All three of them were getting beat to hell, and time wasn't their friend. If they didn't reach the oil platform ladder in the next two minutes, they would fail the mission.

*Assuming we survive for the next two minutes,* Jack reminded himself.

And then there were the gunmen on the oil rig to deal with. But right now, armed killers seemed like the least of their problems.

As if on cue, a rogue wave swelled beneath the speeding craft, lifting the port side out of the water. Jack had shoved the toes of his boots through the safety rope along the rubber deck for purchase but felt himself pitching over the side anyway. Midas grabbed the drag handle of Jack's vest with a sure hand at the last second, saving him from a headlong dive into the angry black sea.

Jack glanced to his right at the other Zodiac just a few yards away. In the green haze of his iced NVGs, he saw

Dom Caruso flash him a quick "Okay?" with his gloved thumb. Jack thumbed him back. No time for chitchat. Ding Chavez drove Dom's boat, his eyes fixed on the GPS locator.

The five special operators of The Campus were a close-knit team, the tip of the spear of the private "off-the-books" intelligence agency known only to President Ryan and a select few of his closest advisers. They were a small organization, but they punched hard—and far above their weight. This mission was proof of that. They did the jobs the CIA or other government intelligence services couldn't do. Or wouldn't.

Tonight was no exception.

Jack ran through the schematics of the oil rig platform in his mind again, particularly the control room and machine shop—his two targets. Gavin Biery's webmaster magic had come through again. If it weren't for him, they'd be going in totally blind.

Gavin's intel brief confirmed seven hostages and six Green Army Faction eco-terrorists, armed and trained. But intel on a hostage-rescue operation like this was always sketchy. John Clark's warning echoed in his head. "Stay frosty out there. You don't know what you don't know."

*True that.*

"It's time," Ding whispered in everyone's comms.

"Roger that," Midas confirmed.

Jack watched Ding's boat veer off at a sharp angle, its bulletproof Armorflate rubber skin shredding water into the turn. The small drilling platform had two access ladders. Jack's boat would take the front; Ding and Dom would scramble up the back. On training runs with the Norwegian MJK (Marinejegerkommandoen) this past week, the weather had been cold but calm and they'd been able to get the timing down perfectly. But out here tonight on a raging North Sea, everything was up for grabs.

The mission had two goals: save the hostages and kill or capture the tangos. The Green Army Faction threatened not only to kill the captured oil workers but also to blow the rig, causing another catastrophic oil-spill disaster like Deepwater Horizon, if their ransom demands weren't met. American policy had always been to ignore ransom demands from terrorists. Meeting them inevitably led to more terror. Any student of history knew that. But some governments and corporations apparently didn't read history.

Those were the people Green Army Faction targeted. Profitably.

But in this case, intel from an informant indicated that the group on the rig had no intention of surrendering after the money transfer. In their sick minds, they planned on "saving the earth" by poisoning the sea in order to fuel more public outrage at the oil industry. Killing the oil rig workers was a sacred bonus, like ISIS butchering captive infidels.

The decommissioned oil rig stood in an abandoned field dead center in the North Sea and in international waters. The Texas wildcatting team was developing new fracking-style technology to revive dead underwater wells. The GAF got wind of it and struck.

When it became clear that the hostages would be

killed, the company's desperate security chief called his friend John Clark, hoping Clark could mobilize some of his old Rainbow Six connections. But with only a four-hour window remaining, there weren't any options.

Except one.

By sheer coincidence, John Clark had arranged for The Campus operators to train with MJK operators for exactly this kind of mission just two hours away. The Norwegian government wouldn't allow the MJK to aid in the assault, but Clark called in a few chits and arranged for the *Møvik*—a Swedish-built CB90-class fast-assault craft—to drop the team off. After that, they were on their own.

The hastily devised plan was that both Campus teams would scale the ladders at the same time and make a simultaneous assault on three of the four buildings on the rig, taking out bad guys along the way. Jack's team would take the front of the platform. Midas and Adara would go for the crew's quarters, where the hostages were probably being kept, while Jack cleared the control room, after which he'd drive toward the machine shop. On the back side of the rig, Ding's two-man team would first assault the drilling and process modules, where the explosives were undoubtedly positioned. After clearing them, they would support the assault on the crew's quarters or machine shop as needed. Each team would drive toward the center of the facility, herding any surviving GAF fighters into the middle and forcing them to surrender—or die.

At least, that was the plan.

They all agreed that clear and constant communication was key to their success. No telling what the real situation was on the rig or the precise number of either terrorists or hostages.

Their biggest challenge tonight beyond the hellish weather was their limited firepower. Each team member carried the same two suppressed weapons systems: short-barreled SIG Sauer MPX submachine guns and SIG Sauer P229 pistols, both in nine-millimeter. They couldn't use larger calibers for fear of overpenetration, and explosives or even flash-bang grenades were out of the question in the highly flammable environment. Brains, brawn, and steady hands were their only force multipliers. Given the makeup of the team, Jack figured that was good enough.

The bow of the Zodiac dipped as Midas throttled down. That told Jack they were close. The rolling swells kept the boat rocking violently, but not so badly that Jack couldn't raise his hands to finally clear his NVGs. The boat was just a few yards away from the platform ladder now. He could barely make out the other Zodiac on the far side of the rig. The sleet turned to thick flakes of snow, reducing the value of the NVGs to nearly zero now.

"Ten seconds," Midas whispered in the comms.

"Rog . . . Go . . . op," Ding replied.

"Say . . ." Midas whispered.

No reply.

"What's wrong?" Jack spoke into his comms.

He saw Midas's lips move but didn't hear anything in his earpiece.

*Comms down!*

As soon as Jack thought it, Midas was already switching to hand signals.

This was going to be an old-school op for sure.

The Zodiac slowed further. Adara reached down for the rope and its hard rubber grapple as Midas cut the engine. The boat was lifted by another high wave and crashed violently into one of the thick steel piers supporting the platform, but the inflated rubber bounced harmlessly off in the direction of the nearby ladder. Adara tossed the grapple and hit a ladder rung on the first try, then she and Jack pulled hard on the rope until the Zodiac was close enough to tie off and secure.

The problem now was the other boat. It was critical that both teams scale the ladders at the same time. Jack pulled his tactical light and flashed it twice in Ding's direction. A moment later someone flashed back.

Jack signaled "good to go" to Midas and Adara. They both acknowledged and Adara took the lead, lifting one boot from the heaving deck to the top of the gunwale, then timing her next step onto the ladder with her other boot to the rising swell, pulling herself up with one hand as the boat lifted to its apogee, all in a singular motion of effortless grace. She instantly began the arduous hundred-foot climb.

Jack watched her in the flickering green glow of his goggles. From down here in the rocking boat it looked like Adara was climbing up into the blackened portal of a rusted steel hell.

The boat pitched down again as Midas took position next. At the top of the next swell Midas stepped up. He landed a heavy boot on a rung and pulled his broad frame up by his strong arms, then began his swift, wordless climb.

The boat plummeted down again, and Jack's stomach with it, hitting the bottom of the swell so hard that Jack's knees nearly buckled. The waves were getting worse.

Jack tugged on his MPX to verify the sling was still snug as he stood back up and planted his right boot on the gunwale. A moment later he felt the massive surge beneath him and the boat rocketed upward, but the hull crashed hard against the steel ladder just as Jack stepped off, throwing him forward. He barely managed to grab an icy rung with both gloved hands as his knees slammed against the sharp steel, boots dangling in midair. A moment later his feet found a rung and he was secure. His eyes tracked the fleeing swell as it crashed against another steel pylon.

His heart raced. *That was close.*

Jack paused just long enough to take a deep breath and gather his wits.

Big mistake.

Out of the corner of his eye he saw another rogue wave suddenly breaking over him in a white-capped fury.

He braced himself against the ladder just as the wave hit.

Too late.

**2**

All Jack could do was hold on grab-ass tight. The wave hit him like a great gray bull, smashing the side of his helmeted face against the ladder's steel, but somehow he hung on.

A second passed and the furious gray monster sped away into the forbidding dark.

Jack couldn't believe his luck. He didn't wait for the next one.

He untangled himself as quickly as he could and began the ascent, spitting and coughing up briny seawater through his mouth and nose. He scrambled as fast as he dared on the frozen steel, driven upward by John Clark's raspy voice ringing in his brain: "Shit happens in threes." Comms going down and a big-ass rogue wave counted for two. He didn't want to think about what the third might be.

The first few soaking-wet steps were easy, but his left foot slipped badly on the next ice-coated rung. Once again his heart raced, but his fast reflexes secured him tightly to the ladder. His mind was clearer now—running from death had that effect on a man's brain—and in a moment he was in his stride, carefully but swiftly alternating hands and feet in the dangerous ascent.

He climbed several rungs before glancing up to locate the rest of his team. They were already near the top and scrambling fast, unaware of his near-death experience. The gunshot to Adara's leg in Chicago last year clearly hadn't slowed her down.

Gaining confidence in his stride, Jack picked up the climbing tempo. The adrenaline was fueling him now, which helped cut the cold, even though he was drenched, and the exertion was warming him up despite the blasting snow. The burning in his thighs was a good sign that he was still alive. Even the seawater still stinging his sinuses helped clear his mind.

So far, so good.

He slowed as he entered the guardrail cage near the top of the ladder, expecting Adara's gloved hand in the open hole to signal him to hold. The plan was for the three of them to rally at the entrance, then split up and assault their respective targets some ninety feet apart. He popped his head up quickly to scan the platform.

Adara and Midas were gone. *What the hell?*

So much for the plan.

Jack cleared the hole and the guardrails and assumed a crouching position on the steel-grated deck, designed to keep seawater from accumulating. Most of the snow fell through, so there were no clear boot prints for Jack to follow. He glanced to his left, where the crew's quarters were located. He didn't see either Midas or Adara, but according to the plan that's where they were headed. The schematics indicated that the entrance door was around the corner from where he was, so if the two of them were positioning there, he wouldn't be able to see them anyway.

Jack checked his watch. If the other team was in place, they'd hit their door in the next thirty seconds.

Time to get to work.

Jack racked the charging handle of his MPX. The terrorists would all be inside in weather like this. Of course they'd be. He smiled to himself. *What moron would be outside in this shit?* The snow fell heavier now in the fierce wind—near-blizzard conditions. Jack brushed away the ice crusting on the back of his gloves.

He tried his comms again but still got no reply. Even if Adara and Midas were squatting here next to him, they couldn't talk to one another—in this wind they'd have to shout, and even if they could hear one another they'd risk giving their positions away.

Jack watched the seconds tick by. He was grateful for the long, tedious hours of training he'd spent over the last week on a platform not unlike this one, especially now that he was finally here in the freezing dark, getting hammered by gale-force winds and with time slipping away. He checked his watch again.

*Go!*

He ran in a low squat past a steel storage crate and rounded the corner when something near the deck caught his eye. "Head on a swivel!" Ding had shouted at him time after time in training reps. It saved his ass again.

Jack froze in place, the toe of his boot just short of a line of snow.

A tripwire.

It stretched across the steel grating, heavy flakes perching on it like fat pigeons roosting on a power line.

Jack knelt low and lit up the tac light on his weapon, following the tripwire to its terminus—an MRUD, a Yugoslavian knockoff of a Claymore mine.

*Tricky bastards.*

Gavin's intel brief didn't mention mines, but Clark said to be ready for anything. Maybe these Green Army Fucks deployed a jammer to screw with their comms, too. But now Jack wondered, *Are the tangos just covering their perimeter, or are they setting us up for something worse?*

Jack stepped carefully over the tripwire, his eyes keenly alert for more of them in the green glow of his NVGs and the falling snow. He saw none as he reached his position to the right side of the outward-opening steel door.

According to the dated schematics, the square control-room building he leaned against was thirty feet by thirty feet—identical to the other three structures on the old platform. Jack was entering on the east wall. On the far west wall was another door, leading to the crew's quarters. On the north wall was a door to the machine shop. That was his goal.

*If I survive the control room,* he reminded himself.

Inside the control room there were no interior walls. All of the control panels, desks, and workstations were along the exterior walls. Once he was inside, there was nowhere to hide.

Jack checked his watch again. Ten seconds to go. He laid a gloved hand on the doorknob and turned it gently. Unlocked. *Good.*

Gunshots rang out on the far end of the platform. Sounded like AK-47s. That meant Ding and Dom were in it. But they weren't shooting AKs. He didn't hear return fire. Maybe the sound of their suppressed guns wouldn't make it to him in this wind.

Jack felt the blood rush. His friends were in trouble. Suddenly he wasn't cold at all. *Time to kick some ass.*

Jack pushed the door open and quickly drew back, pressing against the corrugated steel wall, certain the terrorists would fire at the open doorway.

They didn't.

Jack glanced in for one second and jerked back. He'd seen nothing in his NVGs except the exit door on the north side of the room, slightly open. He was grateful for the advantage the low-light tech gave him.

More loud gunshots blasted around the platform. A few muffled bursts as well. He needed to move his ass.

He dashed low and fast through the doorway—

*BAM!*

Light stabbed his eyes like daggers.

His wide-open pupils in the NVGs turned the light in the overhead lamps into photon shrapnel. Jack hit the deck and rolled just as gunfire broke out from the open north door. He raised his weapon blind, pulled the trigger, and sprayed full auto in the direction of the noise, but as soon as his magazine emptied, the GAF shooter stopped.

Jack jumped to his feet, yanking off the goggles and rubbing his blinded eyes as he bolted for the north wall. By the time he slammed into the wall near the door, his vision had mostly cleared. He wondered if it was a motion sensor or a fast hand that had tripped the room lights. Guess it didn't really matter.

A quick check of his body confirmed he wasn't hit. He wasn't sure why not. The linoleum floor near where he had dropped was shredded.

All Jack could think was *Shit comes in threes*. And that was number three.

But his gut told him that three wasn't the limit.

He loaded a fresh mag and charged his weapon.

Jack knew the north door opened to a short open deck that led to the machine shop. Another outward-opening door would be waiting for him.

So would the shitbird that just took a potshot at him.

And maybe his friends.

He heard more gunfire far away. Could be his team was still in the fight. Or the tangos were killing the hostages.

Without comms, he couldn't know.

No time to lose.

Jack knelt low and did the head-bob thing again. Nobody on the short open deck, and the door on the far end of it was shut.

They knew he was coming. All they had to do was kick open that far door and open up on him. He'd be trapped on the deck with the rails pinning him in—unless he decided to leap over the side into the roiling blue abyss.

"Seven breaths," he told himself. A line from the *Hagakure*.

He ran like hell.

His heavy boots clanged on the steel grates. He kept his eyes focused on the shut door, waiting for it to open.

It didn't.

He slammed into the machine shop wall with a thud. They already knew he was coming. No point in dancing around in the freezing dark.

He wished he had a flash-bang. But he didn't. Just his guts. That had to be good enough. His team was counting on him. So were the hostages.

Jack ran through the room schematic again. Thirty by thirty. Six rooms—stalls, really, only two walls each. Two-by-fours and corrugated steel. Tools and machines in each, he assumed—lathes, welding tanks, whatever.

Which one would the shooter be in?

Jack yanked the door open but stayed out of the doorway. He felt the big-caliber slugs slam into the wall above his head. Glanced up. Saw the jagged steel petals flower a foot above.

That meant the shooter was probably in the northwest corner. A lousy shot—or scared to death.

Or wanting him to think so.

He had to do something to distract the shooter. He reached his MPX around the door frame and fired a short burst, aiming high against the far back wall to avoid hitting a hostage or one of his team if they were close by. He fired another burst, then dashed through the door, diving into the first stall on the left. He slid into a tall mechanic's tool chest.

A woman screamed on the other side of the room.

A short burst of gunfire rang in the distance.

*Damn!* Jack glanced up. A blunt-nosed drilling hammer hung from a peg on the far wall. He dashed over and grabbed it.

"This is gonna hurt!" he shouted as he tossed the hammer like a hand grenade. It bounced and skidded across the steel-grated floor, landing near the last stall on the left, where he figured the tango was located. He hoped the bastard would think it was a flash-bang and cover up.

At least, that was the plan.

Before the hammer finished bouncing and skidding, Jack launched out of his stall and rolled into the second one on the other wall, his weapon pointed at the northwest corner.

Sighted in the center of his scope was a bearded fighter and a short-barreled AKS-74U—almost like a machine pistol. Jack wanted to waste him, but he was hiding behind two platform technicians in oil-stained coveralls. Both women. One brunette, the other a stunning blonde. Even from here he could see the blonde's blue eyes. The bearded man held the two women by their collars in one fist, half choking them. His other hand held the weapon, pointed at their heads.

"Drop your weapon!" Jack shouted.

"I kill them both!"

The red dot on Jack's gunsight centered for a second on the man's face. Jack's finger twitched, but he didn't pull. The first ROE on any op was to save the hostages if at all possible. Putting a slug in this puke was secondary. It wasn't worth the risk. The bastard was scared. Maybe Jack could still talk him down.

In that moment of hesitation the terrorist shifted his position and hid again behind the women. Too late, even if Jack wanted to shoot.

"Drop your weapon!" Jack shouted again.

*"Fick dich, Kapitalist!"*

Jack held up a hand. "Don't be stupid. Drop your weapon. I'll guarantee your safety." Jack didn't budge. He prayed the psycho would expose himself again.

Instead, the terrorist walked the two women forward out of the stall and toward Jack, keeping them in front of him like a human shield, and worked his way toward the steel exit door on the east wall leading toward the wellhead.

Jack stutter-stepped left and right to keep from being an easy target, but he was out in the open—why didn't this guy just shoot him? He kept his weapon trained on the killer, hoping for a clear body shot. If the man escaped, he might take out his friends and blow the rig. But if Jack took the wrong shot, he'd kill the hostages.

The bearded terrorist reached the door. His gun hand searched for the knob, but his eyes stayed fixed on Jack. "Don't even think about it!"

"No, man, we're cool."

The door opened slightly and the Green Army fighter

backed into it—then suddenly thrust the two women forward and slammed the door behind him.

The women ran toward Jack, shouting and crying.

Jack raced for the exit door, but the two women grabbed him and wrapped their arms around him. "Thank you! Thank you!"

"Get back! Please!"

Jack grabbed them both by the waist and shoved them firmly but gently away from the door for their protection. "Are you hurt?"

Both women shook their heads. "No, no. We're okay. Thank you!"

Jack heard two gunshots ring out from the other side of the shut door.

"Wait here!"

The women nodded, compliant, stepping back toward the far wall.

Jack raised his weapon high and approached the door.

"Jack! You in there?" It was Ding's voice on the other side of the door.

*Thank God.* Jack sighed with relief. "Yeah. It's me. Jack." He dropped his weapon to his side.

"All clear?"

"All clear!"

The door swung open. Ding stepped through, a wide grin on his face. Dom was right behind him.

"Where are the others?" Ding asked, as Dom's smile broke into a horrified grimace.

A pistol shot cracked behind Jack. The bullet's overpressure brushed the side of his face, but the slug hit

Dom in the chest. In the blink of an eye another shot cracked and put a bullet in the wall near Ding.

Jack whipped around, raising his weapon to shoot the brunette with the pistol, but it was the grinning blonde who caught his eye as she thrust the tip of an eight-inch knife blade into his gut.

## 3

The tip of the heavy black KA-BAR Tanto blade crashed into one of the ceramic-composite body-armor plates on Jack's vest, dulling the blow. The blade slipped across the plate but didn't penetrate. The force of the strike pushed him back a few inches, stunning him for a moment.

In a heartbeat, the blond terrorist drew back her arm to launch another knife thrust at Jack's exposed face, but her neck exploded in a cloud of arterial spray as three muffled shots rang out, spattering hot blood on Jack's skin. The blonde spun to the ground in a heap like a broken puppet.

Jack's adrenaline-fueled brain slowed the action down to a crawl even as his reflexes accelerated. His eye caught the brunette falling to the deck at the same time as her comrade, two red stains flowering on her chest, pistol clattering to the steel deck.

Adara dashed over to Jack, the barrel of her MPX still

smoking. She ripped the balaclava off her head to get a better view. Her short blond hair was matted with sweat. She touched his chest where the knife had struck. The fabric was torn, exposing the ceramic plate. "You hurt?"

"No—check Dom." Jack feared the worst. His cousin was one of his best friends.

But Adara hadn't waited for Jack's suggestion, and at "No" she sped over to Dom, seated on the floor and leaning against the corrugated wall. Ding had already yanked open Dom's armor vest when Adara pushed him aside and dropped to her knees. The former combat Navy corpsman had patched up wounded Marines in Afghanistan. She'd seen the worst and expected more of the same as she reached for Dom's wound, but she knew she could deal with it.

"Damn! That hurt!" Dom said through gritted teeth.

Adara examined his left pectoral where the slug hit. A huge red welt the shape of the armor plate that saved his life was forming on his skin. "That's gonna bruise ugly, but you'll live, cowboy." Adara fought back a flood of emotion. On the combat field they were teammates, not lovers. She pushed it all back inside for later. There was still a job to do. She stood.

"Anybody hurt?" Adara asked.

"I think we're all good," Ding said. The shortest man in the room spoke with the authority of a trusted leader. Years of service in the infantry, Rainbow, and the CIA had earned him the hard-won respect of everybody at The Campus, especially John Clark.

Midas nodded at the dead blonde on the deck, a nearly headless corpse. "I think she's gonna need a Band-Aid."

"Good shot, by the way. You saved my life," Jack said.

"I was aiming for her head. But you're welcome," Midas said, clapping Jack on the shoulder as he loaded a wad of chaw in his bearded jaw. Adara had put two rounds into the brunette, who was trying to kill her boyfriend.

"I want a fast sitrep, people. Where are we?" Ding asked.

"Nine tangos dead, including these two," Midas said. He didn't need to say that their intel had been wrong.

"Four surviving hostages in the crew's quarters. One lightly wounded, patched and stable," Adara said. "The other three are fine, just shook up."

Ding frowned. "What about the three that didn't make it?"

"Dead before we got there," she said. "Bastards cut their throats." She dragged a finger across her own to emphasize the point.

Ding turned around. "Dom?"

"A simple detonator. Deactivated. A couple of bricks of C-4 are still in place in the drilling compartment, but they're inert."

"I found a tripwire out front, connected to a Claymore knockoff," Jack said. "There might be more. Everybody needs to keep their eyes open. We should do a check and keep the civilians locked down until we get an all-clear."

"Good idea," Ding said as he stepped over to the two corpses. He knelt down, studying them.

In the silence, Jack heard the howling wind outside. Loose sheet metal rattled, chains and pulleys clanged.

Satisfied, Ding stood and turned around. "All in all, a good job, people. We saved lives and ended bad ones and somehow managed to not get our asses blown up in the process. We'll debrief when we get back to base."

"What's the plan for tonight?" Midas asked. The ex–Delta recce colonel was used to being in charge, but like all great leaders, he knew how to follow orders, too, and Ding was running this op.

"Storm's too bad to transport civvies, especially down the ladders, so we'll bunk here tonight," Ding said. "Midas, grab your tac light and head out to the platform and signal the Norwegians that our comms are down and that we're bunking here tonight with four surviving hostages. Ask them to come back when the storm breaks."

"Roger that," Midas said. "What else do you need from me?"

"I hate not having comms. See if you can find the jammer these assholes deployed. And check to see if the rig has some kind of communications unit."

"On it," Midas said. He turned on his heel and headed for the exit door.

"Adara, you head back to the hostages and do what you can for them to make them comfortable. Like Jack said, keep them locked in until we give the all-clear. Apprise them of the situation, that they're safe and that we can't leave the platform until the storm passes, probably tomorrow morning. You need anything else from us?"

Adara tapped her med kit. "I'm good to go." She headed for the door near Dom, still seated, lightly brushing his broad shoulder with her hand as she passed, hoping no one else caught the gesture.

"Dom, when you're up to speed, I want you to secure that C-4. Grab one of us if you need help."

Dom stood, grimacing. "I'm on my way." He stretched out some kinks as he headed for the drilling room.

"Jack, you and I will do the booby-trap search first and clear those. Then we'll search the Green Army people for pocket litter and any other intel we can find on them, then grab fingerprints and DNA samples for the Langley crew to sort out and catalog."

"And then we toss 'em?"

Ding nodded. "They're chum, as far as I'm concerned. It's not like this is a crime scene that needs to get processed." In Ding's mind, what The Campus did here tonight was righteous. It just wasn't *entirely* legal. They had to cover their tracks.

Jack's father, an ex-Marine, had instilled in him a deep respect for the honored fallen, but in this case he couldn't agree more with Ding. The terrorists had almost killed him and his team. These were cold-blooded fanatics who butchered innocent civilians. They'd lost the right to be treated with respect, either in life or in death.

"You good?" Ding asked. He laid a hand on the taller man's arm. Jack nodded, his mind elsewhere.

"Yeah, just processing."

"Nothing else?"

Jack couldn't lie to Ding. He respected him too much for that. "Can't help but feel I screwed up tonight."

"I get it. We'll talk later. For now, we've got work to do."

"Roger that."

_____

Jack vomited again, but nothing came out. The long rolling ocean swells and steady bouncing of the CB90 fast-attack craft made him seasick, but the sickeningly sweet smell from the chemical toilet he was hunched over made things even worse. It was going to be a helluva long ride from the oil rig to the Norwegian coast if he had to stare into this crapper the whole way.

A loud knock rattled the bathroom door.

"You all right in there?" It was Ding.

Jack spat and wiped away a long string of drool. "Freaking fantastic."

"Sounded like you were choking a moose."

Jack climbed to his unsteady feet. "Be right out."

He splashed cold water on his sweaty face, rinsed his mouth out, and toweled off. When he yanked the door open, Ding was waiting for him in the cramped hallway.

"You look like hell."

"I just blew a plate of poached salmon," Jack said. "But thanks." The thumping deck beneath his feet and the close warm air made his head spin again.

"Let's go topside, get you some fresh air."

"Roger that."


The ship's movement on deck was more violent than below, but the cold, fresh morning air and the freezing spray against Jack's face did the trick and his nausea subsided. He held the rail tight and watched the far horizon, almost as dark as evening with the cloud cover and polar night at this latitude. Ding stood behind him to avoid getting hit by any water—he didn't suffer motion sickness of any kind.

Jack ran through the night's events one more time, step by step. He was honest enough to know where his performance was up to grade and humble enough to know when he was luckier than good, especially on this op. The rescued hostages were grateful and in good spirits and would soon be examined by the medical staff at Haakonsvern Naval Base. But Adara was a terrific combat medic, and she'd already treated the minor flesh wound one hostage had sustained.

Clark had called them to offer his congratulations. The CEO of the wildcatting company was thrilled, as were the families of the survivors. By any measure they had overcome extreme conditions and perilous odds and won the day.

So why did he still feel like shit?

"Feeling better now?" Ding asked. He had to shout over the roar of the big twin V8 diesel engines powering the thundering Kamewa hydrojets.

"You have no idea."

"Then why does your face look like you just swallowed an ashtray?"

"I screwed the pooch, Ding. You know I did."

"Why? Because you hesitated?"

"Dom got shot, you could've been shot—and I had a combat knife shoved into my gut."

"Nobody got hurt."

"In spite of me, not because of me."

"At least you own it. That's what's important."

"If I hadn't hesitated, if I had reacted faster, maybe I could've prevented all of it."

"Was it the knife that froze you?"

"No. At least I don't think so. It was the girl. Both women, really. I saw their coveralls and I saw the oil stains, and I 'knew' they were hostages." He didn't have to remind Ding that when they examined the women's bodies, they discovered that the dark oil stains were actually the dried blood from the hostages they had slaughtered with the same knife used on Jack.

"From what you told me, they played their parts to perfection. They obviously planned that stunt from the beginning in case they ever got cornered."

"Well, it worked pretty damn good, didn't it?"

"So what lesson did you learn from this?"

"Always shoot the blonde, I guess."

Ding laughed. "Don't let Adara hear you say that. She'll kick your ass."

Jack nodded, smiling. Adara was a CrossFit monster. She was stronger than most men and knew how to throw a punch.

"I just don't want to ever let the team down like that again, no matter what."

"You won't, if you keep pushing yourself."

"That's the plan. I just hope it's good enough."

"We all make mistakes. None of us is perfect, but we can always get better."

"Thanks, Ding."

"The day I stop trying to improve is the day I walk. You better do the same."

"I'll keep pushing. You know that."

"But there's still one lesson from all of this I need you to drill into *here*." Ding stabbed Jack's chest with his finger. "Never forget that you never know about people. *Never*. You feel me?"

"Yeah, I feel you."

"Good. Now let's head back down to the galley for some hot coffee. I'm freezing my personality off up here."

"You go ahead. I'm fine right where I am."

"Suit yourself. We should be docking in an hour." Ding clapped Jack on the back and headed below deck.

Jack turned back to the rail and faced the horizon, his arms crossed against the chill. He was trying to let Ding's words sink in, but his mind drifted back to the night's events, walking through them step by step, replaying the mistakes one by one, the feeling that he should've done better washing over him like a cresting wave. It hurt like hell, but it was the only way he knew how to prep for the next mission, whatever it might be.

# 4

## USS *BENFOLD* (DDG-65)
## 20 MILES OFF THE COAST OF SINPO, NORTH KOREA

Commander Holly Symonds stood on the bridge, a pair of high-powered Fujinon binoculars wedged against her eyes. Her executive officer was below deck in the Combat Information Center, monitoring this morning's missile launch on the vast array of radar and tracking displays. She was on comms with him and kept fully apprised. Symonds preferred the early-morning sunlight and the sting of the stiff breeze gusting over the slate-gray water to the darkly lit, air-conditioned CIC and the electrical hum of its glowing LED displays.

In a real combat situation she would be down there directing tactical operations, but this was a routine test flight by the North Koreans. Not that anything the North Koreans ever did was routine. Clearly they had gone out of their way to *not* hide today's launch, which definitely wasn't par for the course. Choi Ha-guk's sociopathic predecessor had tested twenty-five rockets in the previous four years—more than the Hermit Kingdom had launched in the previous eighteen. That was a worrisome trend to the Navy brass—and anyone else within targeting distance. Today's test did nothing to allay those concerns.

The USS *Benfold* was one of the Navy's most advanced multiplatform surface combat ships. By deploying the Aegis Combat System—integrating AN/SPY-1 phased array radar, AN/UYK-1 high-speed computers, and a wide variety of missile launch platforms—the Arleigh Burke–class destroyer could track and defeat up to one hundred airborne, surface, and subsurface threats simultaneously.

But the Aegis Combat System was also the world's most advanced antimissile defense platform. South Korea remained vulnerable to potential long-range missile attacks from the Democratic People's Republic of Korea. Until the THAAD—Terminal High Altitude Area Defense—system was fully deployed in South Korea, the United States shielded its ally with the Aegis antimissile defenses as needed.

Given today's SLBM—submarine-launched ballistic missile—test by the DPRK, the USS *Benfold* was deployed as a symbol of that continued commitment, despite the fact that Choi Ha-guk was unlikely to start a nuclear war today. Nevertheless, the South Koreans were nervous, and rightly so, as the North Korean ballistic missile and nuclear weapons programs continued their aggressive expansion.

"Submarine doors opening, Commander," her XO said in her headphone. "Preparing to launch."

"Roger that." Symonds twisted the furled focus ring on her binoculars. By the naked eye the missile would have to rise some five hundred feet above the surface before she could see it at this distance, but the high-powered binoculars would shave some of that off. A night launch would have been spectacular and easier to track with her eyes. No matter. The *Benfold*'s automated video tracking cameras would record the launch and feed the data back to the DIA for analysis.

The sonar operator on duty this morning had ears like a vampire bat, but Commander Symonds had another tactical advantage today. A Los Angeles–class fast-attack submarine, the USS *Asheville*, had successfully deployed an autonomous torpedo-shaped underwater surveillance drone fitted with an array of sensors, including video cameras. The stealth drone had successfully tracked the *Gorae* from its dock at Sinpo to its current location. The *Gorae* was believed to be the first and only ballistic missile–capable submarine in the DPRK fleet. Incredibly, the *Asheville*'s drone was providing a live video feed of the diesel-powered sub and the images were being piped directly into the *Benfold*'s CIC. This was a first for the Navy—eyes-on surveillance of a North Korean SLBM launch in action. Naval intelligence would feed on this data for years.

Little was known about the indigenously built *Gorae*, but it bore a striking resemblance to Soviet-era boats of a similar type and size. It was believed to have the capacity to launch only one SLBM at a time—the KN-11, aka Pukkuksong-1. It had successfully done so just a few months earlier after a number of failed attempts on sea-based barges. Today it was stationed only a mile off-shore from the naval base at Sinpo, submerged in just fifty feet of water—an easy target for the drone's cameras.

The Pukkuksong-1 had an estimated range of just over 333 miles, posing no threat to the United States. In comparison, America's Trident II SLBM had a range of more than 4,000 miles. The DPRK land-based systems were more potent. The Taepodong-3 had an estimated range of 8,000 miles.

Today's launch, no doubt, was to confirm the *Gorae*'s capability, but equally important, it was meant to send a signal to the United States and its regional allies that the DPRK was now in the submarine-launched ballistic missile club. It would take several more years for the North Koreans to build enough SLBMs to alter the regional balance of power. But when the North Koreans mounted a nuclear warhead on the Pukkuksong-1, the strategic situation in Asia would shift forever. According to the most recent DIA and ONI estimates, that was still several years away.

"She's launched!" the XO shouted in Symonds's headset.

The commander knew the first stage of the missile's flight out of the launch tube and into the water was a cold launch. Instead of firing the missile's engine—and risking a catastrophic explosion that could destroy the submarine—the missile was expelled from its tube by a separate noncombustible gas generator, like a spitball through a straw. A few seconds after the missile safely cleared the surface, its first-stage engine would ignite.

"I've got it." Symonds watched the missile's growing

smoke trail climb into the dull gray sky. Several seconds passed. She handed her binoculars to a nearby sailor. The missile was moving too fast to track through the glasses. It was easier to trace the smoke trail with her naked eye.

"Mach One achieved," her XO said. "Vehicle attitude and flight path are as expected."

Symonds's head bent upward as the missile climbed higher.

"Captain, something's wrong," the executive said.

"What is it?"

"The flight path—it's not right."

"I'm on my way."

Symonds bolted for the CIC.

What the hell was going on?

**XICHANG SATELLITE LAUNCH CENTER**
**MISSILE EARLY WARNING FACILITY**
**PEOPLE'S LIBERATION ARMY ROCKET FORCE (PLARF)**
**XICHANG, SICHUAN, PEOPLE'S REPUBLIC OF CHINA**

The steely-eyed People's Liberation Army Rocket Force (PLARF) major stared at the satellite-tracking display, his face illuminated by the monitor's amber glow. "First-stage separation completed. Two hundred and sixty-four kilometers and climbing."

A PLARF captain seated at the adjoining console confirmed, adding, "Terminal velocity achieved, four thousand four hundred meters per second, and holding."

A PLARF colonel stood above them, beaming. "Excellent!"

"Second-stage burn time, sixty seconds and counting," the major said.

The small contingent of PLARF officers were clustered in a secured section of the civilian facility. They tried to contain their excitement. In less than a minute, the Americans were going to be very surprised.

The North Korean missile, misnamed by the Americans as the Pukkuksong-1, was performing exactly as designed. They should know.

They designed it.

In an adjacent room, a civilian engineer was also tracking the missile, avoiding the watchful gaze of the senior supervisor, a hard-line party official. The engineer lifted the receiver of his secure landline. He dialed a number, trying to hide his fear. The call he was making could land him in a secret PLA slave labor camp for the next twenty years—or worse. He let the phone ring exactly three times, then hung up.

He hoped the message got through. That call might have just cost him his life.


**BUCKLEY AIR FORCE BASE, COLORADO**
**460TH SPACE WING**
**2ND SPACE WARNING SQUADRON (SWS)**

The SBIRS GEO-3 infrared missile-warning satellite stood high in geosynchronous orbit over the Asian continent, monitoring the flight of the same North Korean rocket.

The SLBM's trajectory and flight data displayed graphically in real time on the wide wall monitor in the SWS tracking facility, but in accordance with standard procedure, relevant data points were read aloud by the noncommissioned Air Force officers stationed in their specialized departments.

"Second-stage fuel burn complete."

"Altitude four hundred miles."

"We have warhead separation."

The sergeant standing next to the commanding officer, a major, whispered aloud, "Hope it's a dummy."

The major ignored the comment. The sergeant was a real motormouth, especially when he was nervous. Of course it was a dummy warhead. This was a test launch, not a first strike.

She studied the warhead's seven computer-generated probability tracks, each color coded. The farthest reach was twelve hundred nautical miles from the Sinpo launch point, approximately six hundred miles due east of the northern Japanese coast.

The major frowned. She knew the performance specs for the Pukkuksong-1. That outer track was far and away beyond what she had been expecting today from the compact SLBM.

"Major?" the sergeant said, alarm cracking his voice. But he didn't need to say anything. Everyone in the room was watching the wall monitor, including her.

"Missile warhead appears to be breaking up."

The major stepped closer to the monitor, shaking her head. "Holy crap."

"Sir?"

The major was too busy to reply. The seven color-coded tracks suddenly split into twenty-one. She knew the flight was being monitored by U.S. air and ground stations around the world, but the SOP required her to pick up the phone and dial the wing commander now.

That warhead wasn't breaking up.

# 5

## AUDACITY MMA DOJO
## SPRINGFIELD, VIRGINIA

The mixed-martial-arts dojo was located in a strip mall not far from the community college and less than two miles from The Campus's safe house. A light, cold rain fell outside, but after the last training exercise in the North Sea, it felt like the Bahamas to Jack.

The dojo was owned by Hector "Bruiser" Martinez, a former Navy SEAL chief petty officer and now a Brazilian jiujitsu black belt who trained a team of heavy-hitting MMA competitors dominating the professional circuit.

Martinez often used other instructors to round out the martial-arts sparring opportunities for his students. He sometimes invited his friend Dom Caruso to train his team in Krav Maga. Dom first learned Krav Maga from his mentor and friend Arik Yacoby, the former Israeli Shayetet 13 naval Special Forces operator, in Paravur, India—slaughtered along with his family by a bomb detonated by an Iranian-led hit team.

Dom wasn't a certified Krav Maga instructor, but his skills on the mat and his real-life combat experience counted for more than a piece of paper. Dom enjoyed teaching eager young students in the world's deadliest and most practical form of unarmed self-defense, developed through hard years of street combat by the Israeli Defense Forces. Teaching Krav Maga was also his way to honor his dead friend.

Like everybody else, Jack had been exhausted on the long flight home from Norway to Virginia on the company's luxurious Gulfstream G550. But he had a hard time sleeping. He kept running what he now called the "blonde scenario" in his head. Yeah, she'd distracted him, but he had to admit there was something about that knife. Two hours before they landed at Reagan International, Jack woke Dom up with a shake of his lapel. "Need a favor."

"Sure, cuz. Name it."

Jack had trained in hand-to-hand and close-quarters combat, but he wanted to be better prepared the next time he faced a bladed weapon. He asked Dom for help.

"You mean you want an edge," Dom joked, still bleary eyed.

Jack shook his head. "Don't quit your day job."

Before they'd even landed, Dom had called Martinez for advice, and within the week, today's private instruction had been arranged.

Dom and Jack knelt barefoot on the thick dojo sparring mat, waiting for Martinez and the special instructor to arrive. They waited in silence out of respect for the traditions of the dojo, and also in their practice of mindfulness—a spiritual discipline Adara had introduced to The Campus recently. Mindfulness helped foster focus, creativity, and awareness, making the team more productive in every aspect of their work, including combat.

Jack and Dom wore heavy gym shorts and shirts for the training. Their legs, arms, and hands bore purpling bruises and scrapes from the rescue operation. Jack had a black eye from where his head had slammed into the ladder, too.

Bone tired and sore, Jack still leaped at the opportunity to fill in a chink in his combat armor. Around his neck he wore a small silver pendant engraved with the Japanese ideographs for *kaizen*—continuous improvement. It was more than a piece of token jewelry. It symbolized his personal drive to be the very best he could be at everything, no matter the cost.

Jack's exhausted mind began to wander. He knew part of his incessant drive for personal excellence was because of his dad, Jack Senior. Not that his dad ever forced him to do anything or held him up to some impossibly high standard. Just the opposite. His father had shown him only unconditional love and support as he grew up.

There was the old saying that "familiarity breeds contempt," but in Jack Junior's case, just the opposite was true. He had always seen his dad as a heroic figure, even before he was privy to all of the clandestine work Senior had accomplished when Junior was only a kid. So it was hard for Jack Junior not to try to live up to the example his father lived in front of him—not in order to earn his love and respect, but rather out of love and respect for the man he had the privilege of calling Dad.

His mother worried when Junior was younger that he was trying too hard to compare himself to his father. "Well? What did you expect when you named me Junior?" he once joked with her. She shrugged, conceding the point. As the chief of ophthalmology at Johns Hopkins, she was no slouch herself. His parents demonstrated the value of disciplined lives devoted to the service of others. It was the best inheritance any kid had ever received from any parent, and he and his siblings started collecting that inheritance the day they were born into the family.

Jack was pulled out of his memories when Martinez entered the dojo, followed by a dark Asian man, short and slim. He appeared to be at least twenty years older than anyone else in the room, and he carried himself with an easy, determined confidence. The man held a small leather bag in his hand, rolled up like a towel. Jack assumed he was the special instructor Dom had arranged. He and Dom stood.

The four men briefly bowed toward the framed photo of Martinez's Brazilian jiujitsu master on the eastern wall, then Dom and Jack bowed to their instructors, who bowed in return out of mutual respect. Such was the etiquette of a properly disciplined dojo. Jack's father had often said that many of America's problems could be lessened if not solved if the concept of mutual respect was ever recovered. Junior agreed.

Martinez smiled and held out a scarred hand, the skin puckered and slicked by extreme heat. Dom took it. "Bruiser, this is my friend Jack. Jack, this is Sensei Martinez." Jack involuntarily bowed again slightly, but Martinez reached out to shake Jack's hand. "Any friend of Dom's is a friend of mine. Call me Bruiser." They shook.

Martinez then pointed to the man he'd brought in. "This is Master Amador Inosanto, an expert in Kali, Silat, and other fighting arts, but he is known for his work with the blade. He has trained military and police units all over the world. It's an honor to have him back here in my dojo this morning."

Amador's unassuming face broke into a gentle smile. "Such formalities. Please, let's all just be friends." Amador shook hands with Jack and Dom and then finally said, "Let's begin." He motioned with his hand for Martinez and Dom to sit, but for Jack to remain standing.

While Martinez and Dom took to the floor, Amador unrolled the leather pouch on a plastic folding chair standing near the mirrored wall. He removed three knives and carried them carefully to the men, handing one each to Martinez, Dom, and finally Jack.

"These go by many names but most commonly are called karambits. These particular knives I forged myself," Amador explained.

Jack examined the karambit in his hand. The small knife had a razor-sharp double-edged blade that curved inwardly—almost a semicircle—and ended in a vicious point. The knife fit perfectly in his hand, was well weighted and comfortable in his grip. The form and function reminded Jack of a tiger's claw.

The karambit also featured a large round steel finger hole on the end of the handle, and the ring hole itself featured a sharp point on the end. Jack followed Martinez's example and put his index finger through the hole and clutched the curved handle in the palm of his hand.

"This knife is just begging me to use it," Jack said, twisting his wrist in a circular motion.

Dom agreed. "It's a nasty piece of business."

"Ever used one?" Martinez asked.

Dom and Jack shook their heads.

"I've seen them before at the knife shop, but they're so unusual I thought it was a gangster knife or something out of a graphic novel," Dom said.

Martinez rolled his eyes. "More and more LEOs and service members are picking these up. They come in folders with grippier composite handles and pocket clips for concealed carry." Martinez held up the blade Amador had given him. He admired the knife in his hand. "Me, I like the traditional ones."

"Perhaps as you can tell from my accent," Amador began, "I'm from the Philippines. My culture is a traditional blade culture, and in my country, just about every man on the street carries a knife. Sometimes like the one you hold in your hand."

Amador paused as the others examined their blades again.

He continued. "Many of our fighting arts, like Kali, are all about the blade, especially the knife." He turned to Jack. "In close-quarters combat, my favorite weapon is a twelve-gauge shotgun if I can get my hands on one." He smiled.

"Amen, brother," Martinez said.

Amador held out his palm and Jack carefully handed

him the karambit. Amador held it up high. "But if you don't have a shotgun, a pistol, or even a knife, how do you fight with a man who knows how to use one of these?"

That's what Jack wanted to know, too. That momentary freeze on the oil rig after the blond killer stabbed him with the knife almost cost him his life and the lives of his team members. He was still dealing with the idea that she had fooled him, but he also needed to make sure that he was better prepared for fighting with blades.

"There are many techniques for fighting with a knife, and many techniques for defending against one." Amador touched the side of his head. "But there is one basic idea that you must master before any of those techniques make sense. That is why I have come today."

Jack exchanged a look with Dom. *This is going to be an interesting day.*

"Let's start with the basics, okay? Because if you want to fight with the blade or against it, you must first understand the blade," Amador said.

"Is that the idea we must master?" Jack said.

Amador shook his head. "No." He lifted the knife up high so everyone could see it. He touched the various parts of the karambit as he spoke.

"What advantage does a knife give in combat? First is the blade itself. Sharp steel." He dragged the blade slowly in the air above his flesh, making precise motions across and around his free hand and arm. "It will slice through skin, muscle, tendons, cartilage, and even bone. Your fist can't do that. Neither can your foot. And the steel? It feels no pain." He grinned again. "It only causes it."

"Second, the knife extends your reach." He thrust the

blade out in front of him as fast as a cracked whip. "This one? Not as much as, say, a KA-BAR or bowie knife, but still, a three- or four-inch extension is still an extension, isn't it? And in the hand of a skilled enemy? That is enough advantage to kill you."

**6**

Amador pointed out the other features of the hand-forged karambit, then returned it carefully to his leather bag. He then removed two dulled versions—training knives. He stepped back over to Jack, pocketing one as he approached.

"You have trained in martial arts, yes?" Amador asked.

Jack nodded. "Jiujitsu, karate, judo. Even a little Krav Maga, thanks to Dom."

"Good. Then you are familiar with basic blocking and striking with the hands and forearms."

"Of course."

"And the more advanced moves that exploit twisting joints, pressure points, and so on? Like aikido?"

"Yes, but I can always get better. That's why I'm here."

"Good! Me, too! Maybe you can teach me a thing or

two." Amador laughed. And just as suddenly his smile disappeared and his laughing eyes narrowed.

Jack took the hint. He squared up and bowed to his teacher, and Amador returned a slighter bow to his student.

"Let's start with a very basic move, shall we?" Amador raised the karambit high above his head with his right arm. "A common thrust by a street thug or criminal. It takes no training." He stepped slowly toward Jack and lowered the blade in slow motion. Jack raised his much larger left forearm perpendicular to the strike. Amador's arm touched Jack's, and they left both arms frozen in the air, holding the position.

Amador turned to Martinez and Dom. "You see? Jack is well trained. He knew how to block this basic strike." He turned to Jack, much taller than he. "And what does your training tell you to do next?"

Still blocking Amador's right arm with his left, Jack swung a slow-motion right fist toward Amador's midsection until it connected.

"Good! Right out of the textbook." Amador disengaged and took a step back. "Now let's see what an enemy with a little more skill might be able to do."

Amador stepped forward again, raising his right arm high again, and slow-motioned his strike down. Jack repeated his block. But when their arms connected, Amador twisted his wrist and turned his elbow in. The dull practice karambit blade turned sharply into Jack's arm. Faster than an eye blink, the dull blade bit deeper as Amador turned farther and pulled his arm down. The pressure was intense, and the leverage against Jack's arm nearly threw him over. Amador disengaged before Jack lost his balance.

"Of course, with a properly sharpened blade, your arm would be sliced to the bone. You wouldn't think about the counterpunch. Your brain would be screaming—'My arm is cut off!'" Amador laughed again.

Jack was impressed. He rubbed his forearm where the blade had touched him. Dom and Martinez nodded appreciatively.

"You're not injured, are you?" Amador asked, genuinely concerned.

"No, not at all. Just . . . surprised."

Amador grinned. "Good. Let's try one more. Same move by me. But a question first. What is the first thing you're usually taught when you have no weapon but are being attacked by a man with a knife?"

"Attack the knife. Disarm him," Jack said.

"Correct. So this time, I will make my clumsy attack and I want you to seize my wrist with one hand and then rip the knife out with the other, just the way you've been taught."

Amador threw another slow-motion overhead strike, driving the blade down toward Jack's head. Jack countered by seizing Amador's small wrist in his left hand, then reached for Amador's gripping hand with his right in an attempt to seize the knife.

"Stop," Amador said.

Jack froze in place. Amador turned his head to the others seated on the mat.

"You see Jack's firm grip on my wrist? Very strong! It's a good move, isn't it? But watch." Amador simply twisted his trapped wrist and hand, and the curved blade came into contact with Jack's wrist. "A real blade instantly cuts through the muscle and tendons of his left hand before his right hand can grab my knife. The pain in his left hand will also cause it to pull away if it can, and his right hand will involuntarily reach for the wounded one. That allows me to continue my attack."

"Ouch," Jack said. He could imagine the blood spurting out of the resulting wound that would have disabled his hand and maybe even severed it from the wrist.

"Let's do some more work," Amador said. The Kali master coiled, then sped like a skater toward his larger opponent, his shoeless brown feet barely touching the mat, the calluses scraping like a file on sandpaper. Then the slow-motion death dance began again.

They spent the next twenty minutes demonstrating the power of Kali knife-fighting techniques and the vicious striking power of a karambit blade against a trained fighter like Jack. All of Jack's blocks were easily countered with the flick of the blade. Kicks were stopped, too, and countered with slashes across feet, ankles, and thighs. Amador used his free hand and feet for strikes as well. Jack and Amador stopped in the middle of each strike-counterstrike sequence and demonstrated the subtle but powerful techniques Amador deployed.

"Now let's switch up. Jack, you attack me, and I'll defend," Amador said.

"Do I get the knife?" Jack asked, hopefully.

"You don't need a knife. You're much larger and more powerful than me. I'm just a little old man!" Amador laughed. "Begin!"

Now Jack moved in, throwing slow-motion punches and jabs at Amador, easily six inches shorter than he. As in other martial-arts demos Jack had witnessed, Amador used a variety of techniques to dodge or deflect the heavy blows with his free hand but instantly counterstruck with the wicked claw-shaped blade, inflicting slicing wounds across the back of Jack's hands, around his wrists, down the biceps, across the forearms. They no longer stopped to demonstrate at each point of contact but flowed continuously with the fluid motion of their attacks and defenses.

Jack picked up the pace of his attacks, adding straight and rounded leg kicks. Amador matched him step for step, blow for blow, dancing inside and out of Jack's larger frame and delivering crippling knife strikes at the groin, inner thighs, stomach, and face. Other blows were struck with the far end of the knife, the steel retention ring acting like a brass knuckle. It delivered crushing blows to soft tissues, cartilage, and bone in the nose, larynx, and eyes.

"It's like I'm boxing with a velociraptor!" Jack said, admiring the fluidity of Amador's movements matched to the vicious talon in the man's skilled hand.

After the last lethal blow was struck—the curved blade's inner edge striking Jack below the left ear, then dragging the pointed tip across the carotid artery—the shadow fighting stopped. Jack acknowledged his defeat with a gracious smile and a bow.

"Questions?" Amador asked.

"I noticed that a lot of your knife skills were connected to your open-handed martial-arts technique," Dom said. "It was kind of hard to separate the two."

"Good observation. That's because all forms of open-handed fighting were derived from blade fighting. Swords and knives were always preferred in combat. But what happens when a man loses his sword or spear in battle?" Amador held up an empty hand. "He learns to fight with these. Still, don't be confused. Empty-hand fighting is different from knife fighting. They are connected, but different."

"Any more questions?" Martinez asked.

Jack thought about the knife attack on the oil rig that almost killed him. He cleared his throat, carefully picking his words. "Master, it seems as if we would have to study for years in order to master this fighting technique. I would think that Kali, like all martial arts, has a lot of ritual forms and defined movements. How does that translate to real-world knife fighting? Most knife attacks are short and explosive, not like what we did today."

"An excellent question. First, I would say that learning the art of Kali or any other martial art has many benefits beyond fighting. But you already know that, I'm sure. So to answer your question directly, learning the 'ritual forms and defined movements,' as you put it, trains your mind and body to handle the knife and the rhythms of what you call a 'real' knife fight."

"How?" Dom asked.

"There are only three basic moves in a knife attack," Amador said. He held up his knife and demonstrated each movement as he spoke.

"An overhead strike, a forward thrust, and a slash. That's it! An unskilled fighter will rely on one of these moves primarily. The most advanced fighter uses combinations of all three. Kali teaches you all three, and how to put them together in a devastating combination."

Amador stepped closer to Jack. "But I'm not here to teach you Kali or to sell you on the benefits of it. What Bruiser asked me to do was to help you with knife fighting. What I've attempted to show you today is not the technique of fighting but the essence of knife fighting itself."

"The 'basic' idea that we must master?" Jack asked.

"Yes."

"And what is that?"

Amador held up his karambit. "It's not this." He tapped the side of his head with the dull practice blade. "The mind is the knife, son. The blade is only an extension of your will. If a man attacks you with a knife, he is attacking you with his mind. You need to understand the mind of the knife fighter first. Forget the knife. The knife is nothing. It's the fighter that counts. You beat the fighter, not the knife."

Jack rubbed his bearded face, trying to process what Amador was saying.

"But there are knife-fighting techniques," Dom said. "And specific skills to defend against them."

"Yes, there are. But never forget that the best defense against a knife if you have no other weapon is to use these." Amador held up one of his bare brown feet. "Notice my advanced technique." He set his foot back down, turned, and pivoted, taking several short steps away. He called over his shoulder. "Always run away if you can!" he said, laughing.

The three students laughed, too, as Amador crossed

back over to the two kneeling men. He stared down at them. "Now, seriously. If you have no weapon against a knife, escape if at all possible. A knife is very dangerous. Nothing to fool with. Understood?"

They both nodded.

Amador held out his open hands. Martinez and Dom carefully held up the razor-sharp karambits and Amador took them in his fighting grip.

"You saw how powerful one blade was in both attack and defense," the wizened Filipino master said. "Can you imagine what two of these can do in the hands of one who can use them?"

Jack ran through the katas he'd seen in years past. In his mind's eye he threw punches and kicks at the little Filipino, then watched the two karambit blades in the master's hands cutting his limbs like scissors or blocking Jack's unarmored flesh as it struck. Jack felt his two thighs being ripped open at once, his two wrists slashed at the same time, and two pointed claws tearing across his eyes simultaneously. He shuddered.

"Does it matter if we're fighting an opponent who uses two knives?" Jack asked. "Or do we use the same approach as with someone who only uses one?"

Amador's smile faded. "I will tell you what my master taught me when I was first learning the way of the knife and asked the exact same question."

Amador handed the two lethal karambits to Jack, then laid a strong hand on Jack's broad shoulder. His voice lowered. "'Whenever you are faced with a true master of two blades,' he said to me, 'pray to God that He is ready to receive you in Heaven, because in that moment you are surely going to die.'" Amador leaned in closer to Jack. "In other words, my friend, RUN LIKE HELL!"

Martinez belly-laughed. So did Dom. When Amador finally cracked up, Jack allowed himself a grin.

Martinez stood. "Let's grab some breakfast. All this knife fighting has made me hungry. Then we'll come back and Master Inosanto will run us through some more of his drills."

"Works for me," Amador said. "I'm dying for pancakes!"

Dom stood up to grab his shoes, but Jack just stared at the two blades in his hands, feeling their heft and fearing the worst.

## 7

## WHITE HOUSE SITUATION ROOM
## WASHINGTON, D.C.

He'd read somewhere that the Chinese ideograph for the word *crisis* was supposedly composed of the two words for *opportunity* and *danger*. Even if it wasn't true, President Jack Ryan found it relevant to today's meeting.

The President sat on the far end of the long mahogany conference table. All of the tall leather chairs surrounding the table were empty except for the four next to him. In times of national crisis every chair would be filled, and deputy assistants would crowd the rest of the room, either sitting or standing. But today he wasn't facing a crisis—at least, not yet. He certainly saw an opportunity, but he also sensed extreme danger for the nation if he made the wrong choice in the next thirty minutes.

President Ryan was flanked on his left by Mary Pat Foley, the director of national intelligence, and Robert Burgess, the secretary of defense. On his right sat the secretary of state, Scott Adler, and the President's chief of staff, Arnold Van Damm, the only political voice he allowed in the room. Arnie's hair was long gone and the lines in his careworn face were deeper than when the President had first met him, but the pale blue eyes—and the brain behind them—were as keen as ever.

That was it. These were four of his most trusted advisers. Ryan didn't want a cacophony of political opinions or academic theories clouding the room. He needed only the clear, sober, actionable analysis these four would give him in order to make his decision, and quickly.

"Thank you all for coming on such short notice—and for keeping this meeting just between us. We don't need public opinion or the Hill getting ahead of us on this."

They all nodded. "Of course, Mr. President," Mary Pat Foley said. "We understand completely, and we serve at your discretion."

Ryan poured himself a cup of black coffee from the service in front of them and invited the others to do the same. "We don't have much time to make this call. You know I count on each of you for your honest and candid opinions. I know you've all been briefed by Mary Pat, but I want to catch you up on the facts before we proceed. Mary Pat."

The director of national intelligence picked up a remote control and pointed it at one of the big wall monitors. She talked through the video from the SBIRS GEO-3 infrared missile-warning satellite as it played on the screen.

"As you all know, the North Koreans managed to successfully launch a MIRV'd SLBM yesterday at approximately five p.m. EST. The missile carried three dummy warheads, each landing harmlessly, thankfully, in the northern Pacific Ocean, with no loss of life or property damage. Nevertheless, the event is significant for several reasons.

"First, we had no idea that the missile in question—the Pukkuksong-1—had this kind of range. Either the missile has been improved or our intelligence estimates were way off base."

"Or it's not the KN-11 at all," the SecDef said, preferring the American designation. "It could be an entirely different weapon. It has nearly the same performance characteristics as our Polaris A-1, which we first deployed back in 1962."

Jack Ryan smiled to himself. It never failed to amaze him how technologically advanced the United States was compared to the rest of the world. Most of the planet still wasn't able to achieve what his parents' generation had accomplished fifty years earlier.

Mary Pat continued. "Our second concern is that we had no idea that the North Koreans had acquired MIRV technology—another intelligence failure." She frowned when she said this. As the titular head of America's civilian intelligence community, she felt personally responsible for the current crisis.

"Third, because they've acquired MIRV technology, it's only a matter of time before they move from three warheads to seven, ten, or even more on this platform. Multiple independently targeted warheads means that each missile has more target opportunities and greater capacity to defeat any kind of ABM defense with decoys and countermeasures. That changes the strategic equation in Asia, especially when the North Koreans are able to arm them with nuclear warheads. But what's particularly worrisome is the idea of the North Koreans deploying MIRV technology on their land-based ICBM platforms. The Taepodong-3 has a range of eight thousand miles. At that point they become a world power, like it or not."

"And we removed all of our MIRVs from our ICBMs a few years ago," Ryan said. He was a trained security analyst, so it didn't take long for him to process the implications. "If we don't stop the North Koreans from MIRVing, we'll have to go back to it ourselves, and that will launch another nuclear arms race between us, the Russians, and the Chinese."

"Exactly our concerns, Mr. President," Mary Pat said as the SecDef nodded in agreement.

Ryan sighed, frustrated. Like everyone else involved at the time, he had assumed that the coup ousting Choi Ji-hoon two years ago was going to solve the North Korean problem. Obviously it hadn't.

Ryan rubbed his chin, thinking. "Can someone please tell me why the North Koreans are still hell-bent on their strategic nuclear program? They still can't produce enough food to feed their own people."

"We've been asking ourselves that same question since their first nuclear test in 2006," the SecState said. "Power, prestige, leverage, blackmail. Pick one. Or pick all of them."

"They also see it as a deterrent," Mary Pat said.

The President frowned. "Deterrent? From whom?"

"From us, the South Koreans, and the West, generally. And even China, truth be told, especially after the role they played in Ji-hoon's overthrow."

"Nobody is planning on invading North Korea," the SecDef said. "This idea of Western aggression is all a fiction, designed to keep the population under control."

"Agreed," Mary Pat said. "But that's why their missile and nuclear programs are so important. The majority of North Koreans have no access to outside news sources, and most of them have been brainwashed to believe that the United States and our allies are aggressively seeking the chance to invade. But the North Korean people aren't stupid. They see the scarcity of resources, and they're the ones that have suffered the most under this regime. So when they see Chairman Choi spending billions of dollars on nuclear bombs and long-range missiles instead of food and housing, it only reinforces the government's message that the West is hostile—otherwise, why would the 'benevolent' government spend all that money? It's a devil's logic, but it works."

"For the true believers it works. But the dissidents know better," the secretary of state said.

Mary Pat shook her head. "But the dissidents are quickly killed or imprisoned in one of Choi's gulags. Compared to their internal security apparatus, Stalin's NKVD looks like a wedding planning service."

Ryan leaned forward on the table, folding his hands. "So to bottom line this discussion, what we're saying is that the North Korean missile and nuclear programs are about external and internal security, which really means it's all about Choi Ha-guk staying in power. Is that right?"

The others nodded in agreement. Mary Pat added, "So long as any member of the Choi family is in power, the North Koreans will continue to pursue their missile and nuclear programs."

"Okay. So the first question on the table is this: What can the United States do about that? How can we effect regime change unilaterally?"

"Without Chinese cooperation, we can't—and we certainly wouldn't want to risk a conflict with them," Burgess said.

Ryan turned to Burgess. "Forget China for just one minute. Is it even possible for us to overthrow the Choi power structure through overt military action?"

"We've been war-gaming scenarios about this for over six decades—technically, we're still in a state of war with North Korea. Under the best scenario, we would expect mass civilian casualties in South Korea and the deaths of many thousands more in the north. If ever there was a definition of a Pyrrhic victory, this would be it."

Secretary of State Adler quickly added, "Which is why our South Korean allies are completely against any kind of offensive military action."

"What about a complete economic embargo?" Ryan asked.

"For all intents and purposes, there is one—except the Chinese might not enforce it. Without their complete cooperation, it isn't possible," Adler said. "And even if it were, it would only hurt the innocent civilians. The leaders won't suffer. If you include food in the embargo, then another mass famine would result."

"So as far as you all are concerned, we have no unilateral options available to us to stop the North Korean missile and nuclear programs or effect regime change," Ryan said.

Again, all heads nodded in agreement.

"The only hope we have of either is China. They hold all the cards," the secretary of defense said.

"Which is the real reason why we're here," Ryan said. He turned to Mary Pat. "Thank you for the summary analysis." He turned to the others. "Now for the question at hand." He poured himself another cup of coffee as he said, "Scott, tell us what the Chinese have proposed."

The secretary of state squared his shoulders. "I have received an unofficial inquiry from my Chinese counterpart regarding our openness to a face-to-face meeting between the heads of state of China, South Korea, Japan, the Philippines, and, of course, the United States. It would be held next month in Beijing."

"Regarding the North Korean situation?" Burgess asked.

Adler nodded. "President Zhao's government has expressed concern over recent developments."

"They always 'express concern' after every nuclear and missile test. But it's all hot air," the defense secretary said. "The problem is that they're the ones supplying most of that technology."

"Zhao's government is doing that?" Ryan asked.

The SecDef shrugged. "Officially, no. But someone in Zhao's government is. Whether or not it's sanctioned by Zhao is still a question mark."

Mary Pat added, "The South Koreans are convinced the Chinese provided the North Koreans with cold launch capability. It only took them months to perfect it when it should've taken years. Same goes for the MIRV tech, we're certain."

"So the Chinese provided the MIRV technology and now they want a summit with us because they're worried about it? That doesn't make any sense," the chief of staff said.

The secretary of state shook his head, smiling. "Welcome to Chinese internal politics."

"If China holds all the cards, and if Zhao is truly concerned, why doesn't he just take care of the problem?" Ryan asked.

Adler shrugged. "Same answer, I'm afraid. Internal politics. There are factions within the Politburo and within the military that are at odds with Zhao on the issue. Beyond that, we really don't have a clue. Right now we have to ask ourselves what they have to gain and what we have to lose by turning down President Zhao's offer."

"I'm confused. What exactly is he offering?" Burgess asked.

"That was my question to the foreign minister. He was intentionally vague, but he insisted his government is as interested as we are in North Korean regime change. Beyond that, he doesn't want to show his cards until he has a commitment from us to attend the security summit."

The chief of staff frowned. "So we don't know what their specific proposals are for stopping the North Koreans?"

"No. But he emphasized it would be a permanent solution."

"I'm not interested in anything less," Ryan said. "We

need to solve the North Korean problem once and for all before we're all dragged into World War Three."

Van Damm shook his head. "So the President is supposed to fly halfway around the world to find out what Zhao's plan is? That's ridiculous. Why can't he tell us up front?"

"He might be afraid of a leak on our end—a real possibility with some of the old 'China hands' lurking in the bureaucracy. Or he's worried that we'll reject his proposal and then we'll tell someone else about it," Adler said.

"It must be something big," Ryan said. "Something that affects his position or the factions that oppose him. What do we know about the political power structure inside China right now?"

"Frankly, not enough," Mary Pat admitted. "The tectonic plates are still shifting."

Ryan turned to Adler. "Can we trust Zhao?"

"We don't have any reason not to at this point, but frankly, we don't know enough about him, either."

"But he needs to keep his cards close to the vest on this thing. That tells me his position might not yet be fully secure," Ryan said, the wheels turning in his mind. "And the fact that he needs to keep this secret and to do it quickly sounds like this will be a decisive action. Something strategic, not tactical." Ryan turned to his SecDef. "Sound about right, Robert?"

"I think you're onto something, sir."

Van Damm leaned forward. "Excuse me, but I think we're getting a little ahead of ourselves here. If he doesn't want to tell us up front, why can't he fly over here to tell us what's going on?"

Ryan grinned. "Maybe the new Chinese president is afraid of flying."

"More likely, he's afraid of leaving his country. Again, it speaks to the idea he's still consolidating his position," Mary Pat said.

Adler added, "And Zhao must think he needs you standing at his side to carry out his plan, not to mention draw the other heads of state to the summit."

"Or Zhao wants the President standing there next to him holding the bag when the summit goes sideways," Van Damm countered.

Ryan sat back in his chair, tenting his fingers in front of him, thinking. "Scott, what happens if we turn the summit down?"

"If we turn Zhao down and he's committed to North Korean regime change, he'll turn to the Russians, since Zhao obviously can't do it on his own—otherwise, why call us? Given the current geopolitical realities in Europe and Asia, we don't want a renewed Chinese-Russian alliance. That would strengthen China's hand in the South and East China Seas, and that means we'd have to devote even more of our air and naval assets to the region, potentially weakening our ability to respond to any new Russian threats in Europe."

"I agree with that assessment," the SecDef said.

"So do I," Ryan said. "And that ain't good. Now give me the downsides to showing up for this thing."

"This summit might be another huge waste of time, where everyone gets all excited but nothing substantive actually happens," Van Damm said.

SecDef Burgess added, "Maybe the Chinese want us

to waste our time and only appear to be concerned so they can continue their buildup of North Korea." He pointed at the monitor. "They know that we know what's going on over there, and they know we're concerned. This might just be sleight of hand on their part."

"It's also a prestige play for them," Secretary Adler said. "No matter the outcome of the summit, the fact that they invited us to Beijing to solve a regional crisis and that we accepted the invitation reinforces the impression that they are the dominant power in Asia and co-equals with us. And if the summit fails, they'll blame us."

Van Damm added, "To some, it might even look more like a summons than an invitation. Especially since this is the second time you will have flown to Beijing to meet with a Chinese president."

"And perception is reality in politics," Adler was quick to add. "Especially in Asia."

"There's one other possibility," Van Damm said. "You show up and he springs a plan on you that puts us in a bind."

Adler shook his head. "If he does that, we'd walk away and he'd look the fool. I don't think Zhao will offer anything that we can't agree to."

"So there are plenty of downsides," Ryan said. "But despite those, there's still the real possibility that the Chinese have a plan that will permanently change the situation on the Korean peninsula," Ryan said. "That interests me."

The President's eyes narrowed, his mind concentrating. The others watched in silence as he put all of the pieces together. Finally, he leaned forward on the table.

"The dilemma as I see it is this: risk wasting our time and looking like fools at a worthless summit, or risk losing the opportunity to solve the North Korean problem once and for all. Is that about the size of it?"

They all agreed.

Ryan smiled a little. "When I put it that way, the decision seems clear. It's worth the risk, given the possible reward, even if it means another long damn airplane ride. Let's do this."

"I'll contact the foreign minister directly and tell him that we're interested," Adler said.

"I've got a better idea. Arrange for me to speak with President Zhao directly. I want to take the measure of the man myself and show him I'm serious."

Adler smiled. "That's an excellent idea, Mr. President."

Ryan stood, signaling that the meeting was over. The others stood, too. "Thank you all. I'll be in touch."

As the others shuffled out, Ryan poured himself another coffee. The Chinese could be handing him an opportunity for sure. But he also knew from boot camp that the bullet you didn't hear was the one that took your head off.

## BUILDING 19
## PYONGYANG, NORTH KOREA

They met in the underground bunker deep beneath the
drab and unassuming five-story granite building on
the outskirts of the city, far from the central government
district. Nominally it was the subheadquarters of the
State Ministry of Fisheries, just another administrative
organ in North Korea's micromanaged, state-owned
command economy.

Aboveground, harried black-coated technocrats ex-
erted enormous bureaucratic energies administering the
regulations and procedures of the vast ministry, which,
unsurprisingly, had very little productive impact on
North Korea's fishing industry. Most of the bureaucrats'
work was designed to justify the generous food ration
cards they received, the less cramped public housing they
lived in, and the meager but regular salaries their privi-
leged jobs paid them.

What these bureaucrats didn't realize was that both

their work and their lives were meant only as camouflage. Neither the building nor the ministry appeared to have any strategic significance and therefore would hardly qualify for targeting by American or South Korean military planners. But down here, in the nuclear-proof bomb shelter that served as one of the regime's many secret conference rooms, the truly important business of the state was being conducted. Chairman Choi Ha-guk met with his most trusted civilian and military advisers. He trusted them only because they feared him. The three empty chairs around the long teak table were a grim reminder of the cost of failure.

Unlike his cousin Choi Ji-hoon, Choi Ha-guk was a seasoned military officer, leading the elite Army unit that had killed Ji-hoon's bodyguard two years earlier in a violent coup and overthrown the young, spoiled fool. Choi Ha-guk's father, Choi Sang-u, was freed from his labor camp and installed as the new supreme leader of the Democratic People's Republic of Korea. But years of forced labor had destroyed his father's health, and within weeks of leaving the camp, he died. With his father's blessing and the Army behind him, Ha-guk's unanimous election to the nation's presidency, the chairmanship of the party, and promotion to the supreme marshal of the armed forces was assured.

The chairman's first order of business was to repair his relationship with China, grossly undermined by his idiot cousin. Having trained with some of China's top military units and fluent in Mandarin, the chairman had deep personal and political ties with key members of the Chinese Politburo and PLA staff officers.

Changing policy course was vital but difficult. Undermining his cousin's failed initiative potentially delegitimized his own position. Choi Ha-guk was careful to preserve the hagiographies of his violent predecessors—a cousin, his father, his uncle, and his grandfather. North Korea was the inheritance of the Choi family, and he would do nothing to risk that inheritance for himself or his own children, who stood in the line of succession now that his uncle and cousin were dead.

But Choi Ha-guk also had a vision. He knew he was destined to play a decisive role on the world stage and finally elevate North Korea to its rightful place among the nations. Kant and Hegel were essentially right. All of History was marching toward an Idea. What neither philosopher realized was that he, Choi Ha-guk, was that Idea—at least in Asia.

But all of that was at risk now. His next decision would determine the fate of the country, he was certain.

Sitting at the head of the table, Chairman Choi Ha-guk surveyed the row of grim military officers on his left, each stern face directed toward him, their spines stiff, hands neatly folded in their laps. Their hair was cropped uniformly short in the regulation military style, and their broad caps stood in a perfect row in front of them down the table—with the exception of the missing officer and his empty chair. A man who had recently disappointed the chairman.

Each military uniform was resplendent with hard-won badges, medals, and ribbons from the shoulder tabs to the hems of the coats—enough "fruit salad" for a dozen wars and a hundred battles. But not one of them had served in the great Fatherland Liberation War or in sustained combat of any kind.

But the chairman knew these were hard men, highly trained and motivated—one of the great legacies bestowed upon him by his uncle and grandfather. Each of these admirals and generals had been vetted and monitored for their ideological fervor and political reliability, both of which were reinforced by the privileges and perks of their positions, and the extensive kinship networks that linked them by blood to the dominant Choi family.

But even more important, these flag officers were part of North Korea's great warrior class, the sons and grandsons of DPRK troops who fought and sacrificed valiantly, fanatically, and skillfully against the South Korean bandits and later against more heavily armed American and UN invaders. Family honor and patriotic pride drove these men seated at the table like Harpies' whips. They were the Spartans of Asia.

On Choi's right sat his equally focused civilian advisers, each wearing identical Mao-styled black jackets buttoned to the top of their throats and short-cropped hair like the military men. It would be easy for outsiders to dismiss the civilians as bureaucratic sycophants, but they were each as talented, driven, and proven in state security matters as their military counterparts were. Two of the seven chairs on the civilian side were empty. Failure came at a high price.

What each man in the room knew was that, unlike his predecessors, the chairman eschewed fawning subservience. Instead, he demanded flawless performance from his subordinates, a far more difficult and dangerous proposition than effusive bootlicking.

In the back left corner of the room was a secretary who was seated at a small desk, recording the proceedings on a shorthand machine. In the back right corner of the room opposite the secretary sat a young man in a single chair. His face and body screamed military, but he wore civilian clothes. The anonymous man was unknown to everyone but the chairman. He sat in a silent, disquieting strength.

Choi Ha-guk turned toward one of his key spymasters, the new head of the RGB—Reconnaissance General Bureau. "When was this confirmed?"

"My South Korean informant confirmed it yesterday."

"And he is reliable?"

The RGB minister resented the question. The clandestine bureau had spent decades successfully cultivating a vast network of highly placed and reliable South Korean agents. "Perfectly reliable, sir. She is a secretary in the president's travel office."

"How can we be certain she isn't a double agent?"

"She is a loyal daughter of our glorious revolution, working tirelessly for our imminent reunification with the bandit South. But it is also true that her great-uncle is a pensioner in one of our senior public housing units, where he is well cared for by our benevolent government. She has expressed her undying gratitude for his continued well-being."

The chairman nodded. "Very good."

The RGB minister continued. "She forwarded this by courier." The minister passed the single-page document to the man on his left, who in turn passed it along, one after another, until it was carefully placed in front of Choi Ha-guk. He left it on the table in front of him, unread.

"Do we have any specifics about the summit? What is it they plan to talk about? What do they want to accomplish?" Choi turned toward the head of the 225th Bureau, one of several overseas covert operations departments at his disposal. The 225th Bureau's target was South Korea, infiltrating operatives across the border and recruiting South Korean agents.

"Unknown at this time, sir."

The chairman glanced around the table. "Anybody?"

Heads shook.

Choi sighed, frustrated. "We know that the Chinese called the summit, and we know that the Americans and the others can't do anything without their permission or cooperation." He turned to his foreign minister. "So the questions are: What is Beijing up to? And to what lengths will they go? What will they permit the Americans to do to us?"

"I have spoken with the Chinese foreign minister. He was very vague and expressed his government's displeasure at the firing of our MIRV'd SLBM."

That was surprising news to the chairman, but his stoic gaze didn't betray him. His cousin had grossly overreached in his desire for long-range ICBMs that could hit the United States. How could President Ryan *not* respond to such a strategic threat?

But apparently, he himself had also miscalculated the effect that a medium-range MIRV missile test would have on the superpowers. That was troubling, in part because the technology had come from friendly Chinese sources.

Either the power struggle on the mainland had intensified or his so-called Chinese friends had set him up for a fall. Either way, his situation was untenable.

"What assurances regarding our interests did he give you?"

"None."

Another surprise. Choi's gaze held steady. "That's disturbing news."

China had always been North Korea's advocate and shield on the world stage, even when they misbehaved. China shed more than a million lives in the great Fatherland Liberation War after the Americans intervened and threatened to cross the Yalu River. The mutual sacrifice and shared ideology formed a strong bond between the neighboring dictatorships, particularly among the militaristic factions.

Strategically, the North Koreans played a key role in China's foreign policy, keeping Japan and South Korea on edge and at the same time currying Chinese favor to intervene against Pyongyang's ambitions.

But two years ago, President Ling and President Ryan had conspired to initiate the overthrow of Ji-hoon and his reckless policies. Fortunately, the replacement of President Ling by President Zhao had given Choi time to consolidate his position.

What were the two great powers up to now?

W e must assume, then, that regime change is their unstated goal," Choi said. "How will they try to overthrow us? War?" War was always on the forefront of Choi's mind as the commander-in-chief of all military forces and as an ardent student of history.

"We must not preclude the possibility of a full-scale invasion from the south, supported by naval and air assets from the coalition partners," the Korean People's Army Ground Force general said. "And perhaps with Chinese troops pouring across our northern border."

"But it is highly unlikely," Choi said. "There would be horrible bloodshed and widespread destruction. What would be left for them to take over?"

"Let them try. We'll smash them all!" one of the generals said. The military heads all nodded in agreement.

"I don't doubt our military capabilities, gentlemen. But even if we smashed them, they would still surely smash us. War is to be avoided if at all possible, if we want the Revolution to survive." He sat back in his chair. "But as a precaution, let's quietly redirect ten additional divisions north. We'll use the pretense of border security and drug trafficking—no, sex trafficking—but move them at night and under cover whenever possible."

"Yes, sir," an Army general replied.

"What other military options do they have, short of total war or invasion?" Choi asked.

The general of the strategic rocket forces leaned forward. "If I were the Americans, I would make tactical strikes on our missile facilities and submarine pens."

"Our underground nuclear facilities are impervious to aerial bombardment," a technocrat said. "But the Americans will drop chemical or biological agents around our facilities to slow production and transport."

The chairman nodded. "I've thought of this myself. I want a plan drawn up immediately to relocate as many civilians as we can to surround these facilities—new schools, hospitals, whatever it takes. The Americans won't dare strike then."

He scanned the military faces again. "So that's it? It sounds as if the coalition's military options are quite limited."

Heads nodded in agreement.

Choi turned to an economic official. "Besides military action, what else could the coalition do?"

"A total economic blockade," the minister offered. Clearly Choi already knew what the man's answer would be.

"That would only be possible with a complete air and naval blockade," the Korean People's Army Navy admiral said.

"China and South Korea account for the vast majority of our imports and exports. A blockade would hardly be necessary," Choi said. "But I would hate to lose our business with Pakistan and Iran." Some of North Korea's nuclear and missile technology came from them.

"Our submarines can break the back of any blockade," the Korean People's Army Navy admiral said. The KPAN had thirty-five submarines, many of them domestically built, and over seven hundred ships in total.

"I appreciate the gallantry, Admiral, but our subs are

vastly outnumbered by their antisubmarine forces," Choi said. He pulled out a Gitanes cigarette from a fresh blue pack and lit it. He was the only person allowed to smoke in the room. A lead-crystal Baccarat ashtray sat to one side, a gift from one of his young mistresses after her last trip to Brussels. He took a few drags, thinking. His eyes fixed on the oily smoke curling from the end of his cigarette, whisking away into the ceiling ducts by the powerful fans circulating the filtered air—a gift of the Ukrainian Communists decades ago. It gave him an idea. He turned to the foreign minister.

"What will the Russians do if we are blockaded?"

"Given their current status with the Americans, I'm certain they will gladly ignore the embargo if for no other reason than to frustrate President Ryan."

"Contact your counterpart in Moscow. Confirm this, and find out precisely what items and services they might be willing to provide," Choi said.

"Immediately, sir."

Another minister spoke. "There is no question that we can survive an economic embargo. Our people are willing to make the necessary sacrifices for the sake of our country."

Choi stubbed out his cigarette in the expensive ashtray in small, precise movements. "Agreed. We can survive their economic embargo. But I'm not interested in merely 'surviving.'"

The paper in front of Choi caught his eye. He picked it up and read it. Another idea came to him. "We have the meeting confirmed, as well as the time and place. President Zhao, President Ryan, Prime Minister Hironaga, and President Yeo-jin will all be in attendance. Does this gathering of heads of state present us with an opportunity?"

Everyone in the room knew Choi was referring to the 1983 Rangoon bombing by North Korean agents. That attack killed several high-ranking South Korean cabinet officials, who had all gathered for a public event. Dozens of other innocent civilians died as well—collateral damage in the long march toward the Idea. The president of South Korea survived only because the bomb went off before his scheduled arrival.

The head of the Ministry of State Security's foreign counterespionage cadre cleared his throat. "It would be nearly impossible to organize an assassination attempt on Chinese soil, especially in Beijing."

"Nearly impossible, but not entirely impossible, correct?" Choi asked.

"Anything is possible if one has the will," the MSS deputy, a cousin, said. "But a successful outcome would turn us into a pariah with our friends in the Chinese government."

Choi turned to the general of the rocket forces. "What about a decisive blow from one of our missiles, smashing the summit?"

The general froze. Was he serious?

"Would it even be possible?" Choi demanded.

"Yes, it would be possible."

The chairman shook his head. "But not probable. The Chinese air defenses are impermeable."

"But our scientists are working tirelessly to defeat their systems," a civilian offered.

Choi waved a dismissive hand. "Yes, of course. But that doesn't help us now, does it?"

The man shook his head sheepishly. "No, sir."

"Do we have any other options available to us? Something that would at least disrupt their planned summit?"

"Did you have something in mind, sir?" one of the generals asked.

Choi suggested, "Another nuclear test, perhaps."

A civilian technocrat from the nuclear directorate answered. "We might be able to rush one forward, but we risk a failure by doing so, and that would damage our technical credibility in the international community. But if we succeeded it would only reinforce the concerns of the Americans and their lackeys."

"Agreed." Choi folded his hands, thinking.

The anonymous man in the rear of the room fought back a smile. The chairman was putting on quite a theatrical performance.

The room sat in silence. No one dared speak until prompted by the dictator.

"This is quite perplexing, isn't it?" Choi finally said. "The capitalists aren't stupid. They must surely have gone through a similar exercise as we are going through right now. Thanks to our valiant armed forces, they are deterred from significant military action. And another economic embargo won't amount to much in the long run. They must know these things. So why have the summit? A failed summit is terrible propaganda. They must have a plan to destroy us. But how? What do they know that we don't?"

The room waited for his answer.

"Do I have to do all the thinking? Our enemies are set to strangle us. Speak up!"

Shocked by the rare display of emotion, the officers and ministers immediately conferred among one another briefly, then silenced again, confounded.

The anonymous young man stood up, his chair scraping on the concrete floor. Every head turned in unison.

"Chairman, gentlemen, I have a slightly different view of the situation," he began.

The heads around the table turned back toward Choi. Their quizzical faces all asked the same question: *Who is this interloper?*

"Gentlemen, this is Deputy Ri from the General Administrative Services Directorate."

This answered nobody's question. No one had heard of the obscure department. The only way anyone in the room could have known about it was to have memorized the organizational chart of the State Commission for Railroad Construction. They would have needed a photographic memory to recall that near the very bottom of that extensive document was a row of organizational boxes stemming beneath the machine tools division. Further beneath that division was the lubricants and petroleum distillates department, administered by a subunit simply abbreviated as GASD.

In reality, GASD was one of the most important agencies in the vast North Korean intelligence apparatus. GASD was so obscure that its existence was unknown even to the head of the Ministry of State Security. This is why Western intelligence agencies had no idea of its existence. It reported directly to Choi.

Choi watched the room's unresolved confusion turn to frustration. "I trust Deputy Ri's opinions completely."

That was all everyone else needed to hear. The officers and technocrats turned back around and listened in rapt attention to the arrogant young GASD official.

"The enemies of our republic are many and powerful, and they are constantly plotting our destruction." Ri spoke with command authority. The military men recognized it at once even if they didn't recognize him. Ri wasn't his real name, of course. In a previous life Ri had been a noncommissioned officer in one of the nation's elite combat units, but he was plucked from his platoon when his particular genius was discovered.

"Fortunately, their great strengths are matched by a singularly cataclysmic weakness. A weakness my department is prepared to exploit. But it must be done so quickly. A window is rapidly closing."

The chairman sat up. "With what result?"

"Two results, sir. First, the peace, safety, and security of our republic. And second, the end of China as we know it, and the West along with it."

The stone-faced chairman smiled.

# 9

## HENDLEY ASSOCIATES
## ALEXANDRIA, VIRGINIA

**P**aul Brown sat behind his desk studying an Excel spreadsheet dense with numbers, the glow of the computer screen reflecting on his bifocal lenses. The figures danced in his brain the way sheet music played in the ear of a symphony conductor. He loved accounting and forensic auditing in particular, and in his humble opinion, he was pretty good at it. But working at Hendley Associates, a private equity management firm, was the icing on the cake. The company had grown exponentially in the five years since he'd been hired, and both his salary and his responsibilities had grown with it.

In fact, the job had probably saved his life.

Paul was so focused on the task at hand he forgot to finish his morning tea, now tepid in his favorite Iowa State ceramic mug. His leather chair squeaked as he shifted around to alleviate the sciatica pain shooting down his leg—sitting too much was a professional hazard. His executive assistant urged him to get a stand-up desk ("Sitting is the new smoking," she claimed), but he couldn't ever pull the trigger. Probably just a fad, he kept telling himself. Besides, he really liked his desk. It was just the right size. Held everything he needed, right where he needed it. The framed photo of his beloved Carmen stood on the right-hand corner, her plain, gentle smile a constant comfort to him.

God, how he missed her still.

His doctor urged him to lose weight to help with the bad left knee and creaking lower back, but Paul found it a struggle to even mount the stairs at work, let alone attack a gym. Even he had to admit he was beginning to look like Wilford Brimley without the mustache. He couldn't grow one to save his life.

His mother called him "big boned" when he was a kid, but he was an ace on the wrestling mat in high school, placing third in the state championship in his weight class in his senior year and earning him a college scholarship. Those were his glory days, at least physically. But that was nearly forty years ago. A lot of water—and chocolate glazed doughnuts—had passed under the bridge since then. His only concession to physical fitness was a set of Zenith hand grippers that he worked at his desk every day.

"There you are," he muttered to himself, his bleary eyes finally landing on a data cell he'd been searching for. He highlighted it, then pushed his mouse aside. He pulled off his glasses and rubbed his tired eyes. It was only eight in the morning, but he'd come in three hours earlier in order to get a running start on today's work.

Technically he was three days ahead of schedule on his end, and the project wasn't due for another week. But he liked to get his work done ahead of time. His father, a beat cop in Chicago in the fifties and later in Des Moines, where he was killed, had taught him as a kid: "Ten minutes early is on time."

He was thinking about the salami-and-cheddar sandwich in his lunchbox when his intercom buzzed.

"It's Mr. Hendley for you," his assistant said. "Line two."

Paul hesitated. Why was the director of the firm calling him? He picked up. "Paul Brown here."

"Paul, it's Gerry Hendley. How are you?"

Paul smiled. The soft-spoken South Carolina accent sounded quaint in Paul's midwestern ear. He and Hendley didn't speak often, but Paul liked the man immensely. He hoped it was mutual.

"Fine, sir. And you?"

"I could use a favor, Paul. I don't suppose you have a minute to come up to my office?"

Paul glanced at the unblinking computer screen, beckoning. Hours of work lay ahead of him. "Maybe later this afternoon? Say around two?"

"If it's not too much of an imposition, how about right now?"

The gentility of the former senator's voice didn't fool Paul. That was a summons, pleasant as it was.

"I'm on my way."

"I'm grateful. See you in a bit." He rang off.

Paul cradled the receiver, saved his document, and shut his computer down as per the privacy and security protocols his department required. Protocols that he had written himself.

He pushed himself up with his arms and stood, hoping desperately that he hadn't committed some heinous error in his work. He couldn't bear the thought that he might have done something to hurt the firm's stellar reputation or to have disappointed Gerry Hendley. He brushed the powdered-sugar dust off his gray polyester slacks and reached for the matching suit coat hanging on the door, trying to decide if he should be worried or not.

"Not," he said out loud, pulling on his coat. If he'd done something wrong he'd fix it, no matter what it took.

Hendley's secretary was on the phone when Paul appeared in front of her. She covered the receiver, smiled, and pointed him to the tall mahogany door on the far side of the spacious waiting room. "Head on in. He's expecting you." She returned to her phone call.

Paul limped over to the door but couldn't bring himself to just barge in, so he knocked gently with a thick knuckle. He heard voices on the other side, and soft laughter, too. He recognized Hendley's voice. The other seemed familiar. He felt stupid standing there, and he hated to interrupt them, but he was practically eavesdropping at that point. Obviously they hadn't heard him, so he knocked louder. A moment later the heavy door swung wide and Hendley's beaming face greeted him.

"Paul! So glad you're here. C'mon in! I've got a little surprise for you."

Paul forced a jowly smile. In truth, he didn't like

surprises. Not even when he was a little kid, when surprises were usually more benign. As an adult, he found that surprises usually meant trouble.

Hendley laid a guiding hand on Paul's shoulder as he waved him in. A handsome middle-aged man in a fashionably tailored designer suit sat on the tufted black leather couch against the wall. He stood and flashed a bleach-white smile.

"Paul Brown, surely you remember Senator Weston Rhodes?" Hendley asked.

"Of course he does. We're old friends," Rhodes said. He stepped forward, extending his hand. He reminded Paul of a tennis star or a movie actor.

"Senator Rhodes, it's good to see you again," Paul said. They shook hands. Paul noted the athletic build and strong grip. Except for the immaculate silver hair, the senator had hardly aged. Unlike Paul, Rhodes seemed to have won the genetic Powerball. Twice.

Paul stood up a little straighter and squared his shoulders, but Rhodes was still two inches taller. The accountant didn't bother trying to suck in his ample belly. That was a lost cause.

"'Senator'? Please. It's 'former senator' now, anyway. You knew me when I was Wes. Hell, we were both just kids back then, weren't we?"

"Yeah, we were."

"It's been, what, three years since we've seen each other?"

*Five years, three months, and twenty-one days, to be exact,* Paul thought. Carmen's funeral. Rhodes came that day, unannounced. He was an important man back then, too. It was an unexpectedly thoughtful gesture that Paul never forgot. He didn't blame the senator for not keeping in touch with an unimportant guy like him over the years. "Sounds about right."

"Please, let's sit down, shall we?" Hendley said, maneuvering Paul toward an empty chair. Rhodes resumed his seat on the couch.

"Something to drink, gentlemen? Coffee? Tea?" Hendley asked. "Orange juice?"

"I'm fine, thank you," Rhodes said.

Paul remembered his tepid tea and his mouth watered. A cup of fresh hot tea would really hit the spot. But he couldn't bring himself to ask for it in front of two former U.S. senators—one of whom was his boss. "No, thanks."

"Paul, I appreciate you taking the time to come up here," Hendley said, taking his seat behind his expansive desk. "Senator Rhodes has an urgent matter he'd like to discuss with you."

Paul shrugged. "Of course." But his mind was already back at that Excel spreadsheet on his desktop, running through the numbers.

Rhodes leaned forward, clasping his hands. It looked like a prayer, Paul thought.

"First of all, what I'm about to tell you is strictly confidential."

Paul nodded. "I understand."

"Good. Well, as you probably know, I'm now on the board of directors of Marin Aerospace Systems, one of the country's largest defense contractors, and we've set our sights on a really remarkable firm that we think would make an excellent acquisition target. Well, not a 'target,' of course, because it's all very friendly, very aboveboard. We're going to tender a formal offer to their corporate officers in the next ten days, and they've given us every indication they intend to accept."

"Is it a defense company, too?"

"It's a technology firm. Civilian applications, mostly, but very advanced, very innovative. We think they will add tremendous synergies to our side of the equation."

"How can I help?"

Rhodes smiled broadly. "To be perfectly frank, our company has dropped the ball. We signed a letter of intent along with a contract to begin this process—you know how these lawyers are, and their lawyers over there—"

"Over where?" Paul asked.

"Singapore. Didn't I mention that?" Rhodes brightened. "Have you ever been there?"

Paul shrugged. "No, I'm afraid not."

"Oh, you're in for a real treat. It's a marvelous place. A truly world-class city. You have no idea. It's the Paris of Asia, except it isn't filthy and there aren't any French people." Rhodes laughed at his own joke.

Paul shifted uncomfortably. The sturdy club chair groaned. "I'm traveling?"

Rhodes saw the concern in Paul's eyes. "I'm sorry, I didn't mean to get ahead of myself. Let me read you in on the rest of it, then we'll talk specifics."

Hendley smiled. "Paul, I want to assure you that there's no pressure here. I know you don't like to travel much. But if you don't mind just hearing the senator out."

Paul nodded, but he already knew he wouldn't do it.

There was too much work for him to finish here. And he hated flying. He tried to remember how far away Singapore was.

"So here's the thing," Rhodes said. "Our company has been going through a strategic transition—revisioning the mission, as it were. Going back to square one and asking the big questions like who we are, what we're doing, how we want to do it—you get the idea. And what that all means is that we've had several changes in personnel lately, C-suite-level executives especially, and it just so happens that the woman overseeing this particular venture was recently poached by one of our major competitors. What I prefer to believe is that she apparently forgot about the contract of intent, or at least the important details. She hired someone at the last minute—a firm, frankly, I didn't approve of, and I canceled their contract, and that means I've put my company at some risk."

"You need an independent, third-party audit, I take it," Paul said.

Rhodes flashed his million-watt smile. He turned to Hendley. "Didn't I tell you? Paul's the best. Just the best."

"Believe me, I know," Hendley said. "And when we hired him, you were his strongest reference."

Rhodes shrugged. "I just call 'em like I see 'em."

Paul had been grateful for the reference at the time. But even back then, he couldn't shake the feeling that someday he'd have to pay it back.

In spades.

**10**

A firm knock on the door caught everyone's attention. It swung open. Jack stood in the doorway, harried and apologetic.

"Sorry I'm late. There's a wreck two blocks up."

"Jack, it's great to see you," Rhodes said. He and Hendley stood to greet him. After a brief struggle, Paul managed to stand up, too.

Rhodes examined Jack's face. "I like the mustache, Jack. There's something else about you, but I can't quite make it out."

Since the hostage-rescue operation Jack had shaved his beard, keeping only a thick but well-groomed mustache, and cut his long hair short and parted it in the opposite direction. He'd even put on a little base makeup to hide the remnants of his black eye. It wasn't vanity. As the son of President Jack Ryan, Sr., "Junior" liked to change up his looks every once in a while to avoid being recognized when he was out in public.

"You look like a young Burt Reynolds," Hendley said.

"Who's Burt Reynolds?" Jack asked.

"My wife's childhood crush," Hendley said. "Before your time. Say, have you met Paul Brown?"

Jack extended his hand, smiling. "Accounting, right?" He liked Paul's unexpectedly firm grip.

"I'm surprised you remember me. We're on opposite ends of the building and on different floors."

"You do good work," Jack said. But in truth, Jack hardly knew the man. He had met him a couple of times at Christmas parties, saw him in a few general staff meetings. But Paul Brown's reputation was sterling.

"You do good work, too," Paul said. "Or so I hear."

For a moment Jack hesitated. Neither Paul nor Rhodes knew about The Campus, Hendley Associates' "black side" operations. In order to fund those operations, Hendley and Jack Ryan, Sr., also formed the "white side" private-equity management enterprise known to the public as Hendley Associates. The firm had grown exponentially over the years, in terms of both personnel and AUM—assets under management. Jack actually began his work on the white side as a first-rate financial analyst before joining The Campus as a special operator—without his father's knowledge or permission.

"We never worked together, did we?" Jack said.

"No, but you worked with Kevin Hedrick on a project I'm familiar with a few years back. He said you were the sharpest knife in the drawer."

"Kevin was the lead on that one. He just made me look good."

"I know what it is," Rhodes said, like a math student

solving a problem. "You've put on some muscle since I last saw you. Hitting the gym pretty hard these days, eh?"

"You look pretty good yourself, Senator," Jack said, trying to take the attention away from himself. In fact, he'd recently added another five pounds of muscle, thanks to a new training regimen, bringing the total to fifteen since he left college.

"Pilates and yoga, mostly," Rhodes said. "And Whole Thirty."

Jack and Rhodes shared a couple personal stories for the next few minutes, pulling Hendley into the friendly mix. Rhodes had been a frequent guest at the White House and even the President's personal residence when he was a senator. Rhodes had worked tirelessly on behalf of President Ryan's defense agenda in his first term, earning him both Hendley's and Ryan's gratitude and allegiance.

Paul Brown noted the easy familiarity between the three men. Old friends, it seemed to him. Two former senators and the son of a President. Paul felt like an intruder. He was just the son of a beat cop who was raised on his grandfather's dairy farm. "Can I get you something to drink, Jack?" Hendley asked.

"I'm fine, thanks."

They all took their seats, and Rhodes filled Jack in on the part of his presentation he'd already given to Paul. He picked up where he'd left off.

"So the bottom line, gentlemen, is that we need an independent, third-party firm to conduct a 'good faith' audit of their assets, and in the end, you'd both sign a form that would summarize your findings. Nothing too complicated or involved. That way, both parties can be assured we've negotiated a reasonable purchase price."

"Any doubts about that by either party?"

Rhodes shrugged. "We're offering double the current stock price. If they're as good as we think they are, it's more than worth it. But two more sets of eyes on the prize will put a few hearts at ease, including mine."

Rhodes leaned forward. "And as everyone in the industry knows, Hendley Associates has a sterling reputation for this kind of work, and nobody"—Rhodes waved a finger at Paul—"is better at forensic accounting than Paul Brown. I've seen him at work, believe me."

Jack frowned. He'd never seen Rhodes at Hendley Associates before. He wondered when Paul and Rhodes had worked together—and why.

Rhodes said, "Paul, what I'd ask you to do is look at their books—it's all digital now, of course. Root around in there, make sure everything is on the up and up."

"Do you have your suspicions?" Hendley asked.

"No, not at all. Dalfan Technologies is an old and reputable firm in the most honest market and robust economy in Asia. But everyone thought Enron was the golden child, too, in its day. In the current market, large-cap companies like ours can only grow our market share and capture new growth through acquiring smaller, faster-growing companies like Dalfan."

"But your board doesn't want to overpay for the privilege," Hendley said. "Or buy a pig in a poke."

"Exactly. A third-party audit protects everyone's

interests." Rhodes turned to Jack. "I've known Gerry for twenty years, and I cheered him on when he decided to jump into the private sector and start this magnificent firm." He turned back to Hendley. "Wasn't I your biggest cheerleader? Didn't I tell you you'd succeed?"

Hendley smiled. "Guilty on both counts. And I'm truly grateful for your support over the years."

Rhodes turned back to Jack and Paul. "So what other firm would I turn to other than Hendley Associates?"

Hendley saw the hesitant look on their faces.

"It's a great honor for the senator to ask us to do this, and I'd very much like to accept. The remuneration is extremely generous, too. However, he's placed three conditions on our employment. And the first two conditions are the two of you, gentlemen."

Jack and Paul exchanged a confused look.

Rhodes smiled. "I specifically requested you, Paul, because I know your work and I know you understand the value of discretion. There's no one I trust in the world more than you to handle this thing." He paused for effect. "I'd bet my life on it."

Rhodes's little speech seemed kind of over the top to Jack, but by the look on Paul's face, it had the desired effect.

Rhodes turned to Jack. "And I didn't ask for you, Jack. I asked Gerry who his best financial analyst was, and he named you without skipping a beat—which was no surprise to me at all. You're whip smart, just like your father. And given our past history together, I couldn't be more delighted to have you on board with Paul."

"I appreciate that, Senator."

"And if I can't have the two of you, well, it's a no-go for me. Sounds crazy, I know, but that's how strongly I believe in our little team."

"Well, there you have it," Hendley said. "Without the two of you, we don't get the contract."

Jack and Paul exchanged a noncommittal look. They saw in each other's eyes exactly the same thing. Neither wanted to do the job—for different reasons, obviously. But there would be an inevitable fallout for both of them if they didn't take it, Gerry Hendley's disappointment being the worst of it. Jack saw that his boss clearly wanted the gig.

Rhodes saw this silent exchange as capitulation and took it as a sign of victory.

"Paul, if you agree to take the assignment, you'd handle the forensic accounting. I'd want you to turn on that radar brain of yours and cut through all of the haze. I really don't think you'll find anything, and that's as good an outcome as I can hope for." Rhodes paused. "But don't mistake my meaning. If there's something wrong, something fishy, I want to know. I have a fiduciary responsibility to my company, and I'm counting on you to help me fulfill it."

"Of course," Paul said. "But any competent CPA can do that kind of work."

Rhodes pointed at Jack. "Jack, if you sign on, your assignment would be more qualitative in nature. I'd want you to look around, size up the people you meet there, the working conditions, the general feel of the place—

even the city. Is it the kind of work environment you'd want to be in? Are the people happy, productive? What's Dalfan's quality control like? Their security? And I'd want you to take some time to confer with Paul. If he pulled up a questionable file or two, I'd hope you'd burn some shoe leather and check things out, kick the tires. Do you catch my drift?"

"I think so."

"They'll put on their very best dog-and-pony show," Hendley said. "That's to be expected. Just keep your eyes and ears open and try to see what's behind the curtain."

Rhodes added, "I need you both to keep a very low profile while you're over there. If word of what you're doing gets out, it could affect the deal."

Jack and Paul nodded their agreement.

"Questions?" Rhodes asked.

"What was the third condition for the job?" Jack asked.

"Oh, yes, I almost forgot. You would need to leave for Singapore tonight. We're up against the clock and it's a twenty-hour flight."

Paul Brown's eyes got wide as dinner plates. Jack frowned.

Rhodes saw that he hadn't sealed the deal yet. He turned to Hendley. "Gerry, do you mind if I have a private word with Paul here in your office?"

"No, not at all. I want to grab a cup of coffee, anyway, and catch up with Jack about another matter. Will thirty minutes do?"

"That should be fine."

"Call me if you need more," Hendley said. The four

men stood. "C'mon, Jack. They've got prune Danish in the cafeteria this morning."

Jack sighed quietly and followed him out the door.

Gerry Hendley was about to serve him a steaming pile of something, and it sure as hell wasn't going to be prune Danish.

## 11

Hendley poured himself a coffee, but the prune Danishes were already gone, so he grudgingly reached for a blueberry muffin. Jack snagged a granola bar and a bag of Jocko White Tea, his new favorite caffeinated beverage. Hendley led him to a table in the far corner, away from the other patrons. Free breakfast and lunch was one of the perks of working at Hendley Associates. So were eighty-hour weeks. It was a competitive industry and there was always a market open somewhere around the globe. Eating in meant less time away from the building. Adding a cafeteria had been a costly but necessary expense for the firm.

"Ding and John gave me a detailed brief of the rescue mission yesterday," Hendley said. "You and the team did excellent work. I never got the chance to tell you that in person."

"John told us to take some time off. I was sound asleep when you called this morning."

Hendley flashed a conspiratorial grin. "Late night, eh?"

"Started a new Churchill biography I just bought, and binge-watched the whole first season of *Stranger Things*."

"Such a misspent youth," Hendley joked. "But seriously, you doing okay? That was a hairy op you all pulled off."

"Yeah, fine. Still processing a few things. Looking forward to the next one."

"That rescue mission was kind of a fluke. I feel badly about it, to tell you the truth. Things could've gone sideways."

"It was lucky we were training for exactly that kind of mission. It paid off."

"I know. But if you guys hadn't already been in the area you wouldn't have received the call. John and I talked about it yesterday. We're going to try and avoid that kind of thing in the future. Too many variables and too many unknowns on a mission thrown together like that."

"If we hadn't gone in, the rest of the hostages would've been killed. It was worth the risk."

"Now that we know the outcome, I agree. But we could have lost both your team and the hostages, given the circumstances. If anything had happened to you or any of the others, I just don't know what I would have told your father."

"You would have told him we did our best. That's all he'd want to hear."

"You're right about that." But Hendley's mood suddenly darkened. He still hadn't gotten over the deaths of Brian Caruso, Dom's brother, or Sam Driscoll. The Campus lost two good men when they lost the two of them in the last few years. The business they were in was risky, no question, and all of the members of The Campus were willing to take that risk on behalf of the country. But Hendley felt the responsibility to make sure that every effort was taken to mitigate those risks as much as possible. Advanced planning and intelligence were key in that effort, but the rescue mission had largely forsaken both because of the time factor.

"Tell me about this thing with Rhodes. What's really going on?" Jack asked.

"You know as much as I do. He called me late last night and made his pitch. He and I go back a long way. It sounds like an easy gig for the two of you, and you're going to love Singapore."

"It's just that I haven't done any white-side work for a while."

"All the more reason I want you to take this job. Your analytical work for Hendley Associates provides you with fantastic cover, and you need to keep those skills up."

"I like The Campus work better."

"I bet you do. Firing a machine gun must be a little more exciting than reading 10-K reports or all of those other SEC filings. But remember, son, the analytical work is still part of your job description." He took another sip of coffee.

Jack frowned. It wasn't like Gerry to pull rank. "What's this really all about?"

"I'm sorry?"

"I get the feeling you want me in Singapore for some reason you're not telling me about."

Jack wondered if he was being reassigned permanently. It had all been laughed off by now, but last year Gerry was none too happy about getting machine-gunned by Jack with Simunitions belowdecks on a yacht anchored off Carpenter Point. Jack had pulled the trigger too quickly on that mission. On the North Sea rig, he hadn't pulled it soon enough.

Hendley sat upright. "Frankly, you're one of my best analysts, and I really need you to do this assignment for Rhodes. It's that simple. You know him as well as I do. He isn't just connected to Marin Aerospace. He has ties all over town. If we do a good turn for him on such short notice, he won't forget, and that will lead to a lot more work, boring as it can sometimes be. But it's that boring work that keeps The Campus fully funded and operational."

Jack examined Gerry's determined eyes. He was a friend and a mentor even more than he was a boss. He could read between the lines. "And?"

Hendley held Jack's gaze for a moment, then his face broke into a smile. "Well, there is one more thing."

Jack smiled, too, trying not to gloat. It wasn't often anybody called Gerry Hendley's bluff. "Yes?"

The former senator laid a fatherly hand on Jack's muscled forearm. "I just like the idea of you being in Singapore. It's probably the safest city in the world—certainly the cleanest. This will be like a paid vacation. Give you a chance to rest up, see a part of the world you haven't seen before."

"I knew it. You're worried about me."

"Worried? Why would I be worried?"

"Did Ding say something to you?"

"Yes, as a matter of fact. He said you did a good job on that rig, and that anybody could've made the mistake you did."

"And that's all?"

"Anything else you think I should know?"

Jack knew that the senator's southern charm hid a ruthless instinct for weakness and a fishmonger's skill for hard bargains. He needed to tread carefully.

"We're supposed to start the new training module in Colorado next week. I can't miss it."

"John assures me that you're not missing anything significant, and he'll brief you when you get back."

"I don't want to let the team down. If I'm in Singapore and they get the call, I can't be there for them." Jack took a sip of tea. "Or is that the point?"

"Look, you're reading way more into this thing than you need to. It's a job, and I need you to do it. That's all. If I wanted you off The Campus, you'd be off, right?"

"Yeah, for sure." Having once lost his place on the team before winning it back, Jack worried he could lose it again. He hoped this white-side assignment wasn't the first gentle shove out the Campus door.

Hendley tore off another piece of his blueberry muffin. "I understand that an analytical assignment in Singapore isn't a shoot-'em-up. I can only imagine the adrenaline rush that kind of thing must be."

"It's not just that. It's about playing my part on the team."

"Which team? You work for Hendley Associates and The Campus. We're all one big team. You have different roles to play on both sides of the company because you have more than one talent. Not everyone in The Campus can do what you do."

"Thanks."

"But there's a bigger picture here I don't think you're seeing. Do you know the old proverb 'For want of a nail'?"

Jack remembered it vaguely. He recited it once while at St. Matthew's Academy. "'For want of a nail the shoe was lost, for want of a shoe the horse was lost, and for want of a horse the rider was lost.'"

Hendley held up a finger. "Ah! And for want of the rider, the battle was lost, and then the *kingdom* was lost. Sometimes you get to swing the sword in battle, but sometimes you're just mucking the stalls—God knows I did enough of that back on the farm. But they're all important parts to play, and we must each play them. Jack, I need you to play this part for Rhodes."

Jack felt Hendley was still hiding something. He didn't want to let Hendley down, but he didn't want to let the operators of The Campus down, either. He was torn.

"Jack, you know you've earned everyone's respect around here, especially The Campus. You always show up to do the job, no matter what is asked of you. I'm asking you to see that this is your job, too."

Hendley stood, scraping his chair against the tiled floor. "Take an hour and think about it and let me know your decision."

"I don't need the hour, Gerry. Of course I'll do it."

Hendley smiled broadly. "Great. Trust me, it'll be more fun than you know. And it's a good chance for you to get to know Paul. He can be a hard egg to crack, but he's a good man."

*More like a soft-boiled egg,* Jack thought. But Gerry Hendley didn't make suggestions lightly.

Hendley turned around and caught someone's eye across the room. In a moment he was over at another table, joking and glad-handing like he was running for county commissioner.

Jack got a sinking feeling. He would rather jump out of an airplane than spend it sitting next to a man whose idea of a good time most likely was watching subtitled reruns of *Gunsmoke* on the hotel cable channel. He didn't exactly relish the idea of spending the next ten days in a city so uptight it outlawed chewing gum, either.

But like his dad used to say, at least he wasn't shoveling shit in Louisiana.

# 12

"What did you need to talk to me about?" Paul asked. He'd watched Rhodes close the door after Hendley and Jack left, then shut the curtain to the sidelight window.

Certain they were alone and unobserved, Rhodes crossed back over to Paul, who was seated in the club chair again. Rhodes took up a position directly in front of him, leaning against Hendley's desk, towering over the heavyset accountant. The ex-senator's instincts told him he should do a bug check to make sure no one was listening in, but Gerry Hendley was an old friend and a straight arrow, and he certainly didn't want to spook Brown.

"Paul, everything I told Gerry and Jack before about the purpose of this assignment was absolutely true. I need you to believe that."

"Okay."

"And I need you to believe I really did ask for you to be on this assignment, and when I said you're the best forensic accountant I know, I wasn't just blowing smoke. We both know your skill set. You're even a certified fraud examiner—perfect for this job. And we both know that CFE title isn't an easy one to acquire."

Paul shrugged, uncomfortable with the compliments.

"I also know you're a man of . . . routine. And plucking you out of this place, out of your comfort zone and your work schedule at the last minute, and hurtling you to the other side of the planet on a moment's notice isn't the kind of thing you relish."

"It's just that I'm right in the middle of a major project, and my team—"

Rhodes raised his palm like a traffic cop, silencing him.

"You don't need to explain yourself, Paul. You're absolutely right. You already have important responsibilities here. And I want to assure you that you don't have to do this thing if you don't want to. But I know you, and if you'll let me tell you what's really going on, I think you'll jump on board."

"Okay. I'm all ears."

Rhodes slipped into the empty club chair next to Paul—two old friends now, conspiring against the world.

"You know the Chinese are hell-bent on expanding their military forces. They've been increasing their defense spending by double digits for the last twenty years, and they're not showing any signs of slowing down. Worse, their technological advances have been staggering. They seem to match us step for step in the development of stealth fighters, radar, drones—you name it. And the hell of it is, most of their technology has been stolen from us. The PLA cyberwarfare division is second to none.

They let our corporations spend billions of dollars in research and development, then steal it away from them with the stroke of a key."

Paul nodded. "It's worrisome."

"Well, large companies like mine have done a pretty good job lately locking things down. We suffer thousands of hack attacks every day—most of them from low-level criminals or hacktivist malcontents, but some are quite serious, particularly the state-sponsored ones. So far our firewalls and defensive measures have proven impervious, and we have new antihacking and antivirus technologies coming on soon. But like I said, we're a multibillion-dollar technology company. We should be good at this kind of thing.

"But as you can imagine, our government is determined to keep it from happening in the first place. By and large, American companies are getting up to speed. So the Chinese government is turning its attention to smaller foreign companies. Companies like Dalfan Technologies."

"Do you think there's a problem?"

"Actually, no, I don't. I've been over there a couple of times when we first began exploring the option of buying them up. They have a first-rate IT department. And the man who founded the company, Gordon Yeoh Fairchild, is the son of a British expat. He's about as pro-Western as you can get in that part of the world. But we did a little digging around and we found out he's had some business dealings with firms in Hong Kong and on the mainland."

"So has your company," Paul said.

"Of course we have. We're an interconnected global

economy now. Free trade benefits everyone. The challenge in this case is a little more complex. It's one thing for us to sell a widget to a Chinese firm—even one with ties to Beijing—because that's a simple transaction, an exchange of product for cash. But if we merge with Dalfan, that means our software, mainframe computers, cloud servers, and other IT infrastructure will intermingle. What our friends at Langley fear is that the Chinese may have already planted software and hardware at Dalfan that might be used to break through our cyberdefenses. Sort of like inviting the fox into the henhouse without even knowing it."

"I'm not really an IT guy, let alone an expert in cybersecurity."

"But I know someone who is. And that's why he gave me this." Rhodes reached into his coat pocket and handed Paul a USB drive.

Paul pushed his glasses back up on his nose with one finger. He brought the drive close to his face for examination. "What's loaded on here?"

"The cyberwarfare specialists at the CIA came up with a diagnostic program that can sniff out all kinds of nasty malware, worms, bots, and what have you inside of a computer system, no matter how complex. I've been tasked with making sure that the USB in your hands gets installed into a computer that has access to the Dalfan mainframe. Naturally, I thought of you."

"I'm still a little bit confused. No offense, but why would the CIA give this assignment to you and not to one of their SAD operatives?"

If Paul's question stung, Rhodes didn't show it.

"One of the advantages of my position on the Marin Aerospace board is that I'm kept in the loop on major developments, and when it seems appropriate, I keep our government informed, especially on matters that affect national security. When the Dalfan venture was first proposed, I let Langley know."

"So you're spying on your own company?"

"No. I'm helping my government win the war on terror and defend against all known enemies, foreign and domestic, including the Chinese."

Paul frowned. "Isn't that a conflict of interest? Secretly telling the government insider information about what your own guys are doing?"

Rhodes shook his head. "Not at all. Whatever is good for my country is good for my company. But even if it were a conflict of interest, I'm a patriot, and I put my country first." He glanced at the American flag lapel pin on Paul's department store suit. "And I know you're a patriot, too."

Paul sat back, processing. "You left the Agency, what, twenty years ago?"

Rhodes smiled. "We never really leave, do we? I mean, I don't take a paycheck from them anymore, that's for sure. But whenever duty calls, men like us always answer."

Paul turned to Rhodes, trying to read the man's face. He and the senator had a history from years before. He thought Rhodes was many things, but he was always a patriot. He was born into it. Rhodes was a third-generation Yalie, a blue-blooded Yankee for sure. Rhodes's grandfather served with the OSS, the CIA's wartime predecessor, and Rhodes's father was a deputy director under Bill Casey, Reagan's CIA chief.

"So all of the other stuff about the audit and letter of intent really is just a cover," Paul said.

"Not at all. Like I said, every bit of it is true. This is a real deal that my company is pursuing, and we need Hendley Associates' services to make it happen."

"That's the real reason why you fired that other auditing firm at the last minute?"

"The CIA handed this to me at the last minute. I didn't know anybody on the other team, but I knew Hendley Associates, and I knew you."

"Makes sense, I guess."

"But this extra little assignment—should you accept it—is a security add-on. A prophylactic, as it were. And truthfully, I expect that absolutely nothing will come of it. But because our company is so important to the national defense effort, Langley wants to take extra security precautions."

Paul twisted and turned the USB drive in his chubby fingers, thinking. Rhodes worried that Paul might hand it back over to him.

"Look, we both know you're too polite to say it, so I'll say it for you. You want to know why I'm reaching out to you to do this when we haven't been in touch for years."

"Yeah, something like that."

"Well, not staying in touch is completely my fault, and I apologize. You knew how ambitious I was back then. I hate to admit it, but I've only gotten worse over the years. It's easy to forget old friends from back in the day when you're busy making new ones, scrambling up the corporate ladder. I'm sorry."

Paul shrugged. He'd never known Rhodes to apologize for anything. "No, I get it. You were a busy man—heck, a senator. Not a lot of time to grab a beer with your old buddy in accounting."

Rhodes laid a manicured hand on Paul's thick thigh. "But you know that I never forgot what you did for me. Never."

Paul shifted uncomfortably again. "That was one night, a long time ago. Water under the bridge."

Rhodes smiled. "You know, when I told my friend in the Special Activities Division that you would be the point man for this, he was thrilled."

Paul frowned, incredulous. "Why?"

"Because they still remember you over there."

"Really?"

"How could they not?"

Paul stopped twisting the drive in his fingers. He stared at it, calculating. "So if I were to do this, what are the conditions?"

"Good question. There are a few things. First, we can't tell Jack or Gerry about any of this."

Paul was confused. Ryan and Hendley were friends of Rhodes's and as patriotic as anybody. "Why not?"

"They're both first-rate men—trust me, I know them well. But they're not on the need-to-know list as far as Langley is concerned, and the fewer people that know about this, the better. More important, there is the extremely slight possibility that you will get caught doing this. It's better for them, and for the firm's reputation, if they genuinely have no idea what you're doing."

"Plausible deniability."

Rhodes nodded. "It's really to protect Hendley

Associates. You remember what happened to Arthur Andersen after the Enron fiasco."

"I get it."

"Along the same lines, we obviously can't let Dalfan know what you're doing. If we give them a heads-up, and if there really is an internal problem, they might put up a defense against the probe. On a personal note, I hate to call a potential partner a Chinese spy before we've even begun the relationship—especially since I don't think that little sniffer in your hand is going to find anything. Make sense?"

"Sure."

"Also, if word got out about what you and I are doing, it could kill the merger and tank our stock price, along with theirs. And like you suggested, this really would appear like a gross conflict of interest—at least in the eyes of the SEC. They'd crucify me and my board if they got wind of this. Fines, maybe even jail time. Not to mention the fact I'd be fired. And quite frankly, I've gotten used to the big paycheck they hand me every year."

"I can only imagine." Paul was well compensated for his work at Hendley Associates, but the kind of money Rhodes made as a board member would be several orders of magnitude greater. "Anything else?"

"Yes, and it's the most important one. You must get this drive inserted into a computer that's connected to the Dalfan mainframe no later than midnight local, six days from now." Rhodes took the drive from Paul's hand and pointed at a tiny LED light on the far end of the thumb drive. "Just insert the drive into any USB port and the program will automatically launch. When you insert it, the light here will turn red. As the program executes, it will begin flashing red, and when the program is ready to launch, the light will turn blue. The program then asks for a four-digit passcode that you'll provide, and then you're done. The whole thing should take no more than thirty seconds."

He handed the drive back to Paul. "I take it you're in?"

"Yeah, I'm in."

"Good, then there's just one more thing."

While Rhodes opened up his buffalo-leather laptop case, he explained that the USB drive he was giving to him needed to be biometrically encrypted, setting it up exclusively with Paul's thumbprint so that only Paul could use the drive, and nobody else, including Rhodes. Using the software on Rhodes's computer, they finished the brief procedure and Paul pocketed the drive.

"Can't have this falling into anyone else's hands, can we?"

"No worries, Wes. I'll guard it with my life."

Rhodes smiled. "I doubt it will come to that, old boy." His smile faded. "But whatever you do, don't fail the mission."


## FALLS CHURCH, VIRGINIA

After kissing his young wife good night and watching her ascend the staircase to their master suite, Weston Rhodes retired to his private study and locked the door.

It had been a good day—and a close call, for sure. He knew he could handle Brown, though he was surprised at the man's initial resistance. It was Jack Ryan, Jr., that was the hard sell. Thank God for Gerry Hendley.

Rhodes unlocked a lower cabinet on the floor-to-ceiling bookcase and removed the small fingerprint-activated gun safe. The hinge popped open, revealing a Kimber Micro Crimson .380 ACP pistol with a checkered walnut grip—not his primary weapon.

Lying next to the Kimber was a small black Faraday bag, designed to block Wi-Fi, Bluetooth, and cellular signals. A no-name generic cell phone was inside. He removed the burner phone from the bag and placed it on the blotter of his Italian nineteenth-century turned-walnut writing desk. He then opened a desk drawer and removed a box of paper clips, opened it, pulled out a SIM card from the box, and inserted it into the phone. He powered the phone up with an instant cell-phone charger he kept in yet another drawer, then dialed a number. It rang until the man on the other end picked up.

"It's in play," Rhodes said. A barrage of questions followed. He answered each. "He'll contact me as soon as the drive is installed. No need to worry. Like I said, Paul's the best. I'll keep you posted."

Rhodes rang off when the conversation had run its course. He never mentioned Jack Ryan, Jr. That was his affair.

Jack was his insurance.

# 13

**G**erry Hendley had kindly arranged for a Town Car to pick them up and shuttle them to the airport after they both went home to pack. They were dropped at the airport in plenty of time for their red-eye flight to London.

Jack led the way through the terminal. He was rolling just one smartly designed eBag, his clothes neatly folded and stacked in packing cubes. He liked to travel light and figured the hotel where they would stay would have laundry service, so there was no need to pack a lot. Hendley also told him that because it was a strictly white-side assignment, he wouldn't be allowed to bring his sat phone or any other covert gear. He wouldn't need it, and there was no point in raising any kind of red flags as he traveled through various customs and security stations along the way. No arrangements were made for him to pick up any weapons locally in Singapore, either.

Paul followed behind, pushing a luggage cart that

carried his overstuffed garment bag, a yellow hard-sided American Tourister that had seen better days, a bulky nylon duffel bag, and his laptop carrying case.

Jack wasn't surprised that Paul had a valid passport. It was a requirement for current employment at Hendley Associates—The Campus, too. "You never know where your work will take you on short notice" was the company policy. Fortunately, Singapore didn't require a visa from an American traveler staying less than thirty days.

They made their way to the Virgin Atlantic check-in counter, where their boarding passes awaited them, and checked their baggage.

Paul's carry-on was the nylon duffel bag that pushed the size and weight limit, along with the laptop slung over one of his shoulders. He was in the same gray suit he had been wearing earlier in the day.

Jack's carry-on was a hand-tooled leather messenger bag for his Kindle, iPhone, and iPad. At home he'd showered again and changed into business-casual attire. He preferred comfortable athletic wear on long flights like this, but he was representing Hendley Associates and decided to dress it up a little bit. It was going to be a long seven-hour flight that started in Washington and landed in London tomorrow morning, where they would switch airplanes and catch an even longer thirteen-hour flight to Singapore.

In flight hours it was less than a day, but because of the time changes, they would land two calendar days after they departed Dulles International. In Jack's mind that meant fitful hours of uncomfortable boredom interrupted by bouts of intermittent sleep and the inevitable onset of jet lag, coming and/or going.

Yeah. Fun.

At least the security-check lines were short this time of night and they passed through quickly, making their way to Terminal A to catch their flight. The flight was full but mercifully not oversold, and they boarded shortly after the first-class passengers. Hendley said he couldn't spare the company's luxurious Gulfstream G550 for the flight over and certainly couldn't leave it parked on a tarmac for ten days waiting for the return flight. That meant flying commercial, and Rhodes's executive assistant wasn't able to secure upper or first class on this last-minute booking.

Jack couldn't help noticing Paul's pronounced limp as he made his way down the aisle through the first-class cabin, then the upper-class section, and finally toward their premium-economy-class seats. He offered to carry Paul's heavy duffel, but Paul politely declined. "Window or aisle?" he asked when they arrived at their row.

"Doesn't matter. Whatever's best for you," Jack said.

"Same for me."

"It might be better for your leg if you can stretch it out. The aisle might be the way to go," Jack offered.

"If you really don't mind."

"Of course not." Jack set his carry-on in the overhead compartment and slid into the window seat as Paul heaved his bag onto his empty seat and unzipped it, pulling out a small down pillow and an inflatable neck pillow before zipping the bag back up and tossing it into the same compartment. A few impatient passengers huffed in line behind him until Paul finally fell into his seat with a big sigh of relief.

They both buckled up, Paul shoving the small pillow behind his lower back. He saw Jack watching him. "L4–L5 disk degeneration."

"Must not be comfortable."

"It's hard to sit for long periods of time."

"I get antsy myself," Jack offered. *Just twenty hours and fifty-nine minutes to go,* he thought.

"I should probably tell you now that I'm not a very good flier," Paul said.

"Nervous?"

"Airsick. Well, and nervous."

"My dad hates flying, too."

Jack tried to keep from rolling his eyes. *It was going to be a very long flight.*

"I brought some Dramamine from home." Paul shook the pill bottle. "It's beyond the expiration date, but it should still work." He craned his head around. "Maybe the stewardess can get me some water."

*Stewardess? Geez, when was the last time this guy flew on a plane?* Jack wondered. "I'm sure the flight attendant will be glad to get you some." Jack pushed the call button, and a handsome middle-aged woman appeared a few moments later with two small glasses of champagne on a tray and passed one to each of them.

"Welcome aboard, gentlemen. My name is Sally. Is there anything else I can get you during boarding?"

Jack lifted the glass. "How do we rate?"

"It's our way to say thank you for flying premium economy."

Jack admired the bubbly in his hand. Suddenly the wide leather seats seemed a little more comfortable. "When you get the time, would you mind getting my friend a bottle of water? He needs to take his medicine."

"Sure thing, soon as we get everyone settled in."

"Thanks."

Paul sighed with relief. "I should've taken it in the terminal, but I was afraid we were going to be late."

"It's not a problem."

Jack raised his glass for a toast.

"Cheers."

"Cheers." Paul's glass trembled slightly as he sipped from it.

Five minutes later the flight attendant reappeared with a bottle of water, and Paul downed two Dramamine—he took an extra one because they were old. Fifteen minutes later the plane screamed down the runway and clawed its way up into the night sky, Paul's hands clutching the arm-rests in a white-knuckled grip. A few minutes later they leveled off, and Paul relaxed.

"You don't mind flying?" Paul's face was pale and clammy.

Jack wanted to say he preferred jumping out of planes rather than sitting in them, preferably HALO or HAHO. "You know you're more likely to die in a car wreck than a plane crash, right?"

"Not a big fan of car wrecks, either."

"How's your stomach? Feeling queasy?"

Paul thought about it. "I don't feel any turbulence. I think I'm good."

"Good. They'll be serving dinner soon."

Paul checked his watch. "It's nearly seven. I'd like some hot chamomile tea."

"Why? Is your stomach upset?"

"I always have a cup of tea at seven. It's just a habit I have."

The flight attendant appeared a few minutes later with her service cart, and Paul requested his chamomile tea. She apologized and said she didn't have that particular flavor, so Paul requested a cup of hot water and fetched a zippy bag crammed with Celestial Seasonings chamomile tea bags from his duffel. "I packed some for the hotel just in case they didn't have any," he explained. Jack was content with bottled water.

When the beverage service cart cleared, Jack decided he needed to take a leak. He apologized to Paul as he crawled over him and headed for the restroom in the back of the plane because the first-class cabin was partitioned off with a curtain. He had to wait a couple of turns until one vacated. He slipped into the cramped little facility and did his business hunched over, his large frame ill suited for the angular geometry of the phone booth–sized john. He flushed, then washed his hands, and practically fell out of the folding door and back into the aisle.

When he emerged, the overhead cabin lights were dim, and the darkened interior was gently lit by purple accent lighting. When Jack reached his row, he saw that Paul was sound asleep, mouth agape and lightly snoring, his neck wedged in his inflatable pillow. The Dramamine had hit him hard. Jack was a little disappointed. He took Hendley's advice to heart and was determined to try to get to know Paul Brown better. He seemed nice enough, though painfully shy. There would be plenty of time on this trip to find out more about the man.

Jack opened up the overhead compartment and fetched his Kindle, then climbed as carefully as he could over and around the beefy accountant so as not to wake him. He finally managed to fall into his own seat and buckle in. With any luck he'd be able to finish the Churchill biography he'd started the other day. But a few electronic pages into his read his eye caught the flight attendant walking toward them with a tablet in her hand, followed by a silver-haired captain. A moment later they stood over Paul.

"That's Mr. Brown, Captain," she whispered.

Some of the passengers around them cast furtive glances in their direction.

Jack wondered what kind of trouble his partner was in. It was against FAA rules for the pilot to vacate his cockpit while in flight. Something was wrong. He nudged Paul. "Hey, buddy, better wake up."

"Wha . . . ?" Paul woke with a start.

"Paul Brown," the captain whispered. "I don't believe it."

Paul blinked heavily. Squinted. His face broke into a smile. "David Miller. What are you doing here?"

"Flying, supposedly. Babysitting the autopilot is more like it." The tall aviator held out his hand. Paul shook it. "I saw your name on the manifest and just wanted to make sure. I'm so glad you're on this flight. What brings you my way?"

Paul was still groggy. He pulled his glasses off and wiped his eyes. "Business trip. Oh, I'm sorry. This is my associate, Jack Ryan. Jack, this is David Miller. An old friend."

Jack extended his hand. "Nice to meet you, Captain."

"Same." A firm, steady grip. But the captain clearly wasn't interested in a conversation with Jack. He turned his attention back to Paul. "Is Sally taking good care of you?"

Jack saw the respect in Miller's eyes. Or was it something more?

Paul smiled. "She's been wonderful."

The flight attendant beamed. "Thank you, Mr. Brown. It's been a pleasure. There will be a regular food service in half an hour, but if there's anything special I can get you before then—"

"Oh, no. I'm fine, thank you."

Jack tried to hide his utter confusion. She was acting like he was a celebrity or something.

What the hell was going on?

The captain leaned close and lowered his voice even further. Jack could barely hear him say, "Look, Paul, I just checked with Sally. There was a last-minute cancellation in first class. I want you to take it."

"Me? No, I couldn't—"

Captain Miller grinned. "I insist. For old times' sake."

Paul turned toward Jack, his neck still wedged in the inflatable pillow. "How about you, Jack? Why don't you take it?"

Sounded like heaven to Jack. Hot facial cloths, mixed drinks, steaks. "You need to take it. Your back and your knee will do a lot better in first class if you can stretch out."

"You sure you don't mind?"

"I'll be fine. I'll just be reading, anyway."

Paul rubbed his knee. "Yeah, maybe you're right."

"Good," Captain Miller said. "Sally will help you with your things. I need to get back to the salt mine. Good to meet you, Jack. Have a pleasant flight."

Captain Miller turned and headed back toward the cockpit while Sally helped Paul gather his things. He wouldn't let her carry the heavy duffel, though.

"See you in London, Jack. Hope you sleep well."

"Thanks. Have fun up there."

Jack watched Paul limp up the aisle, following the flight attendant through first class. A few envious passengers leaned out to watch the portly accountant pass beyond the first-class curtain, where travel nirvana—and a twenty-thousand-dollar private suite—awaited him.

Ten minutes later Jack was back into his Kindle when Sally reappeared with a small tray and a tall red cocktail adorned with a wedge of pineapple. She handed it to Jack with a smile. "Courtesy of Mr. Brown, with his compliments."

Jack took it gladly. "What is it?"

Sally smiled. "A Singapore Sling, of course."

*Of course,* Jack thought. He took a sip. He tasted gin, brandy, Cointreau, Bénédictine, and pineapple juice. Incredible.

"Do you like it?" Sally asked.

"My new favorite. Tell Paul thanks for me, will you?"

"Sure thing. Enjoy." She turned and headed back to first class.

Jack lifted the glass in a mock toast. "You're okay, Paul Brown." He suddenly remembered how much he liked to travel and that he'd always wanted to go to Singapore. Hendley was right. Maybe this was going to be a great little vacation after all.

But he still wanted to know. *Paul Brown, who the hell are you?*

**14**

By the time they finally boarded their next flight, Jack was fried. Mechanical problems, a switched plane, and crew delays from a transit strike turned a scheduled three-hour layover into a nine-hour debacle. A frustrating business trip was suddenly worse.

What really bothered him, though, was the utter waste of time. If he'd only known about the delays, he would've grabbed a taxi and headed into London to see Ysabel Kashani. It killed him to be this close to her and not say hello in person; to say he was sorry for the way it ended, on a hurried phone call between flights they both had to catch, without even a last kiss good-bye.

Paul was happy as a clam, though, and fresh as a daisy. Captain Miller had given him a pass to the Virgin Atlantic Clubhouse, where he enjoyed a hot shower and a shave, along with champagne and breakfast. He even got his suit cleaned and pressed. At least one of them was having a good time.

Jack, on the other hand, had cleaned up in the public restroom, his face nicked by the cheap razor he'd bought in the terminal. Still, he was happy for Paul. The only explanation Paul was willing to offer about the extraordinary attention Captain Miller had paid him was that he and Miller had known each other years ago. Beyond that, Paul wouldn't get more specific. Jack let it go. There were still another thirteen-plus hours of flight time and a whole week on the ground to decipher the growing enigma that was Paul Brown.

Jack was also exhausted. He hadn't been able to sleep on the overnight flight to London, partly because a man in the row behind him snored like a jigsaw ripping through a tin roof. He certainly couldn't sleep in the stiff-backed Heathrow terminal chairs, anxiously waiting to board their flight while Paul worked his Sudoku puzzles.

Now that Jack was finally settled into his plush reclining leather chair, he could catch some shut-eye. He stretched out his seat as Paul fired up his computer. "I need to keep working on my other project," Paul said, but Jack was already sound asleep.

Paul worked diligently on the last spreadsheet he'd been combing through when he first got the call from Hendley and Rhodes. When the dinner service finally arrived, he dove into it, and he ordered a cup of steaming-hot water for his private stash of chamomile tea just before he went to sleep.

When the breakfast service rolled around, Paul decided to wake Jack up with a gentle nudge.

Jack stirred out of his dead slumber. "Something wrong?"

"Heck no. Breakfast is coming, and it smells great."

Jack yawned and stretched. "Sounds good." He raised his seat. "I miss anything?"

"Like what?"

Jack rubbed the sleep out of his eyes. "A hijacking. A monster on the wing trying to tear it apart. The usual."

"No, not really. You've got a couple of options for breakfast."

"I'll have what you're having."

"I'm going for the full English selection. And just to be a little crazy, I'm going for the Earl Grey tea. I could use the caffeine."

"Order for me—but with black coffee. Back in a flash."

Jack excused himself, crawled over Paul, and used the cramped facilities, splashing water on his face and running his fingers through his hair to try and bring some order to the chaos on top of his head. He checked the scabbing razor nicks on his face and hoped he could buy or beg a toothbrush and toothpaste from the flight attendant before they landed.

Jack made his way back up the aisle, passing three men scattered around the cabin: a German, a Bulgarian, and a Ukrainian. Jack didn't notice them. He wasn't supposed to.

But each of them was keenly aware of Paul Brown.

The "Singapore girl" flight attendant, wearing the airline's distinctively colorful *sarong kebaya*, arrived with breakfast just as Jack retook his seat. His mouth watered as he started tucking in.

As they ate, Jack decided to pick up where they last left off on the flight to London, hoping Paul's defenses were finally down.

"I never did thank you properly for that Singapore Sling."

"I had two. Knocked me out cold."

"I take it you and Senator Rhodes have a history."

Paul chewed a crumbling biscuit. "We worked together a long time ago."

"Just like you and that Virgin Atlantic captain."

"Something like that."

Jack cut another piece of sausage. "What was Rhodes like to work with?"

Paul set his fork and knife down and wiped his mouth with the heavy cloth napkin. "Everybody loved Weston Rhodes where we worked, especially the ladies. I think even Carmen had a little schoolgirl crush on him. He was just so darned handsome and charming. You know how he is."

Jack had to give him that. Even as a middle-aged man, Rhodes still turned younger women's heads.

Paul chuckled. "He never met a stranger."

"A natural political talent."

"We all knew he was destined for great things. I wasn't surprised at all when he was elected to the Senate. I was shocked that he didn't run for reelection. I just assumed he was setting himself for a run at the Oval Office."

"The Senate doesn't pay as well as Wall Street." Jack decided to press his luck. "Neither does the Company."

Paul frowned. "He told you about his past?"

"Didn't have to. He was born and bred to clandestine service. It's practically a family business. But a man like Rhodes has a hard time with authority, unless he's the one in charge."

Paul smiled but didn't comment. He picked up his silverware again and went after his potatoes.

Jack pushed a little deeper. "Were you and Rhodes close back in the day?"

"Not really. I was downstairs, he was upstairs, both literally and metaphorically. Ivy League and all of that."

"I know the type." Jack had attended Georgetown University, a first-rate academic institution, and his dad was a Boston College grad. Jack was grateful for his education. He didn't care that he didn't have the Ivy League connections. Like the Jesuits taught him, it was character—not pedigree—that determined one's destiny.

"I met your dad once," Paul said.

"Really?"

Paul continued. "A few months ago, Gerry asked me to drop off some paperwork at his place out in the country. I had to wait on his front porch with the Secret Service detail because your dad was inside. But when Gerry came out, he invited me in for a beer. He grabbed one for me from the fridge and told me to follow him into the den, where your dad was. We all just sat around and drank a beer together, and talked about college football for a few minutes. Nice guy. Not stuck-up like most politicians."

"I'm a fan, too."

Paul finished the last bite of buttery eggs, licked the fork, and set it down on the tray.

"So, I have to confess. I wasn't completely honest with you back in Gerry's office yesterday."

"How so?"

"When I said I knew you by reputation, that was true enough. But I also know you through Susan Styles."

Jack struggled to remember the name. "Sorry, drawing a blank."

"She's an executive assistant in my department. Older woman, heavyset, plain. A real hard worker and smart, but not the kind of woman a man pays much attention to. Anyway, she told me the whole story."

Now Jack was squirming. Had he done something wrong to this woman?

"It was raining cats and dogs one night, and she was driving way too fast when her tire blew. She almost lost control but managed to pull over on the side of the road, shaking like a leaf. Just as she threw on her emergency lights, an SUV pulled up in her rearview mirror. The guy jumped out, got soaking wet, and asked her if she was hurt. She said she wasn't, then he offered to change her tire. She didn't have Triple A and she didn't know how to do it herself. So the guy changed her tire. He was muddy and drenched when he finally got done. She offered him twenty dollars for his trouble and he refused it. Even insisted on following her home to make sure she got there okay. When she pulled up in her driveway, he honked the horn and waved good-bye. Who does that kind of thing anymore?"

Jack shrugged, a little embarrassed. "It was no big deal. Just a tire."

"So when I said you did good work back in Gerry's office, I was really talking about the tire."

Jack smiled, accepting the half compliment. "Did you finish catching up on your other work?"

"Not yet. In fact, I need to get back to it."

As soon as their trays were carried away, Paul broke

out his laptop and dove into his spreadsheets. Jack opened up his, too, connected to the onboard Wi-Fi, and started doing research on the Dalfan corporation. He wanted to hit the ground running.

An hour before they landed, the flight attendant passed out customs declarations cards. Jack glanced at it. Standard stuff.

Except for the big bold red letters in an extra-large font at the bottom of the card:

**WARNING**
**DEATH FOR DRUG TRAFFICKERS**
**UNDER SINGAPORE LAW**

**15**

## CHANGI AIRPORT
## SINGAPORE

Voted the world's best airport year after year by Sky-trax, Changi didn't disappoint in either beauty or efficiency. Jack would have enjoyed checking out the butterfly garden or the rooftop sunflowers, but the two of them had customs to get through and baggage claim before meeting up with the car service that would shuttle them to their hotel.

Having nothing to declare, Paul and Jack proceeded swiftly through the green corridor at customs, then headed for the Terminal 3 baggage area. Jack was stunned by the architecture in the wide and open space. The gray-and-white stone floors were patterned like an IBM punch card, complementing the cantilevered panels that opened in the high ceiling like silver windows. But the cold modernity was offset by soaring walls covered in a green hanging garden and stately palm trees planted in the floor. It felt more like a space station biodome than an airport terminal.

The added bonus was that their luggage was already rumbling along on the wide rubber plates of the conveyor belt.

"How is that even possible? I'm usually waiting for my luggage longer than the flight lasts, back in the States," Jack said.

Paul stood with his rent-free luggage cart—unheard-of in American airports. "I read online that they used to have a rule at Changi Airport—no longer than twelve minutes for the first bag on the airplane to reach the belt. I guess it's still in effect."

"If Singapore runs the rest of their country like their airport, they'll soon run the world."

They gathered up their bags and headed for the exit, where they saw a cluster of black-suited limousine drivers holding placards and tablets in a wide variety of languages and scripts. But it was a woman about Jack's age that caught his eye. She wore an open-collared white shirt, a powder-gray suit jacket and slacks, and a near frown on her beautiful but serious face. No jewelry. Obviously Asian, but taller than most, and also mixed race. Stunning.

Standing to her side and slightly behind her was an Asian man about as wide as Jack but not as tall, in a pair of slacks, a polo shirt, and a tight-fitting sport coat, the seams strained by a muscled torso. Jack guessed the square-jawed security man was Korean. His dark eyes bored into Jack's.

The woman stepped forward, extending her hand. "You must be Jack Ryan."

Jack took her firm grip. "And you're Lian Fairchild, head of Dalfan security."

She tried to hide her surprise. "You did your homework."

"It was a long flight and I had good Wi-Fi."

She extended her hand to Paul. "Mr. Brown, I hope you had a pleasant trip."

"Very much so, thank you."

"This is Park, one of my senior security staff."

Park nodded curtly.

"What branch of service?" Jack asked, curious if the stone-faced hulk would answer.

"Marine Corps," Park said. "Republic of Korea."

*No one to screw around with,* Jack noted.

Lian pointed toward the exit. "We should get going. Traffic is heavy this time of day."

A few minutes later they loaded into a black luxury Range Rover and navigated the heavy airport traffic. The windshield wipers slapped away a light rain. Paul was visibly nervous about the fact that they were driving on the wrong—English—side of the road but didn't say anything.

So close to Malaysia and Indonesia, Jack had been half expecting a Third World megacity, overcrowded and dysfunctional, until he did his research on the plane. From the highway he could see the ultramodern Western-style metropolis and its towering skyline. Most of the cars around them in the bumper-to-bumper traffic were late-model vehicles, many of them bearing luxury name plates like Lexus and Mercedes. He could've been on a freeway in Los Angeles or New York, except the cars and roads in both of those places were in far worse condition.

"I hope you don't mind, but we've changed your plans," Lian said from the front seat.

"We're not heading for the hotel?" Paul asked.

"You won't be staying at a hotel. I've made better arrangements for you."

"That's very generous of you, but it's not necessary," Jack said. What he really wanted was to fall into a bed after a shower and a shave, or at least a change of clothes, before meeting the CEO of Dalfan Technologies.

"Of course it isn't necessary, but it's my father's wish."

Jack and Paul exchanged a look, surprised by the hostility in her voice.

"I hope the two of you are not too tired from your journey. My father wishes to meet with both of you this evening."

"We're happy to meet him. That's why we're here," Jack said.

"Good. I trust it won't be too unpleasant."


Twenty-five minutes later they found themselves just west of the Singapore Botanic Gardens, in one of the oldest and wealthiest neighborhoods in the island nation-state.

The two-lane road was lined with dense foliage and trees on both sides. Steel gates broke up the tree line occasionally, and through them Jack spotted large modern homes nestled far back from the road. The area reminded him of the one-percent zip codes in Washington, D.C., and elsewhere around the country he'd had the pleasure of visiting.

Two guards stood discreetly in the shadows of a broad entryway. The fortified gate slowly opened for the Range Rover as the guards waved them through. The Range Rover's tires burbled on the driveway's cobblestones as it rolled up the slight incline toward the mansion, nestled inside an expansive, well-manicured lawn. Off to the side of the house stood a tall sprawling tree, like an oak, with long, sturdy branches and a thick trunk.

"What kind of tree is that?" Paul asked. "Must be seventy feet tall."

"It's called a *penaga laut*. That one is over one hundred years old. My father has been extremely careful to preserve it. He says that tree is as much a part of our family as he is."

"Beautiful specimen."

"My father's modest home," Lian said. "I hope you don't mind, but we've prepared a small reception for you."

"Modest?" Jack said. "It's spectacular."

The red-tiled roof contrasted brilliantly with the white two-story structure. It was obviously old construction, though renovated, and similar to several elegant bungalows they had passed earlier.

"Thank you. But it's not quite as large or famous as the house your father lives in, I'm afraid."

"My dad's place is bigger, but it's older and it's just a loaner," he said.

Jack couldn't tell if there was a smile on her face in the passing shadows, and the tone in her voice didn't provide any clues, either. She might have been paying him a compliment—or mocking him. Maybe both.

"My father's house is the last privately owned bungalow of its kind on the island. There are only about one hundred left. The rest are owned by the government and leased out, mostly to wealthy British expats longing for an authentic colonial experience."

The Range Rover rolled to a gentle stop in front of the mansion. Two men in casual uniforms scrambled down from the porch to open the doors, while a third, taller than the other two, called out.

"Mr. Ryan, Mr. Brown, welcome to Singapore!"

Lian, Paul, and Jack approached him. It was still warm outside and slightly humid after the rain, but pleasant.

"Dr. Fairchild, it's a pleasure to meet you," Jack said. The man was just a few inches shorter than Jack, but he was broad in the shoulders and lean for his age, which Jack guessed to be in his late fifties, judging by the flecks of gray in his hair and the lines on his face. Like his daughter, he was a mixed-race Asian, though his Caucasian features were more pronounced than hers.

"Please, call me Gordon, both of you." They shook hands. Dr. Fairchild's smile was wide and infectious. Lian slipped under her father's arm and he gave her a hug and a kiss on the head. "You've met my daughter, obviously. Pardon a father's pride."

"How long have you been head of security?" Jack asked.

"Only two years."

"My daughter's being modest. She served ably under her predecessor for three years and before that was a sergeant in the Special Tactics and Rescue Unit with the Singapore Police Force."

"That's quite an accomplishment."

A sleek Protonic Red BMW i8 roared through the gates. Every head turned.

Dr. Fairchild was clearly annoyed at the spectacle but tried to hide it behind a forced smile. "Come in, please. I know how tired you both are after that long journey. I've made it too many times myself. We have dinner prepared for you."

"That's very kind of you, sir," Paul said.

"It's a humble meal, but I hope it will satisfy."

The i8 screeched to a halt behind the Range Rover and the gull-wing doors lifted. The driver leaped out and dashed over to the porch. "Sorry I'm late, Father. A small emergency at the office."

Dr. Fairchild's smile disappeared. He began to say something but held his tongue. "Gentlemen, this is my son, Yong Fairchild, the chief financial officer of Dalfan Technologies. Yong, this is Paul Brown and Jack Ryan from Hendley Associates."

Yong was taller than his father and as handsome as his sister was beautiful. Broad shouldered and narrow waisted, the CFO carried himself like a fighter. Like his sister, he owned a firm grip and smiled as he looked Jack straight in the eye.

"We've been looking forward to your arrival," Yong said. "I hope the two of you will forgive my lateness."

"We just arrived. It's not a problem at all," Jack said.

Dr. Fairchild pointed toward the front door. "Now that we're all finally here, we should eat."

**D**r. Fairchild took the tall leather chair at the end of the expansive table, flanked on either side by his son and daughter. Jack sat next to Yong and Paul next to Lian. Two Indonesians, a husband and wife, began the service by bringing in the dishes as a third servant poured ice water into crystal glassware. The dining room, like the rest of the house, was modern with traditional touches, featuring dark wood timbers and white walls. The architecture and furnishings felt both tropical and colonial but not garishly so. It was an homage to history and the local culture, and impeccably stylish.

Dr. Fairchild raised a glass. "To our honored guests, and to our two countries. Peace and prosperity for us all."

"Thank you," Jack said. Paul agreed.

They feasted like kings on melon-and-mango salad, chili crabs, *xiao long bao*, pork rib soup, curry rice, tandoori chicken, and other exotic delectables, each dish a reflection of the wildly diverse cultures that inhabited Singapore—British, Malaysian, Chinese, Indian, and Indonesian. In a nod to his proud English heritage, Dr. Fairchild served frosty porters and Tanqueray gin.

Dr. Fairchild began the evening's conversation formally, lightly touching on global economic conditions, the Federal Reserve's latest meeting, the Bank of Japan, and other financially oriented subjects—something he knew Jack and Paul were familiar with. Lian and Yong offered few questions and even fewer opinions, allowing their father to drive the discussion. Jack felt like it was a warm-up to a sparring match.

As the meal progressed and the liquor began to take hold, Dr. Fairchild opened up the conversation.

"How well do you know the history of Singapore, gentlemen?"

"Only what I read coming over," Jack said. "It's an amazing place."

"If you want to know the history of the island, just look at my family." He beamed with pride, lifting his hands like a blessing pope.

"Let's take our dessert and coffee in the library," Dr. Fairchild suggested. "Or do any of you take tea?"

"Tea would be fine, thank you," Paul said. "Chamomile, if you have it."

"Certainly."

Dr. Fairchild stood and led the group into a two-story library with floor-to-ceiling mahogany bookcases. Jack stopped in front of one unit and scanned it. The shelves in front of him were full of history texts and war biographies. Other shelves featured science, engineering, and technical works. Around the room on display tables or on shelves Jack spotted black-and-white photographs of English soldiers from the two world wars as well as the Korean War.

Jack stepped over to a display case featuring a well-worn Webley revolver—standard issue in the British Army for decades. Prominently featured high on the far wall in a display case was a captured Imperial Japanese Army battle flag, bullet ridden and burned on the edges. Jack was something of a World War II buff, his grandfather having served in the 101st Airborne at the Battle of the Bulge.

"You have an amazing collection of books," Paul said.

Dr. Fairchild shook his head with mock embarrassment. "You should see my Kindle! It's even worse. Father was an avid reader. I'm afraid I picked up the habit myself."

Jack and the others took their seats on plush leather couches and rattan chairs as the servers brought hot coffee and tea services along with plates and bowls of exotic desserts, setting them on the low tables in front of them.

"These are two popular local desserts, durian mousse with *gula melaka* and pandan chiffon cake. I hope they're not too sweet," Dr. Fairchild said, sipping a cup of strong black coffee.

Jack was already overstuffed but didn't feel comfortable refusing the colorful offerings. He tried both. The pandan cake was moist and delicious. It tasted like hazelnut, one of his favorites. But he wasn't as crazy about the durian mousse, with its strange textures and odd flavors—almost like buttermilk and almonds. The coffee was a smooth, dark-roasted Sumatran. He'd never tasted better.

"I mentioned before that if you want to know the history of Singapore, you need only know about the history of my own humble family. My father was a lieutenant with the British Army, Malaya Command, stationed at Fort Singapore with the 30th Fortress Company, Royal Engineers, when the Japanese invaded. When the British Army surrendered, my father disappeared into the rain forest, eventually joining up with a Malaysian rebel unit, where he met my mother. In between blowing up bridges and shooting Japanese, they fell in love. They married after the war."

Dr. Fairchild pointed at the Japanese battle flag. He smiled broadly. "My father kept several souvenirs from the war, including me. He decided to stay in Singapore rather than return to Blighty, and started a small firm, which has since become Dalfan Technologies."

"Impressive," Jack said.

"I attended university here, where I met my wife, the mother of my two precious children. She was half Chinese and half Indian. She and I spent the first years of our marriage in London, where I earned my doctorate in electrical engineering, before returning here to start our family."

Jack had read his wife's online obituary on the plane ride over. "I'm sorry for your loss. Dr. Fairchild was an accomplished woman."

"Thank you. I miss her still."

Paul's research into Dalfan hadn't included the personal stuff. He was touched by Fairchild's grief, an emotion he understood too well.

Yong set his coffee down. "As you can see, we are a proud Singaporean family, but typical of our people. We work hard, obey the laws, take risks, create wealth, pay our taxes. Singapore is successful because it has allowed families and companies like ours to prosper."

"Sounds a little like the American Dream," Jack said.

"Or what used to be the American Dream," Yong said. "Your national debt, government corruption, and massive trade deficits put all of that at risk. The 'end of history' has a different meaning for the United States these days."

Jack understood the reference. He had read Francis Fukuyama's seminal 1989 article years before at Georgetown. Fukuyama's thesis was that all of human history was progressing toward a final, culminating idea of liberal democracy that marked the "end" of historical development, and the United States was the epitome of that idea. Fukuyama's argument seemed unassailable in the 1990s, after America won the Cold War. Fascism and communism had been defeated by Western liberal democratic ideals. But America's challenges and Europe's crises in the twenty-first century suggested that liberal democracy itself might have seen its best days, at least in the declining West.

"Don't count us out yet," Jack said. "My country has a habit of coming back from behind to win."

"I'm a huge fan of your father," Dr. Fairchild said. "If anyone can revive the United States, it's him."

"I'm a fan, too, sir. But the country is too big for one man to fix all by himself. My father always does what he thinks is best for all Americans. Hopefully, there are enough of us who will do the same and follow his example, no matter what it takes."

Dr. Fairchild nodded approvingly. "I have great hopes for your country and mine. The West has its problems, but the world as we know it—at least the best parts of it—is Western to the core, even here in Asia." The Dalfan CEO shot a sideways glance at his son. "Don't you agree, Yong?"

"No question, Father. But China is undoubtedly on the rise, and America's influence in Asia is in decline."

"Do you agree with that statement, Mr. Ryan?" Lian asked.

"The upcoming summit will help shape peace in the region for years to come, I'm sure."

"A very political answer," Lian said.

Dr. Fairchild smiled playfully, leaning forward, feigning conspiracy. "Care to share any specifics about the agenda?"

Jack smiled and shrugged. "I don't have any. I'm just making an educated guess. My father doesn't talk about financial investments with me, and I don't talk politics with him."

"I understand." Dr. Fairchild nodded thoughtfully. He muttered absentmindedly, "Fathers and sons."

Lian spoke. "We are honored that you and Mr. Brown have come here, and we hope you know how much we want this deal to go through with Marin Aerospace Systems."

"As a third-party auditor, all I can promise is that we will be as fair and evenhanded in our analysis as we can possibly be."

"We would expect nothing less," Yong said. The muscles in his jaw flexed. "My department will make every effort to assist you in your work. But trust me when I say that you will find all of our accounts in order and the financial strength of our company uncontestable."

"I wasn't suggesting otherwise," Jack said, surprised by the sudden hostility. "I apologize if I've offended you."

"Of course you haven't," Dr. Fairchild said. "My son

runs a tight ship. He's not used to someone running a gloved finger along the windowsill, looking for dust."

"Good, because that's what we've been hired to do. Paul will handle the quantitative analysis, and I'll be checking in with your division heads and asking a lot of questions to help me get a better sense of your operations."

"Whatever access you need will be provided to you. My son will be your primary contact person for the audit, and my daughter will see to your security needs."

Jack shrugged. "Security? I thought Singapore was one of the safest cities on the planet."

Dr. Fairchild tented his fingers in front of his smiling face. "Yes, I suppose it is, isn't it? Still, precautions are in order."

"I will also be your tour guide. I imagine you will want to see the sights and get a feel for the city," Lian said. "You can't separate our company from our country. The two go together, hand in hand."

Jack smiled. "We look forward to it."

Yong shifted in his chair. "Tell me, Mr. Ryan—"

"Please call me Jack. As much as we'll see each other, there's no point in being formal."

"Okay. So tell me, Jack, can you tell us your opinion of Mr. Rhodes and Marin Aerospace Systems?"

"In what regard?"

"Are you of the opinion they still want to go through with the merger?"

"I'm confused. Why would you ask that? If they weren't interested, we wouldn't be here, would we?"

"Humor me, please."

"We're a neutral third-party examiner. I don't think my opinion is worth much."

"But as a neutral third party, you are in the best position to form an unbiased opinion about the two parties in question."

Jack glanced at Paul. *You wanna help me out here?*

Paul shrugged. *You're on your own.*

Jack dove in. "As far as I can tell, Marin Aerospace is very eager to proceed with the merger. And while our job is to provide a thorough and unbiased analysis of your firm's net worth and operations, my impression is that Mr. Rhodes is hoping that we will be able to sign off as quickly as possible."

"That's good to hear," Dr. Fairchild said. "When Mr. Rhodes canceled the audit, I was concerned Marin Aerospace was reconsidering their offer."

"Not at all," Jack said. He didn't feel comfortable revealing that Rhodes and his team had simply screwed up.

"Your visit is pro forma. That's the term of art, I believe," Yong said.

"As per the contract of intent," Paul countered. "Signed by both parties."

"Do you have any questions for us, Mr. Brown?" Dr. Fairchild asked.

"Call me Paul, please. Just one for now. From what I've read, your company has been extremely successful. Why do you want a merger with Marin Aerospace? Most companies prefer to remain independent."

"Beyond the obvious advantages that additional capital will provide, the fact remains that the world marketplace is terribly competitive. We won't survive for much longer without a strong infusion of liquidity and the global resources that a company like Marin Aerospace can provide."

Jack watched Yong. The man's gaze shifted around the room and his mood darkened.

"You don't fear losing your autonomy as a company?"

"If we're wiped out by competition, we won't be autonomous anyway," Dr. Fairchild said. "The reason why I chose to merge with Marin Aerospace was Senator Rhodes's promise that we would remain an independent entity under their corporate umbrella."

"What else would they say?" Yong asked. "You wouldn't have agreed to the proposal otherwise."

Dr. Fairchild stiffened in his chair. It was clear to Jack the two men had had this conversation before.

"I trust Weston Rhodes and the board." He turned to Jack and Paul. "Barring any unforeseen mishaps, the merger will be going through shortly, and that's my final decision."

"My understanding is that the agreed-upon stock purchase price is substantially higher than the current market price," Jack said, trying to drain the tension out of the room. He looked at Yong. "Your family will be very rich."

Dr. Fairchild nodded. "My legacy to my children. What else is the duty of a father than to provide for his heirs?"

*So that's the real reason you're doing this,* Jack thought. He wondered if Dr. Fairchild had some health issues. Something to look into later.

Lian checked her watch. "Excuse me, Father, but it's late and our guests are probably tired. I should get them to their residence."

"Of course. How thoughtless of me." Dr. Fairchild stood. The others followed suit. "I've enjoyed our conversation very much, gentlemen. I hope you'll be my guest here again soon."

"We look forward to it. Just as soon as we get our work done."

The Dalfan CEO smiled. "Excellent."

**16**

Lian and Park, her South Korean bodyguard, pulled inside the electric gate and into the driveway of a newly constructed two-story home in a newer and more crowded neighborhood. It was much closer to the Dalfan corporate headquarters near Changi Airport than Dr. Fairchild's mansion was. The rain had stopped.

Lian's bodyguard helped Paul and Jack unload and carry their luggage into the foyer.

"It's a modest house," Lian said, "but it has all of the modern amenities. We keep it available for visiting guests like you."

"We're honored," Paul said.

Lian pointed at the umbrella stand. "Feel free to use those. It's monsoon season now, you know."

Jack had checked the weather before packing, but clearly Paul hadn't, judging by the stunned look on his face.

"Yes, we know," Jack said, covering for Paul.

Outside, the home was mostly stucco and glass, with

a sloping red-tiled roof—obviously influenced by the architectural style of traditional homes like Dr. Fairchild's. He had laughingly described the style of his home as "tropical Tudor-Elizabethan."

Lian gave them a quick tour of the place, including separate bedrooms with private bathrooms, a fully stocked kitchen, satellite television, and high-speed Wi-Fi.

She opened the back door and led them to a detached garage. She activated the automatic garage door opener and handed Jack a set of keys.

"The Audi TT is a company vehicle, completely at your disposal. Of course it has a satellite GPS system, should you need it." Lian pointed at the far wall, where two bikes were chained up. "Sometimes it's easier getting around on one of those than driving."

"You've thought of everything."

"My father wants you to be comfortable. If you need anything, you have my number. Also, meals will be provided to both of you at the office. Any questions?"

"A hotel would've been fine with us."

"Isn't this better?"

"Much better, thank you." *And easier for you to keep an eye on us,* Jack thought.

"Then we'll leave you to get settled in. I imagine we'll see you tomorrow?"

"First thing."

"Good. We'll talk about our security arrangements then."

She didn't offer her hand, only a curt nod. She and Park marched across the lawn toward a side gate and straight for their vehicle. Jack and Paul headed back into the house.

Paul made a beeline for the kitchen. He found an electric kettle with water and plugged it in. "I need another cup of tea to settle me down before bed."

"My biological clock is all messed up, too. It's morning back home right now. We need to get on local time quickly if we want to get any work done."

"I'm boiling extra water."

"Sounds good."

Paul grabbed two cups out of the cupboard and set them on the counter, then limped into the foyer. A luggage zipper zipped open and closed before Paul returned to the kitchen with a box of tea bags. "Chamomile is good to help you sleep."

"Thanks."

Paul poured boiling water into the waiting cups.

Jack took a seat. "What did you think of Dr. Gordon Yeoh Fairchild?"

Paul opened up the cupboard doors, doing an inventory. "Nice man, smart. Seems like he really wants this deal to go through."

"His son wasn't as keen. I think he'd be just as happy if we got on the plane tomorrow and never came back."

Paul smiled. "I know the type. He's defensive because he's good. In his mind, there's no need for an external audit because his numbers are perfect and any reports he's filed are flawless. It's a good sign, actually. It's when the accountants are overly cheerful and compliant that you know something's wrong, because most of the time, there is. There are way too many *i*'s to dot and *t*'s to cross, especially on the ledgers of a complex international company like Dalfan." Paul found a bottle of Glenfiddich single-malt scotch. He pulled it down.

"You're probably right."

"I know I'm right." Paul unscrewed the cap and tipped an ounce into his tea. He pointed the bottle in Jack's direction. Jack shook his head. *No, thanks.* "What did you think of Lian, his daughter?"

"Still forming an opinion." Night had finally fallen. Jack checked his watch. "Let's hit the ground running tomorrow. We'll leave here at seven, if that's okay with you."

"I'll be ready."

Lian's Range Rover was speeding along the tree-lined East Coast Parkway when her cell phone rang. It was Yong.

"Where are you?" Lian asked.

"On my way home. Have you dropped them off?"

"Just a few minutes ago. What do you want?"

"I saw the way you were looking at them, especially Ryan. I'm concerned."

"You needn't be."

"They're not our friends. These men have been sent to find something wrong with our company. Rhodes sent them to find a way to drive the purchase price of our stock down."

"Are you certain?"

"Don't be naive."

Lian frowned. "They won't find anything, will they?"

"Of course not. How can you even ask me that? But that doesn't mean they won't lie or make something up."

"Jack and Paul didn't strike me as liars," Lian said. "They're just doing their jobs."

"Their job is to screw Father out of his money, or worse. Rhodes isn't stupid. He sends the President's son to make a big impression. But it's obvious what he's up to."

"I'm not so sure."

"You don't have to be. Just keep a close eye on them, especially Ryan. I'll have someone keeping close tabs on Brown. Let them do their audit, but let's not give them the chance to cause any trouble for Father. Agreed?"

"Agreed."

"Besides, we already talked about this. If something were to happen to the President's son while he was here, there would be hell to pay. And Father would be humiliated."

"Nothing will happen to Ryan. I'll keep close to him. You have my word."

"Thank you, Sister. That's all I ask."


The bedrooms were upstairs. Paul took the one at the far end of the hall, overlooking the street, Jack the one closest to the stairwell. Paul wouldn't let Jack help him with his heavy suitcase or duffel as he limped his way up the stairs. Paul was obviously out of shape, but the way he slung the luggage around told Jack that there was still some power left in those flabby arms.

Jack unpacked his suitcase and put his things away, then decided to grab a shower before bed. He felt grimy after traveling in the same clothes for more than twenty-four hours in closed spaces and breathing recirculated air.

Before stripping down, he decided to do a quick check of the room. He was being paranoid, he knew. But there was something about the way Lian studied him. At first he thought it was because he was the son of the American President. As hard as he tried to hide that fact, it invariably got out. It wasn't surprising that the head of corporate security would've discovered that, but even more likely, Rhodes had told her. He probably thought it was a real coup that Jack Ryan's son was doing his audit.

The other possibility was that she thought he was a good-looking guy. But she wasn't throwing off any kind of vibe that led him to believe she was sexually interested in him. Too bad. She was a real looker.

Over the course of the meal he finally figured out that she watched his every move and carefully analyzed his words. She was intensely interested in him, for sure, but in the end, she was just doing her job.

And if he were her and the job were to collect intel on a visitor, he'd bug the joint he put them up in.

Maybe he was being overly cautious, but better safe than sorry. He thought about sharing his concerns with Paul but decided against it. No point in thinking or acting like a spook in front of him, especially if there wasn't any proof yet. But he didn't know what kinds of things they'd be discussing regarding their findings at Dalfan, and he didn't want that information to be shared without his consent.

Jack went to the shower and turned the water on full blast, along with the faucets in the sink. If his rooms were under audio surveillance, the sound of rushing water could defeat all but the very highest grade of noise-reduction software.

He started in the bathroom and moved to the bedroom, running his fingertips along edges of frames and sills, checking curtain hems, zippers, drawers. He didn't spend more than five minutes searching. It was only a spot check, hoping for a random find, but really all he wanted to do was silence the nagging voice in the back of his head. When he started he doubted he'd find anything anyway, and he was right. If Lian and her team were deploying sophisticated equipment like long-distance laser microphones or electronic bugs wired into appliances, he wouldn't find them, and he didn't have the electronic countermeasures he needed to defeat them. This was strictly a white-side job, Hendley had said. But Hendley forgot that there was a lot more corporate spying in the world than government spying.

Not exactly satisfied but not willing to exert any more effort, Jack stripped down to his birthday suit and hit the hot, steaming water.

It felt good to be getting clean again.

Paul stuck his head out of his bedroom door to make sure Jack wasn't out in the hall or moving around downstairs.

He shut his door again and locked it, then headed for his luggage. He unzipped his laptop bag and opened a pocket that contained the USB drive Rhodes had given him with the CIA software he was tasked to install.

He held the USB drive in his hand again. Lian had said that they would be discussing security measures tomorrow morning. What did that mean? Obviously, security measures deployed by Dalfan at Dalfan headquarters. They'd be looking for exactly the kind of thing now sitting in the palm of his hand. If drug dealers got the death penalty here, what was the penalty for spying?

He put the USB drive back in the laptop pouch and zipped the case back up. He'd have to find a way to sneak the drive onto the floor before he could even think about installing it—that would be a whole other headache. He'd think about that later. Right now it was time to floss and brush his teeth.

"Security measures," he repeated to himself. What would those be? He ran through a list of the protocols he would deploy in a similar situation. It wouldn't be at all impossible to find a way to get the USB drive past their security, and even if it was found, what would they do? Probably just tell him to leave it at home. But if they seized it and examined the contents? Like Rhodes said, the mission was designed such that if someone had to fall, it was Paul and only Paul. He accepted that. But it would be better to not get caught in the first place. He needed to find a way to get that drive past security and then a way to install it. Might as well start tomorrow.

A thought struck him. He turned off the bedroom light and crossed over to the window. If he were running a security operation, he'd put security people on-site and keep the target under surveillance at all times. Certain that he wasn't backlit, he carefully pushed the curtain, just half an inch, and glanced out to the dimly lit street.

A sedan was parked in the distance in front of a different house. He couldn't quite make anything out. He pulled his smartphone out of his pocket and pointed it at the vehicle, then used the 6x optical telephoto magnification. The camera's lowlight feature and zoom helped him see the shadow of a man in the passenger seat who seemed to be looking up in his direction, but he really couldn't tell. If he had to guess, he'd say he looked Caucasian. The moonlight striking the windshield created a glare that blocked the view of the driver's side.

Paul felt like a voyeur. This was stupid. If that was one of Lian's security teams, so what? Keeping them under observation was for their own protection, wasn't it? Besides, there were a lot of houses in the area. It was relatively early in the evening. He put the camera down.

Another man dashed into view just then, flung open one of the rear doors, and fell in. The car's headlights popped on, the engine fired up, and the car sped away down the street.

*What was that?*

Probably nothing, Paul decided. Just people in the neighborhood. Lian's security team wouldn't quit this early.

That USB drive was making him crazy.

Paul flipped the bedroom lights back on and headed for the bathroom. Maybe if he brushed his teeth and put on some pajamas he'd be able to fall asleep. It was going to be a long day tomorrow and he was going to need his wits.

# 17

## DALFAN TECHNOLOGIES HEADQUARTERS
## SINGAPORE

It took Jack a few moments to acclimate to driving a car seated on the right side of the vehicle, and even longer to get used to driving on the left side of the road. His first clockwise roundabout was an eye-opening experience. Paul clutched the overhead hand grip and shoved his feet into the floorboard, and Jack began laughing out loud after he got stuck on the inside and had to run the circle again before shooting out onto the correct street. What struck him as particularly funny was the near-frantic tone in the constantly changing voice commands from the GPS navigator as he whipped past the half-dozen exits on the roundabout.

The crowded early-morning traffic on the main thoroughfare was slow but organized compared to the free-for-all scramble that characterized most big cities in the non-Western world. It only took them seven minutes to find the techno-modern four-story steel, concrete, and green glass Dalfan building. He pulled into the gated driveway and gave the security guard their photo IDs. After a check against the data on his tablet, the unarmed guard smiled and waved them through the gate. Ten minutes after that they stood at the front desk of the main entrance on the ground floor.

"Jack Ryan and Paul Brown for Ms. Lian Fairchild."

The young and demure receptionist smiled and called back on her phone. Jack saw the broad open floor and workstations on the other side of the secured glass wall. A minute later Lian appeared.

"Gentlemen, welcome. Any trouble finding us?"

"No problem at all. It's your GPS that's gonna need therapy. I think I drove that woman crazy—pardon the pun."

"How about some coffee or tea before we get started?" Lian asked.

"We already had breakfast back at our place, but thanks."

"Tea later would be nice, though," Paul said.

"Of course. Anytime you like. Please, follow me."

Lian flashed a card, unlocking the heavy security glass door, and led them through into the next suite. Glass-walled offices and conference rooms with glass doors were located on both sides of the room, and on the floor itself were two dozen occupied computer workstations.

On their immediate left as they entered the suite was the security office, another glass-walled room but without a door. A serious young man, maybe fresh out of college, stood behind a desk with a computer workstation off to the side.

Lian gestured toward him. "Gentlemen, please."

"What's this?"

"We have strict security protocols beyond this point. We must check your bags for contraband items and inspect your electronic devices if you want to be able to bring them inside."

"I'm not comfortable with that," Jack said.

Paul shook his head. "Me, neither."

Lian shrugged. "Then you have the option of leaving your bags with us and using only our equipment, or you cannot go in at all."

"If we don't go in, we don't do the audit," Jack insisted. "Your father won't be pleased."

"He'll be even less pleased if I allowed two strangers to smuggle in equipment that hacked or stole our most important data. There is no Wi-Fi in this facility. Every computer is air gapped and hardwired to our mainframe, which has a secure Internet connection."

"Is corporate espionage that big of a problem?" Paul asked.

"It has been in the past. Not anymore."

Paul and Jack set their bags on the table along with their smartphones.

"Please, do you mind opening them?" the security guard asked. "And power up your devices and enter your passcodes."

Jack and Paul complied as the security guard snapped on a pair of surgical gloves—computer keyboards were dirtier than toilet seats, collecting bacteria, fecal matter, and other unsanitary deposits. The first thing he did was to swab each device with a cotton trace detector.

"You're checking for explosives?" Jack asked.

"Standard operating procedure," Lian said.

The security guard tossed the swabs, then did a quick check of the applications folders on their laptops and phones. Seeing nothing obvious, he returned the items to them.

"Thank you." The guard tossed his gloves in a garbage can and began inspecting their bags. He frowned when he rifled through Paul's opened clamshell bag. His finger touched an object tucked beneath the material lining the fold, and with some effort, he finally managed to extricate a USB drive.

"Sir? Is this yours?"

Paul felt the floor fall out from under his feet. He swallowed hard. "Yes, I suppose it is."

Jack saw Lian glowering at his partner. What was Paul trying to hide?

Paul shrugged. "It must have fallen down there. Sorry about that."

The friendly security guard suddenly wasn't as friendly. He took the drive and slipped it into the USB port on his computer.

Paul watched him tap a few keys, studying the contents intently.

Jack glanced at Paul. Shot him a look. *Something you want to tell me?*

Paul shrugged again and shook his head.

The guard's computer beeped and he ejected the drive. "Nice photos, sir. Washington, D.C., isn't it?"

"My last trip to the Smithsonian. I was wondering where that drive was. Thanks for finding it."

"I'm afraid I'll have to keep the drive here. You can pick it up when you leave."

Paul shrugged. "Okay, sure."

Lian asked the guard a question in Mandarin. The guard shook his head as if to say "No problem."

Lian pointed the way out. "All right, gentlemen. Please follow me."

She led them toward the far end of the room, where there was yet another glass security wall, shut and secured by a card reader as well. They passed a steel emergency exit door leading to the stairwell, which was next to a large kitchen and dining area where someone was making coffee.

Lian showed them the rest of the floor beyond the security glass and pointed out the offices along both walls for the senior analysts following global markets and related research. Junior analysts sat at workstations on the floor.

At the far end of the room Jack saw another glass partition wall, but on the right side of the room leading up to it was a large glass-walled conference room. A dozen people were seated around a long table.

Lian motioned toward the door. "Gentlemen."

When Jack and Paul entered, everyone else stood, all smiles. They were mostly in their thirties and forties, men and women, from East and South Asia, intense and earnest but friendly, like tech executives Jack had met all over the world.

Lian introduced them to several department heads and their assistants from around the company, including production, marketing, sales, and accounting. She further instructed her employees to answer any and all questions that the Hendley Associates auditors might have. "And they insist you call them by their Christian names, Jack and Paul."

The brief meeting ended with more handshakes and smiles, and Lian led them to the next security door. She flashed her key card and they passed into the last section of the floor. Across the room along the far wall opposite the glass partition was Dr. Fairchild's expansive office, spanning the entirety of the outer wall. On the left side of the inner wall were two offices—Yong's and Lian's. On the opposite wall were two more offices, both empty. Lian pointed at them. "Those are yours for the duration."

Jack and Paul stepped over to one of them. They were spartan accommodations. Each office had just a desk and computer terminal with a landline phone, a small laser jet printer, and a single storage cabinet full of office supplies.

"Your laptops can't be connected to the mainframe without the installation of proprietary software, so any work you need to do will have to be done on one of our terminals."

"Can we download data from your system to our laptops so we can do work off-site?" Paul asked.

"No. For the purposes of the certification audit, our data remains on our hard drive. Of course, once our firms merge, Marin Aerospace will have complete and total access to all of our data, mainframe, and storage. Until then, the two of you are welcome to take notes on your machines or print hard copies of anything you need, but we can't allow any kind of machine interface between your equipment and ours. That includes the use of any portable drives. Is that clear?"

"Perfectly," Paul said.

He was screwed.

Lian checked her watch. "We just have time to visit the second and third floors before your assistant arrives, Mr. Brown. He'll walk you through the accounting databases and software and be available to you for any further questions."

"What about me? Don't I need a minder?" Jack asked.

"You have one. Me."

Jack half expected a playful smile or a coquettish shrug, but she was all business.

Lian guided them back out onto the main floor and past the kitchen area, explaining that for security purposes, the stairwells were never to be used except in the case of an actual emergency.

They exited the suite and took the elevator to the second floor, which had the same strict security protocols as the first. Lian assured them the protocols were the same on all four floors. Clearly, Dalfan and Lian Fairchild took their security seriously. Jack was glad he wasn't on a clandestine black-side operation. He wasn't sure if he could crack this high-tech safe.

Lian introduced them to Dr. Chen Tao, the head of their virtual reality department. Jack couldn't help noticing the lovely spray of freckles across her nose. For some reason it made him think of a Beach Boys song. They set a meeting time.

Lian then took them to the third floor, where they met the head of their Steady Stare research program, Dr. Mahindar Singh, who assured Paul and Jack of his complete cooperation. Jack made an appointment to see him tomorrow.

"What about the fourth floor?" Jack asked.

"That's where we keep our mainframe secured. It's also where Dr. Heng's department is located."

"His team is doing some very interesting work," Paul said.

"Unfortunately, he is at a conference right now. But you can meet him on Saturday if you like."

"We're in no hurry. That works for us," Jack said.

Jack was genuinely looking forward to seeing the demonstrations Drs. Singh and Tao had promised, and what their two departments were developing. From what he saw, it was all cutting-edge stuff. Dr. Heng's work was harder to grasp but still impressive, judging by the corporate reports. No wonder Marin Aerospace wanted to do this deal.

After the brief tour, Lian escorted them back to their offices across from hers on the first floor and reintroduced them to the young man named Bai from accounting they'd met earlier in the conference room. He would be Paul's assistant.

Lian also handed both of them security badges and cards that would permit them to enter any room in the building. "Except for the mainframe facility," she said.

"No need for us to be in there," Jack assured her.

"I'll leave you to start your work. Please contact me if you intend to leave the building."

"Sure," Jack said. He had no intention of heading out today anyway. Tomorrow? *Well, we'll see,* he told himself.

"I hope you'll both join us for lunch. We have a chef who comes in and prepares a meal for us."

"That would be great," Paul said.

"It's another chance for both of you to get acquainted with our staff and ask all of your questions."

*It's also another way for you to keep an eye on us,* Jack thought. The car. The house. Yeah, it was all so very convenient, wasn't it?

# 18

The first thing Paul's assistant, Bai, did was set up their computers for security, starting with their usernames. He handed each of them a USB drive with digital read-outs. Digital numbers already flashed on them.

"What are these?" Jack asked.

"Those security fobs generate passcodes. When you log on with your username, you have sixty seconds to type in the number generated by the fob. If you don't, you can't log on, and you must wait another sixty seconds for the next number to generate before you can try to log on again. That make sense?"

"Perfectly."

"You only get one of those each. Please don't lose them, and if you do, report it immediately."

"Of course."

Bai then detailed the rest of their security instructions. "First of all, you're free to use your laptops, but as Ms. Fairchild explained earlier, there is no Wi-Fi or cell access in the building, and there's no way for you to connect physically to our main server without first downloading our encrypted security interface, which is not allowed."

Bai then pointed at a USB port on the computer keyboard. "You are not allowed to insert your own private USB drive into this port or into any other Dalfan machine. But even if you did, it wouldn't work. The USB ports are passcode-encrypted, just like the computer."

*That's not good,* Paul thought. *How will I be able to load Rhodes's USB drive if the port is locked?*

Bai pulled a USB out of his pocket. "Only a Dalfan-encrypted drive like this one will interface with our machines."

"Will we be given one of your encrypted USB drives for our personal use?" Paul asked.

Bai frowned. "Not allowed. Too dangerous." He turned to Jack. "Any other questions?"

"We understand the need for tight security," Jack said. "We'll just have to work around your protocols as best we can." Jack stood. "See you later, Paul. Have fun."

"You do the same."

Paul spoke to Bai. "Might as well get my feet wet." He opened up his desktop as Jack headed back to his office.

Bai pointed Paul to the file containing the general ledger—the controlling document that contained all other subledgers and accounting files pertaining to all financial and nonfinancial data of Dalfan Technologies. Paul's focus was on the financial side. He opened up the first big file folder labeled "Assets." There was a lot of work to do, and not much time to do it. But his mind was somewhere else. He sighed.

"Something wrong, Mr. Brown?"

"Any chance we can grab a cup of tea before we get started?"

Bai stood. "Follow me."

Jack was looking forward to not being monitored by Lian or anyone else from Dalfan, but just as he sat down in his executive chair, there was a knock on his glass door.

Jack turned around. *Crap.*

"Feng," the man said, offering a small, crooked smile of yellowed teeth. "I'm the vice president of Dalfan operations."

Feng reeked of stale tobacco. He was the oldest employee in the building Jack had met so far. He wasn't in the conference room earlier. He carried a tablet in his left hand.

Ryan stood and offered his hand. "Jack."

"I'm here to give you a general overview of the corporation. We will review its organization, facilities, and personnel, and I will answer any questions you might have."

Jack forced a smile. "Great. Let's get started."

Jack opened up the Dalfan desktop with his passcode fob as Feng tapped on his tablet. They spent the next few hours reviewing organizational charts, personnel records, operating budgets, and facility locations around the city—including an FBO hangar at nearby Seletar

Airport. By the time they finished reviewing all of these documents, it was lunchtime.

"Will you be joining us in the dining room?" Feng asked, standing.

"Not today, but thanks." Jack stood, too.

Feng frowned. "That's disappointing to hear. I'll let Ms. Fairchild know."

*Of course you will,* Jack thought. "See you after lunch."

It had been a long first half of the day for Jack and Paul, but productive. Their biological clocks were still messed up, and they were both beat and famished.

Jack half expected a fight from Lian when he confirmed that he and Paul wouldn't be eating with the Dalfan employees, but instead she suggested a good local restaurant about ten minutes away.

Jack asked, "Will you be joining us?"

"I think you can handle the chili shrimp without my assistance," she shot back. "But don't be surprised if you have a few friends nearby."

Jack offered to let Paul drive, but the taciturn accountant wasn't interested in figuring out how to navigate on the wrong side of the road from the wrong side of the car, especially in a downpour. Ten minutes later they found themselves seated in a comfortable, low-lit restaurant populated by locals. They both ordered the house specialty, chili shrimp. For drinks, Jack went for the mango iced tea and Paul ordered a vodka tonic.

"So, tell me about what you found out," Jack began, sipping his iced tea. He scanned the room. His eye landed on Park, Lian's bodyguard, glowering at a menu, sitting by himself on the far side of the restaurant. No doubt there to keep an eye on them.

Paul frowned. "The first thing I found out was that my assistant is sticking closer to me than a remora on a manta ray. I half expected him to follow me into the john this morning."

"You get the feeling you're being watched?"

"More like handled. Friendly enough, don't get me wrong. Happy to answer any questions I had. But the man had no interest in leaving me alone, even for half a second."

Paul went on to describe the bulk of his research that day, mostly comparing tax filings against corporate reports going back over the last ten years.

"Everything lines up. It's almost too good. Not one decimal point out of place. You know, sort of how an escaped fugitive might drive a little under the speed limit so as not to draw the attention of the traffic cop?"

"You think there's a problem?" Jack waved a server over.

"Not necessarily. Only that the fact that the books are perfect—at least so far—isn't proof that everything is on the up and up."

The young server flashed her lovely smile. "Sir?"

"That man over there? By the window?" Jack nodded at Park, then pointed at the drink menu. "Send him one of these on me, will you?"

She giggled. "Right away, sir."

Paul tapped his vodka tonic. "And another one of these, too, please."

She nodded and scurried off.

"Sorry, Paul. You were saying?"

"I already said it. Everything looks good so far, but I'll keep digging. What did you find?"

Jack outlined his research for the day, including going over the personnel files. "Just trying to get a handle on employee retention, hiring practices—the usual. Started digging into their benefits program, too. Turns out most of the senior management have stock options. They're going to make out like bandits when Marin Aerospace swoops in and pays twice the current price per share."

"No wonder those people in the conference room were so glad to see us today."

Jack watched the server deliver a tall red drink to Park's table. He examined it, his eyes frowning with confusion.

"Our boy Park just got his delivery," Jack said.

Paul turned around just in time to watch Park flip them both the bird.

"What did you send him?"

"A Shirley Temple. I figured he wasn't allowed to drink liquor while on the job."

Paul cracked a smile. "I don't think you want to mess with that guy."

"What else is there to do?"

The server arrived bearing platters of sizzling-hot shrimp, steaming bowls of rice, and crisp stir-fried vegetables. They dug in.

Paul enjoyed the sweet and fiery spicy chili sauce and the crunchy stir-fried shrimp, but his mind was still on Rhodes's USB drive. He was glad he had run his little experiment today with the dummy drive. He assumed their protocols would catch something like that, but he wasn't sure. If that really had been Rhodes's drive the guard had discovered in his bag today, he might be sitting on a plane right now flying back to the United States, or pacing in a cramped Singaporean prison cell. The good news was that they didn't do a body search. Dalfan was serious about their security but not paranoid. *A mistake on their part,* he told himself.

He chewed quietly, working the puzzle. Even if he'd been allowed to keep his dummy USB drive, he never got the chance to try and load it on his Dalfan computer today for a test run, and according to Bai, it wouldn't have worked anyway, since it wasn't loaded with the Dalfan encryption code.

Bai himself was a security barrier, Paul decided. If he was going to stay that glued to him, he'd never get the opportunity. Odds were he was going to fail the mission or quite possibly get caught in the attempt. Neither scenario appealed to him. Rhodes even said there probably wasn't a problem to begin with—this was all just precautionary. Sitting here, it suddenly didn't seem worth the risk. Time to try a third option. Maybe get the mission canned altogether.

"So, if you didn't find anything and I didn't, either, maybe we should just sign off on this thing and go home early," Paul said.

Jack laughed. "Why? Are you as bored as I am?"

"Something like that. Dr. Fairchild wouldn't care if we wrapped this thing up."

"Rhodes seemed to want us to do some serious digging while we're here."

"But he still wants us to sign off in the end." Paul

drained the rest of his glass. He didn't want to seem too eager or oversell it. "I mean, you never seemed big on this assignment anyway, and I need to get back, so, whatever you want to do, I'm up for it."

Paul hoped to God Jack would take the bait. He didn't think his nerves could stand this for another four days. If they were sent home early by Fairchild, then he really couldn't be blamed for failing the mission, could he?

"I don't know. We're here, we might as well do the job right. Let's keep painting by the numbers and see what turns up."

"Okay. Sounds good to me." Paul fought the panic welling up inside his chest. When he saw his server rush by, he held his empty glass up high at her and jiggled the ice. "Another one of these."

She nodded and headed for the bar.

Paul sighed. It was going to be a long week.

**19**

"Mind if I ask you a question?" Jack asked.

"Sure."

"What made you want to become a fraud examiner?"

Paul stabbed another glistening shrimp. "Well, I was always pretty good at numbers, and my mother said that accountants could always find work, so I decided to go that route in college. In my junior year I had a professor who was a JD and a CPA, and he had retired from the FBI before going into teaching. He told us all kinds of great stories from his time in the Bureau—he described it like being a detective or a spy hunter, but instead of using guns, he used numbers. So what's a fat kid from Iowa gonna do? He's going to become a forensic accountant."

"And you were in government service?"

"Briefly."

Paul's clipped answer told Jack not to probe further—at least right now. He changed subjects.

"And you enjoy fraud examination?"

"It's really interesting. Never a dull moment."

Jack fought the urge to roll his eyes. Was he kidding? The thought of drilling down into accounts-receivable ledgers and hunting for misplaced decimal points made him want to shove his chili-stained chopstick in his eye. "Interesting . . . how?"

Paul's drink finally arrived. He said, "Chili's pretty hot, isn't it?" as if that were the reason he was about to take a sip from his third vodka tonic.

"Hot but good. I'm glad we came here."

"Me, too. What were we talking about? Oh, yeah. Why the job is interesting. Well, for me it's interesting because in the end it's never about the numbers, it's always about the people. People are creatures of habit and pattern. Turns out numbers are pretty good at revealing habits and patterns, and the kinds of fraud people commit generate habitual patterns of numbers and data sets, too."

"Is there a certain kind of person more likely to commit fraud?"

"From what I've read, there's no one exact trait or indicator that the psychologists can agree on—maybe they'll find a gene for it someday, but I doubt it. But when people do commit fraud, they're generally one of four types." Paul paused and took another bite of rice.

Jack picked up another shrimp and plopped it into his mouth.

"A fraud expert named Allan characterized them as the bully, the egoist, the control freak, and the mouse. People who commit fraud either crave approval, demand control, are territorial, or want to keep things the way they've always been."

"Where's the mouse in that lineup?"

"The mouse is interesting. That's the gal or guy who is quiet, doesn't make any waves, and doesn't draw any attention to themselves—except that they stand out as the perfect employee."

"Perfect—as in *too* perfect?"

"Yeah. Extra-long hours, taking on extra projects, never complaining, never asking for a raise. Of course, all that means is that they're trying to hide the bad stuff they're doing."

*You never know about people.* Ding's words on the deck of the fast-attack boat rang in Jack's head.

"So those are the kinds of people that commit fraud. I suppose their motivation is just greed?"

"Not necessarily. There's an acronym—MICE. Have you heard of it?"

*Only about a million times,* Jack said to himself. "Remind me."

"Money, ideology, coercion, and ego. So, yeah, sometimes it's about money, but as often as not it's those other motivating factors, and usually a combination of them."

"I think I read somewhere that terrorists and traitors fall under the MICE paradigm."

"That's right."

Jack shrugged. "Makes sense. If you're committing fraud, it's kind of like an act of terror or treason against the company's management and stockholders."

"I never thought of it that way. I suppose you're right."

"So how do you go about finding these fraudsters? I'd think if they were smart enough and motivated enough to cook the books, they'd be smart enough to cover their tracks."

Paul offered a rare smile, then took another sip. The ice tinkled in his glass. "Oh, believe me, they try."

"So what's your secret weapon?"

"I have a bunch of them, but data analytics is my best one. In the old days I'd break open some dusty old ledger book and run my fingers down the columns. Now I let the software do all the work. I'll give you one example—it's really interesting."

Paul pulled a mechanical pencil out of his pocket and snagged a napkin.

"Hey, wait a second, I have one of those." Jack reached down and pulled up a pen he kept clipped to the inside of his pants pocket. "That's a Zebra F-701."

Paul grinned. "I didn't know you had one, too."

Jack clicked his. "Mine's ink, not lead like yours."

Paul held his Zebra between his two hands, admiring the iconic shape of the solid stainless-steel barrel. "I've been using Zebras for decades."

"I started using these the day I graduated from college—my dad gave me a set of them. Told me my Zebra would never let me down."

"Small world," Paul said. He pulled the napkin closer. "Have you ever heard of Benford's law?"

"No."

"This is pretty cool stuff." Paul stopped. "Wait, am I boring you?"

"No, it's interesting. Really."

Paul smiled, grateful for Jack's white lie. "Benford was a physicist who began noticing a pattern in numbers. So one day he took a bunch of random figures—numbers he found in a magazine, the surface area of bodies of water, molecular weights—a whole series of uncorrelated data sets, and then he analyzed the numbers, and what he discovered is fascinating and, frankly, hard to explain."

Paul sketched out a two-by-two graph, with percentages listed on the *y*-axis and numerical digits 1 through 9 on the *x*-axis. He plotted his graph out as he spoke.

"Turns out, no matter where you look in nature, there's a uniform pattern in numbers. What Benford discovered was that the first digit of any number is going to be the number one about thirty percent of the time." Paul marked an X at the intersection of thirty percent and 1.

"The number two will occur in the first position almost eighteen percent of the time, the number three about twelve-point-five percent, and so forth." Paul filled in the rest of the graph. "The number nine will be the first number less than five percent of the time."

"So . . . if you find patterns of numbers that don't correspond to Benford's law, you think you've found fraud?"

"If I find a break in the Benford's law pattern, then I know it's something worth looking into. But then again, there are lots of reasons why it can be broken. For example, if a company has a regular purchase of an item that costs $97.86, and if that's the most purchased item on their books, well, that's not going to conform to Benford, is it? There are many other patterns and incongruences my software can check for besides Benford, but you get the idea."

"So I take it your Benford template hasn't pulled up anything?"

"I haven't run it yet. It would take several weeks to do a decent audit of Dalfan's books, so all I'll be able to do is a few random spot checks."

"I still think we need to keep at it."

"I get paid either way." Paul swallowed his disappointment as he drained his glass. He fought back a monstrous yawn. "Mind if we grab a cup of coffee before we head back? I'm beat."

"Sure." Jack waved at the pretty server. She smiled and came over.

"A coffee for my friend here."

"Of course. Cream and sugar, sir?"

Paul nodded. "Please."

Jack nodded over at Park again. "And be sure to give me his check. I think the two of us got off on the wrong foot."

After lunch, everyone got back to work, including Jack and Feng. Feng pulled information about the two small manufacturing plants they operated in the city not far from where Jack was sitting, the only other buildings that Dalfan owned on the island. Jack quizzed him about working conditions in those places, security protocols, and production schedules. Anything Feng couldn't answer he made notes about and promised to get back to Jack with the answers as soon as possible.

Jack's analytical brain absorbed all of the information, but he also took copious notes on his laptop. He enjoyed this kind of work, pulling all of the puzzle pieces out of the box and trying to fit them back together. But he still hated being here. Less than two weeks ago he was fighting for his life on an oil rig in the North Sea in the middle of a blizzard.

His biggest risk right now was a paper cut.

While the rest of The Campus was on a training mission in the Colorado Rockies, he was sitting at a desk, sifting through leasing contracts, employee benefits plans, and production reports.

"I need to stretch my legs, Feng. How about you show me the outside of this place?" Jack figured the old smoker was craving a cigarette pretty badly by now. Feng brightened at the prospect. "Glad to."

Feng's first chance to light up was on the roof, where Jack checked out the palm trees and sun deck and spectacular views of the city. A half-dozen butts later, Jack had seen everything else the Dalfan building had to offer, all the way down to the loading dock and parking lot, with a quick run through the garage, where the company vehicles were parked, and even the boiler room for good measure. Jack had a good eye for architectural details—especially the kind that came in handy during an emergency.

By the time they were done and back at his office, it was quitting time. Jack shook Feng's hand again and thanked him for the tour, then tapped on Paul's door.

"You ready to roll?"

Paul turned around in his swivel chair, yawning. Bai looked pretty frazzled, too.

"Is it already that time?"

"Yeah. Let's get out of here."

Lian knocked on the door frame. "Gentlemen, how was your first day?"

"Productive," Paul said.

Lian glanced at Bai. The young accountant nodded. "Very."

"You can go home now," she said to Bai.

"Thank you, ma'am." Bai stood and grabbed his jacket. "See you tomorrow, Mr. Brown." He nodded toward Jack and said, "Mr. Ryan," as he stepped past him and out of the door.

Lian watched him leave. When Bai was out of earshot, she asked, "I'd like to take the two of you out for dinner and drinks. Show you some of the city."

"What's the occasion?" Jack asked. He was hoping she was actually becoming human.

"It's my responsibility to show you my city as well as my company."

Paul fought another monstrous yawn. "I'm sorry, I need to take a rain check."

"I understand," Lian said. She looked at Jack. "You're probably exhausted as well. Perhaps another time."

Jack shook his head. "No, I'm good. Let's go."

Paul yawned again as he stood.

Jack jerked a thumb at him. "After we drop him off."

# 20

They sped along the East Coast Parkway toward the bay front, passing the Singapore Flyer, the world's second tallest Ferris wheel.

From inside Lian's Range Rover, the Marina Bay Sands resort dominated the breathtaking skyline. Its three fifty-five-story towers were wide and narrow and slightly curved, and they were topped with what appeared to be a starship. The entire structure was brightly lit and bathed continuously in a shifting wash of accent lights. It was an architectural marvel. No wonder it was one of the most photographed buildings in the world.

But it was the view from the spaceship—technically, the SkyPark—that blew Jack's mind. The view around the bay and the downtown core was like a scene out of *Blade Runner*. Skyscrapers ran nearly to the horizon, a cacophony of shifting lights and dramatic shapes that glowed purple and blue and white beneath the low-hanging clouds. The Flyer's giant spokeless circle of light rotated slowly, like a vertical space station, and traffic flowed along the ECP in a wide amber river of light, spanning the coast. In the distance, Jack saw the lights of a hundred freighters moored offshore, and as many docked beneath the towering cranes of the bustling port.

Just below them was the ArtScience Museum, which appeared like a giant half-open concrete lotus flower. In the distance was a small forest of giant "supertrees"— twenty-five- to fifty-meter-tall metal-and-concrete structures with canopies that spread wide to the open sky like upheld hands. Like everything else in view, they were stunningly lit.

The whole effect was ethereal, made even more surreal by the laser light show on display from down below, the thin green beams slicing through the cloudy haze.

The thousand-foot-long SkyPark itself was a stunning piece of architecture, topped with nightclubs, bars, and restaurants but made world-famous by the nearly five-hundred-foot-long infinity pool that disappeared along the edge of the cantilevered platform. Even at this hour it was filled with swimmers snapping selfies, standing waist deep in water at the edge of the sky.

Jack and Lian sat in the crowded poolside SkyBar of the Cé La Vi nightclub, throbbing with techno-beats and horny tourists. Jack wasn't hungry enough to take advantage of the nightclub's award-winning restaurant, so they settled for sushi and beers at a small table along the glass rail beneath a red umbrella overlooking the bay. The view was better here anyway, and the cool, damp breeze felt good.

"If you were trying to sell me on your city, you've

closed the deal," Jack said. "It's one of the most beautiful places I've ever seen."

Lian allowed herself a small smile. "We're very proud of it. It's a metropolitan wonder carved into the heart of a beautiful rain forest."

"Between the botanical gardens and the green laser lights, Singapore reminds me a little of the Emerald City."

"It may be the Emerald City, but even Oz had its flying monkeys."

Jack laughed. "I thought you guys didn't have a crime problem."

"Not one that you can see. But where there are people, there are always problems."

"Is that why you left the Singapore Police Force?"

"No. My plan was always to join the family business. I wanted the practical and technical experience that I knew the SPF would provide."

"You're very proud of your company, aren't you?"

"Is there something wrong with that?"

"No, not at all. I didn't mean to offend. I guess what I was trying to say was that your sense of place in the world is strongly tied to the city, your company, and your family."

"Yes, it is."

"So how do you honestly feel about the merger? It won't affect my judgment, and I won't say anything to my bosses. I'm just curious."

Lian took a thoughtful sip of her Tsingtao, her third so far. Jack popped another piece of tuna sushi into his mouth while she formulated her answer, wondering if he needed to order a second beer himself.

"In truth, I'm not happy about it because I fear the loss of control. But my father is a very wise man and I trust his business acumen, and he believes it is not only a good move but a necessary one, so I defer to his judgment."

"Thanks for being honest."

"What else would I be?"

"You've been pretty hostile the whole time we've been here. Hostile people tend to lie."

"Hostile? Have I been rude to you or Paul?"

"No, not rude. But you're obviously angry that we're here. I'd think you'd be happy about the merger because it's going to make you very rich."

Lian frowned and shook her head. "You think being rich is something that matters to me?"

"Finding out that you're going to be wealthy isn't exactly like finding out you've got terminal cancer."

"Tell me, Jack, is money the thing that motivates you?"

Jack shrugged. "No, not really. But then again, I don't own a company like your family does."

"No, but you work for a financial firm. Why do you do that kind of work if you don't love money?"

*Because I secretly work for The Campus, working for my dad and defending my nation,* Jack wanted to say. Instead, he said, "It's interesting work, and I'm pretty good with numbers."

"I'm terrible with numbers, but I'm pretty good with a gun and I love my father, so I do everything I can to protect the company because I'm also protecting him."

*I guess we're not so different after all,* Jack thought.

"So, Mr. Jack Ryan, I apologize if I have seemed

hostile or defensive. I suppose I should be fawning over you and showering you with attention because that's what you expect."

"Why would you say that? Because of my dad?"

"What? No. Because you're so good-looking."

*Didn't see that one coming,* Jack thought. *Must be the alcohol.*

"I don't know about that."

"Haven't you seen all of the women ogling you around here? You probably have a lot of girls back in the States."

Jack shook his head as he peeled back the label on his empty beer bottle. Ysabel's face flashed in his mind. "My work doesn't exactly allow for a social life."

Lian stared at a happy couple at the next table over. "I understand, believe me."

A waiter approached with a tray loaded with a giant tropical fruit drink, a massive wedge of pineapple sticking out of it.

"For the lady, a mai tai, compliments of those gentlemen," the waiter said, nodding at a table across the way. Three large white men in their twenties smiled lustily at Lian. The one with the bulging biceps, and seemingly the oldest, lifted his own half-consumed mai tai in a toast.

"That thing is as big as your head," Jack said. He remembered the Shirley Temple he'd sent Park earlier that day. *Karma is a bitch.*

Lian told the waiter, "Tell the gentlemen thank you, but I respectfully decline the generous gift."

"What's wrong? Don't you like mai tais?" Jack asked.

"I love mai tais. Just not from strangers."

The waiter blanched. "Ma'am, the gentlemen mean no harm. It might cause them offense if I returned it."

"You can call security if they make trouble," Lian insisted.

The waiter said, "Better if no trouble is started. *Lah*." His smile, a plea.

"How much did they tip you?" Jack asked.

"Ten dollars, Australian." The waiter leaned in close and whispered, keeping his eyes on the three lecherous musketeers. "I'm afraid they will get angry if I return the drink. Best if you accept it, my lady. They'll leave soon enough."

Jack pulled a Benjamin Franklin out of his wallet and held it up. "That's one hundred dollars, American. It's yours if you take that drink away right now."

The waiter snatched the bill and pocketed it before grabbing the drink and scurrying away.

"We should go," Lian said. "Those men are trouble."

"Friends of yours?"

She flashed a knowing smile. "No, not at all. But they're men, aren't they?"

"I'm enjoying myself. Let's stay put."

"Are you sure?"

Jack looked her straight in the eye. "Yeah, I'm sure."

She studied his face, then stole a glance at his powerful hands and shoulders. "Yes, you are, aren't you?"

"Let's just say I'm a good judge of character."

"We'll have to see about that, won't we?"

They ate in silence for a few minutes, Lian casting wary glances at the table full of trouble between bites, her street-cop instincts on full alert.

Jack refused to look at them, but in his peripheral vision he saw them finally get up and leave. Once they cleared the bar, he waved the waiter back over.

"Sir?"

"A mai tai for the lady."

The waiter frowned in confusion. "Sir?" He glanced at Lian for guidance. "Ma'am?"

She smiled.

"A mai tai sounds good," she said, "but that thing was as big as my head. You better bring two straws."

The waiter laughed. "Okay, *lah!*"

# 21

While Jack was enjoying the mai tai and the spectacular view, Paul was drinking hot tea and sweating bullets.

He sat at the kitchen table, staring at Rhodes's USB drive as well as the dummy drive containing his Smithsonian photographs.

His test of the security system went about as expected. Well, he'd *hoped* Dalfan's security was lax, but he expected it to be like other high-security environments in which he'd worked, and his expectations proved correct. That wasn't good for him.

Pretending to hide a USB drive in the bottom of his computer bag was Paul's way to test how thorough their search procedures were. He was a little surprised Dalfan went to the trouble of opening up his personal USB drive to check the contents instead of just handing it over to him. If there had been a virus on that drive, it would have infected the security station computer, but that also meant that the security computer wasn't connected to the mainframe, so all Dalfan would lose in an infection scenario was one computer.

Smart.

The fact that Dalfan security also checked for explosive residue meant they were very serious about both kinetic and digital threats. Paul now assumed that at least some of Lian's security team must have been concealing weapons as well.

Bai was a pain in his rear end. The guy never left his side. But his explanation of the electronic lock on the USB ports of every Dalfan computer was useful. No USB drive could be loaded without the encryption code.

The only problem was that Paul didn't have the encryption code.

That meant he couldn't load Rhodes's USB drive directly.

Which meant he couldn't complete the mission.

Which meant that he was seriously and irrevocably cornholed.

Paul picked up Rhodes's USB drive and examined it again. Was there something he was missing?

The only good news was that the Dalfan people didn't do a full body search. It might, in fact, be possible to smuggle Rhodes's drive into the facility by hiding it in one of his pant cuffs or a shoe. But even if he did that, what good would that do?

And just because Dalfan security hadn't wanded him or patted him down last time didn't mean they wouldn't do so on his next visit. Getting caught trying to smuggle in a USB drive he couldn't load anyway was a special kind of stupid.

He also couldn't connect his laptop to a Dalfan computer or the mainframe—the same encryption code prevented it.

Paul took another sip of tea. He formulated a list of questions for himself.

*How can I defeat the USB port encryption lock?*

*How can I distract or get rid of Bai?*

*How do I not get caught doing any of this stuff—and avoid getting thrown into a Singapore jail for espionage?*

The only good news was that there were still four days to try and figure out these questions.

The bad news was that there were only four days left to try and figure out these questions.

Paul wondered if he should call Rhodes and tell him he just wasn't up to the job. Tell him the security protocols were far more stringent than they had realized.

Wait. Didn't Rhodes say he'd already been to Dalfan headquarters? If he had, then he would've known how strict the security protocols were. Why didn't he tell Paul?

Maybe because Rhodes knew that he wouldn't have agreed to do the assignment if he'd known how tough it was going to be.

Rhodes was a manipulator. That was part of his job. Or at least it was when Paul knew him back in Bulgaria in 1985. He also remembered that Rhodes didn't tell him all the gory details in advance about that night so many years ago, either.

Rhodes had a high estimation of himself and his

abilities, and a corresponding poor estimation of others. Both defaults were a function of his class and his breeding, his education and his training. So naturally he would believe he had to manipulate others around him in order to accomplish his objectives through them.

Now the picture was becoming clearer. The old-boy network at Langley had called on one of their favorite sons again—a CIA legacy, no less, the grandson of an OSS hero—and that dutiful son, Rhodes, had answered that call yet again. It was only natural for Rhodes to reach out to someone who could actually carry the water on this mission, and so Rhodes cajoled Paul into the assignment. Rhodes had handed him a rock too heavy to lift and then told him to lift it.

But then again, the more he thought about it, the more Paul began to see the logic. No doubt the reason the CIA didn't run the op themselves was that they couldn't figure out a way to pull it off, either. So they called in Rhodes for ideas, and apparently Paul was his best. "If anyone can pull this off, it would be Paul Brown," he imagined Rhodes telling them. And that would be true, because Paul had certain unique skill sets, and Rhodes knew that.

So that would've been a compliment.

Hard to get angry about that.

"But what if he can't pull it off?" Paul imagined the Langley Special Activities officer asking. And in his mind's eye, he saw Rhodes shrugging and saying, "Then he doesn't pull it off. We're no worse off for trying."

"Unless he gets caught," Paul whispered aloud, still speaking as the imaginary SAD man.

Paul shrugged. *So just don't get caught.*

So how could he avoid getting caught? The only way to definitely not get caught was to not try at all, but that wasn't an option.

He didn't want to let Rhodes down. More important, he didn't want to let his country down. He had to try something.

But what?

Paul checked his watch. It was time to call Rhodes. He wasn't going to be happy.

After several rings Rhodes finally picked up. "Paul?"

"One and the same."

"It's good to hear your voice."

"Yours, too, Wes. I hope I didn't wake you."

"Not at all. Just got back from the gym. How's the weather over there?"

"Warm, scattered showers. A lull in the monsoon season, I'm told."

"We're expecting snow this evening. I think I'd rather be where you are. How do you like it? The city, I mean?"

"It's an amazing place. I've never been in such a clean, well-ordered city. It feels more like Disney Epcot than New York or Chicago."

"I thought you'd like it. So, how is everything? Has Dr. Fairchild taken good care of you and Jack?"

"Very much so. Jack's out on the town right now with Lian Fairchild."

"Outstanding. How's work?"

"Uneventful, as we suspected."

"That's good news." The senator paused. He was waiting for the coded message Paul was required to deliver.

"I only have one complaint about this place. I can't find a good cup of chamomile tea."

There was a long silence on the other end. Finally, "That's disappointing to hear. But keep looking. I have no doubt that you'll find it, and soon. Tell Jack I said hello and send my greetings to Dr. Fairchild."

"Will do."

"Stay in touch."

Paul rang off. He could hear the disappointment in the senator's voice.

There had to be a work-around. He hoped he had the time to figure out what it was, but he doubted he had the skill.

Still, he had to try.

And if he got caught? Well, if the prison was as clean and well run as the rest of the city, maybe it wouldn't be so bad.


*F uck, fuck, FUCK!*

Rhodes paced around his library, his cell phone still clutched in his hand.

This wasn't good. He was sure Paul would've already loaded the USB drive. He knew Dalfan's security was tight, but Paul was smarter than any IT security department. Or at least he thought so.

And if smart wasn't enough, luck was even better. *Paul has that in spades, the fat bastard.*

Rhodes stepped to the library door to make sure the maid didn't have her ear pressed against it, even though she wasn't due in for another hour. His young wife was off to her hot yoga class, which meant Rhodes had the place all to himself.

Rhodes retrieved his burner phone, SIM card, and battery pack and hit the speed-dial button. His father had taught him a long time ago the only way to confront trouble was straight on. Unfortunately, the man on the other end was a brick wall, and Rhodes was running into it headfirst.

"What's the status?" the voice demanded.

"Still working on it."

"Then why have you called?"

"To keep you informed."

"Do I need to remind you that time is running out?"

"There are still four days left. I'm confident he'll figure out a way to make this happen."

"You know what happens if he doesn't."

Rhodes swallowed hard. He'd bet heavily on this operation by borrowing heavily, including a second mortgage on the McMansion he was standing in. Crashing Dalfan's stock price was a guaranteed way for him to cash in with leveraged calls—like betting against a boxer you knew was going to throw the fight. "I'll lose a great deal of money."

"That's the least of your worries." The voice rang off.

Rhodes stared at the phone in his hand, trembling with rage.

"Or yours, asshole."

Rhodes paced the room.

*How in the hell did I get myself into this mess?*

# 22

His favorite hotel was a cozy boutique closer to the city center, but the women were always more impressed with the view of the Potomac from the seventh-story suite his family had owned for more than thirty years. Rhodes had recently updated it in mid-century modern, a phase he was going through at the time.

He stood on the balcony despite the chill air, staring at the lights of the Capitol, eager to begin the night's festivities. The little blue pill had already kicked in, as had his first gin and tonic, and the twins from the escort service were due at any moment.

Over the years it had never been a problem for a man as handsome and well built as Rhodes to pick up women in bars, hotel lobbies, gyms, and even libraries. But the time and energy expended in the pursuit were too taxing for him now, as he balanced his role as board member of a major defense company with marriage to a young and eager trophy wife, the mother of their toddler, Weston Porter Rhodes III, his only son and heir. Better to spend his limited time and energy in the physical act of wanton sexual congress and avoid the inevitable emotional entanglements engendered in the women he seduced.

Or, as his father used to say, better to just pay for it.

Rhodes used a particularly well-stabled and discreet service called The Sorority, specializing in college coeds seeking to finance their expensive private-school educations in the Washington, D.C., metroplex. The girls in this service were also medically certified and psychologically screened. Most came from middle-class families and saw their employment as both adventurous empowerment and practical necessity.

The women he reserved for tonight were two of his favorites, partly because of their physical endowments, but mostly because of their shamelessness. The twins— in truth, Tri Delta sisters born on the same day, not genetic siblings—were pricey but worth it, and never failed to please.

They were also running late.

But Rhodes didn't mind. It was part of their immature charm, a childish but calculated ploy to whet his insatiable appetite.

They needn't have worried.

Just thinking about the coming revelries stirred a familiar ache in Rhodes, and the gentle ring of the doorbell nearly set him off.

He crossed the living room eagerly, brushing past the white tufted Harvey Probber modular sofa, where he intended the evening's first consummation after drinks and, for the girls, Ecstasy. He yanked the broad door open, a lascivious smile plastered on his square jaw and a prominent erection bulging against his tight-fitting pants.

"Hello, Weston."

Terror shot through Rhodes like a bolt of lightning. It wasn't the twins.

H ow?" Rhodes asked, hand still on the door handle.

The thickset man in the hallway smiled, revealing yellowed teeth nestled in a gray, well-groomed beard that matched his well-cut slacks and suit jacket. The top left corner of his forehead was hidden by a green felt fedora with a wide brim, pulled low and angled steeply.

"Aren't you going to invite me in?"

Rhodes recognized the heavy Bulgarian accent, but it was Zvezdev's black, piercing eyes he most remembered.

*Where the hell is my SIG?* Rhodes asked himself, his mind fogged and frightened all at once. *In the bedroom,* he remembered.

Too far away.

Zvezdev read his mind. His smile faded, his eyes hardened. "If I wanted to kill you, you'd already be dead."

Rhodes swallowed hard. "The last time I saw you, you *were* dead."

Zvezdev smiled again. "I thought so, too. Fix me a drink and I'll tell you the story."

Rhodes hesitated. Tervel Zvezdev was a dangerous man, and he'd found Rhodes, after all these years. Rhodes wanted to run or, better yet, strike him down.

*But how do you kill a ghost?*

They sat on the white modular couch across from each other, separated by a teak-and-glass coffee table. Rhodes absentmindedly rubbed the couch fabric with one hand, a subconscious reminder of what could have been.

Zvezdev lifted the tall glass to his lips for another sip of gin and tonic. His green felt hat sat on the couch next to him. The massive divot in the man's forehead where his skull had been caved in at the hairline and repaired—inexpertly, in Rhodes's mind—was now clearly revealed. The puckered skin looked like melted plastic. Rhodes tried not to stare at it. His eyes flitted between the golf ball–sized divot and the USB drive on the table glass.

"I can't work for you," Rhodes finally said, trying to be firm. But he saw the look in Zvezdev's narrowing eyes and quailed. "I'm sorry."

"Perhaps I wasn't clear. I only need you to do just this one thing." He smiled. "And did I mention it will make you very rich?"

"I'm a lot of things, but a traitor isn't one of them."

Zvezdev shook his head. "This has nothing to do with your government, nor does it affect American national security. It's purely business."

"So you're a businessman now? I remember you being a Communist, working for the Second Directorate of the Committee for State Security for the People's Republic of Bulgaria."

Zvezdev set his glass down. "Then you weren't paying attention. Yes, I was a Party man with a license to kill the enemies of the state. But all that meant was that I was a businessman with a gun."

"You mean a gangster."

"Ha! Exactly!" Zvezdev leaned forward. "But you never really caught on, though, did you?"

"In the end I did." Rhodes's eyes shifted involuntarily to Zvezdev's divot. "Obviously."

"The Bulgarian CSS was already a criminal enterprise, and we were connected with other elements in security services all over the Eastern Bloc who were, shall I say, equally as enterprising as we were. When the Iron Curtain fell, we formed our own organization, expanding our operations and profitability as opportunities presented themselves—which they did, enormously. We're a global organization now. If we were a legal corporation, we'd be listed in the S&P 500."

"Glad to see you made out so well."

Zvezdev wagged his head, grinning. "Not too bad. Of course, I have worked very hard. So many things to do these last thirty years." The Bulgarian's smiling eyes turned menacing. "Naturally, I wanted revenge against my enemies, and against those who had done me harm."

Rhodes felt the blood drain from his face.

"But thirty years is a long time, Weston. I was too busy making money, fucking too many women, and having such a good time that, well, maybe I'm just an old man now, but killing for revenge seems like such a waste of time. Better to make friends and make money, yes?"

"I certainly think so."

"Ha! Of course you do! Look at you, still handsome,

still rich, right? Oh, sorry about the girls tonight. I know you had big plans."

"Mind telling me how you knew?"

Zvezdev grinned. "Because they're my girls! My organization runs the service you use—along with half of Capitol Hill! Ha!"

"Well, as much as I appreciate your newfound civility, and while I always want to make money, the fact of the matter is that I'm just not interested. I have too much to lose, and frankly, I'm already rich."

"Can a man be too rich?"

"If all those millions put a man in jail, then yes, a rich man in jail is too rich."

"Then tell me this: Can a dead man be too rich?"

"Really, Tervel? You're going to be that obvious? You used to have more finesse."

"If you don't do this thing, Weston, then I'm the dead man."

"Who would want you dead?"

"You don't want to know." Zvezdev didn't dare tell Rhodes about the North Korean, or his savagery.

"And why is any of this my problem?"

"Because if I'm a dead man, well, I hate to be alone in the dark." Zvezdev took another sip of his drink.

Rhodes turned up his hands. "Even if I wanted to help you, what can I possibly do?"

"Like I said before, install this software program." He pushed the USB drive closer to Rhodes.

Rhodes picked it up, examined it. "I'm no techie."

"All you have to do is insert it into a USB drive on one of the Dalfan computers. When the light turns from red to blue, you insert your own four-digit code and you're done. Thirty seconds at most. How hard can that be?"

"And tell me again what this program does?"

"Dalfan Technologies is registered on the Hong Kong Stock Exchange. The software on that drive is designed to crash the value of Dalfan stock at a specified time and date for just a few seconds—but long enough for my HFT experts to short the stock and make millions."

"HFT?"

"High-frequency trading. Most stock transactions are done by computers these days, and the faster computers get, the better the deals. But we've decided we can be the fastest if we can predict the future—and get the best deal of all."

"That's cheating."

"Only if we are caught."

"I don't know." Rhodes set the drive back down on the glass. "I've been to the Dalfan facility. Their data security seems impregnable."

"Then impregnate it."

"How?"

"How do you impregnate any reluctant woman? Seduction. You're good at that."

"What does that even mean? I don't know how to breach their security protocols."

"Not my problem."

"It is if I fail."

"Then do us both a favor and don't fail." Zvezdev grinned. "And I think you wouldn't mind becoming very, very rich."

"I have a fiduciary responsibility to Marin Aerospace

and, by extension, Dalfan Technologies, which we're about to acquire, which you no doubt know, otherwise you wouldn't be here."

Zvezdev pursed his lips, his head bobbing. "Well, yes, a 'fiduciary responsibility' is something to consider. But so is this." He pulled a smartphone out of his pocket, punched a few buttons, and handed the phone to Rhodes.

Rhodes read the screen, then reddened, angry and embarrassed. It showed Rhodes owned thousands of stock options with Marin Aerospace but he couldn't exercise them for another three years. And even though he earned a good salary, his lavish lifestyle, two divorces, and a recently acquired gambling habit put him behind the financial eight ball. He tossed the phone back to the Bulgarian. "How did you get this?"

"The identity-theft company you're signed up with? We own it." Zvezdev tapped the side of his head with a thick index finger. "I know you need the money, Weston. And it's easy money."

Rhodes glowered at the fat Bulgarian, a pockmarked peasant from a failed state: a lesser man in every sense of the word. Yet somehow it was Rhodes who was the threadbare beggar. He resented Zvezdev's easy smugness. This wasn't a negotiation. The Bulgarian held all the cards, and he was broke. The only thing Rhodes hated more than treason was poverty.

Zvezdev drained his glass with a flourish and wiped his bearded mouth with his hand. He set the glass on the table. "So what shall it be?"

Rhodes sank back into the sofa, thinking. Years ago they worked together. Zvezdev was CSS and he was CIA.

Natural enemies. And yet they managed to form an uneasy partnership back then, forged in the fire of mutual self-interest. In truth, they were using each other for their own ambitions. In that regard, they weren't so very different.

In truth, Zvezdev could've come in here, guns blazing. He had every right. After all, Rhodes had left Zvezdev for dead all those years ago. No doubt he had files, evidence. Things that could destroy Rhodes worse than bullets.

But the man sitting across from him seemed to bear no grudges, only gifts.

"You know, there just might be a way. I know somebody—"

Zvezdev raised his eyebrows, smiling. "Who?"

Rhodes started to say but stopped himself. He smiled. The irony was too rich. "Never mind who."

"This man you're thinking of can't be traced back to me. Are we clear?"

"Who said it was a man? But don't worry, I'm your firewall. How much time do we have?"

Zvezdev pulled on his hat, securing it over his wound as he stood. "You have until midnight on the twelfth local to do this thing. Not one second later, or the program fails."

"That's only a little more than two weeks from now. I'll need more time."

"That's all the time we have." Zvezdev marched toward the front door, Rhodes at his heels.

"But it's a day's travel just to get to Singapore from here."

Zvezdev stopped at the door, gripped the handle. "Then you better get to it first thing tomorrow, yes?"

Rhodes frowned, worried. "No. I should probably start tonight."

"You can't start tonight. You're going to be busy." Zvezdev opened the door. The twins stood in the hallway, smiling.

Rhodes smiled back. "Hello, girls."

"You see, Weston? I take care of my friends." Zvezdev whispered in Rhodes's ear. "My treat, on the house." He winked and nudged Rhodes in the ribs. He nodded toward the girls as he pushed past them, then turned around. "And stay in touch. I need to know the moment it's accomplished."

Rhodes had already slipped his arms around the waists of the two busty coeds. "I will. And thanks."

"I have a plane to catch." Zvezdev threw him a mock salute, turned on his heel, and headed for the elevators.

Rhodes steered the twins toward the bar, wondering if the cagey Bulgarian was doing to him what he was planning to do to these girls tonight.

# 23

Lian did most of the heavy lifting on the mai tai. Jack took a few sips, just to be social, after hitting his limit on beer. In the back of his lizard brain Jack wondered if Lian's flirtation mixed with copious amounts of rum and beer might lead to something more interesting, but he pushed the thought away. He would never take advantage of an inebriated woman.

When the last of the drink was consumed, Jack paid the bill and the two of them made their way to the elevator and the subbasement floor, where her vehicle was parked.

"You okay to drive?" Jack asked.

"I think so. But just to be certain, do you mind?"

"Not at all."

She handed him the keys as they headed back to the northeast corner of the huge garage where the Range

Rover was located. It was a beautiful evening, the sushi was good, and he'd had enough to drink to feel completely relaxed without being impaired.

That's when he heard Ding's voice in his brain again. "Head on a swivel, kid!" He couldn't help smiling to himself. Situational awareness was always a good idea, even in paradise.

Every parking space was full. That made sense. The hotel, casino, restaurants, and other amusements were packed shoulder to shoulder with tourists and locals as they had passed through upstairs, but down in the garage no one else was around. Lian's gait was steady but a little slower than before, so Jack slowed down as well. Their footfalls echoed on the concrete. Making their way to the farthest row, Jack noticed that the security camera on the concrete pillar was disabled by a disconnected cable and the overhead light nearest the Range Rover was smashed.

"Wait here," Jack said.

"What's wrong?"

"Nothing." Jack scanned his surroundings again. Didn't see anything. He pushed the alarm disable on the key fob. The Range Rover beeped twice and the interior lights came on.

Just enough light to shine on the muscled mai-tai punk leaning against the SUV. He grinned.

"Hallo, mate."

Jack noted the thick Aussie accent. "You looking for a ride home, bud? I can call you a cab."

The Australian straightened up to his full height. He

was even bigger than Jack remembered, at least an inch taller and twenty lean pounds heavier than he was.

"You see? I come down here for a friendly little chit-chat and all I get is more rudeness." He pointed a thick finger at Lian. "Her I get—she's a stuck-up little bitch. I know the type, believe me. And you? A Yank, and rude little wanker you are, too. Manners is what you need."

Lian shouted from behind, "Get your hands off me!"

Jack whipped around just in time to see Lian struggling in the grip of another thug from the bar, his ropy arms wrapped around her from behind. He was smiling and whispering something in her ear that made her growl and struggle even harder.

Jack started to move in her direction when he caught sight of the shadow of the third man from the bar circling around behind him.

Jack turned back and faced the ringleader, older and larger than the others. He recognized the tat on the big man's cabled forearm. The sword Excalibur, with flames. SASR—Special Air Service Regiment.

Australian Special Forces.

Jack lifted his hands chest high, palms out, a surrendering gesture. "Dude, look, I don't want any trouble."

"Well, mate, you found it just the same."

The man who was circling in the shadows stepped out. He stood to Jack's left, four feet away.

The tattooed leader darkened. "I just wanted to buy the lady a drink—"

Jack stepped cautiously toward him, just three feet away now, his eye on the Rover's interior light.

"I know. I'm sorry. I was in a bad mood—"

"And flashing your filthy money around."

Jack stepped his right foot forward, closing the distance, and reached with his left hand for his left rear pocket. "Money? Sure. No problem."

Just then, the interior light snapped off.

Just what Jack was waiting for.

He lunged forward and threw a sharp jab at the big man's throat with his open left hand. The man tried to scream but gurgled instead, clutching at his windpipe.

Jack stepped backward and pivoted left, turning forty-five degrees, using the momentum of his twisting torso to help propel his exploding right fist straight into the nose of the other man charging directly at him. Jack felt breaking cartilage and hot blood gushing onto his knuckles as the man's head snapped back with a crack. He crashed to the ground at Jack's feet, splayed out in front of the gasping thug, now on his knees.

"FUCK!" echoed off the concrete behind Jack. He spun around in time to see the last Aussie doubled over in front of Lian, clutching his balls. Lian launched a kick, the toe of her shoe slamming underneath his jaw. Jack winced at the crack of his breaking teeth. The man flew backward, arms high in the air, knocked out cold before he thudded into the concrete in a heap.

Jack ran over to her. "You okay?"

"Caught me by surprise." She turned to the downed man. "Bastard!" She spat at him, started to lunge at the body, but Jack seized her by the arm.

"You already nailed him. No point in killing him."

She whipped around at Jack, her eyes blazing. "Let go of me!"

Jack let go, lifting his hands in mock surrender. "You win."

She ran a hand through her long hair to get it out of her face. The gesture calmed her down. "It's those assholes from the bar."

"Really?"

She shot him a look.

"Sorry." Jack glanced around the garage. Still nobody around.

Lian picked up her purse, dropped at her feet when she was grabbed from behind. "I'm calling the police."

"I wish you wouldn't."

"Why not?"

"I think they've suffered enough—"

"JACK!" Lian screamed.

The tatted thug was rushing straight at Jack, his big hands open, grasping for his waist.

Jack stepped aside just in time and threw a punch at his temple as the man was sailing by. It landed. The force of the perfectly timed blow crashed the man's brain against his thick skull, knocking him out instantly. The Aussie tumbled to the concrete, smacking it like wet meat.

Jack rubbed his knuckles and turned to Lian. "Like I said, they've suffered enough, and I'd like to avoid any publicity. So would you, I'd think." He pointed out the disabled security camera. "Nobody upstairs saw anything." He nodded at the downed thugs. "And they sure as hell won't file a complaint."

"Maybe you're right." She looked at the two bodies Jack had put on the ground. "Not bad for a financial analyst."

"Let's hurry, before someone shows up. Grab any ID you can find." Jack pulled out the big man's wallet and shoved it into his pocket before seizing him by the boots and dragging his unconscious body between two parked cars, careful to get him out of the way of any traffic. Lian pilfered the smallest man's wallet, then grabbed his shoes and did the same while Jack hauled the last man up by the lapels and propped him against a pillar.

"Let's get out of here before they wake up," Jack said.

"Give me my keys. I'm driving."

Jack tossed her the keys. "You sure?"

"Trust me, I'm sober now."

"I'd hate to see you in a fight when you weren't drunk."

She fought a smile as they climbed into the Range Rover. She fired up the engine and pulled away, careful not to draw any attention to their departure.

Lian sped east along the East Coast Parkway, heading back to Jack's place. Jack kept checking his side-view mirror, scanning for any cars that might be following. He noticed Lian doing the same in the rearview mirror. Confident they weren't being followed, Jack pulled out the big man's wallet and rifled through it.

"According to his Australian driver's license, your boyfriend with the drinking problem is named Archy Hamilton, from Melbourne." He didn't find any military identification. Maybe he was just a wannabe special operator or had a relative in the service.

Lian hit her turn signal and merged into the next lane. "I have a good contact in the SPF. I'll run all three IDs through her first thing tomorrow."

"Any ideas?"

Lian shook her head. "I'd say they were just three punks looking for trouble."

"I guess they found it." Jack wasn't so sure. Lian caught the tone in his voice.

"You think we were being set up?"

"Did you see the man's tattoo? On his forearm?"

"Yes. It looked familiar."

*I bet it did,* Jack said to himself. *Especially if you're the one that hired him.* He checked the side-view mirror again. "Special Air Service Regiment. Australian Special Forces. Some seriously badass operators."

"What would an Australian operator be doing here?"

"Oh, I dunno. An *operation?*"

Lian's face masked with confusion. "You're kidding, right?"

A few drops of rain hit the windshield. The automatic wipers turned on.

"Just have your friend look into it. Maybe they can get access to his service records, if he has any." Jack knew that if the man really was black ops, his identity would be hidden from the prying eyes of a metropolitan police inquiry.

"You know, not every ex-serviceman is a hero. Sometimes bad apples fall into the barrel. I'd bet you another mai tai that if he is ex-service, he has a criminal record."

"Yeah, maybe you're right." Jack dropped the subject for now. If Lian or her brother were behind this, she'd cover it up.

He stole another quick glance at her. The shadows of the raindrops on the windshield marred her otherwise perfect face.

# 24

Jack dashed in the front door of their guesthouse, caught in a sudden downpour. He shook himself off just as Paul approached in his slippers and pajamas with a bowl of cereal in his hand. He wiped away a drop of milk perched on his lower lip.

"Have fun?"

"Fun? Yeah. I guess so."

Paul frowned when he saw Jack's red, swollen knuckles. "Anything I need to know about?"

"No."

"Seriously. You okay?"

"I'm fine." Jack pushed past him. "I just need a shower. And a drink."

Paul wondered what the hell Jack was up to. And why was he being such an ass? He crammed another spoonful of cereal into his mouth.

*Must have had a bad night.*

If he had to guess, Paul thought it looked like Jack

had been in a fight. But Jack was a financial analyst, not a street brawler. If he'd been in a fight, why wouldn't he just tell him that?

Paul stood chewing his cereal in the foyer, thinking. He wiped away another drop of milk dribbling down his chin, running through the possibilities.

*Booze? Drugs? Brain chemistry?*

*Maybe.*

Or maybe Jack wasn't the man Paul thought he was, after all.

Paul was nervous. He wanted a drink. Needed one, in fact. But he needed his mind clear more.

After thinking about the Dalfan security protocols all day, Paul finally figured out a way to work around them. Like most brilliant solutions to complex problems, it was frighteningly simple. It was also kind of crazy.

His plan had only a few moving parts: Download the CIA program onto his laptop, then copy the CIA program from his laptop to a Dalfan encrypted USB. Once it was infected, Paul would then install the Dalfan USB into a Dalfan desktop and, thirty seconds later, his mission would be completed.

Tonight was the easy piece. All he had to do was download the CIA program from Rhodes's USB drive to his laptop. Easy.

Unless it didn't work.

*Relax,* he told himself. *One step at a time.*

He double-checked the lock on his bedroom door to

make sure Jack wouldn't suddenly walk in. No point in getting him tangled up in this mess.

He then sat on his bed and opened his laptop in order to load Rhodes's CIA drive onto his computer. But what did Rhodes say? It was an automatically executing file. But it would execute only after he used his thumbprint to unlock it and typed in his verification code. Once he did those two things, the program would automatically launch.

That was a problem. Paul didn't want the program to launch automatically—otherwise, he might not be able to copy it.

But Paul figured out a crack in the system. He inserted the CIA drive into the USB port, then pressed his thumb against the thumb pad. The drive recognized Paul's print. It unlocked, as expected, flashing red, then blue.

The laptop screen then flashed a dialogue box, asking Paul for his security code, which would initiate the program launch. Paul ignored it. Instead, he opened up the USB drive icon on his laptop and examined its contents.

Paul saw a single unnamed file folder. The file didn't appear to be doing anything. So far, so good.

He swallowed hard, then dragged the unnamed CIA file onto his laptop. A copy progress bar opened up. It was going to take about two minutes to transfer. Paul drummed his fingers nervously, waiting for the transfer to complete . . .

. . . waiting for an explosion.

It never came.

The progress bar completed, and the CIA file was successfully copied to his machine's desktop. He ejected the CIA drive, and the passcode dialogue box disappeared.

Paul stared at the copied file on his screen. It didn't seem to be doing anything.

What was really interesting to Paul was that his MilSpec-grade antivirus software wasn't picking up anything. In theory, the CIA program hadn't launched inside his computer because he hadn't entered his passcode.

Paul's heart raced as panic set in. How could he enter his passcode and launch it on the Dalfan machine without the CIA drive inserted? Maybe the CIA program wouldn't run on the Dalfan machine without it.

A second later, a new passcode dialogue box generated by the copied CIA file opened. The copied CIA file was now ready to launch. That meant a copy would run from the Dalfan machine without the CIA drive inserted. Paul sighed, relieved.

Tomorrow he would copy the CIA file from his laptop to an encrypted Dalfan USB drive, then install the infected drive onto a Dalfan desktop. The copied CIA program would ask him again for his verification code, and once he entered it, the program would launch and his mission would be complete.

At least, that was the plan.

There was still one problem. He needed to acquire an encrypted Dalfan USB.

But how?

# 25

The next morning, Jack did two of his three S's in quick succession and brushed his teeth. He pulled on a pair of chinos and a blue oxford shirt with a pair of his favorite urban hiking boots—super-comfortable and just dressy enough for the business-casual atmosphere at Dalfan. They were also waterproof. There was the strong possibility of thundershowers again today.

He'd promised Paul he'd be down in twenty minutes, and his watch told him it had already been twenty-two. But Jack needed to do one more thing before heading out the door.

He pulled out his iPhone and tapped on his Photo Trap app—the best ninety-nine cents he had ever spent, as far as he was concerned—and then went around to his closet, his clothes drawers, and his bathroom sink. At each stop, he pressed the + button to record the date and time of an initial photo. Later this evening he would come back and stand in the same position and take secondary photos and then compare them on the app by hitting the manual flip function, which switched back and forth between the comparison photos to see if anything had been moved.

It was standard operating procedure at The Campus to establish personal security checks when on assignment—foreign hotel rooms were notorious surveillance traps for any visitor, especially Westerners. But beyond electronic devices, it wasn't uncommon for hotel security—or, worse, national security personnel—to enter one's private hotel room and search around in person for contraband.

Of course, this wasn't a Campus assignment, but the habits drilled into him by Ding and the others were hard to break, including this one. For an extra thirty seconds of effort, the Photo Trap icon would scratch an itch that would otherwise drive Jack crazy and would keep Ding's nagging voice silent. Besides, Clark told him to always trust his gut, and Jack's gut was telling him to stay vigilant.

Until recently, the way to find out if someone had broken in and searched around was to place a single piece of lint on a drawer lip or leave a zipper slider at an exact location on a piece of luggage, but most skilled surveillance people knew these kinds of tricks because they employed them themselves, and that meant they knew how to spot and defeat them. The great thing about the Photo Trap application was that it took a picture of everything, so that if anything was even slightly out of place, Jack would know someone had been in his room and what they had touched.

Not that he had anything to hide. But he hated the idea that someone would have been snooping around and he wouldn't know about it.

He thought about telling Paul to do the same thing, but he didn't want to give Paul any reason whatsoever for him to suspect that Jack was anything but a financial analyst for Hendley Associates. Finance guys on business trips didn't do OPSEC. The less Paul knew about him, the better.

Paul and Jack arrived at the Dalfan building and split up. Paul was met by Bai, and the two of them headed for his office.

Jack waited for Lian, who arrived a few moments later, clearly off her game. She greeted him formally, then escorted him to the third floor for his appointment with Dr. Singh. She didn't say a word on the elevator ride up. Neither did Jack.

Dr. Singh greeted Jack and Lian at the security desk and directed them toward the floor. He was taller than Jack but thinner, with a lean, handsome face that was heavily bearded. His turban was brilliantly white and perfectly wrapped. Dark, smiling eyes were framed by square glasses with stylish clear acetate frames.

"Are you familiar with our Steady Stare program, Mr. Ryan?"

"Only what I read from your materials. It's a twenty-four-hour-a-day drone-based surveillance program for civilian applications."

"That's correct. But when you put it that way, it

sounds rather boring, doesn't it? What I want to show you today is how we put it all together, and what it really means for the bottom line for our customers and for Dalfan."

"Can't wait."

"Good. Please, follow me."

The Steady Stare floor was organized into two main divisions, much like the one downstairs. The first division was composed of offices and computer workstations.

"This is where we write our own proprietary software for GPS navigation, autopiloting, image correlation, and so forth," Singh explained.

"What's proprietary about any of it?" Jack asked. "Lots of people are writing software like that."

Singh's eyes shifted to Lian. She nodded.

"It's the artificial-intelligence software we've written, and the means by which we're applying it to each phase of the other software and hardware components, that make Steady Stare a unique product," Singh said.

"AI? That's what Google and the other big boys in Silicon Valley are trying to figure out. You're facing some stiff competition."

"We believe we're holding our own."

He led Jack and Lian over to a computer-aided design station. "And here is one of our hardware design platforms. We use CAD to create and build our own devices—optics, sensors, communications, and the Steady Stare unmanned aerial vehicle itself."

"And you manufacture all of these components here in Singapore?" Jack said.

"The proprietary ones," Singh said. "We utilize a lot

of off-the-shelf technology, too. Some of that we import from trusted sources."

"Trust is hard to come by these days."

"Rarer than the rarest earth element," Lian said. "But we have our sources."

Singh then introduced Jack to several of his top programmers and designers, all young. Like everyone else in Singapore, they were all fluent in English, no matter their ethnicity or mother tongue.

Jack quizzed them on the particulars of the projects they were working on, but they answered in technical jargon, pointing at the CAD diagrams or lines of code on their screens. He could follow their trains of thought, but he didn't have the engineering or programming expertise to drill down further. It was clear they all knew their stuff, though. He thanked them and pushed on.

Singh then led Jack to the second part of the floor that was separated by a glass security wall—again, just like downstairs, but a blackout curtain was on the other side of it. Singh explained that his designers and programmers didn't need access to the operations room, and that some of what was going on in there was strictly off-limits. "Privacy concerns," he explained, as they passed through the curtain.

The operations suite was dark and laid out like a mini mission control room, with workstations and video monitors all manned by technicians watching their screens and speaking into headsets.

At the far end of the room was a nearly wall-to-wall video screen displaying what appeared to be a live overhead shot of Singapore. It looked like a satellite video.

There was a lone control station facing the screen, unmanned. Singh led them to it.

"This room is the heart of the Steady Stare operation," Singh said. "Our Steady Stare UAVs remain on station for twelve hours at a time, and we put two in service every day, providing twenty-four-hour coverage."

"What powers your drones?"

"Solar."

"You're able to fly for twelve hours on solar power?" Jack was incredulous.

"In theory, Google's unmanned solar-power plane can fly continuously for five years without landing. Of course, theirs is a much larger platform. Our small airplane relies on our own solar cell and lithium battery storage designs—another example of the value we bring to the project. There is also a backup battery on board, and a small petrol engine for emergency use."

"So the idea is that these drones fly over the city for twenty-four hours a day and provide video monitoring."

"Exactly."

"How do you manage that during monsoon season?"

"It's a challenge for sure. We launch the planes with their batteries precharged, but even on cloudy days there can be a good deal of radiation."

Jack frowned. "Why is your system of aerial observation particularly useful or unique, especially in civilian applications?"

Singh cleared his throat and shifted his attention to Lian.

"Aerial observation has many advantages," Lian said.

"But we provide a highly efficient, low-cost aircraft to perform it."

"Do you have any idea how many hundreds of low-cost, high-capacity drones have been or are being developed?"

"We're aware," Lian said.

"Then you know you can't make money in that business."

"We're not idiots." Lian smiled.

Jack pointed at the video monitor. "Then what is it that your system does that would make me believe this is a revenue generator?"

Lian crossed her arms, thinking and clearly conflicted. Finally, she nodded toward Singh. "Go ahead."

Relieved, Singh smiled. "Do you believe in time travel, Mr. Ryan?"

**26**

"Time travel?" Ryan shook his head. "I like sci-fi as much as the next guy, but no. It's not logically possible."

"Actually, it is possible. Let me show you."

Singh led Ryan to the back wall, then picked up a tablet from the nearby empty control station. The screen at the control station was a mirrored image of the wall screen.

"What you're seeing on the screen is a live video feed of Singapore from five thousand meters—approximately sixteen thousand feet." Singh tapped a virtual key and performance data appeared for altitude, speed, latitude, longitude, and the like.

"Can you fly your bird from this control station?" Jack asked, pointing to the one he was standing next to. There was a joystick, a keyboard, dual monitors, and a wireless mouse on the desk.

"In theory, we can fly our UAV from any of the stations you see in this room. In the future, we plan to fly multiple UAVs from each station. For now, the Steady Stare vehicle that's aloft is being run from a control station at Seletar Airport—"

"At the Dalfan hangar?"

"Yes."

Jack turned to Lian. "I'd like to see that facility when we're done."

"I'll see what can be arranged."

Singh tapped more virtual keys on his tablet. "Now let's focus in more closely." The camera zoomed in like a dive-bombing hawk. The image finally resolved on the Dalfan building in the center of the giant screen.

"There, do you see that delivery van that just pulled up at the security gate?" Singh asked.

"Yeah, but I can't make out anything except that its roof is blue," Jack said.

"Imagine if that van was loaded with explosives and was driven by terrorists. Imagine further that it passed through the Dalfan gates and onto our property—just like it's actually doing right now—and say twenty meters in, it exploded, killing whoever was in the van and completely destroying the vehicle."

"Okay."

"In a situation like this, how would you normally set about trying to determine the identity of the killers and the location of their hideout?"

"Usually, the investigating authorities would look for forensic evidence on the scene—fingerprints, photo IDs, VINs, a license plate—any kind of physical evidence that would begin to provide a clue."

"Correct. But the likelihood of discovering usable

physical evidence from a catastrophic crime scene like this one is extremely remote. However, if a police department or government agency had a time machine, it wouldn't need any of the things you mentioned. All they would need to do is travel back in time to a point before the explosion."

Singh tapped a few more virtual keys and the blue van suddenly reversed direction. He tapped another key and the van sped up 2x.

"Please observe."

The van backed out of the Dalfan driveway and onto the main boulevard—the street name clearly identified on the screen now, just like a Google map—and drove away in reverse, along with the rest of the traffic. The clock on the video monitor was also running backward as the van sped through the industrial park area, pulling in and out of a few more driveways until it finally arrived at a warehouse some five miles away, where it stopped in front of a loading dock.

Singh froze the image. "So, this is the origination point of our theoretical 'terrorist' van. But we still don't know who our theoretical 'terrorists' are." Singh resumed the reversing image and two men exited the van and walked backward, climbing the stairs to the loading dock in reverse.

"All of this data is stored on your mainframe?"

"In this case, yes, because we're still analyzing the data from our field testing with our first client."

"Who is that?"

"The Singapore Police Force. They're also storing all of this data on their cloud storage server. Anyone who leases the program from us in the future is free to store it on their own servers, in the cloud, or wherever it suits them. Storage is the easy part." Singh held up the tablet. "It's the software that powers the aircraft, cameras, and the surveillance packages we've developed that really counts."

"How hard is it to use?"

"Quite simple, really."

"Then show me."

"No," Lian said. "Dr. Singh has already shown you everything you need to know about the system to understand its profit potential."

"Ease of use will be a key factor in your ability to sell it to public agencies. If it isn't easy to use, you won't make any money from it. So I need to see how easily it works."

Lian glowered at him. "Fine," she finally said, throwing a dismissive hand up.

Jack was troubled by her hostile reaction, especially given the fact he probably saved her from a gang rape last night, or worse. He knew she was no damsel in distress, but most people would be more grateful under the same circumstances.

A thought occurred to him. *Unless she knows I didn't save her at all.* Maybe the incident was all a setup by her to scare him off or test him. She seemed capable of such a thing.

But he had no reason to believe that. She kicked the shit out of that one guy. If she had hired that poor toothless bastard, she owed him a bonus, or at least a dental plan.

More likely, she might have just been embarrassed by the whole evening. She did, in fact, flirt with him, and he didn't respond in kind. Not because he wasn't interested, but only because he was raised to be a gentleman, and she was a little drunk. *But she wouldn't know that about me, would she?* And technically she was the security last night, but he was the one who saved her. *Yeah, she's embarrassed for sure.*

Or not. Who the hell knew? Sometimes he felt like he knew how to handle guns better than he did people, especially women.

Singh handed Jack the tablet. "The video manipulation is completely intuitive. See for yourself."

Jack took the tablet and hit the play-button icon. The video image began running forward. He paused it again and ran it in reverse with a slider, back to the point where Singh had stopped it before.

"So I want to follow these guys back to their original locations. How do I do that? Just run the image backward until they get there?"

"You can do that manually exactly the way you were doing, but that might take minutes, hours, or even days, depending on your target. The easier way is to let the program's tracking and facial-recognition software do the work for you."

Jack handed him the tablet. He watched closely as Singh tapped a few more icons. On the big screen, both delivery men were surrounded by boxed target reticles, one red, one yellow. The men separated. One fell into a car, the other climbed onto a motorcycle.

Singh zoomed out, clicked more icons, and the virtual camera lens zoomed back out so that the entire city could be seen again. The two men were just yellow and red dots. A moment later a red line and a yellow line sped away in different directions from the warehouse, snaking through the city streets. Both lines ultimately landed in two separate locations on either side of the city. It took less than a second for the Steady Stare software to accomplish the feat. Singh paused the program.

"Wow," Jack said.

"I set a time limit of only two hours."

"How far back can you go?"

Singh shrugged. "That depends completely on how much data you have stored. If a client keeps video records for a year, they could trace those two guys—or anybody else—for a year."

"Storage is the key, isn't it?" Jack said. "Depending on what you want to do with the data."

"Storage is another profit center," Lian interrupted. "Make sure you note that in your report."

"I will."

"Have you seen enough?" Lian asked.

Jack studied Singh's face. Singh's eyes locked with his. A silent invitation.

Jack shook his head at Lian. "I'm guessing there's still more to all of this."

"Maybe there is," Lian said.

**27**

Paul and Bai grabbed two cups of steaming-hot tea and settled into their seats back in Paul's small office. Bai was on Paul's elbow, as usual, and intensely interested in Paul's every keystroke. Paul spent the first thirty minutes doing another random survey of the various subledgers, especially accounts payable and accounts receivable.

He then turned his attention to the statement of financial position and pulled up the shareholders' equity statements. After all, the overall purpose of this accounting exercise was to help assure both Dalfan and Marin Aerospace that the agreed-upon price for the stock purchase was a fair value for both parties. There were a few technical details and also terms in Mandarin script that Bai needed to clarify for him early on, but overall it was an uneventful exercise in due diligence as Paul plodded on, line after line, figure after figure.

Though initially attentive and alert, Bai's focus began

to wane. The young accountant began pecking away at his own laptop, hardwired into Dalfan's LAN. Paul couldn't see Bai's screen, but he could see the reflections of an intense video game playing on the lenses of the young man's glasses.

What Bai couldn't have suspected was that Paul was running a subroutine in his brain's CPU while he was overtly working on his accounting assignment. Paul thought he might have found a way to override the encrypted electronic lock on the Dalfan computer he was using, but it would be a multistep process, and the first step in the process was wearing Bai down.

So far, so good.

From yesterday's work session, Paul had learned that Bai had a fast metabolism and was nearly ravenous by the time lunch rolled around. Paul pushed on with his mundane accounting work until he could hear the boy's stomach mewling like a drowning cat.

"We have a problem," Paul said.

Bai's attention was fixed on his laptop screen. "I'm sorry, did you ask me something?"

Paul turned in his squeaking swivel chair. "I said, there's a problem."

Bai's eyes snapped up. "Problem?" He slammed his laptop shut.

"Yes, a problem. I can't do my job if I can't connect my laptop to the mainframe."

"It's not possible. You know the security protocols."

"It's not possible for me to do my job if I don't."

"Why?"

"Because I'm finished doing my preliminary survey. Now it's time for me to do my formal examination of your records."

"I thought that is what you were doing."

"No. That was only a survey—an overview. To give me the thirty-thousand-foot perspective. Now I need to drop down and hit specific targets."

"But why do you need to connect to the mainframe with your laptop?"

"That's where my accounting software is located."

"That's not possible, sir."

"That's why we have a problem."

"What kind of software do you use?"

"Analytical software."

"We have CaseWare IDEA analytical software already installed on our computers. If you don't know how to use it, I can show you."

"IDEA is an excellent program and I've used it many times. But I prefer my own software."

"Why?"

"Because it's mine. I wrote it."

Bai blinked a few times, his face blank with confusion, his brain stuck in a continuous logic loop. Finally he blurted out, "I'm sorry, it's just not possible."

"Then how else am I supposed to be able to download all of these data sets?"

Bai shrugged.

"Oh, I have an idea," Paul said. "You can load all of the data points I need by hand into my computer within the next twenty-four hours. It's probably not more than half a million numbers. And, of course, you can't make a single mistake while you do it. Would that work for you?"

"You're not serious."

"How else can I get the data into my laptop?"

"Let me speak with Mr. Fairchild." Bai exited the office and headed across the suite to Yong's office. Through the glass partition, Paul watched the two of them speak. A few moments passed and Yong glanced up, glowering at Paul. Paul waved meekly. Yong rose and crossed the suite, entering Paul's office with Bai in tow.

Paul remained seated.

"Please explain your problem again, Mr. Brown?"

"Please, call me Paul."

"The problem?"

"I can't do my forensic audit without my software. Bai has explained to me that I can't download the encrypted security passcode onto my machine or have any other direct interface."

"Why can't you use our analytical software?"

"It isn't as good as mine."

Bai whispered something in Mandarin. Yong nodded. "Would it be possible to upload your software onto our machine?"

Paul shrugged. "Are you sure you want to do that? The whole point of not allowing alien machines to connect to your mainframe is to prevent malware from infecting your system. Call your IT person, but I bet they'd have a real problem with that."

Yong nodded at Bai, who grabbed a desk phone and speed-dialed a number. Paul guessed it was the IT department. Bai and the party on the other end of the line chatted in Chinese for a bit. Bai hung up. "Mr. Brown is right. They don't want to upload his software."

"Even if they check it?" Yong asked.

"No, sir."

"There is one other possibility," Paul suggested. "If you can loan me one of your encrypted USB drives, I can download the data I need and transfer it to my machine. That way my machine is never in direct contact with your computer."

"Why can't you just use Bai's?"

"I prefer one of my own."

"Why?"

"It would be a violation of the International Auditing and Assurance Standards Board auditing protocols to allow a Dalfan employee—or a Marin Aerospace employee, for that matter—to have access to the data and records I'm examining. Surely you see how that would be an ethical violation?"

Yong rubbed his face, thinking. "Yes, I suppose it would be." He turned to Bai. "Get him one of our drives—and wipe it clean. Then make sure he's registered with it and the serial number is recorded."

"Yes, sir. Will he have to turn it in each day before he leaves?"

"Yes, of course." He turned to Paul. "Is that a problem?"

"No. I'll BleachBit the drive clean each day, just to keep things . . . ethical."

"You must also return the drive to us when you're

finally through with it. It's proprietary, and we keep a strict accounting of each device."

"No problem. I'm sorry for the inconvenience. It's just that I have a job to do."

"I understand. Hopefully this will be the last hurdle for you to jump in order for you to complete your assignment."

Paul smiled. "That's the plan."

It was mostly bullcrap, of course.

Paul had to lie. It was his only choice. But he wasn't happy about it.

Bai was right. IDEA was a great piece of analytical auditing software, and just about anything Paul needed to do on this "due diligence" audit could've been done with it. Paul's software was even better because he'd written the macros and templates himself, based on his years of experience in fraud analysis. But to do a proper fraud investigation would take several weeks for a company this size. What Paul really needed was the Dalfan encrypted USB flash drive. That didn't solve his problem, but it got him one step closer to completing his mission.

Or so he hoped.

In the meantime, he had work to do. Rhodes had told him that the audit was legit but that it was in addition to his more important task. Paul couldn't shake the feeling that the auditing assignment was just a cover for the software upload. A giant waste of time. That didn't make sense, either, though. Rhodes was paying a lot of money to send him and Jack out here. But then again, it wasn't his money, was it?

Paul pushed that idea aside and opened up his program. Time to eat the elephant.

Even if he had all the time in the world, on a project this size the trick was to cut it up into bite-sized pieces rather than try to swallow it whole. If there was some kind of fraud or illegal activity taking place, and if whoever was behind it was careless enough to record the transactions somewhere in the general ledger, his auditing software might be able to sniff it out. It would take a great deal of luck to find anything, since all he could do with so little time available was perform random checks of selected data sets. But Fortune was a lady, and she favored the bold, statistically.

Paul had constructed thirty discrete tests to perform, most of them numerical, but some were qualitative, searching and comparing the names and addresses of vendors, banks, warehouses, and products, as well as key words related to transactions, assets, destinations, and personnel. Connecting people, places, and patterns of behavior sometimes proved more valuable in cracking a fraud case, especially when the fraudsters were good at hiding the numbers. In fact, one of the Singapore banks that did business with Dalfan had been connected to the North Korean rare-earth-element debacle a few years ago, though no charges were ever filed. It was an interesting coincidence he would check out later.

But it was number crunching that dominated Paul's work. He believed that most fraudsters weren't as good at hiding the numbers as he was in finding them, and he had the track record to prove it. But he was no fool, and it usually took a combination of both investigative approaches to crack the hardest cases. As far as he knew, Dalfan was innocent of any wrongdoing, but for the sake of this exercise, he was going to assume they were hiding something, and hiding it very well.

Would he find Dalfan vendors that changed bank accounts frequently? Had any Dalfan employees authorized multiple payments for items below a certain threshold limit to avoid triggering a limit alarm? Were there invoice receipts paid for amounts greater than the goods receipts they were matched to? How many purchase payments were made that exceeded the purchase-order amounts?

And then there was his Benford's law search engine.

Paul rolled up his sleeves. It was going to be another long day, but it was still going to be a lot of fun. It was hard for him to believe that anybody could find this kind of work boring.

**28**

"O kay," Jack said. "So what else is there?

"Mostly technical details," Singh said. "Maybe not that interesting."

"Try me."

Lian's eyes narrowed, calculating.

Jack flashed a roguish smile. "I'm sure those technical details will look really great on that report."

She nodded to Singh, defeated. "Fine. Go ahead."

Singh pointed at the video wall. He punched another button.

The red and yellow terminal points flashed specific addresses, then a list of names and accompanying photos of the occupants of each residence on record. Singh paused the program again.

"Where did you get that data?" Jack asked.

"What you see on the screen right now is all OSINT. Facebook, Twitter, LinkedIn, YouTube—these are all big platforms in Singapore, just like the U.S. We also utilize phone number listings, tax records, and all of the public filings." Singh paused. "But because this is a pilot project for the SPF, we're also linked into their databases—immigration, prison records, internal security, civil defense, and even Interpol. So we can get virtually any information we need about anybody at any time if they're in Singapore."

"And you're pulling all of them together into one analytical platform?"

Singh beamed with pride. "My teams write great algorithms. That's our secret weapon, Mr. Ryan."

"Even more impressive."

Singh then highlighted the photo of a twenty-eight-year-old male named Ho who was living in the red terminal point. He tapped another key and more data came up. "You can see that Mr. Ho is employed by the delivery company we've been tracking. So now we have a good confirmation that he's one of our targets."

Singh hesitated.

"Is there a problem?"

Singh glanced at Lian one last time for a final nod of confirmation.

Singh continued. "If we let the software keep tracing their movements from the previous day, week, month, or year, we can collect all sorts of interesting data. Every time they enter a building we can determine who they are meeting with. Then we can trace the movements of those new targets as well. In this way, we can reconstruct entire networks of people, establish relationships, property locations, patterns of movement, et cetera, and all in far less time and for far less cost than traditional methods."

Jack ran the calculations in his head, multiplying the number of policemen times the number of hours in stakeouts, surveillance ops, shift rotations, vehicle miles driven, and a dozen other cost factors that added up to hundreds of thousands of dollars in salaries and expenses for even small intelligence operations over a decent length of time.

"Let me show you a quick example. We've been running this test program for the last sixty-four days. So let's see what Mr. Ho has been up to."

Singh tapped several more keys. First, he cleared the screen of the yellow line representing the other delivery driver, then extended the time-trace parameter to sixty-four days. Nearly instantly, the screen filled with a crazy spiderweb of red lines, all tracing Ho's movements, and all centered on Ho's residence. The red lines mostly tracked along the same routes, with a few loose strands snaking around the island to parks, recreation areas, and shopping centers.

"Now, if I hit another key, the software will show me Mr. Ho's five most visited locations as measured by length of stay." Singh executed the new function, isolating five specific locations, and took away all of the red spiderweb trace lines to clarify the image.

"As you can see, two of those five locations are his home and his place of work. A third looks to be a local bar, and the fourth a horse-racing venue. The fifth . . ."

Singh tapped more keys. "Is the residence of this

woman." A photo popped up, along with her personal stats. It was a thirty-two-year-old single woman, plain and somewhat heavyset.

"So Mr. Ho spends quite a bit of time with this woman. For the sake of her privacy, I won't pull up her name. But just for fun—"

"Dr. Singh—" Lian said, but too late.

Dozens of tracer lines, each in a different color, radiated out from the woman's apartment. The home terminal of each line appeared, along with the images of their occupants—all men, of various ages and races.

"It seems Mr. Ho's 'friend' has a lot of other friends." Singh raised an eyebrow. "If you catch my meaning."

"Friends who are friendly by the hour, judging by the time stamps," Jack added.

"That's enough, Dr. Singh."

"Yes, ma'am." Singh tapped another key and all of the data disappeared, leaving only the live overhead image of Singapore on the screen.

Jack shook his head. "I'm utterly amazed. You're putting a beat cop in the sky. A beat cop with a perfect set of eyes and a perfect memory."

Singh nodded thoughtfully. "More or less, yes."

"This is what military and intelligence agencies have been doing for the last ten years," Jack said. "I know you've written your own AI programs, but what's your value-added?"

"You know how these government systems run. A Predator operation might have eighty, a hundred, even two hundred people in the loop, everyone from the ground-control station and flight crew all the way back to the Pentagon, with civilian and military analysts added in for good measure." He held up the tablet again. "Here's your analysis team. The UAV we've developed can be transported in the back of a truck, unloaded, assembled, and made ready to launch in less than thirty minutes by just two people with a wrench and a screwdriver. Compared to the large military systems, Steady Stare is cheap, easy to use, and requires very little manpower." Singh flashed a smile. "And, of course, Dalfan is prepared to provide any or all of those manpower services if the client requires them. If not, Dalfan provides all of the training and technical support they might need."

Jack glanced around the room. There were four analysts sitting at workstations with headsets on, speaking. "How does a police department actually use a system like this?"

"The SPF is responding to various calls around the city every day. If they conduct their initial investigation and can't identify the culprits in a crime—for example, a hit-and-run car accident—an assigned detective will call us and give us the street address of the accident, and then we perform a 'time travel' search function like the one I just showed you. We would then call in the terminal address of the alleged vehicle to the detective and officers would be dispatched to the location. We're not replacing police work, we're just making it far more efficient."

"Politicians will love it because their police departments will be solving far more crimes for less money," Lian said. "And when word gets out, it will deter crime. If every speeding vehicle automatically gets ticketed because of Steady Stare, fewer people will speed—that means fewer accidents, lower insurance costs, and fewer injuries and deaths."

*No wonder Marin Aerospace wants a piece of this,* Jack thought. He ran his hand through his hair, considering the possibilities—and the profits.

Jack turned to Lian. "Now I'm getting a better idea why Dalfan has such tight security. The Chinese would love to steal this kind of technology."

"They've already tried." Lian smiled. "And not just the Chinese."

Jack checked his watch. "This has been fascinating, Dr. Singh. I'd like to see the airport facility."

"When?"

"Why not now?"

Lian shrugged. "Fine. Let's go."

The Dalfan hangar at the Seletar Airport was unremarkable, a duplicate of several other leased hangars on the property. A single-wide trailer was parked next to it.

Singh, Lian, and Jack parked the company car and headed into the hangar, big enough to accommodate two Cessna 172s or a medium-sized executive jet. Inside was neither.

"That's the Steady Stare UAV," Singh said.

The pilotless plane had no cockpit, of course. Its wingspan was about sixteen feet, and the fuselage about half of that. It had a six-bladed propeller. Singh pointed at the glass-orbed housing on the belly. "Our camera, sensor, and communication payloads are mounted in here. Optical, infrared, night vision, laser range finder, GPS—you name it—everything can be interchanged. They're all modular and designed to fit in the unit."

"What kind of runway length do you need to launch?"

"None." Singh nodded toward the corner. Four lengths of aluminum pipe were welded together with smaller, thinner pieces, forming a ten-foot-long piece of scaffolding. "That's a spring-loaded catapult. It launches the Steady Stare into the air, so no runway is needed."

"What if you don't have the catapult?"

"Then I'd go get it. Right now it's not equipped for a conventional takeoff, but it's designed to attach landing gear. We didn't see any advantage to doing that over the catapult."

Jack tapped on the fuselage with the tip of his finger. It was hollow.

"The fuselage is made of carbon-fiber composites. Super-strong and lightweight."

Jack shook his head. "I'm trying to find another word besides 'impressive,' but I can't. I'm sold on the concept. It looks as easy to use as you say, and I've seen what the cameras and software can do. What are the downsides to this system?"

"High winds will ground the system, and night flying is only possible if the operating and backup batteries are fully precharged. Of course, you can always deploy the auxiliary internal combustion engine if needed."

"I only see one problem, and I don't know how you overcome it."

"What's that?" Lian asked.

"In the United States, the Fourth Amendment to the Constitution prohibits warrantless searches, and I know that some legal scholars would consider continuous surveillance like this a violation of civil rights."

"Our sales team has encountered this issue on several occasions in the States, but American cities keep finding out about us and still contact us," Singh said. "You're right, it's still a contested legal issue, and we suspect that our American operations won't really pick up for another few years. But until then, Asian police departments have shown a tremendous interest in our product, and my best guess is that Western governments won't be far behind. After all, they already deploy closed-circuit surveillance cameras everywhere, don't they? That's just an inefficient version of what we offer, and it fails to deliver our nearly perfect results."

Lian added, "Police departments are our first target market, but any government agency that needs to track the movement of people—polluters, poachers, illegal immigrants, pirates—will all demand a system like this."

Singh nodded in agreement. "We also believe there will be an even bigger market for private companies. For example, trucking firms that want to track their delivery vehicles or auto insurance companies that want to determine the actual cause of car wrecks."

*Terrorist groups and crime syndicates would love to "time travel," too,* Jack thought. *So would outfits like The Campus.*

"If history teaches us anything, it's that human morality follows technology, and not the other way around," Lian said. "It's only a matter of time before your crime-infested urban areas come around to our way of thinking."

Jack agreed. He understood all the advantages of this kind of program, and it made sense for governments to deploy it on behalf of their citizens' safety.

But he couldn't help wondering, What happens when a government can't be trusted? Dictators and tyrants would definitely use this kind of technology against their own people. But even in the United States, lone wolves in federal agencies like the IRS, the FBI, and even the CIA used their power to persecute domestic political enemies.

Jack glanced up into the hazy sky. He couldn't see the Dalfan drone circling overhead, but he knew it was there, and he hated the idea that it was watching him. It was irrational, he knew, but it was already changing the way he was thinking about himself and his personal security—and he wasn't one of the bad guys.

He ran a hand over the smooth fuselage again. It seemed just like an ordinary airplane, but today's demonstration proved it was anything but ordinary.

"Have you seen enough, Mr. Ryan?" Lian asked.

"Yes, thank you. Quite enough."

*At least for now,* Jack told himself.

This was just the kind of dog-and-pony show Gerry Hendley had warned him about. There was something more they weren't talking about, but he sure as hell was going to find out what it was.

## 29

Paul Brown played poker in college, shaking down wealthy Greeks in their smoke-filled fraternity basements and beer-soaked-carpeted game rooms across the Iowa State campus. He made enough to cover his books and tuition for two years and stopped only when a three-hundred-pound lineman threatened to break his spine after Paul relieved him of five hundred dollars in a single hand.

His keen numbers brain allowed him to accurately calculate the odds in a hand, but he excelled at the game because he knew that in poker you don't play the cards, you play the man, and Paul had developed the world's stoniest poker face. A poker face he had used to great effect today.

The first time he used it was when Bai appeared in the office with the encrypted USB drive Yong had promised and handed it to Paul. He took it as nonchalantly as if Bai had handed him a glass of tepid tap water. Inwardly, Paul was dancing for joy. He was now decidedly one step closer to fulfilling his mission for the CIA.

Coolly and calmly, Paul began downloading data from the Dalfan computer to the Dalfan USB, then loading that data onto his laptop. His own machine didn't require the encrypted passcodes on the Dalfan drive, so it ignored them.

Bai tried stealing glances over Paul's shoulder every now and then, on the pretense of stretching or fetching hot tea or office supplies. Bai's job obviously was to get a sense of the kinds of files Paul was pulling down, but Paul shifted around in his chair and adjusted his posture to keep Bai at bay, and when that failed, he simply turned to the young accountant and said, "I'm sorry, but I need my privacy."

That was enough to get Bai to back off, but Paul knew that Bai wasn't his only problem. Someone in the Dalfan accounting department was likely monitoring his work. If it were him, he would've set up some kind of remote mirroring program—the same kind that allows a technical-support person in Bangalore to conduct remote repairs on a client's computer in Baltimore. Every file he opened, and every data set he pulled down from the Dalfan desktop, would've been seen and probably recorded by the remote observer.

That was fine by Paul, because the important work he needed to do he accomplished on his private machine. Unfortunately for Dalfan, the security protocols that prevented Paul from logging on to their machines prevented Dalfan from logging on to *his* machine. Air gapping worked in both directions. Acquiring the encrypted Dalfan USB drive allowed him to download their data onto his secure laptop.

But the real reason why he wanted the drive was the drive itself. As soon as Bai left the room for his first bathroom break, Paul plugged the Dalfan drive into one of his laptop USB ports and screen-grabbed the make and model and stored it in a file. He needed that information if he wanted to go out and buy a duplicate one. He wasn't sure that he even could; at this point, he was still improvising. Unfortunately, he still didn't have any idea how to defeat the Dalfan drive's encryption.

In the meantime, he needed to keep his hand to the plow and try and find any fraud in the Dalfan books. He got back to his auditing work.

As the day wore on, Paul's proprietary auditing screens had come up negative in his searches. For the most part, Dalfan appeared to be a well-run and highly profitable company. Yong and his team had done an excellent job organizing and maintaining their general ledger over the last five years.

Bai's eyes continued to flit between his own screen and Paul. Paul hid his disappointment behind his poker face. The joy of the job of a fraud examiner was the discovery of actual fraud. The hunter who came home from the field without the kill, or the lothario who didn't have a woman to bring home to his bed, hadn't the faintest glimmer of the kind of disappointment Paul felt when he couldn't find the clues he needed to uncover the criminal act. But Paul felt it was generally bad form for a CFE to show that kind of disappointment when no fraud was found at a reputable firm, just as it was bad manners to gloat excessively when a crime was finally discovered.

It had taken him years to realize that he loved the job because it was exactly like a game of poker, only harder, playing against a brilliant but unseen opponent holding a million invisible cards. Paul's job was to play the man—or woman—but first he had to find out what the cards even were and to see what kind of hand his opponent was playing.

After he and Bai went to lunch in the Dalfan cafeteria and devoured steaming bowls of dumpling soup and heaping plates of chicken and rice, Bai returned to one of his video games and Paul resumed his game of blind poker.

An hour later, Bai glanced up from his screen. "Everything okay, Mr. Brown?"

Paul Brown the poker player shrugged, fighting the joy welling up inside of him. One of Paul's more mundane search screens had just signaled a hit.

"Yeah, I guess so."

"Find anything yet?"

"No. So far, everything looks fine."

"Good." Bai returned to his game.

So did Paul.

The search screen had pulled up the letter combination *QC* enough times to meet the screen's frequency parameters. Paul naturally assumed it was an abbreviation for "quality control," and Dalfan, apparently, was concerned with it. But what caught his attention were the document references pertaining to the QC hits. They didn't square up with his idea of quality control, and he couldn't reconcile their connection to particular budget documents.

He dug a little more and discovered that much of Dalfan's QC concerns were connected to certain items that it produced and sold to an importer in Shanghai that seemed equally concerned about quality control—in fact, no other company Dalfan did business with made any reference to Dalfan's quality-control issues.

Strange.

Not that doing business with a Shanghai importer was a problem. Nor was the fact that the company exported its Dalfan products to the People's Republic of China. The whole world traded with China, including the United States, which had been running chronic trade deficits with Beijing for decades, transferring hundreds of billions of dollars of wealth to the Communist dictatorship decade after decade, allowing them to grow their economy and expand their military at America's expense.

But as Calvin Coolidge once said, the business of America was business, and such matters were far beyond Paul's pay grade.

However, Lenin was only half right when he said that a capitalist would sell the rope to the Communist who would hang him with it. In fact, while the United States government was more than happy to foster trade with China, it took a dim view of exporting goods or services that directly affected American national and economic security.

To that end, the Department of Commerce's Bureau

of Industry and Security created and maintained the Commerce Control List (CCL), which listed thousands of general and specific items that could not be exported to problematic countries on the Commerce Countries Chart (CCC).

Of course, the People's Republic of China was on the CCC and there was at least one item listed on the CCL with the Export Control Classification Number 5A002.c, and that item had two letters in it: QC.

It was probably just a coincidence, but it was the closest thing to a clue that he had come across in two days of searches, so he decided to keep digging. He never could confirm the meaning of QC in the Dalfan files, but his investigation led him to that obscure file with a running list of invoices and payments that didn't quite make sense. It was just a thread. But sometimes pulling on a thread led to unraveling the whole suit.

He flagged the file on the Dalfan mainframe and made a mental note to return to it later, when he had the time to chase it down.

The old Thai trainer was dark like mahogany, with a hard, round belly beneath his T-shirt and a bald head like the Buddha of Yong's childhood memory, the one on the shelf in his grandmother's kitchen. Only the ageless Thai never smiled.

Yong stood barefoot and shirtless in his bright yellow Muay Thai silk shorts, hands up, ready to launch against the thick square pads in the trainer's skilled hands, held up on either side of his head. The sinewy muscles in

Yong's torso and limbs were tightly wound cords beneath his glistening skin.

Yong exploded on his left foot and threw his right foot high, whipping around so fast that his heel strike against the pad sounded like a shotgun blast. He instantly repeated the move, again and again and again, four strikes in blindingly quick succession.

The Thai muttered a command in his own language. Yong acknowledged it and switched directions, his left foot now striking six inches higher than the trainer's head.

"It would be an advantage if the deal goes through," Meili said in Mandarin. She was small but well toned, with a heart-shaped mole just above her upper lip. Her hair was pulled back in a short ponytail. She wore red training shorts and a tight black tank top, and her hands were taped for practice sparring.

Yong understood her perfectly, despite her heavy mainland accent. His own Mandarin was heavily influenced by his mother's Hokkien dialect, which was also practically another language—the second of four he spoke fluently, English being his first.

Yong took a couple of deep breaths, his eyes focused on the square pads now held chest high and pointing down at a forty-five-degree angle.

"My father wants the deal," Yong said. "My sister wants the deal because Father wants the deal." Yong's right leg exploded forward, his weight leveraged on his back leg. His foot struck against the pads in four rapid strikes, smacking them so hard it knocked the sturdy Thai back onto his heels.

"Did I hit a nerve?" The diminutive Ministry of State

Security agent asked. She kept one eye on the Thai. Yong had assured her before that he spoke only Thai and no Chinese dialects of any kind, but she was still suspicious.

Yong hissed through gritted teeth. "I won't have it!"

Yong reversed positions and launched four more crushing blows against the Thai's hands. The trainer grunted with each strike.

Meili didn't speak when Yong threw his kicks. There was no point—the noise was deafening. She shuddered at the thought of being on the other side of those heel strikes. She was hoping to convince Yong of the strategic advantage a merger with Marin Aerospace would have for him, and for her agency.

Yong was breathing hard now. He turned to face his Chinese contact. "And that wasn't our arrangement."

"No, it wasn't. I just wanted to be sure you had considered the possibilities."

The Thai trainer shouted and Yong spun effortlessly on his heel, throwing a vicious right elbow strike across the left pad, then whirled around in the opposite direction and crushed the left pad with a left elbow reverse. Yong shouted, then repeated the exact strikes six more times in a single flowing movement.

From Meili's perspective, Yong looked like a spinning rotary blade. The elbow was the hardest bone in the human frame and Muay Thai used it to great advantage, one of the "eight limbs" of its fighting discipline— elbows, shins, knees, and fists. More and more MMA fighters were incorporating the Thai martial art into their combat repertoire.

"And you're certain Ryan won't find anything?"

"As certain as I can be. After all, I designed the accounting system."

"Is that enough?"

"I've done my part. But it would be best if he and Brown just went away—the sooner, the better."

Yong barked an order in Thai for the trainer to leave for the day. The trainer grunted and bowed slightly, shutting the door behind him as he exited. The gym was an outbuilding behind the main house on Yong's estate, not far from his father's mansion.

"What are you suggesting?" the woman asked.

"If something happened to them, they might be tempted to leave early."

Yong slipped his fingers into the elastic band of her shorts and pulled her close to him.

"Send me their itinerary. I'll see what I can—"

Yong's mouth devoured hers greedily as he lowered her to the sweat-stained mat and took her without much resistance.

Paul made a big show of downloading data from his Dalfan desktop onto his encrypted USB, then loading it into the port on his personal laptop.

"Man, this USB data transfer is really speeding things up. Thanks again for all the help, Bai."

Bai smiled. "You're welcome, Mr. Brown. Happy to be of service."

Paul stretched his flabby arms high and wide and

yawned like a bear coming out of hibernation. "Man, I'm tired."

"You want some tea, maybe?"

"Oh, wow. That would be great. Something sweet, too, if you can find it."

Bai nodded. "Be right back."

"Thanks, Bai."

Paul turned back to his laptop, pretending to be focused on the screen but desperately trying to keep Bai in his peripheral vision, waiting for him to turn the corner into the kitchen and—

*Hurry!*

Paul whipped his fingers across the mouse pad and keyboard, opening the CIA file and dragging the contents over to the Dalfan USB to copy them. The progress bar popped up. Two minutes and counting. Just like last night.

It would take Bai at least that long to brew a cup of hot tea and find a pastry or something, and another thirty seconds for him to walk back to the office.

Unless the hot water machine was broken and the pastry box was empty.

A minute passed, then ninety seconds. Thirty seconds to go.

"Hope you like doughnuts, Mr. Brown."

Paul nearly jumped out of his skin. He swiveled around in his chair, using his wide body to block the screen from Bai, who stood in front of him, smiling and holding out a cup of tea and a chocolate doughnut with brightly colored sprinkles.

Paul forced a wide smile. "Outstanding, sir. Thank you."

Bai frowned, lifted his chin, trying to see over Paul's shoulder.

"Something wrong, Bai?"

"What's on your—"

"OW!" Paul jumped out of his chair, his pants drenched.

"What's wrong?"

"I spilled hot tea on my trousers! Quick, get me some paper towels! Please."

"Oh, yes, of course. Be right back!" Bai scurried out the door.

Paul spun around to face the computer. His scalded thighs screamed with pain, but he ignored it. He set the half-empty cup down with his left hand and shook it off, then jammed the doughnut into his mouth with his right as he checked his screen.

The USB message read INSUFFICIENT STORAGE CAPACITY.

"Thit," Paul breathed through his doughnut. His fingers flew again. The USB drive only had one gig of storage. He heard Bai's softly padding feet running toward the door.

"Thit!" Paul trashed the CIA file just as Bai yanked the door open, wads of paper towels from the men's restroom balled up in his fists.

"Here, Mr. Brown!"

Paul turned around, the doughnut still in his mouth. He pulled it out. "Thanks." He took a bite of doughnut and started blotting the hot tea from his trousers. Out of the corner of his eye he watched as Bai cast a glance at his empty laptop screen.

"Anything else, Mr. Brown?"

"No, thanks. This should do the trick. Sorry for the trouble."

"No trouble, Mr. Brown. More tea?"

"Eh, no, thanks. I think I've worn enough tea this afternoon."

"Yeah, *lah*."

Paul was glad he'd dodged a bullet, but his plan was shot to hell.

*How in the heck am I going to get around Dalfan security now?*

# 30

Jack arrived at the second floor with Lian on his hip and processed through the security desk, where they were met by Dr. Chen Tao. A smile creased her round, pleasant face as she extended her right hand to Jack; her other hand held a tablet. Jack noticed a bulge in one of her jacket pockets.

"A pleasure, Mr. Ryan. Please, follow me."

The second floor was divided into three sections separated by security glass and passcodes like the floor below, but this place looked like a Hollywood production studio—which essentially it was.

After leaving the security station, Dr. Tao led them through the central section with video-editing bays in the offices and software programming stations on the floor.

Jack passed a workstation where three earnest programmers argued passionately over the densely packed lines of code on the screen. Jack felt the energy in the room all around him, full of creative and brilliant young minds attacking problems he could barely understand.

Dr. Tao pointed out graphic designers, artists, mathematicians, software developers, and even a few physicists as they walked by. She asked Jack, "What do you know about VR—virtual reality?"

"It's the next big thing in video gaming."

"Why do you suppose that is?"

"Obviously because it makes games seem more realistic."

"And it does. The challenge all VR programmers face is this: Is there a way to make virtual reality so realistic that it's no longer possible to discriminate between the virtual and the real?"

Dr. Tao slid her pass card into the reader for the glass door leading to the rear section of the floor.

"Is that even possible?" Jack asked. "By definition, 'real' means that which actually exists. How can software and sensors ever be as 'real' as reality?"

Dr. Tao pulled open the door and pointed them through a blackout curtain. "I suppose that depends on your definition of 'reality.'"

"You sound more like a philosopher than a computer programmer."

"One of my undergraduate degrees was in psychology, actually. I've found it to be extraordinarily useful in my present position."

"How so?"

"Psychology is the study of the human mind. The whole point of computer programming is to mimic the mind and, when possible, exceed it, in order to improve the human condition."

"Exceed the mind? You mean artificial intelligence," Jack said.

"Yes. AI and machine learning are transforming everything, from simple devices like home thermostats to combat technologies on the battlefield. AI is central to our VR and AR development."

"AR—augmented reality?"

"Exactly. Between you and me? I think AR will be much bigger than VR in the coming years."

"Because AR is an overlay of reality, and easier to create?" Jack offered.

Dr. Tao nodded approvingly. "You catch on quickly, Mr. Ryan. Ever considered a career change?" She opened the security door and led them into the third section of the floor. It was an open area divided in two by a thick curtain. The first part of the open area was a high-tech movie theater with luxurious recliners and a massive 4K monitor on the wall.

"Sometimes it's better to see the work you've created on a small monitor put up on the big screen," Dr. Tao said. "And it's always useful to hear and see an audience react to your work."

"So your work is focused on entertainment?"

"Not primarily. We're developing tools that will make any virtual reality experience entirely real. That might include entertainment like video games and movies, but the primary application we're making with our VR tools is with simulators."

"I'm sorry, but there's that dichotomy again. How can 'virtually real' be 'entirely real,' Dr. Tao? That's not logically possible."

"Like I said, it depends on your definition of 'real.' My definition of reality is that which is grounded in human psychology and physiology. The brain is real. The central nervous system is real. The five senses are real. Do you agree?"

"Of course."

"We interact with the real world through our experience of it by means of our senses and the way our brains process those interactions. In other words, reality is data, and how our brains interpret those sensory data inputs is what we perceive as reality."

"In other words, you're saying perception is reality."

"How can it be anything else?"

"Things exist in reality outside of my perception."

Dr. Tao smiled. "Now who sounds like a philosopher?"

"You got me."

Dr. Tao waved a hand at the room. "Do you see any apples in this room?"

"No."

"Do you believe that apples are real?"

"Yes, because I've experienced them before."

"And right now we can only talk about apples in the abstract because we don't have a real apple in our hands to eat." Tao picked up a tablet and tapped a few keys before showing it to Jack. It bore the picture of a bright red apple.

"Is this apple real or virtual?"

"I'd say virtual, because it's only the picture of one. It doesn't exist in reality."

"The picture is real, though. What do you mean 'it' doesn't exist?"

"The apple itself."

"An apple defined as?"

"The sum of its attributes: weight, three dimensions, color, taste—that sort of thing."

"Exactly." Dr. Tao reached into her pocket and tossed a bright red apple at Jack. He caught it.

"Is that apple real?" Dr. Tao asked.

Jack rolled it in his fingers, felt the weight of it in his hands. "Sure."

"Assuming your brain is normal and your senses are normal, your brain is correctly telling you that you have just encountered a real apple. Not a virtual apple. Not the idea of an apple. But an actual apple."

"Agreed."

"Why?"

"Because my brain and my senses tell me it is."

"Exactly so." Dr. Tao smiled. "Have you ever experienced virtual reality, Mr. Ryan?"

"No. I'm not really into video games."

"Then perhaps we should start there."

**31**

Dr. Tao escorted Jack and Lian to the next room, a wide-open expanse but dark like a theater, with markers on the floor and sensors in the ceiling. Two technicians were illuminated by the glow of computer workstations behind a glass wall on one side of the room.

Dr. Tao directed Jack to a table outside of the workstation room. On it were black gloves, pull-on boots, and an unusual set of goggles that Jack picked up. The face of them was a huge rectangular opaque lens.

"That's our own wireless VR goggle design, though it's not terribly different from others on the market, like Oculus Rift or the HTC Vive."

"I take it that the flat piece is like a personal movie screen," Jack said.

"Exactly. There's also a wireless stereo headset that goes with it."

Jack was drawn to a leg holster and a Glock 19 pistol. He picked up the gun and felt the familiar knobby plastic grip in his hand. His thumb touched the wide mag release. A Gen4. It was the right weight and dimensions, but the barrel was capped in orange plastic, the magazines on the table were empty, and there wasn't any ammo.

"A practice gun."

"Have you ever fired a real pistol, Mr. Ryan?" Dr. Tao asked.

Jack shrugged. "Once or twice."

Dr. Tao frowned with concern. "If you're not comfortable with guns, I can arrange a different kind of demo—"

"No, I'm fine, really."

"Good. Let's get you suited up and we'll get started."


Ten minutes later, Jack was geared up with his boots, gloves, and weapon, and he held his goggles in his hand.

He stood next to Dr. Tao in the center of the room. She was kitted out, too, and holding her goggles as well. She demonstrated the intuitive hand and finger gestures that functioned as his controllers within the various simulations.

Jack held up one gloved hand, rotating the wrist, flexing the fingers. *Perfect.* The only thing that ruined the illusion was that his hand floated free, disconnected from an arm. But in a few seconds he didn't notice that quirk anymore.

"You'll notice that everything on you is wireless, so it allows for complete freedom of movement. We're able to accomplish that because we've developed optimization software, allowing us to broadcast far more data in smaller packets. Normally, only hard cables can handle the data transmission loads these systems usually require."

"Wireless is great. I don't want to be tripping over cables if I'm moving around."

"Ready to get started?"

"Sure."

Jack pulled on his goggles and couldn't see a thing. A moment later, the lights popped on and Jack stood in an all-white room in front of a white table. A red apple sat in the middle of it, and Dr. Tao—or, rather, her avatar— stood on the other side. She was dressed the way he was: gloves, goggles, gun.

"Looks familiar," Jack said, looking at the apple.

"Pick it up."

Jack reached for it.

"I don't believe it." He felt the apple in his hand, a definite shape and weight. "Haptics in the glove?"

"Micro-actuators are vibrating throughout the glove, making your hand feel as if an apple is in it. We can add temperature to the gloves, and we're perfecting different tactile sensations."

"It's so real I almost want to take a bite of it."

"Turn around and throw it."

Jack turned around and tossed the apple. It sailed through the air and hit the white floor twenty feet away.

"Now shoot it."

Jack glanced down at his holstered Glock. He reminded himself he couldn't actually see it; he was viewing a virtual representation of the gun on his leg. He reached down and wrapped his fingers around the practice pistol—it was real enough, no haptics needed—but the gun and gloved hand he saw were virtual. He raised the pistol, aimed it, and pulled the trigger.

The gunshot exploded in his ears—the sharp, earsplitting crack of a nine-millimeter round. The spent brass cartridge arced out of the chamber and *tink*ed on the floor to his right, and the gun jerked in his hand. The apple disintegrated into pulpy chunks.

"The gun has haptics, too?"

"That's what made it jump."

"That was loud."

"That's what it would really sound like. Do you want me to turn it down?"

"Better than going deaf."

"Try it again." As Dr. Tao spoke, a paper target appeared, hanging in midair over the apple shards.

Jack took aim and fired three shots in quick succession. Three holes punched dead center; the paper target shook and the gun jumped in his hand. But instead of three gun blasts, he heard three squeaks from a rubber-ducky toy. Jack laughed.

"Cute, Doc."

"It's all about options."

Jack holstered his pistol as he turned around.

"Not bad shooting for a guy who doesn't really like guns," Lian said in his headset.

"You're watching this?"

"Of course."

"I've got to admit, this is really cool technology," Jack said. "The couch potato brigade's gonna love it."

"VR has more important applications than games."

Jack suddenly stood in an abandoned surgical ward.

"What's this?"

"Could be a combat assault, or a police hostage rescue operation."

A metallic sound crashed on the far side of a swinging door.

Jack stepped past a surgical table and pushed against the swinging door, his right hand reaching for his pistol. He felt the weight of the virtual door press against his glove as it gave way. He went into a tiled washing area with stainless-steel sinks, his pulse racing. He started to clear the room but caught himself. This wasn't the time to tip his hand.

"Interesting, but don't military guys just build themselves practice rooms like this?" Jack asked, holstering his pistol.

"They do, but they can't do it as fast as this."

Jack didn't move, but the venues changed in rapid succession, one after another: a hotel lobby, an Afghan village, a department store, an elementary school classroom.

"A training coordinator can lock or open doors; move walls; cause weapons to fail; change up opponents; change the time of day, weather, season—you name it. Complete control and customization of any training scenario at the touch of a button."

"I can see where that would be handy," Jack said, hiding his shock. Any special operations team would love a training system like this. John Clark would go nuts. "But still not as good as the real thing, I'd imagine."

"It's a supplement to physical training, not a substitute. Ready for something else?"

"Sure."

Suddenly Jack was standing on the edge of a windswept mountaintop, a deep chasm falling away at his booted feet. His stomach tingled at the thought of falling off, which he knew he couldn't, since he was actually standing on the floor of the Dalfan building.

*Right?*

An eight-inch-wide board spanned the twenty-foot chasm. On the other side stood Dr. Tao's avatar. She waved to him.

"What do you think, Mr. Ryan?"

Jack spun around 360 degrees, taking in the rugged, snowcapped mountain range. A stiff breeze whistled in his ears.

The view appeared to be utterly real, better than the best 4K television he'd ever seen. Elation swept over him, the sense of utter freedom he always felt climbing in the mountains.

"This image quality is amazing. I'd swear I was really standing on a mountain. No lagging or pixelating."

"We created 12K images by stitching 4K videos together. Optimization algorithms maximize the streaming on your screen."

"Is that mostly what you do? Take existing technology and improve its performance?"

"Exactly correct, though we have amazing graphic arts, video, and audio departments." Dr. Tao's avatar waved for him to cross. "Care to come over?"

"Sure." Jack's legless left boot stepped onto the narrow board, followed by the right. The wind picked up in his ears. He glanced down at the chasm. Far below, a river raged. His sense of balance was already under assault.

"Feels pretty darned real, Doc. The audio quality is shockingly good."

"Our five senses are our gateway to reality. Sound and sight are the two most important."

"I don't suppose you've developed smell-o-vision yet." Jack took a few more steps.

Dr. Tao giggled. "We're working on something, but it's not quite ready."

The board creaked as it bent beneath his feet.

"Haptics in my boots?"

"Just like your gloves. The micro-actuators in your boots can alternate pressure points on the foot, simulating inclines and declines, as well as textures like pebbles, rocks, and even sand. We're working on both a full-sized helmet and a full-sized bodysuit for a completely immersive experience."

Jack stepped farther along the board, his arms intuitively lifting to his sides for balance. Halfway across the chasm, the plank cracked in his ears and the board began breaking in front of his toes. Jack's pulse quickened.

"Wow, this feels so—"

Jack's words were cut short by the piercing screech of a falcon. He glanced up in the direction of the sound and saw the bird circling overhead.

"Sounds like a falcon, but I wouldn't be surprised if it was a vulture."

Dr. Tao said, "Hold out your hand so he can land."

She showed him her extended arm and hand, held flat and perpendicular like a karate chop, with the index finger on top.

Jack raised his right hand in the same manner. A moment later a golden-brown falcon swooped down, flapping its wings in his face to slow enough to perch. It was magnificently rendered. The sound of the beating feathers in his ears caused him to lean back, trying to avoid getting pummeled by the wings. The falcon's claws tightly gripped his index finger.

"Glove haptics again."

"Precisely."

"I can even feel the bird's weight."

"That's partly haptics, partly illusion—your brain fills in the details. It's the 'phantom limb' effect."

Dr. Tao's avatar held up a hand and snapped her fingers. She disappeared, and Jack was standing amid the giant crescent dunes of the yellow Sahara. Windblown sand spattered in his headset.

In the blink of an eye, Jack was in the middle of a howling blizzard.

In the next blink, he stood on top of the Eiffel Tower, the gleaming City of Lights glittering in the dark below him.

"Can you load any video image into this system? Say, something like Google Earth?" Jack was actually thinking about the NGA's Map of the World program. If Gavin could marry the MOTW to a virtual reality program like this one, The Campus could virtually plan missions all over the world without ever leaving their Virginia headquarters.

"In theory, any 2-D video can be rendered in 3-D, then deployed within a VR system. Streets, buildings, rooms, villages, space stations. It's up to you. You can take a walk on the moon or along the ocean floor—anything and everything is possible. And if you don't have actual footage, simulations can be created by digital artists."

"Virtual travel, virtual education—I'm beginning to see the possibilities," Jack said, admiring the dawn breaking over the Parisian skyline.

"Do you have a few more minutes, Mr. Ryan? There's more."

"Sure."

Paris disappeared. Jack stood in the middle of a perfectly white room again. On his left wrist was a virtual heart monitor. The tip of his right index finger was a glowing laser scalpel. Suddenly, a beating human heart appeared suspended before his eyes, the beats thundering in his ears. He raised his left hand and touched the throbbing flesh, feeling the violence of its contractions on his palm.

"We can let new surgeons practice on a virtual heart instead of a real one. Care to try?"

Jack glanced at the laser, then the heart. He imagined gushers of blood pulsing onto the floor with each cut. "No, thanks."

The white room turned black and the heart disappeared. Now the heart monitor on his left arm was a graphic artist's palette for brush sizes, shapes, and colors, and his right index finger was a paintbrush.

"Try it."

Intuitively, Jack selected a brush head—clouds—and

a color. He dragged the brush through the air, leaving a trail of puffy, translucent mustard clouds. He ran the gamut of brush types—pencil points, duct tape, roller— and a dozen colors. Twenty minutes later he'd created a three-dimensional turquoise tree studded with purple fruit and surrounded by crudely drawn stars and birds and geometric shapes in a rainbow of colors. The art was crude and childish, but it was his, and he was surprisingly proud of it.

Jack laughed as he stepped into the middle of his 3-D painting, then through it, and spun it around before crouching down beneath it, utterly delighted and amazed.

"I think this is my favorite thing so far," he said.

"Mine, too, actually," Dr. Tao said. "But imagine designing a home, a new prosthetic limb, or a race car."

"Or a weapon." Lian's voice spoke in his ear.

Dr. Tao said, "The strong emotional response the VR experience evokes greatly enhances the learning and memory functions of its users."

"I get that now," Jack said. He'd felt elation, awe, fear, and joy in the demonstration. Those emotional responses were real. That was the true power behind this technology. Jack saw the enormous potential of the system for combat training but also every other kind of creative human endeavor.

The simulation ended. Jack pulled off his goggles. Dr. Tao and Lian stood in front of him.

"Now you see why video games aren't the direction we're most interested in," Dr. Tao said. "But then again, imagine how fun it would be to play soccer on the pitch with your favorite World Cup team, or a round of golf with your favorite pro teaching you the game."

Jack looked at Lian. "You've got your work cut out for you. This technology is more valuable than all the gold at Fort Knox."

"There are many ways for thieves to break in to steal." She nodded at Park, glowering in the corner, his thick arms crossed. "My team is trained to prevent all kinds of corporate espionage."

Lian turned a withering gaze back at Jack. "Unfortunately, some forms of theft are legal. Those are the ones I am powerless to stop."

It was quitting time, to judge from the number of Dal-fan employees gathering their belongings and heading for the exits.

Jack stopped by Lian's office and tapped on her door. She glanced up from her computer keyboard, a pair of bold neon-orange reading glasses perched on her nose.

"Yes?"

"I was wondering if we had any plans for tonight? I mean, the three of us."

"I thought it best if the two of you had some time to yourselves this evening. If you want to tour the city, I can recommend a few spots."

*Ouch.*

Jack shook his head. "No, I think we're heading back to the barn to try and catch up on some sleep. See you tomorrow."

"Good night." Lian returned to her keyboard.

Jack swung by Paul's office and gathered him up, and the two of them headed back to the guesthouse.

"Any plans for dinner?" Paul asked in the car.

"I saw a couple of steaks in the fridge. I thought I'd fry those up for us. Maybe with some onions and potatoes."

"I'll throw together a salad to go with it."

"Sounds like a plan. How do you like yours cooked?"

"Just wave it over the top of the pan before you drop it on my plate."

"Rare it is."

A half-hour later, Paul cut into his steak. He watched the bloodred juices sluice into the pile of fried potatoes and onions heaped up on his plate—just the way he liked it. He took his first bite, sweet and peppery.

"You ever slaughter a cow, Jack?"

"No, but I've eaten plenty of them. How's your steak?"

"Perfect. If you ever decide to quit Hendley Associates and open up your own steakhouse, I'll be your first customer."

"Thanks. I'm not great in the kitchen, but I'm hell on wheels on a Weber grill."

"I prefer a *kamado* grill, myself."

"Is that what a Big Green Egg is?"

"Yeah. It really locks in the flavor, like a smoker. Keeps everything moist."

Jack decided to let his hair down tonight and decompress with a glass of Bushmills—not that he was under a lot of stress at Dalfan. In fact, it had been one hell of an exciting day. He was still reeling from the virtual reality demonstration. If America had a couch potato problem now, he couldn't imagine what would happen when teenagers locked on to VR gaming systems.

"How was the demonstration today?" Paul asked.

"Funny, I was just thinking about that. Pretty freaking awesome. I need to get you up on the second floor to check it out for yourself."

"I'm not much of a gamer."

"Me, neither. Trust me, you need to see it to believe it. How was your day? Any interesting discoveries?"

"Actually, not much. I was finally able to download some of the Dalfan data sets I needed so I could begin running my screening software. Not a whole lot turned up, except . . ." Paul had also indulged in a glass of the same Irish whiskey Jack was drinking.

"Except what?"

"Well, I hate to cast aspersions, but I found a file that didn't make a whole lot of sense."

"What do you mean?"

"I ran a ratio analysis for some AR and AP reports on a product line that Dalfan sells to a firm in Shanghai—you know, maximum/minimum pricing over set time periods. The closer the ratio is to one, the happier I am."

"Why is that?"

"If the ratio between the highest price and the lowest price paid for an item equals around one, that means that the overall price paid for an item is relatively stable. But if suddenly the maximum price paid for an item skyrockets—or if the minimum price suddenly bottoms out—that's usually a pretty good sign of fraud. What bothers me is that in the last six months the price ratio nearly quadrupled. And the number of units sold doesn't quite add up."

Jack took another sip of Bushmills. "What kind of product are we talking about?"

"Cell phones." Paul took another bite of steak.

"Wait. Dalfan is selling cell phones to China?"

"Disposable cell phones, too, according to the invoices." Paul was still chewing when he spoke.

"That's like me selling sand to the Saudis."

"Like I said. It doesn't make a whole lot of sense."

"Where does Dalfan make them?"

"Here, in Singapore. They store and ship them out of a separate warehouse on the west side of the island."

Jack ran through the list of facilities that Feng had shown him earlier. He didn't recall a separate warehouse facility owned by Dalfan. "Maybe I should check it out tomorrow."

"Only if you want to. Like I said, it's odd, but it's not really a big deal in terms of the overall financial picture. Probably just a data-entry error."

"We're getting paid good money to do our due diligence, so I might as well take a look. It's that or crack open the books again." Jack stabbed his salad with a fork.

Paul watched the younger man eat. Over the last few days he'd gotten to know Jack Ryan, and he seemed like a decent fellow and whip-smart, for sure. Everything in him wanted to ask Jack for help in carrying out the mission for Rhodes, especially now that he had hit a wall, but he knew he couldn't ask him—and not just because

Rhodes had forbidden him to do it. Paul was trying to protect the young analyst. If he pulled Jack into this operation and it went sideways, the President's son could wind up in a world of hurt.

And then again, he still wasn't sure if he could trust Jack, either. Jack was pleasant enough around the office, but he had obviously been in a fight last night and didn't want to talk about it. If it was in self-defense, why hide it? Maybe the whole Mr. Nice thing was just an act.

No, he'd have to do this one without Jack, Paul decided, but he knew he couldn't do it by himself.

He poured himself another whiskey and drained it.

**A**fter dinner, Jack and Paul loaded the dishwasher and cleaned up, then both headed for bed. Paul was yawning his head off and Jack wanted to finish his Churchill biography.

But before brushing his teeth and heading for bed, Jack grabbed his iPhone and opened the Photo Trap app again. Photo Trap listed the photos he had taken this morning, and he pulled the first one up—his clothes-closet picture. The program prompted him, READY FOR PHOTO 2. He crossed over to the clothes closet and tapped the READY prompt, and the camera function on his iPhone pulled up a faint ghosted image of his closet so that he could match his new, live comparison shot to the original, lining up the edge of the closet door, a blue oxford shirt, and a few other markers so that the photos would exactly match. The Photo Trap app also provided directional arrows, telling Jack which way to rotate or tilt the camera on its axis to help match the first and second image. When the directional gauge grayed out all the arrows, he snapped the photo, then he manually flipped back and forth between the first and second photos to compare any differences, however subtle.

He repeated the process for the photos he took of his dresser drawers and bathroom sink. After he had manually flipped back and forth several times, it was clear to Jack that somebody had been in his room and searching for something. And if they had searched his room, they had probably searched the rest of the house as well.

Jack had an idea about who might have done it and what they were looking for. He thought about telling Paul about it but decided against it. Paul seemed distracted enough as it was, and there wasn't anything the accountant could do about it. Jack gave his room a thorough inspection for electronic microphones and cameras but didn't find anything—or so he hoped.

He suddenly felt very exposed.

Utterly exhausted, Paul headed upstairs to his bedroom and took a shower. Unlike most Americans, he preferred to shower at night and get the day's dirt off and climb into bed clean. It was a practice Carmen had taught him.

Beneath the hot, steaming water, Paul's Dalfan encryption problem occurred to him again. He'd been racking his brain all day, and if he was being honest with himself, the booze wasn't helping matters. The shower was pushing away the cobwebs, but he'd needed the booze tonight. Grief had fallen on him again, as unbidden as the plague. The only way to loosen its grip and keep the tears away was the booze. Better numb than despondent. At least he could work that way.

Paul had come up with half of a plan, but he couldn't figure out a way to finish it. Suddenly it dawned on him that he knew someone who could.

Gavin Biery, Hendley Associates' IT director, was a man Paul grudgingly acknowledged was damn good at his job, even if he was a total smart-ass.

Paul toweled off, putting the final pieces together. What he needed next was for Gavin to write a piece of software to capture the Dalfan encryption code on the Dalfan USB drive he now had. Gavin's software had to be written in such a way that when Paul installed the Dalfan USB into his personal laptop, the code would be captured. After capturing the code, he would load it onto the CIA drive, and then he could install the CIA drive directly on the Dalfan desktop.

But none of that would happen if Gavin didn't write that software, and write it fast. The deadline was only three days away.

Unfortunately, Paul also knew Gavin was up to his eyeballs in IT requests at the busy financial firm. He had to find a way to jump to the front of that line and convince Gavin to drop everything else he was doing and write him that piece of code, ideally within the next twenty-four hours, if that was even possible. Knowing Gavin, it would be a long shot to capture his attention, let alone get him to jump through a major hoop on such short notice.

Paul needed to come up with a compelling reason for Gavin to do this for him without compromising his mission for Rhodes. But how?

Paul pulled on a pair of pajamas, then opened up his laptop's browser and typed in the private Web address for Hendley Associates. He clicked onto the employee portal and logged in with his Hendley Associates passcode. He searched through the company directory until he found Gavin Biery's secure-message link.

He crafted a short message he hoped would not only grab Gavin by the short hairs but also get him to respond right away so he could explain everything to him. He wouldn't be able to talk to him at Dalfan with cell service jammed, so he'd have to check the Hendley Associates portal regularly. He needed to find a way to talk to Gavin, though, and not just message him. Talking was much better.

It was easier to lie that way.

**33**

Paul had checked the Hendley Associates portal several times last night and early this morning, but Gavin hadn't yet responded. Even when Gavin wasn't in the office—which was rare, because the man had no social life—he was known to check his messages frequently. Either he was ill or unable to access his machine. Either explanation was a disaster from Paul's perspective. He checked again one last time on his smartphone before they arrived at Dalfan, just in case.

And there it was. The text from Gavin he'd been waiting for. Sort of.

> I'm in the hospital. This better be
> as important as you say it is.

At least Gavin was online. Paul messaged, **Can you talk?**

A second later, Gavin responded:

> **As soon as I'm discharged.**
> **About an hour.**

That was good. That gave Paul enough time to find a way to get clear of the Dalfan building and its cell-jamming system to call him. It occurred to him that he should probably show some concern for his colleague. He typed:

> **Why are you in the hospital?**
> **Everything OK?**

Without a second's hesitation, Gavin typed back:

> **Penis reduction surgery.**

Paul sighed.

> **LOL. Seriously. Nothing major, I hope.**

> **Broken foot. Slipped on the ice outside**
> **of my place. Emergency room wait was**
> **killer. All good now except for the**
> **excruciating pain and the endless**
> **requests for IT help from work.**
> **But thanks for asking.**

> **I'll call you as soon as I can. Thanks.**

> **Don't mention it. Sorry I couldn't**
> **respond earlier. Any hints?**

**Better if we talk. It's complicated.**

**You have my number. Ciao.**

"Must be important," Jack said. "You're texting a dictionary."

Paul shrugged, poker face in place. "That project I was working on before? Just a couple follow-up notes."

"It's late back home." Jack checked his watch. "Almost eight o'clock. You're working whoever's on the other end of that text pretty hard."

"That's the idea," Paul said, as they pulled into the underground garage at Dalfan headquarters.

Jack and Paul entered the Dalfan building, followed the usual security routine, and headed for their offices.

Jack hadn't slept at all the night before, feeling certain he was under observation even though he had no evidence of it. It was like when someone talked about lice. It didn't matter that the lice infestation happened across town or even in the previous year; just the thought of the nasty little vermin made him start scratching his scalp.

The idea of his privacy being violated really pissed him off, but the thought that Lian and her team assumed that Jack and Paul were thieves made him even angrier. There wasn't any question in his mind that Lian was behind the break-in. His anger compounded by his lack of sleep, Jack was livid when he and Paul showed up at Dalfan that morning.

Jack spotted Lian in Yong's office, the two of them engaged in what appeared to be a heated conversation. Jack's plan was to read her the riot act this morning about the break-in. He was certain it was one of her security people that searched their place. The only reason he could come up with was that they were probably trying to find out if Jack or Paul had stolen any valuable secrets. He still wasn't convinced they hadn't planted any surveillance devices, either—and probably for the same reason.

Judging from the energy she and Yong were throwing off behind the closed glass door, Jack decided to postpone his confrontation with Lian for the time being.

Since she was highly distracted at the moment, it was the perfect time for him to go and check out the warehouse that Paul had told him about last night.

**P**aul was just sitting down at his desk when Bai appeared, bleary eyed and yawning.

"Long night?" Paul asked.

"My cousin's birthday party. I think I drank a little too much, but lots of fun and lots of pretty girls. *Lah*."

"Feel free to take a nap. I'm just sitting here, working."

"I might get a cup of coffee. Do you want something?"

"No, thanks."

Bai stepped out of the door just as Jack stepped in.

"I'm heading over to the warehouse now. You want to tag along?"

"I've got plenty to do here, but thanks."

"I'll call you if I find anything."

"Be careful, Jack."

"Careful? Why? We're talking about a case of bad bookkeeping, not an Al-Qaeda bomb-making factory."

"Just watch your back."

"You, too."

Lian was still talking to her brother when Jack walked past her door. They locked eyes for a moment, but she didn't stop speaking to Yong as Jack marched away. She did, however, pick up a phone.

Jack approached the security desk. Park was on the phone and standing at the security desk, towering over the young woman who manned the station. He glanced up just as Jack was passing through.

"Do you need anything, Mr. Ryan?" Park asked.

"Nah, I'm good. Thanks."

"Going somewhere?"

Jack flashed a smile. "Aren't we all?" He pushed against the security door to leave, but it was locked.

Jack turned around. Park was smiling at him, the phone still in his hand.

"Tell your boss I don't need a babysitter. I'm just taking a drive."

"I'm happy to drive you to wherever you want to go."

"I've got my own car."

"It's not an easy city to navigate."

Jack's foul mood suddenly boiled over. He stormed over to Park and got in his face. The ex–ROK Marine didn't flinch. They stared daggers at each other. The young woman they were standing over was afraid they were going to throw punches. "Eh, guys?"

Jack took a deep breath, realizing he'd lost control. He took a step back. He pointed at the phone still in Park's hand. "Let me talk to your boss."

Park bounced the phone in his hand like he was weighing it before finally handing it to Jack.

"Listen, Ms. Fairchild. Me being followed around isn't part of the deal. I'm heading out, and I don't want or need anyone to tag along. Is that clear?"

"Perfectly," Lian said on the other end of the line. "May I ask where you are going?"

"Sure, you can ask."

Lian waited for him to tell her, but soon realized he had just made a joke at her expense. "Fine. But be sure to obey all traffic laws. Our police force is very efficient."

Jack was going to say something else smart-ass, but he thought better of it. "Thanks for the warning." He slapped the phone receiver into Park's wide hand.

"Someday I think you and I are going to have a little talk," Park said.

Jack grinned. "I'll use small words."

Jack pushed on the exit door again just as the electronic lock clicked open, and headed for the elevator that would take him to the underground parking facility.

Park waited for the elevator door to close before he punched a speed-dial number and issued instructions to one of his team waiting in the garage.

**34**

Jack stared at the security camera in the elevator. It was like every other security camera hanging in almost every corner of every room in the Dalfan building—all four stories of it.

The elevator dinged and the door opened and Jack saw the security camera attached to the support pillar directly in front of him. He winked at it. Dalfan took its security seriously, and no doubt whoever was monitoring the cameras today was watching Jack head for his company car.

He chided himself for losing his temper upstairs. He knew that lack of sleep was partly to blame, but mostly it was poor judgment on his part. It was also the disrespect that Lian and now Park were showing him that was grating on his nerves. If he was being honest, his pranking Park the other day was also disrespectful, and Lian's feelings about what happened the other night were about her pride. What he really needed to do was to pull his head out of his ass and apologize to both of them. After all, they were just doing their jobs. It was about time he started doing his like a professional.

He unlocked the silver Dalfan Audi TT and climbed in. He pushed the starter button and the 220-horsepower engine roared to life. He then selected the navigation module on the virtual cockpit and entered his destination—the live Google map displayed between the virtual tachometer and virtual speedometer while he drove. He shifted into gear and carefully pulled out of his parking spot and, opting for the fastest possible route, which would take about forty minutes to drive, headed for the exit.

J ack pulled up and out of the garage and onto Changi North Crescent, then over to Upper Changi Road North, where he picked up the Pan Island Expressway (PIE), a three-lane freeway running the length of the island, closer to the center of it and away from the busy congestion of the southern downtown core abutting the Singapore Strait.

Jack's affection for the city was growing day by day. Even Singapore's freeways were beautiful. The well-maintained asphalt cut through the middle of a rain forest, with palm trees and colorful tropical flowers flourishing in the median strip. The light traffic on the PIE flowed smoothly.

In fact, traffic was so light and smooth that morning, it was easy for Jack to keep an eye on the black Land Rover following him several vehicles back. There were two occupants, a male passenger and a female driver, but he didn't recognize either. He'd picked up the tail just as he got onto the PIE, and he hadn't done anything to let them know he was aware of their presence. He did tap the brakes a few times to slow down to see if they would keep their distance—which they did—and when he accelerated they matched his speed, keeping the same traffic interval at all times.

The good news was that they were driving strictly by the book. The better news was that as far as Jack could tell, there was only one vehicle tailing him.

Jack wouldn't allow himself to get angry again; the people back there were just doing their jobs, too. But now it was time for Jack to do his.

Jack took the Clementi Avenue 6 exit heading south, then took the Commonwealth Avenue West heading east, until he passed the Darussalam Mosque, and then turned a sharp left again onto one of the smaller streets, then left again onto a red-bricked road that ran between rows of tall apartment buildings. He watched them match him turn for turn, but they were falling farther and farther behind.

Jack kept making left turns, then right, driving around as if he were a tourist just taking in the sights, finding narrower roads with heavier traffic, until he came back out on a series of numbered Clementi streets—2, then 5, then 4, then 3, and back around again. Jack wondered why this Clementi fellow was so important that he had several tree-lined streets named after him, even if they all ended in numbers.

In the many twists and turns and congested traffic,

there was no way for a single vehicle to follow him successfully without being noticed, and clearly they'd been
given the orders to do both. Not willing to expose themselves, they apparently opted to drop out. Now Jack
could proceed to his destination.

Paul checked his watch. He'd been working for exactly
one hour. Gavin should be free right about now.

"I need to go stretch my legs," Paul told Bai, standing up.

"It just started raining outside," Bai said.

Paul reached for his raincoat. "I like the rain."

"I wouldn't mind a walk myself." Bai also rose.

"By all means, do so. But wherever you go, I'll meet
you back here in thirty minutes."

Bai took the not-so-subtle hint. "Okay, Mr. Brown."

Paul stood and waited for Bai to gather his things and
leave before he headed for the exit, hoping like heck that
Gavin could save his bacon.

**35**

**P**aul saw the torrential downpour through the front-door entrance. He couldn't stay in the building if he wanted to use his cell phone, and he was sure the land-lines would all be monitored. He borrowed an umbrella from the security guard at the front desk, who remotely unlocked the door for him as he headed out into the heavy rain.

Paul surely must have looked like a fool to the secu-rity guard as he stepped outside for a walk, but he didn't have an alternative. He figured he didn't need to get more than a block away from the Dalfan building. He doubted the local authorities would allow Lian's security system to rob the entire industrial park of cell-phone service.

The pounding rain beat his umbrella like a drum skin, and the tires of the cars whizzing past him hissed through the standing water in the street. The slanting wind drove the rain beneath his umbrella, soaking his suit coat. *At least it isn't cold,* he told himself. *We're too close to the equator.*

Paul needed to find a quieter place to make his call. He spied a canvas awning on a building across from the Dalfan block and on a quiet side street. Paul waddled toward it as fast as his gimpy leg would allow.

Finally under cover, away from the traffic noise, Paul dialed Gavin's cell phone. After a few rings, Gavin picked up.

"Paul Brown from way downtown. How's it hanging?"

"Fine. How's the foot?"

"In a boot for six weeks. Messes up my tango lessons, but other than that, not too bad. So what's this about an emergency regarding Jack?"

"No one can hear this conversation, right?"

"I'm working from home. Nobody but me and the goldfish. So what the hell is going on?"

"I think we've got a security issue developing here," Paul began. He'd carefully rehearsed the lies he was about to tell, but he'd memorized them in order, so he hoped he could keep them straight.

"'Security' as in national security?"

"I think so."

"You're full of it." Gavin served as the IT director of both Hendley Associates and The Campus. Paul Brown didn't know about The Campus or Gavin's role in it.

Paul was startled by Gavin's reaction even though he'd anticipated it. Of course it was a lie, and Paul wasn't good at lying, but he had to make it work. "It's a security situation involving Jack."

"Jack? Why him? He's a financial analyst, not a spy." Gavin was covering for Jack's role in The Campus—a piece of information Paul Brown need not be privy to.

"I know. But I think he's having an affair with one of the corporate principals, and I'm convinced she's working for the Chinese."

Paul's heart sank. He felt terrible lying about Jack, but he knew that Gavin would do anything to protect him.

"Good for Jack," Gavin said. "In my youth, I had my way with a few ladies myself."

"I bet you did. But how many of them worked for the Ministry of State Security?"

"If you know for sure she's MSS, we need to tell Jack right now."

"No, I don't know for sure. That's why I called you. I only have my suspicions. What I need is proof. I have a plan, but it requires you to write a piece of software for me."

"You're making me nervous. Maybe we should bring Gerry in on this."

"No! Are you kidding? What if I'm wrong? Jack and I are here to help close a deal between one of Gerry's old friends and the company this woman runs security for—in fact, she's the daughter of the owner."

"I don't like the way this is sounding."

Paul began to panic. Gavin was about to blow the whistle on him.

"Look, Gavin, if this woman really isn't MSS but word gets out that we think she is, it will kill the merger. And if word gets out that Jack is having an affair with this woman, it might get him in trouble with Gerry, whether or not she's a spy."

"But especially if she is."

"Which is why we need to find out for sure without Gerry or anybody else knowing. That way, we can protect Jack and protect Gerry's client all at the same time."

"Okay, I get it. I'll keep my mouth shut, at least for now. So what exactly do you need?"

Paul laid out what he was trying to do—find a workaround of the encryption on the USB drive, which was true. The lie he told was that he needed to be able to breach Lian's computer to find out if she was working for the Chinese. He was under strict orders from Rhodes that nobody could know about the CIA spyware, and that included Gavin.

"That's a tall order," Gavin grumbled.

A woman dashed past Paul with a paper mask on her face and a clear plastic umbrella over her head. He stopped talking and kept his eyes on her until she was out of earshot.

"I think I've figured out a way to beat it. But it requires you to write a piece of software I can load on my laptop that will capture the encryption code on her USB drive when I load it."

"That won't be too hard," Gavin said. "But once you've captured the encryption code, what do you plan on doing with it?"

"Load it onto one of my personal USB drives and use it to break in."

Gavin whistled. "That might be a problem." A long silence followed.

"Gavin?"

"Thinking."

Paul heard keys tapping on the other end of the line. Gavin finally spoke up. "Any chance you have the model and serial numbers for it?"

"Yes, actually. I'll forward those right now."

"Good. It just so happens I know a gal over at NSA who's put together something that might do the trick."

"Can you get it from her?"

"Are you kidding? What woman can resist my masculine charms?"

*Then we're screwed*, Paul thought. "Of course. What was I thinking?"

"Besides, she owes me a favor. Let me reach out to her. But you still might have a problem."

"What's that?"

"Most security systems require two-factor authentication. Even if you grab the encryption code and load it on your drive, you'll probably need her personal passcode to break in."

"I've got that covered, thanks." Paul didn't tell him that the two-factor passcode for the CIA software was actually his. "Anything else?"

"I should be able to get that snatchware to you in the next twenty-four hours."

"Not soon enough."

"You don't think I have anything better to do than run errands for you?"

"It's Jack we're talking about. Twenty-four hours won't work."

Gavin sighed. "Fine. I'll figure something out. Call me if you need anything else."

"Thanks, Gavin. For Jack's sake."

"I'll be in touch."

Gavin rang off just as the rain broke. Paul collapsed his umbrella and shook it out, suddenly excited by the possibility that his long shot of a plan might actually have a chance of working.


The wipers on his Toyota rental minivan slapped away the heavy monsoon rain thudding against his windshield as he turned toward Changi Airport. He followed the white arrows on the red asphalt lanes toward the pickup area outside the stunning glass-and-steel structure of Terminal 3.

While he made the run to the airport, the German left his Ukrainian and Bulgarian associates back at their posts in order to keep a close watch on Paul Brown.

The noise of the rain pounding on his roof suddenly stopped when his vehicle passed beneath the large steel overhang in front of the terminal. He spotted the lone figure with the smart leather satchel and flat driver's cap standing by the giant number 4 gate marker, just where he should be. The German recognized the narrow-shouldered man instantly. He'd never worked with Wolz before, but knew him well by reputation. Everyone in the organization did. So did the foreign intelligence services. But no one knew Wolz better than his victims.

The German shuddered.

Wolz's narrow face sharpened even further with displeasure, either because of the inclement weather or because of the fact he had to wait nearly two minutes before being picked up.

Or both.

The German pulled the silver Toyota minivan up to the curb and stopped, turning to make eye contact with Wolz, but the middle-aged man with the pencil mustache and angry blue eyes just stared straight ahead as if the van didn't even exist.

Taking the hint, the German swore under his breath and crawled out of his seat and scrambled around to the other side of the vehicle. He opened the sliding rear passenger door and Wolz finally acknowledged him with a quick study of the German's face and, finally, a curt, humorless nod.

Wolz stepped into the rear of the minivan and took a seat in the center of the bench, carefully setting his hand-tooled satchel beside him as the German dashed back around the Toyota and crawled into the driver's seat, hurrying to avoid the airport police, who he knew circled the terminal in regular four-minute intervals in search of parking violations.

The German pulled away from the curb and eased into the departing traffic. They rode silently toward their hotel, where a special meal was being prepared for Wolz's particular dietary needs by the Romanian woman the German had picked up two hours earlier from the same terminal. Wolz was the last member of the team needed to carry out the mission. Paul Brown's movements had been carefully tracked and recorded, and both vehicles and weapons had been secured.

With Wolz finally in position, all they were waiting for now was the word to engage.

**36**

Jack made his way back to Clementi Avenue 6 and connected with the Ayer Rajah Expressway (AYE) heading
west, then turned south on Pioneer Road, making the
final turn onto the side street that dead-ended at the
building he was looking for down near the port.

Jack wasn't completely surprised to see that the building was surrounded by cyclone fencing and razor wire or
that there was a guard shack and a barrier arm. What did
surprise him was the fact that the guards, dressed in
street clothes, were armed with weapons printing beneath their baggy shirts. They were hard and serious
men—not your typical Asian rent-a-cops. His gut told
him they were operators, but he couldn't prove it. But a
wolf always recognizes another wolf, even when he's
dressed like a lamb.

Jack pulled up to the guard shack and rolled down his
window. The taller of the two guards stepped out of the

shack and leaned over toward Jack's window while the other one picked up a phone.

"Sir?"

"My name is Jack Ryan and I'm with Hendley Associates doing an audit on behalf of the Dalfan corporation. Here are my credentials." Jack handed the man his Dalfan security pass and identity card.

The guard examined them briefly. "Wait." He returned to the guard shack and conferred with the other guard, who now examined Jack's credentials while still talking on the phone.

Jack drummed his fingers on the steering wheel. What the hell was the problem? A moment later a four-passenger golf cart pulled up to the gate and four more beefy security guards jumped out.

The tall guard came back out of the shack and handed Jack his credentials as the man on the phone hung up and stepped outside.

"Not permitted entrance." The guards who arrived in the cart now surrounded Jack's Audi TT on all four sides. None of them had unholstered their weapons, but none of them looked like they were shy about the possibility.

"What do you mean 'not permitted'? I have access to every Dalfan property in this city."

The guard scowled. "Leave."

Jack pointed at the phone in the guard shack. "Pick up that receiver and call your boss, Lian Fairchild, or better yet, call her dad, Dr. Fairchild. They both know who I am, and they sure as hell know why I'm here."

The tall guard straightened and pointed at the road behind Jack. "You leave now."

*And if I don't?* Jack wanted to ask. But there was no reason to. He clearly wasn't going to make his way in today, even if he had a weapon. More important, Rhodes had given explicit instructions to keep a low profile. That was probably a good idea anyway for all parties concerned, especially him.

"I must be mistaken. Sorry for the trouble." On a hunch, Jack beckoned the tall man with his index finger to come closer. The man leaned over and Jack snapped a photo of him with his iPhone, then gunned the engine and threw the car into reverse. The two guards now behind his car bolted out of the way, afraid he was going to run them over. Instead, Jack eased his way out of the drive lane and onto the street that would lead him back to Dalfan headquarters, but not before snapping two more photos of the irate and embarrassed guards cursing him in Mandarin.

Jack did a slow 180-degree turn, stopping just long enough to glance in his rearview mirror. The guards stood clustered in a loose formation, watching him leave and making sure he didn't change his mind and turn around. He didn't. He punched the gas and sped away.

Pulling back onto Pioneer, he wondered for just a moment if maybe Paul had gotten the address wrong or if there was some other kind of mistake. But his gut—the one that Clark told him to always pay attention to—told him there wasn't any mistake, at least not on his part.

After turning back onto the AYE, he texted the photos of the guards to Gavin and spoke a text requesting an ID of them ASAP.

"How ASAP?" Gavin replied.

"Yesterday."

"Sure. I've got nothing better to do." Gavin didn't dare tell Jack that he was working his tail off for Paul.

"Thanks," Jack said. "It's important."

Jack stormed into Lian's office. She was on the phone. "You had no right to block my entrance to that facility."

Lian spoke into the phone: "I'll call you back." She slammed the receiver down and stood. "How dare you come into my office with that attitude. You're the one that took evasive action today and lost my security escort."

Jack saw that several people in the area were staring at them, including Paul and Bai across the suite. Jack stepped farther into her office and closed the door.

"I never asked for a security escort. In fact, I said I didn't want one."

"I suspended my people for failing to keep track of you. I'm tempted to fire them."

"It's not their fault. I take responsibility for what happened today."

"Why would you take responsibility? Oh, yes, because somehow you managed to throw off two highly trained security personnel. How did you manage that?"

"What are you implying?"

"It takes training to defeat training." She stepped closer, examining his face. "Yes, Jack Ryan, I think you have training."

Jack thought of a quick lie. "Of course I have training.

My father taught me how to shake a tail when he taught me how to drive when I was a teenager. It was a game we used to play." He flashed a boyish smile.

"You're a lot of trouble, that's what you are." She crossed back over behind her desk and fell into her chair. "Tell me why you were so eager to go it alone today."

"It's a violation of international auditing protocols to allow a client to observe an investigation." Even Jack was surprised how good he was getting at lying on the fly.

"I have never heard of such a rule. But then again, we've never allowed any outsiders like you to come so far inside our organization."

"My job is to make sure that Marin Aerospace and Dalfan Technologies reach a fair and equitable agreement on stock valuation, and part of that valuation is dependent upon your profitability as a company and the accuracy of its financial records."

"Have you found a problem?"

"That's what I was trying to determine."

"Where did you go?"

"You know where I was."

Lian frowned. "No, I don't. You lost my tail, remember?"

"You had me blocked from entering."

"I did no such thing."

"You didn't tell the guards to not let me in?"

"Again, if I didn't know where you were, how would I do that?"

"They called you."

"No one called me about you." She frowned. "What were you looking for?"

"Just checking up on a loose end. I'm sure it's nothing."

"Nothing—and yet you had to ditch my security team to look for it. I want to know where you were."

Jack wasn't sure what to tell her. If she was the one behind the hidden warehouse, he didn't want to tip his hand. But then again, he wanted to get inside, and if she was on the level, she could arrange that. The trick was to give her just enough information to suss her out but not enough to allow her to interfere with his investigation.

"I was at your warehouse facility on the west end."

Lian frowned. "We don't have a warehouse on the west end, or anywhere else. Why don't you take me there and we'll check it out together?"

Jack cursed himself. She gave him the worst possible answer. If she was innocent, that's exactly what she would say. But if she was trying to interfere, she'd want to find out what it was he had discovered.

"No need. It's my mistake, I'm sure. Sorry for the trouble."

Jack turned to leave, but Lian stopped him. "One second, please." She punched the speed dial and engaged the speakerphone.

"Yes?" Yong answered.

"It's me. Question for you: Do we have a warehouse facility on the west end I don't know about?"

"No. Why do you ask?"

"Just tying off a loose end. Thanks." Lian hung up. "I hope that clears things up for you."

Jack smiled, lied. "It does. Thanks."

"And if you change your mind about riding out there together, I'm happy to oblige."

"I appreciate it."

Lian watched Jack leave, more curious than ever about what he was up to.

B ack at the warehouse across town, the tall guard that had turned Jack away stood in the wood-paneled office near his boss's desk with his arms crossed behind his broad back. He was trying not to listen to the woman's conversation, but he kept stealing glances at the heart-shaped mole above her upper lip. His blood surged at the thought of her mouth and what he would do to her if she were willing, and the pleasure it would bring both of them.

His boss stood just a few feet away from her, tugging on his collar and patting away the beads of sweat on his forehead with a handkerchief. The guard didn't know the woman's name, only that she was from Beijing. The guard, however, knew his boss—a ruthless bastard, and a Party man to the core. If his boss was scared of her, the guard knew he needed to watch himself, no matter how desirable she was.

He had reported the incident with the man who identified himself as Jack Ryan to his boss, who in turn reported it to this woman. When she arrived, she demanded to speak to the guard and to see the security footage herself before confirming Jack Ryan's identity.

*Whoever this Jack Ryan guy is,* the guard thought, *he better watch his ass.*

————

**H**ow did he find out?" Yong demanded. He was on the other end of the line.

Meili glanced at the tall guard, studiously ignoring her, judging by the blank expression on his broad, cunning face. She turned around, her back to him.

"No idea. But I don't have to tell you he can't come back."

"Obviously."

"How can we stop him?"

Yong laughed. "You mean besides running over him with a car?"

Meili didn't laugh.

"I'm joking."

"Don't. This is not good. For either of us."

"I have an idea."

**Y**ong ended the call, but his hand still gripped the receiver. Jack Ryan was becoming a problem, quickly, and he needed to be dealt with.

He told Meili that killing him wasn't an option, but he wasn't sure if she agreed with him. If Jack Ryan couldn't be discouraged from further investigation, he needed to be driven away for his own sake or else she would deal with him, one way or another.

# 37

Jack and Paul put in a full day's work at Dalfan, continuing to sift through the mountains of data and reports they were required to examine before signing off on the Dalfan-Marin merger. Jack decided to hold off on further physical investigation of the warehouse facility until he heard back from Gavin.

Given Lian's harsh reaction to his accusations, Jack was suddenly less confident that what he'd stumbled across today was a Dalfan location after all. But there was something definitely there, and whatever it was, it was kept under lock and key. And if it turned out it was a Dalfan facility, it was better to know who he would be going up against when he broke into it.

Jack and Paul picked up some Indian takeout food from a nearby restaurant Bai recommended and headed back to their guesthouse.

They unloaded several cardboard containers and filled their plates with spicy chicken biryani on beds of basmati rice and ladled up bowls of rich vegetable curry. Jack poured two glasses of iced mango tea he fetched from the refrigerator as Paul laid out the silverware.

They began eating in silence, both lost in their own thoughts about the events of the day, neither feeling as if they could talk to the other about them. Ironically, they were both waiting for a phone call from Gavin, and neither knew about that, either. The food was quickly disappearing.

"This is great," Jack said.

Paul forked another mouthful of chicken. "Bai said we wouldn't be disappointed."

"Do you still think he's reporting everything he sees to Yong?"

"No question. But that's his job, and I don't blame him for doing it."

"Nothing much for him to report, I imagine."

"I play dumb, he plays video games. It keeps him out of my hair." Paul swallowed. "What little of it is left." He heaped more chicken and rice onto his plate. "You didn't mention how your trip to the warehouse went."

"It didn't exactly go the way I'd planned. I couldn't get in."

"You showed them your credentials?"

"Yeah. Didn't matter. What's weird is that Lian said she had nothing to do with it."

"But somebody's hiding something."

"No doubt."

"How do you plan on getting in?"

Jack grinned. "My winning personality."

Paul picked up the nearly empty box of curry. "You want any more?"

"Knock yourself out."

The back door burst open.

J ack leaped to his feet as men in tactical gear charged in, guns drawn. But two powerful hands shoved him back down by the shoulders from behind as the cold steel of a rifle barrel pressed against his face.

Paul sat in his chair, mouth open and full of curry, gasping like a carp in the bottom of a boat.

The men in black tactical gear all had POLICE blazoned across their bulletproof vests. Jack heard boots thundering up the stairs and shouts in English and Mandarin.

A short, powerfully built man with lieutenant's bars sewn onto his collar stepped forward, holstering his pistol.

"You are under arrest!"

"On what charge?" Jack demanded.

"Possession of drugs."

"What are you talking about?" Jack ignored the crashing, banging, and thudding on the ceiling. It just meant their rooms were being torn apart upstairs.

Another policeman lifted Paul to his feet, his jowly face white with panic.

"Arms behind your back!"

Paul nodded, complying. Plastic cuffs zipped behind him, pinching his wrists. He winced with pain.

The lieutenant pointed at Jack. "You. Stand up. Hands behind your back."

"You've made a mistake," Jack said, standing. Another cop zip-cuffed him.

Something crashed on the floor above them. Paul startled, staring at the ceiling. The lieutenant noticed.

"Mistake? Then why is your friend so scared? Afraid my men will find something?"

"You won't find any drugs," Jack said. "Not even a stick of Juicy Fruit."

The lieutenant got in Jack's face. "Don't you realize the penalty for drug smuggling in Singapore is death?"

"Yeah, I read about that—"

"What's going on here?" Lian barked as she marched into the kitchen, Park right behind her, his face a brutal mask.

"Who are you?" the lieutenant demanded.

"Lian Fairchild. I own this place. What's the meaning of all this?"

The cocky lieutenant softened. "Fairchild? I know that name. Weren't you with STAR?"

"Yes. What of it?"

"And your father—"

"Answer my question, Lieutenant!"

"My unit received an anonymous tip that there were illegal narcotics stashed in this place."

Lian pointed at Jack. "You think this man is an international drug smuggler?"

The lieutenant scowled. "The tip was legitimate—"

"Do you know who he is?"

"Do you think I care? If he's breaking the law, he's a criminal."

"You're a fool, and you've been played like one." Lian spat out a string of syllables in Mandarin in a low, violent growl. Jack didn't speak the language, but he could tell by the look on the lieutenant's panicking face that it wasn't good for him.

"Release them!" The lieutenant shouted orders into his shoulder mic, and the racket overhead stopped instantly. By the time Jack's cuffs were cut off, the other tactical officers were down the stairs and racing out the doors.

The lieutenant told Lian, "You take full responsibility for these men?"

"I do. And I'll be sure to call your captain and tell him."

The lieutenant gave Jack and Paul one last suspicious look, turned on his heel, and marched out of the back door, slamming it behind him on its busted frame.

Jack turned to Lian. "I guess we should say thank you."

Paul rubbed his aching wrists. "Yes, thank you, Ms. Fairchild."

Lian crossed over the door-frame splinters on the floor. "What a mess." She turned to Park. "Call somebody to come over here and fix this door."

Park pulled out his cell phone and headed for the front room.

"If you'll excuse me—" Paul pushed past Jack and headed upstairs.

"You want to tell me what just happened?" Jack asked.

Lian shook her head, seemingly perplexed. "Somebody made a mistake—or was sending you a message."

"A message like 'Get the hell out of Dodge'?"

"Dodge?"

"An expression. Someone doesn't want us here and tried to scare us away."

"Who would do that?"

Jack fought the urge to laugh. "Gee, I wonder."

Lian frowned. "You think I did this?"

"I don't know what to think. But it was awfully convenient of you to show up at just the right moment. Otherwise, I might have called the American embassy, kicked up a ruckus."

Lian shook her head. "You are one arrogant prick, you know that?"

Jack wasn't expecting that kind of pushback. "I've been called worse."

"I came here tonight to apologize to you for my boorish behavior this afternoon. I was very angry."

"I could tell."

"And now you accuse me of this?"

"If you were me, wouldn't you think the timing was awfully convenient?"

Lian blew air out of her clenched teeth. "I don't know what to think, either, so maybe it's best if I leave." She turned to go.

Once again, Jack was at a loss with this woman.

He was usually pretty good about reading people, but this one kept throwing him off balance. Up until this moment he was sure she was jerking his chain, but her emotional turn made him question himself. He couldn't shake the feeling he was being played.

Who was Lian Fairchild, really?

She was a loyal sister, and clearly her brother opposed the merger. But she was also a loyal daughter, and her father wanted it. And she was a trained security professional. Was she merely bouncing between conflicting loyalties, or was she playing some kind of game with him? And if she was playing a game, what game?

She was ethnic Chinese, at least in part. Could she possibly be working for them? What better way to infiltrate Dalfan security than by recruiting her?

But if she was a Chinese spy, she wasn't very good at her job. A real spy would try to put him at ease, not express constant hostility.

Unless that was her game.

Jack swore to himself. He didn't have a clue. And if he was being completely honest with himself, he sounded a little paranoid.

Jack touched her arm and tugged on it—gently. She turned around.

"Look, I'm sorry. I'm not sure what the hell is going on. If you really weren't part of this, well, I guess I'm an idiot."

She didn't soften. "No guessing is required."

Park came back in. "A man will be here first thing in the morning to make the repairs."

Lian looked at the door. "What about that?"

Jack picked up a chair and shoved it against the creaking door. "We'll be fine tonight. Don't worry about it."

"I suspect those policemen made quite a mess upstairs. Do you need Park's help cleaning up?"

"No, we'll manage." Jack softened. "And thanks for stopping by. Otherwise, we'd be in jail right now."

"You will both be coming to the office tomorrow morning, then?"

"Soon as your guy fixes the door."

"Very well." She turned to leave.

"Hey, let me make it up to you. I know a place downtown that serves a great mai tai."

Lian offered a sad little smile. "I don't think so."

Jack saw Park fighting back a smirk. *Loser.* He fought the urge to backhand it off the Korean's sneering face.

"Good night," Lian said over her shoulder, heading for the front door. Park threw Jack one last mocking look as he turned to follow her.

Jack started to say something but decided there wasn't room in his mouth for any more feet.

**38**

A bomb had exploded in Paul's room.

Or so it seemed to him as he stood in the doorway, examining the wreckage.

He stormed past the socks, underwear, bedsheets, hangers, pillows, and suits scattered across the bedroom floor. He stopped to pick up the framed photo of Carmen he kept at his bedside, and set it back on the dresser— even though the glass was cracked—and marched straight for the bathroom.

An empty plastic pill bottle cracked as he stepped on it while reaching for the spring-loaded shower curtain rod lying on the floor. He picked up the end of the rod closest to him. The rubber cap was off. He turned the rod around, pulled the other cap off, and reached into it with one of his chubby fingers, struggling to try and reach something. It took several attempts, but he finally pulled out a clump of toilet paper pinched between his finger and the side of the rod and tossed it. He tilted the rod even farther down, and the USB drive Rhodes had given him slid out.

Paul let out a sigh of relief. Lucky for him whichever cop was searching in here was too lazy to check both ends, or maybe that's when the lieutenant called them all down. Either way, Paul could breathe easier now. Time was running out for him to finish the mission, but it would be immeasurably more difficult, he told himself, if he lost the USB drive altogether. He held the drive in the palm of his hand.

"What's that?" Jack asked, looking at all of the pill bottles and toiletries scattered over the floor. "And what the hell happened in here?"

Paul glanced up, startled. "This? Nothing. Just a USB drive."

"That you hid in the shower curtain rod?"

"This? No. It was in my pocket. I was checking out the shower curtain rod to make sure they weren't trying to plant any drugs on us."

Jack picked up an empty bottle of Tylenol. All of the little white tablets that used to be in it were scattered all over the floor and on the counter.

"Somebody doesn't want us around."

"Yong?" Paul stood with a grunt, using the tub for leverage.

"Or Lian. Or both. Or somebody else. Who knows?"

"I don't think it's Lian. She seems . . . smitten."

"What? No. Trust me."

*Trust you?* Paul thought. He glanced at the floor. "This place won't clean itself up. We better get started."

Jack surveyed the damage. "Do you want me to help? We can do your room first, then hit mine."

"If you don't mind, I'll take care of my room on my own. I like things in a certain order."

"I understand. I think I'm gonna get something to drink first."

Paul looked around at the disaster that awaited him. "Good idea."

After he and Jack knocked down a couple shots of Bushmills, Paul limped back upstairs with a broom and dustpan and got to work. He didn't bother trying to save the OTC drugs scattered everywhere, but he bagged them all and tied off the bag, wondering where he could dispose of them. He didn't want to dump them in the toilet or in the trash—there were already hundreds of millions of pounds of pharmaceuticals getting flushed into public water supplies every year and probably even more contaminating the soil. He didn't know how he managed to gather such random facts, but they were always there, and when the facts demanded certain moral actions, he tried to act accordingly.

It took him another two hours to finally get everything back in order just the way he preferred. The repair guy would need to fix one broken drawer, and one of his polyester suit coats had a big black boot print on the sleeve. He'd have to ask Bai for a dry cleaner recommendation tomorrow.

Paul wondered if Jack believed him about the USB

drive. He had to assume he didn't. He liked Jack well enough, but he didn't really know him, and he was definitely the curious type. Instead of putting the USB back into the shower curtain rod, Paul retrieved one of his shoes and wedged the small device in the toe with a dress sock to keep it in place.

Finally settled down, Paul decided to take a shower.


He found his phone on the nightstand and saw he'd missed a call from Gavin. He listened to the voice mail and swore softly, cursing Gavin's childish behavior but grateful he had access to him as a resource.

"Paul Brown, you're not downtown. But I just uploaded a zip file in your Dropbox with the program you requested and a README file with instructions, but it's all pretty straightforward. I'm still not exactly sure how the program is going to help you catch your Chinese spy, but so long as you're keeping an eye on Jack Junior, I'm in your corner, and I'm still keeping my mouth shut, at least for now. Let me know if you have a problem—I mean besides the obvious one staring at you in the mirror. And yes, you're welcome. Ciao."

Paul powered up his laptop, opened his Dropbox account, and found the two files Gavin had promised. He double-clicked on the README file and read Gavin's instructions:

1. Download the unmarked SNATCHWARE file onto your laptop.
2. Install the target USB into your laptop.

3. The SNATCHWARE will automatically find and capture the encryption code on the target USB. You don't have to do anything. It will create a file called BigDaddyG.
4. Remove the target USB and install your personal USB.
5. Transfer the BigDaddyG file to your personal USB.
6. Install your personal USB into your target computer.
7. Enter the target two-factor authentication password when prompted.
8. You're in.
9. Buy two steak dinners for Gavin Biery and one special lady friend at Mastro's.

Paul shook his head. "BigDaddyG?" *Give me a break.* Mastro's would set him back a few bucks, but the price was well worth it.

He opened up the unmarked snatchware file. Paul was no coder, for sure, but he could read it well enough. It was tight, elegant, and powerful. The proof of the pudding would be in the eating of it, he told himself, or at least the downloading and execution of it.

He downloaded it without a problem. Now his computer was ready to capture the encryption software on the Dalfan USB tomorrow. *Then we'll see how smart your smart-ass really is,* Paul thought.

Once he captured the encryption program located on the Dalfan USB—which couldn't leave the Dalfan HQ premises—he would transfer it to the USB drive Rhodes gave him, and then all he would have to do is load it into a Dalfan computer, type in his personal passcode, and let it work its magic.

Easy as pie, so long as everything worked exactly as planned and he wasn't caught red-handed in an act of international and corporate espionage.

The thought elevated his blood pressure. He put on his slippers and limped downstairs for another two fingers of whiskey to quiet his nerves.

**39**

The next morning Jack and Paul arrived at the security desk on the first floor and were handed a note asking them to head straight for Yong's office.

Yong was seated behind his computer when Jack knocked on the door frame. Yong motioned them toward the two open chairs in front of his desk.

"You wanted to see us?" Jack asked.

"I heard about last night. Quite disconcerting."

"For us or for you?"

"Both, of course."

"Yes, of course."

Yong shook his head. "Your bad manners haven't improved, have they? But that brings me precisely to my point. I have found your work and your presence both disruptive and ineffective to my company."

"I'm sorry you feel that way."

"I don't 'feel' that way. This is not a matter of feelings. It's business. And I'm simply stating a fact."

"The fact is you really don't want us here, do you?"

"Have I shown you any discourtesy?"

"That's not answering my question."

"My father wishes you to be here, so I wish you to be here."

"But if your father wasn't the CEO? If you were? What would you prefer?"

Yong leaned back in his chair. "To be perfectly frank, I'm not sure what advantage there is to partnering with an American company at this time."

"A massive cash infusion, operating synergies, global brand, and marketing reach. Those don't sound too disadvantageous."

"All short-term stimulants. In the long run, America is in decline, and America's role in Asia is diminishing each day."

"While China's is on the rise," Paul said.

"Unquestionably. But I wouldn't seek a merger with a Chinese firm, either. Both of your countries are going the way of the dodo bird. You're both too large, too socialist, too complex, and too corrupt. The future belongs to small nation-states like Singapore, led by enlightened visionaries like Lee Kuan Yew."

*Or Yong Fairchild,* Jack thought.

"Only nine percent of Americans trust their Congress, but seventy-four percent of Singaporeans trust their government. And if Americans don't trust their own government, why should anybody else?"

Yong hit a sore point with Jack. His father was working hard to restore America's trust in its government by being honest with the American people and always trying to do what was best for the country, even at his own political expense. He'd read in a political science course at Georgetown that in 1964, seventy-seven percent of Americans believed that the federal government could be trusted to do the right thing most of the time. America's political class had squandered that great legacy. It was going to take decades to restore it.

"I wonder why your father is so keen on the merger, then," Jack asked.

"He's old school, raised on his father's white British knee, hearing stories of the heroic resistance against the cruel yellow invaders from Nippon."

"You're saying your father is a racist? He's half Asian himself."

"My father is an Anglophile, and pro-Western to the core. That doesn't make him a racist. It just means he isn't a realist, despite his great wisdom in so many other areas."

"We appreciate your candor. Perhaps we need to make this known to the Marin Aerospace board. They may think twice about a merger with a company with a hostile future CEO."

"If you report any such thing, I'll deny it and I'll sue you over it. What I've shared are merely private thoughts. I adamantly support the merger and anything else my father wishes. Am I perfectly clear?"

"Yes."

"If anything, I should call Senator Rhodes myself and tell him how the two of you have completely overstepped yourselves and killed the deal."

*That won't be good for Gerry or Hendley Associates,*

Jack thought. As much as Yong obviously didn't want the merger, a lot of other folks did. Jack knew he needed to back down rather than give Yong the excuse he needed to kill the deal. Suddenly, the politics of this white-side assignment seemed more difficult than dodging bullets in the North Sea, and nearly as hazardous to his career.

"I apologize if I've said or done anything to offend you. I'm just trying to do my job."

Paul nodded his agreement. "We're just doing a quick, standard fraud audit, and we're trying to keep as low a profile as possible."

"So then what was all this nonsense with the police last night?"

"We have no idea. It was bizarre, to say the least. Good thing your sister showed up just in the nick of time."

Yong cocked his head. "What are you implying?"

Jack wasn't implying anything. It seemed pretty damned obvious. Was he supposed to believe the phony police raid was pure coincidence? "Nothing at all. Thanks to her intervention, your country avoided an embarrassing diplomatic incident with my country on the eve of a historic summit."

"My sister is a remarkable woman and fiercely loyal to her family. But she's also no fool." Yong grinned. "As amusing as it would have been to see the two of you caned publicly, it would be wrong. She knows you and Mr. Brown aren't drug smugglers."

"Good to know, because whoever was stupid enough to pull that idiotic stunt last night isn't bright enough to understand that it won't discourage us from doing our jobs while we're here."

"I'm glad to hear that."

"And we are genuinely grateful that she got us out of that jam."

"I'm glad to hear that as well. She seemed quite upset when I spoke with her last night. She is a proud woman. I can hardly believe she came to apologize to you."

*Technically, she didn't,* Jack reminded himself. "She surprised me for sure."

"My sister had made special plans for the two of you this morning, but she assumed you wouldn't want to participate after the way you treated her last night."

"I was caught off guard last night. After it was over, I told her I was an idiot." Jack wanted to add, *But I was an idiot only if I was wrong about her, and I'm pretty sure I'm not.* But he thought better of it. "We're more than happy to hang out with her this morning—I just have an appointment with Dr. Heng later this afternoon."

"I'm sure you can keep it, and my sister will be delighted."

Paul shifted, anxious. He whispered in Jack's ear, "I've got work to do."

Jack ignored him. "We couldn't be more excited."

Yong stood and extended his hand. "I'm glad we had this little chat today, gentlemen. It's always good to clear the air."

Jack shook his hand. "Just a few more days, Mr. Fairchild, and we'll be out of your hair."

"Hopefully an uneventful few days. If you'll excuse me, I have a lot on my plate this morning," Yong said with a dismissive wave.

Jack and Paul left, looking for Lian. Jack was beginning to think that Paul was right all along—maybe they should just sign off on the damn paper and get out. It seemed now like they were only spinning their wheels.

## PYONGYANG, NORTH KOREA

Chairman Choi Ha-guk's wide desk was empty except for an ashtray. Unlike his predecessor's, the chairman's office was spartan. Its only adornments were a plain couch, two chairs, industrial carpet, and bookshelves neatly stacked with technical books in three languages. He sat stiffly in his low-backed chair in a cloud of smoke across from Deputy Ri, the head of the Services Administrative General Directorate.

"Why hasn't it happened yet?" A Gitanes cherry-tipped in the chairman's yellowed fingers as he took another drag.

"I have every confidence in the Bulgarian. He's proven himself utterly reliable in the past."

"That doesn't answer my question."

"There are unanticipated security measures to be overcome. But he assures me they will be overcome."

"When?"

"Soon."

"We're running out of time." Chairman Choi stabbed his butt out in the crowded ashtray. "You're running out of time."

"But there is still time, and the software my department has written is flawless."

The chairman opened a desk drawer and pulled out a

fresh pack of cigarettes. He slid his thumbnail beneath the cellophane wrapper, thinking. "I'm giving you direct command of any foreign RGB units you may have need of."

"Director Kang will object, and I—"

The chairman cut him short with a raised finger. "This operation takes precedence over all others. I will inform Director Kang myself."

"Thank you, sir."

The chairman offered the blue pack to Ri. "Cigarette?"

Ri hid his surprise. He nodded and took one. "Thank you."

The chairman slid his Zippo lighter across the desk. Ri lit up. They smoked in silence for a few moments, until a curt nod from the chairman ended the meeting.

**40**

## SINGAPORE

Lian took Jack and Paul on a tour of her city, starting with historic Emerald Hill and its restored colonial splendor, then over to the colorful Arab Street in the Muslim quarter, featuring the gold-domed Sultan Mosque, hipster boutiques, and street art. When she noticed Paul's limp getting worse, she waved off on a walking tour in the Cloud Forest and instead drove them around Orchard Road—Singapore's version of Rodeo Drive.

They ended their brief tour at a hawker food center— a kind of mini mall for Singapore street food.

"Our national pastime is eating," Lian explained, standing in front of one of dozens of stalls. "Food is one of our many national treasures, and hawker food is the most famous of all."

Lian indulged in a bowl of spicy fish-head curry. Paul's appetite wasn't whetted by the black eyes and sharp teeth of the fish head swimming in red sauce, so he opted for a plate of chicken and rice at a different vendor, and Jack went a few stalls down to find a skewer of glistening chicken satay—spicier and sweeter than he'd had in his favorite Thai restaurant back in Alexandria.

They slurped and chewed as they sat together on a plastic picnic table, surrounded by the high-pitched babble of animated Singlish and a dozen Asian and European dialects in the food center crowded with tourists. Jack failed to notice a Bulgarian and a German standing far back in the milling crowd, their attention focused on Paul Brown.

"So you got everything put back in order at your place?" Lian had avoided the subject until now.

"Yes, but we're still waiting to hear from that lieutenant about the identity of the anonymous caller," Jack said. "I'm sure he knows how to trace a call."

"I hope you're not waiting for an apology. Our police force takes drug offenses quite seriously. They felt they were doing their duty."

"Even though they were wrong?"

"Being wrong sometimes comes with the job, doesn't it?" She took another bite of curry. "Now that you've had time to think about it, who do you suppose made the call?"

Jack shook his head. "It's either someone's idea of a joke or it was somebody who wanted to get rid of us."

"I promise you it wasn't someone from Dalfan."

"How can you be so sure?"

Lian blinked, processing. "I suppose I can't be absolutely sure, can I?"

"I don't want to risk offending you, but I have to ask: There's no chance it was your brother who did this?"

Lian nearly spat out her curry. "Yong? No way! Not his style."

Jack's phone vibrated in his pocket. "Excuse me." He pulled it out and answered as he began to step away from the table. "Gavin—thanks for calling. What did you find out?"

Paul pretended he didn't hear Jack say Gavin's name as he moved away, but Paul's round face flushed with concern. *Why is Jack talking to Gavin?*

Those photos you sent of the security guards—or whatever they are—came up a big fat zero," Gavin said.

"Nothing?"

"Nada. I broke into a few official databases where you are and I didn't get any hits. OSINT didn't yield anything, either. I'd say their identities were scrubbed."

"Clandestine service?"

"That's as good a guess as any."

"But who? Why?"

"I've given you all I've got. Sorry."

"Keep digging, will you? And while you're at it, I need another favor."

"Sure."

"Can you hack the Singapore Police Force cloud server?"

Gavin sniffed. "Okay, now you're just being insulting. What do you need me to find?"

"I'll let you know."

# 41

As promised, Lian delivered Paul and Jack back at Dalfan by three o'clock, just in time for their appointment on the fourth floor with the head of the department, Dr. Melvin Heng.

Unlike the other two research floors, this one was nearly as quiet as a library, with no sounds other than the click of keyboards and soft whispers between computer stations. Several of the young coders wore thickly padded noise-reduction headphones, heads bobbing to unknown rhythms as they attacked their keyboards.

Dr. Heng led them to his own small office. "Coffee? Tea? Anything to drink?"

"We just ate, thank you," Jack said, as he and Paul took their seats.

Heng took the seat at his desk, brushing his long, graying hair behind his ear. "I apologize that my floor isn't as interesting or fun as the other two research departments. It's almost like a funeral parlor in here, but the silence is more conducive to our efforts. How may I serve you?"

"As you know, we're here conducting a very informal audit in order to sign off on a final document that will complete the merger contract between your company and Marin Aerospace."

Heng smiled. "We're very excited about the merger, especially the senior management."

"Senior management stands to profit handsomely," Paul said.

"The beauty of capitalism."

Paul pushed on. "Is that why you left your research post with the Centre for Quantum Technologies at the National University?"

"Technically, I retired from the CQT in order to start the department here."

"Your research specialty was quantum cryptography."

"Precisely. That's the reason why Dr. Fairchild hired me. Is there a problem?"

"Not at all. We're just trying to get the big picture. Along those lines, we've been sample-auditing various departments and we found a few files that we believe are linked to your department," Paul said. "Specifically, we found a file marked 'QC,' which I originally assumed was the abbreviation for 'quality control,' but your department is developing quantum cryptography, correct?"

"Exactly. We're primarily focused on the software side of QC. Quantum algorithms in particular."

Jack leaned forward. "What exactly is quantum cryptography?"

"That's a very good question, and it requires a very

long and complicated answer—unfortunately, it's mostly technical jargon. Let me see if I can put it in some perspective." Heng leaned back in his chair. "I'm sure you're both aware that cyberwarfare is the new battlespace that the great powers are racing into. Financial markets, transactional commerce, energy infrastructures, military forces—virtually every aspect of modern societies is controlled, maintained, or directed by networks of computers that communicate with one another and, increasingly, with other computer networks globally.

"If a hostile nation or terror group wants to destroy a modern industrial economy like the United States or its military forces, the most vulnerable points of attack are the computer networks, and this is why so many resources are being deployed into cyberwarfare."

"Where does Dalfan play in all of this?" Jack asked.

"I'm coming to that, if you'll indulge me for just another moment." Heng gathered his thoughts. "Cyberwarfare is the latest offensive technology being deployed by the great powers and, to a lesser extent, smaller state actors like Iran, and even non-state actors like criminal gangs and terror groups. But history teaches us that every new offensive technology gives rise to a defensive countermeasure, and quantum cryptography is the defensive countermeasure against cyberwarfare. The country that first masters it will have a strategic advantage over those actors who haven't, and the quantum-cryptography arms race is raging in full force. I'm proud to say that Dalfan is on the cutting edge of that race."

"I'm sorry, Dr. Heng, but I'm still somewhat unclear as to what quantum cryptography exactly is," Jack said.

Heng smiled, embarrassed. "I apologize. I'm not used to speaking with non-industry people anymore, only physicists and software engineers. Are you familiar with the basics of quantum mechanics?"

"The Heisenberg uncertainty principle, Schrödinger's cat, and all of that?"

"Precisely. Until recently, the best defense we could come up with against cyberattacks was complicated mathematical algorithms—essentially, passcodes. But mathematicians and coders came up with even more aggressive attacks, including the use of Shor's quantum algorithm to solve these highly complex mathematical passcodes. So now we're turning away from mathematical defenses to the world of physics—using quantum mechanical means such as entanglement to establish and maintain secure communications networks."

"Entanglement?" Jack asked.

"Yes, as it turns out, we've known since the 1930s that certain pairs of particles seem to 'know' each other." Heng pointed the ends of his two index fingers at each other, manipulating them to illustrate his point. "They are entangled in such a way that when one of them is measured for, say, spin in one direction, the other particle will register spin in exactly the opposite direction at the exact same moment."

"How is that even possible?"

"I can show you the equations that prove it. I can even show you experiments that demonstrate how you can change the state of one entangled particle in the future and it will change the state of a particle in the past, even after the first one has been destroyed."

Paul shook his head. "I'm sorry, but that doesn't even sound real."

Heng shrugged. "I know. That's why Einstein called it 'spooky' science. But believe me, quantum entanglement is real. In fact, it's so real that the Chinese just launched the very first quantum satellite into space last year. It's testing not only quantum entanglement but quantum teleportation for use in secure communications."

Jack rolled his eyes. "Teleportation? You're kidding, right?"

"Not like in *Star Trek*, where you're beaming bodies up and down in transporters. Quantum teleportation is a fancy way of saying instantaneous communication. In other words, if two particles are entangled across a great distance, you can 'talk' to one particle on one end and you 'hear' on the other end at exactly the same moment. There's nothing flying through the air to intercept, no software to hack. Best of all, there's no time lost."

"So if you had a quantum radio transmitter on Jupiter you could speak to a quantum receiver on Earth with no lag time," Jack said.

"Exactly, though that kind of device is many years away. But quantum entanglement is what will finally allow for an unhackable quantum Internet."

Jack threw up his hands. "Okay, mind blown. What's Dalfan's role in all of this?"

"The Chinese are trying to build their quantum network, but there are still some big holes in it. In fact, all of the quantum networks have problems on two levels. We're attacking some of those problems."

"Be gentle with me, Doc, but explain to me in the simplest possible terms what problems you're attacking."

"On the first level, we're developing new quantum algorithms. The truth of the matter is we don't have the software we need to run the hardware. It's all completely new stuff. Google's new D-Wave quantum computer is thirty-six hundred times faster than the fastest supercomputer—a hundred million times faster, literally, than your laptop. But those superfast quantum computers and the quantum encryption we need to protect them with all run on quantum algorithms—something everyone is still trying to figure out, including us." Heng smiled. "But we're doing okay."

"And the second level?"

"Right now, quantum networks depend on expensive equipment linked by fiber-optic cables. We're many years away from a practical, ubiquitous quantum Internet."

Heng opened a desk drawer and pulled out a smartphone.

"What the Chinese and the other quantum powers need is an ability to link their quantum satellites up there," Heng said, pointing at the ceiling, "with quantum-encrypted cell phones down here." Heng tapped the cell phone in his hand. "Only when that happens will you have a practical, working quantum network, because cell phones are now the primary device in use on the planet for communication and for Internet access."

Jack pointed at Heng's smartphone. "And you think eventually we'll have quantum cell phones?"

Heng laughed. "No question about it. It's a matter of when, not if." He tapped his phone. "We're developing the software that will enable that to happen, too, and that's when the QC revolution really begins."

"Are you selling any of this software to the Chinese?"

"No, of course not. Not only would that be completely illegal, it would be completely self-defeating. The Chinese will be our biggest competitors in this field. If we want to dominate the global market, we need to keep this technology to ourselves." Heng leaned forward. "Why would you even ask me that?"

"We found evidence that Dalfan is selling cheap burner cell phones to the PRC at a helluva profit."

Heng shrugged. "Don't look at me. My department doesn't sell anything, especially cell phones. We're pure research. As far as I can tell, we're a net drain on Dalfan's balance sheet."

"But you're the tip of the spear in these technologies," Jack said.

"And that's why Marin Aerospace wants to buy Dalfan," Paul said.

Heng smiled. "Exactly."

"The Chinese must be very interested in what you're doing here," Jack said.

"Everybody is. At least, anybody who knows anything about QC."

"And you're completely confident in your operational security?"

"One hundred percent. As you probably know, humans are always the weak link in any technological system, including security. But I will vouch for any member of my team."

Jack and Paul stood. So did Heng. "Thank you for

your time, Dr. Heng, and for the information. You're doing amazing work here."

"I'm happy to show you around, but there really isn't much to see. And if you have any more questions, don't hesitate to stop by."

They all shook hands, and Paul and Jack left for their offices on the first floor.

Inside the elevator, Jack pulled out his smartphone, clicked on his White Noise app, and selected "Crowded Room." Confident that their voices were now masked from anyone who might be eavesdropping, he asked Paul, "What did you make of all that?"

"The man or the technology?"

"Both."

Paul shook his head. "Fascinating technology. I can't even pretend to comprehend it. Quantum algorithms are a little beyond me."

"And Dr. Heng?"

"He seems like he's a straight arrow. But then again, if he is a Chinese spy, he wouldn't be worth much if he acted like one, would he?"

"I still think there's a problem with that warehouse and those burner phones."

"You don't think they're smuggling QC software on those phones, do you?"

"They wouldn't need to. They could do that with a USB drive." Jack locked eyes with Paul.

Paul's heart raced. What was Jack implying? "That's right. What was I thinking?"

"If anything, the burner phones are just a way to make illegal payments to whoever is stealing the QC software.

The Chinese are the buyers. I need to get back into that warehouse to see if I can find out who the seller is."

"The warehouse that Lian says she didn't know existed?" Paul asked. "How do you plan on getting in this time?"

Jack shrugged. "I'll try and find a hall pass somewhere."

"I wouldn't do anything illegal if I were you. You're not even sure there really is a problem. It could all just be a coincidence."

"That's why I need to get my hands on one of those phones."

The elevator dinged and they got off.

Paul told Jack, "I need to catch up on some work in my office."

"Me, too. Let's break at five and head home."

**42**

**B**ack in his office, Paul logged on to his computer, the conversation about quantum cryptography still swirling in his mind. Lucky for him, Dalfan computers weren't quantum encrypted yet, but getting past the conventional encryption on the Dalfan drive was still going to be a challenge.

His handler, Bai, was situated at his desk, occasionally casting an eye on Paul but mostly paying attention to his own computer screen and grabbing refills of hot tea. Paul was a man of routine and he appreciated the routines of others, including Bai's, and a few days of observation told Paul that after his third cup of tea, Bai would be heading to the restroom—which he did.

As soon as Bai cleared the bathroom door, Paul casually inserted into his laptop the Dalfan USB he was allowed to use while on the premises. Paul knew that Gavin's program would grab the encryption code on the Dalfan drive. Then all he'd have to do was load the Dalfan encryption passcode onto Rhodes's drive and he'd be in business.

Gavin's instructions said it would take several minutes to effect the capture but that his program would do the work automatically in the background. Paul wasn't quite as worried about getting caught on this leg because he was authorized to have and use a Dalfan USB drive. He was just waiting for the dialogue box to appear that read CAPTURE COMPLETE before he could breathe a sigh of relief.

Four minutes and counting.

After hearing Dr. Heng's discussion of an unhackable network, Paul was now glad he was part of the CIA's effort to ensure that China wasn't stealing this technology from Dalfan or finding a back door into America's defense establishment. It made him feel that his mission was even more important than he had realized.

He just hoped he was up to the task.

The CAPTURE COMPLETE dialogue box appeared. Paul clicked it away just as Bai came through the door. He'd have to wait to try and load the encryption code onto the CIA drive until later. Not a problem. He still had more than twenty-four hours to meet the deadline.

Easy as pie.

Jack and Paul drove the short distance back to their guesthouse in silence, the Dalfan security team that Jack had ditched earlier clearly in tow.

"Something wrong?" Jack finally asked as he turned onto their street.

"No. Why?"

"You're awfully quiet. I figured something was bothering you."

"Just thinking, that's all."

Something was bothering him, but Paul didn't want to share. When he was finishing up his work at Dalfan, he suddenly realized he had messed up his calendar.

Because they had flown halfway around the globe, they were technically on a different day in Singapore at the moment than they would've been back home. But home was really his reference point, and that meant today was his wedding anniversary.

The icy grip around his heart was tightening fast.

"Anything you want for dinner?"

Paul hardly heard him. "What? Oh, no. Not really."

"I might just fix a sandwich, then. You can eat when you're hungry."

"Works for me."

Jack parked the car as the electric gate swung closed behind them, and they headed for the house. The Dalfan security team parked at the curb, determined not to let Jack shake them loose again.

Jack wound up boiling water and making himself a bowl of ramen noodles—a flashback to his college days. As terrible for his body as they were—nothing but processed carbs and powdered chicken broth loaded with who knows what chemical compounds—the flavor was comfortingly familiar, and he could use the carb boost for what he had planned tonight.

While Jack was pouring himself a glass of cold unsweetened tea from the fridge, Paul fetched a bottle of Bushmills from the pantry. He tossed the first glass down and poured a second.

Jack wanted to say something but held off. Paul's soft eyes had turned to dark wounds in the last few minutes, and he shuffled around the kitchen as if Jack weren't even there—or maybe it was Paul who was somewhere else. Jack needed to talk to him at some point about the drinking. Paul could definitely hold his liquor, but in the last few days he'd increased his intake considerably. It couldn't be from stress—what the hell was there for him to be stressed about? So he must be battling an addiction, Jack reasoned, or a demon—a battle he was clearly losing at the moment. He'd talk to him tomorrow. Tonight he had other plans.

Jack rinsed his dishes and put them in the dishwasher, then scrambled upstairs. He changed into a pair of black jeans and a dark blue T-shirt, a pair of boots with thick laces, a dark raincoat, and a black-and-purple Baltimore Ravens ball cap. He checked his watch. It was 7:18 p.m. According to Google, sunset tonight would be at 7:21 p.m., and a glance outside his window told him much the same thing. It also confirmed his two Dalfan handlers were in their Range Rover, parked against the curb.

Time to get going.

Jack headed back downstairs and into the kitchen, where he found Paul at the stove, scrambling eggs. That was a good sign.

"Smells good," Jack said.

"Want some?"

"Already ate, but thanks." Jack put his hand on the back door, the busted doorjamb recently repaired.

"Where you headed?"

"Back to the warehouse. I need to see what's inside."

"I thought they wouldn't let you in."

Jack smiled. "I made the mistake of asking for permission the first time."

"Be careful—and don't get caught."

"I will, on both counts. First thing I need to do is ditch our friends out front."

Paul spooned his scrambled eggs onto a plate. "And call me if there's a problem."

"Okay, Mom."

Paul glowered at Jack. Something violent stirred behind those pale gray eyes. It caught Jack off guard, but he ignored it.

Too much to do.

# 43

Jack dashed for the garage, careful not to make too much noise. Gerry had told him this was a strictly white-side mission and that he wouldn't need any tools of the trade for his black-side work, but tonight he felt the need to take a few things along. He found a toolbox and quietly rifled through it, pulling out a couple pieces and pocketing them.

He suddenly got the feeling he was being watched, and he checked the corners of the garage for remote cameras but didn't see any. The Dalfan security team was making him jumpy. He shrugged it off.

Jack stepped outside, closing the door behind him as quietly as possible, just in case the crew out front had their window down and might hear the noise in the backyard and get curious.

He scaled the painted concrete wall facing the property in the rear. He crossed through the neighbor's yard onto Goodman Street, which ran perpendicular to

Crescent Road, where the Dalfan team was parked and, he hoped, still oblivious of his movement.

Jack headed west along Goodman, past a series of beautifully maintained homes, a blend of traditional, modern, and ultramodern middle-class dwellings, all fronting a tree-lined school of some sort. He could've been in a suburb of Los Angeles or Dallas—only the occasional Buddha statue, Singapore national flag, or cars driving on the other side of the road would have told him otherwise.

He walked swiftly but was careful not to run or draw attention to himself, and he kept his face down and away from any prying cameras, but not so down that he appeared suspicious in the prosperous suburban neighborhood. He didn't want to look like he was casing the joint or running from the cops, and he assumed the Singaporeans organized vigilant neighborhood-watch programs like they did back in the States.

When he arrived at the corner of Goodman and Broadrick, he pulled out his phone and tapped the Uber icon he'd registered under an alias and linked to an untraceable Campus credit card.

Fifteen minutes later a Lexus sedan picked him up, and they shot across town west on the PIE and exited south on Pioneer Road North toward the address that Jack had uploaded into his Uber app—not his actual destination. In fact, he was dropped off several hundred feet away from the warehouse he had intended to infiltrate, taking advantage of Singapore's lush tropical topography.

Crowding both sides of all the streets in this part of

town were steel buildings and concrete prefab structures housing every form of industrial and commercial enterprise, and many of them serviced Singapore's extensive shipping and oil-refining industries.

Jack had scouted out a shipyard adjacent to the Dalfan warehouse after he had left there. It was fronted by a stand of tall trees that rustled in the moderate breeze that was blowing down here by the water. All he had to do was jump the waist-high fence when traffic cleared and he'd be able to work his way around back.

Jack paused, suddenly aware of his surroundings. *Why am I doing this?* He was supposed to be conducting a white-side audit, not running a black-side op. Technically, he was about to break the law and, if caught, get himself and Hendley Associates in big trouble, and no doubt blow the merger.

But he couldn't help himself. His gut told him that there was something more going on behind the scenes, especially after the meeting with Dr. Heng and the whole quantum-cryptography conversation. This might be a real national security threat. That alone was worth taking the risk.

Had Gerry actually suspected something was wrong at Dalfan? Gerry knew Jack's tendency to break the mission profile. Maybe that's the real reason why he sent him to Singapore in the first place.

At least, Jack wanted to think so. But probably not. If he was being honest with himself, he'd admit he resented the white-side assignment. He was a black-side operator now. What did Gerry expect him to do? Just put all that away and sharpen his pencils?

Jack sighed, watching the traffic stream by, weighing his options. He should call Clark right now and read him in on the situation and get his advice before doing something stupid. That would be the safe play.

But what would his options be? He couldn't go to the authorities with just a hunch. And he couldn't confront the Fairchilds armed only with an accusation. If they were innocent, they'd be pissed, and the merger would get called off. If guilty, they wouldn't admit it and, worse, would cover their tracks before he could collect any evidence they were selling secrets to the Chinese.

So that's why he was here, right now, getting ready to jump the fence. If he could get in and out of the warehouse without getting caught, he would have proof that something was going on between Dalfan and the Chinese—or not. Either way, the truth would be known.

It was worth the risk. And technically, the break-in would be a problem only if he got caught.

"So don't get caught," he whispered.

As soon as the traffic cleared, Jack jumped the waist-high fence. Once over, he kept as close to the corrugated steel wall as he could, noting that the cameras fixed on the high walls were pointed toward the street and harbor. He made his way past the large commercial boats dry-docked on giant trailers waiting for repairs or refurbishment, careful to avoid the sight lines of the cameras behind him.

He stopped frequently, crouching low in the shadows of the ships he was hiding behind. He marked the slow, methodical rounds of the two security guards he'd counted so far, walking the wide expanse of the shipyard, talking and smoking as they patrolled. When he'd driven by the shipyard earlier, Jack saw only one security guard at the front gate, but the man was more focused on the boxed lunch in front of him than on any passing American. Jack bet that security would be even more lax at night, especially with the yard shut down, and so far that bet was paying off. Once the two guards passed to the far side of the yard, Jack bolted in a low crouch toward the cyclone fence bordering the Dalfan property and dropped down behind a rusted orange forklift parked against it.

Unlike the shipyard, the rear of the Dalfan property was well lit and open. The rear of the warehouse featured four large rolling doors, all of which were shut for the night. Where he was kneeling, he didn't hear any activity inside the building or out on the asphalt.

Jack pulled out a pair of wire cutters. These were meant to snip electrical cords or household nails, not steel fencing. Jack thought about climbing the fencing, tossing his coat over the razor-wire barrier on top so he could scale the hazard, but the fence was eight feet high and the razor wire another eighteen inches taller. He could stand on top of the forklift and toss the coat up from there and probably land it properly, but he was certain security on the Dalfan side would be tighter, and he didn't want to be straddling razor wire nearly ten feet in the air if Dalfan security guards came charging at him with their guns drawn.

Instead, he opted for patience and took his time, clamping down hard with the wire cutter and rotating it back and forth, forcing the sharp teeth to bite deeper into the steel mesh than they were designed to do. He had to switch hands frequently as they tired from the strenuous effort, the handles digging deep into his palms. He paused each time the cutter snipped through a wire link, shaking the fence, making sure the noise wasn't raising any alarms on either side. Thirty minutes later Jack had managed to cut a hole big enough for him to scoot through. He just wasn't sure what to do next. There wasn't anyplace to hide on the other side. His only choice was to make a run straight for the building and hope there weren't any guard dogs or security men hiding in the shadows. He saw evidence of neither. He wished he had a pair of NVGs to scope out the area, but why would he, since this was an easy, no-risk, white-side mission?

He asked himself again, *What the hell am I doing*? If he got caught, there'd be hell to pay. And there was still the distinct possibility that the warehouse wasn't even a Dalfan property.

But his gut.

His gut.

Jack double-checked behind him to make sure the shipyard guards were still out of sight, then crawled through the fence and dashed across the empty yard, racing for the nearest wall of the warehouse, careful to keep his face down and away from the cameras he'd spotted on the corners of the roof.

His pulse raced and his breath shortened as he sprinted the two hundred yards, expecting to hear gunshots or snarling dogs at every step. But he hit the corner of the building without raising any alarms.

So far, so good.

Jack caught his breath and glanced around again. Thanks to the bright sodium lights, he could see across the compound behind him, and all along the loading dock in front of him. Nothing.

Strange.

Whatever work they were actually doing in the building was clearly not being done at night. That was a lucky break for him.

Jack leaped up onto the loading dock and ran past the first rolling door, testing it with an upward tug of his hand, but it didn't budge. He dashed to the next two doors and tried them as well; both were locked down tight. The fourth door was bolted shut as well, but on the other side of it was a regular-access steel door at the top of the stairs leading down from the dock to the asphalt. He glanced around again to make sure he wasn't in the line of sight of any cameras, then tried the door-knob, hoping against hope it would open.

It didn't.

*Shit.*

Jack knelt down by the round steel knob and examined the simple key lock, then scanned the yard once again to make sure no one was watching him. He reached into his front pants pocket and pulled out two large heavy metal paper clips he'd borrowed from his office-supply drawer at Dalfan earlier in the day.

Dom had taught him last year how to pick just about any kind of lock with a set of Sparrows Vorax lock picks—some of the best picks in the business. The only problem on this trip was that carrying a set of thief's tools in his luggage would have drawn the attention of the TSA or Singapore customs authorities. Besides, he'd had no idea he'd be breaking into a building.

Fortunately, Dom had also taught him how to improvise with a pair of paper clips. The last time they did the paper-clip trick they turned it into a drinking game, the loser taking the vodka shot to further impede the manual dexterity needed to pick even a simple lock. Somehow after losing the first two rounds, Jack managed to finally beat Dom at the game. Maybe the booze loosened him up. If so, he really needed some now.

Jack pulled out a pair of needle-nosed pliers and used them to fashion a right-angled tension rod with the first paper clip, which took only a few twists, then spent the next two minutes forming a W rake pick with the other paper clip. The W rake took longer because it meant bending the straightened end of the clip into semiprecise angles like the letter *W*, as well as reshaping the other looped end into a sturdy handle.

Jack took the tension rod in his left hand and inserted it into the bottom of the door lock without applying any torque, then slid the W rake all the way to the back of the lock. Now using his sense of touch in his fingertips and listening carefully, he quickly dragged the W rake back toward him with upward pressure, trying to push the lock pins into their set position while maintaining a light torque on the cylinder.

The first time he raked the lock he thought he heard two driver pins set into place, so he kept torquing the cylinder with the tension rod so the pins wouldn't fall back out. He did this a few more times, his mind and his senses intensely focused on the task at hand. He thought he felt another pin set, and he hoped like hell it was a standard five-pin door lock.

Jack was laser-focused on finding the next driver pin to set when the rolling steel door next to him rattled. For a split second he thought someone was opening it, but then he felt the gust of wind against his face and he knew the door wouldn't be opening. That split second was just enough to distract him, and he dropped the tension on the cylinder just a fraction, and that was enough to cause all of the driver pins he'd already set to fall right back into place.

*Damn it!*

He repeated the process, more determined than ever to pick the lock and see what was inside, if for no other reason than so he could brag to Dom that he'd done it and make him buy a couple of rounds when he got back to town.

It took Jack a good three minutes to knock out four pins, jiggling and popping the W rake, careful to keep the tension just right on the cylinder with the tension rod.

Voices whispered in the dark. Jack froze again, but he was careful not to release the tension this time. He took a deep breath and glanced over at the sound in the distance. He could barely make out the two shadowy figures walking the yard on the other side of the fence—the two guards he'd dodged earlier, just making their rounds and making small talk. Jack seriously doubted they'd look this way, but if they did, they were more likely to call the police than intervene. But who knows? Best to get back to it and get out of the light.

Knowing he had only one pin left, he used the W rake

like a traditional pick, trying to imagine the first sharp
bend of the rake as a single point, and used his mind and
touch to will that single point to find the final driver pin.
He felt it click into place, and Jack was through.

*Thank God.*

Jack stepped inside and nearly shit his pants.

**44**

**E**mpty.

The whole damn warehouse was empty.

Jack started to pull off his ball cap to scratch his head, but he caught himself. No point in winding up on a camera now.

He was frustrated as all crap. Did he have the wrong address?

No. Not possible.

Whoever had cleaned the place out had kindly left all the lights on. And why shouldn't they? There was nothing to see.

And they obviously wanted him to see that.

Jack knelt down and studied the narrow rubber tire tracks that had been left behind by a forklift turning sharp angles and obviously carrying a heavy load. They could've been made ten months ago or ten hours ago.

About the time Lian was keeping him occupied on the tour earlier today.

Jack tried to imagine stacks of pallets or crates of something he wasn't supposed to know existed. But what?

He walked around the wide, empty floor, looking for clues. An oil stain, a piece of crumpled packing tape, a cigarette butt.

Nothing.

Whatever was in here yesterday, guarded by a platoon of burly goons without any official identification, was gone now.

Moved in a hurry.

*Why?*

*Where?*

Standing here with his metaphorical dick in his hands wasn't answering any of those questions. But he thought he might know a way to get them.

He pulled out his phone and tapped his Uber app again. If his hunch was right, time was not his friend.

Time to play the Gavin card.


S orry, Jack, I tried," Gavin said, a rare note of humility in his voice.

Jack couldn't believe his ears. "I thought you said it would be a piece of cake."

"I know. I was wrong. The Singapore Police Force cloud server is better protected than I thought it would be. I can keep hammering on my end or even call in a few favors. But we're talking several hours, maybe days."

"There isn't any time."

"I feel crappy about this."

Jack wanted to curse. He was frustrated, but it wasn't

Gavin's fault. He shouldn't expect the man to pull his bacon out of the fire every time he hit a wall.

His Uber driver pulled up to the curb. "No worries, Gav. Gotta run. I'll find another way."

Jack climbed into the Toyota Camry knowing that a long night was ahead of him. He had one other option, and he needed Paul's help to pull it off. He just hoped the pudgy accountant was up to it.

Jack snuck in the back kitchen door the same way he had left, careful to avoid the Dalfan security car out front and eager to enlist Paul in tonight's clandestine effort. He heard a noise in the living room and headed there.

Paul sat on the couch in the living room, a half-empty bottle of Bushmills on the coffee table in front of him. His eyes were red rimmed and rheumy. He forced a smile. "Hello, Jack."

Jack prayed it was the first bottle. *Paul won't be any help tonight*. He crossed over and sat down next to him, patting his fat knee. "What's wrong?"

"Have a drink with me?"

"What's going on? Seriously. You can tell me."

Paul sighed. "I really miss her."

"Your wife."

"Carmen was the best."

"You're not so bad yourself."

"You don't know me, Jack." Paul stiffened. "Or anything about me."

"You're a great accountant. You have impeccable taste in ballpoint pens. What else do I need to know?"

Paul poured himself another drink, spilling some on the coffee table. He then filled an empty glass next to it. "Have a drink with me."

"I was actually heading back out—"

"Have a drink with me. Please."

"Okay." Jack picked up the glass. "What's the occasion?"

"Today's my anniversary. Carmen and I would've been married thirty-two years today." He lifted his glass.

"That's amazing." Jack touched his glass to Paul's. "To Carmen, and to you."

Paul's lower lip began to quiver, like a child's. "I miss her, Jack."

"C'mon, buddy, drink up. You've got a lot to celebrate."

"Like what?"

"Like fantastic memories of a woman you clearly adored, and who adored you, too. Not everybody gets that in this life." Jack smiled warmly. "My mom and dad have that. I envy them—and I envy you and Carmen." Jack tossed back his drink.

Paul brightened. "Yeah, you're right. I am lucky." He tossed his drink back, too.

Jack stood. "I'd stay and hang out with you, but I've got some running around to do."

"Want me to come along?"

*Yeah, if you weren't already hammered and if it would keep you from drinking yourself into a coma,* Jack thought. "Not this time. But thanks."

Paul grinned wide. Waved a fat finger at him. "Oh, I get it. It's that woman, isn't it? Lian? Oh, boy. She's a beauty. Good for you." Paul poured himself another drink. "We should toast to that."

"Another one of those and I'll *be* toast. Rain check?"

"Sure! I understand. Not everybody can hold their liquor good as me." Paul burped.

"Can I get you something to eat before I go?" Anything to get him sobered up, Jack thought.

"Nah, I'm fine. But thanks."

"Okay. Call me if you need me."

"Don't do nothing I wouldn't do," Paul said, snickering. But then he darkened. "But you treat her right, you hear me? Or you'll answer to me."

Jack nodded gravely. "Of course."

Jack turned on his heel and headed for his bedroom to take care of some business before paying another visit to the garage. Jogging up the stairs, he swore to himself, frustrated that the night was going to be even longer than he'd expected.

**45**

Jack Uber'd over to Dalfan headquarters but had the driver drop him off a few blocks away. He knew from the vice president of operations, Feng, that Dalfan shut down in the evenings, maintaining only a skeleton crew of security in the building. But it wasn't unusual for a few of the hardworking employees at Dalfan to stay late or even overnight if they had hard deadlines to meet.

Jack had asked Feng for a tour of the entire facility as part of his auditing duties, but he'd also been taught by John Clark to always scout the terrain wherever he found himself, even if it's just a movie theater or restaurant. He could still hear Clark's voice drilling the questions into his skull. "Where are the exits? Where is the quickest egress? What are the sight lines? What are the most defensible positions? Where's the men's room?"

"Why the men's room?"

"In case you have to take a leak."

Feng's tour had been quite revealing. For the most

part, Dalfan relied on electronic security for the building, with alarm systems, sensors, and cameras doing most of the heavy lifting. Dalfan's most valuable commodity was their IP—intellectual property—and that was stored on the Dalfan mainframe and workstations, and those were passcode protected. There really was very little crime in Singapore, so they felt comfortable with a single guard at the front station in the lobby monitoring the remote cameras, which Jack had also taken note of.

With his security pass and other Dalfan credentials, it wouldn't be a problem at all for Jack to just walk in the front door and present himself to the guard at the security desk with a story about needing to finish up some paperwork. He had no doubt whatsoever that the guard would let him in. He had even less doubt that the guard would log him into his system and quite possibly discover that Yong or Lian had red-flagged him, requiring the guard to notify one or both of them if Jack suddenly appeared in the building after hours. That wasn't going to work. For the work ahead of him tonight, Jack preferred to remain anonymous, if at all possible, at least until he got the job done.

He suddenly had a better idea.

Back at the guesthouse, Paul tipped the bottle, teasing out the last ounce of whiskey into his glass. He ran his finger around the mouth of the bottle, catching the last glistening drops on his fingertip, then ran it over his teeth, sucking away the very last of it as he set the bottle down with a thud.

He prided himself on his ability to hold his liquor, a gift from his Irish-German cop father, long dead, killed in the line of duty. The man could shoot a pistol—Paul displayed his father's marksmanship trophies in a case back home—but his real gift, the old-timers told him, was his dad's ability to drink any man in the precinct under the table and still be able to walk home in a straight line directly into a tongue-lashing from Paul's teetotaling mother.

Paul knew he was drunk, but the key to mastering the condition was to be cognizant of it, and Paul was fully aware that he was not in his right mind. But it was only in his inebriated self-aware state that he was finally able to put some distance between his heart and the light-absorbing black hole of inconsolable pain spinning inside his chest. For the first time that evening, Paul didn't feel like crying. The booze allowed him to escape the gravitational pull of grief that never let him go while sober. Sober, at least, he could work, blinding his mind from the sense of loss with an intense focus on whatever task was at hand. But when his mind was idle for more than a few moments, he was invariably sucked back into the abyss. It wasn't right, and it wasn't even normal, but it was the way things were. Carmen was his soul mate, and his soul was torn in two.

Now that he was drunk, the iron bonds of grief were slipped, which allowed for a certain clarity of thought, or at least perspective. He had the overwhelming sense that Carmen was watching him at that very moment, and he was certain she was unhappy with him. Not just unhappy, but ashamed.

"You have important work to do. Have you forgotten? Why are you just sitting there, feeling sorry for yourself?"

He nodded, agreeing with her. She was right. Carmen was always right.

"I'm sorry, Carmen."

"Prove it."

Paul shut his eyes, willing her voice away. He picked up his glass and lifted it to his lips, but he couldn't drink it. Not now, at least.

He stood and wobbled toward the kitchen table, where he had laid his laptop shoulder bag. He struggled with the zipper but finally managed to get it open, and a minute later the machine was powered up. He blinked furiously, trying to remember what he was supposed to do next. Through the fog it finally came to him.

He zigzagged his way to the staircase and climbed up with some effort to his bathroom. He tugged on the spring-loaded shower curtain rod, but he pulled too hard and the whole thing came crashing down. Didn't matter. He'd fix it later.

Paul pulled the cap off the far end, trying to fetch Rhodes's drive, but his fat fingers couldn't feel the tissue paper. He looked inside the rod. Nothing.

Someone had stolen the USB drive.

His heart raced as panic flooded over him, dumping enough adrenaline into his bloodstream to sober him up a little. He suddenly remembered something.

He dropped the curtain rod and marched over to his closet and picked up the shoe that he'd stuffed with the sock, and in it found the USB.

Snatching up the drive, Paul practically ran back downstairs and loaded it into the drive port on his laptop. He heard himself breathing heavily through his nose as a throbbing headache crept into his skull.

"This is too important to fool around with," Paul told himself, repeating what he had heard Carmen tell him.

"Coffee," Paul told himself. He took a minute to try to clear the cobwebs, then figured out where the coffee, filters, and coffeepot were located. Ten minutes later he sat back down in front of his computer, a giant steaming cup of Sumatran coffee in hand, creamed and sugared like a cheesecake. He slurped it down as fast as he could, then opened up his laptop again and got his bearings.

He found the file containing the captured Dalfan encryption code where Gavin's program had placed it. He opened it and scanned the lines of software. He blinked hard. It might as well have been Sanskrit. Paul could write basic software and create macros for his Excel spreadsheets easily enough, but encryption algorithms made his head spin. He closed the file back down.

After missing the slot a few times, Paul finally inserted the CIA drive into the drive port on his laptop. When the drive icon appeared on his desktop, he dragged the Dalfan encryption code onto it. A minute later, the file was copied to the CIA drive.

Paul sighed through his nose. His plan was actually working.

He felt the warmth of Carmen's approval flooding over him. He picked up the cup of coffee but didn't see the point in drinking it now. His work was done for the evening. Time to finish up the last of the whiskey still waiting for him in the living room. He had reason to celebrate.

He stood and headed back to the living room. The heavy rain thundering outside jogged his memory.

Where the hell was Jack?

# 46

Jack thought his "better idea" was pretty solid until the sky opened up and torrential rain poured down in sheets. He was already twenty feet up in the air and still climbing the exterior drainpipe at the back of the Dalfan headquarters building.

His feet slipped against the rough concrete wall a couple times, but his hands were locked tight on the pipe—John Clark taught him a long time ago that grip strength was the key to overall power and stamina, and it was paying off in spades tonight.

The slashing, sidelong rain whipped his face, but his Baltimore Ravens cap stayed fixed to his skull. He was halfway to the rooftop. Climbing down at this point would be just as hazardous as continuing the climb up, and it wouldn't get him to his goal anyway. His arms were tired, but the prospect of plummeting to his death on the asphalt below strengthened his resolve, and he took advantage of the steel brackets supporting the pipe for extra foot grips. As he finished looping an arm around the top of the roofline, the rain suddenly stopped—*of course!*—and he hauled the rest of his rain-drenched body over the edge and headed for the roof access door.

Jack had taken a flathead screwdriver he'd borrowed from the garage and was working against the latch bolt in the door when the rain came crashing down again. When Feng had shown him the roof his first day on the job, Jack noticed that the strike plate was hardly worn, suggesting that the plate was set too deep in the door frame. That meant the deadlocking plunger probably didn't engage when the door was shut.

Sure enough, it took only a couple twists with the flat blade of the screwdriver to push back the latch bolt and open the door. Jack had also noticed that the door hadn't been secured with an electronic alarm or even a magnetic sensor. There weren't any cameras on the roof, either. Feng's sand-filled coffee can was flooded over with water, the butts washed out onto the roof, all around Jack's feet.

Jack slipped inside and took a second to pull off his cap and coat and shake them out, trying to dry off as much as possible. Once he was inside he would get picked up on security cameras; if the guard on duty bothered to check the cameras and if they actually saw him dripping wet, he might guess Jack's entry into the building was less than conventional.

Jack sped down the steel stairwell but did his best to keep as quiet as possible. No point in alerting any-body by thundering down the steel steps. He reached the third-floor access door and paused for a moment, listening to see if anybody was nearby. He didn't hear anything, so he waved his security card past the reader and the door clicked open. He wondered how he'd explain his actions when Dalfan checked their security logs tomorrow, but that was another problem for another day.

The first thing he did was dash into the men's room, where cameras were thankfully not present, and he used fistfuls of paper towels to finish drying off before heading back out to the main floor. Nobody was around. He had the place all to himself.

Jack made his way past the second glass security wall with another wave of his security card, then headed straight for the workstation that controlled the Steady Stare surveillance drone system. He logged on with his passcode and accessed the window for the live feed and found exactly what he expected—nothing. In weather like this, the drone would be grounded. But it wasn't a live feed he was looking for.

Jack pulled up another window, which allowed him to access the stored video data for the last twenty-four hours. "Time for a little time travel," he whispered.

I t took Jack just a few clicks to find the video data files he was looking for. His concern was what he would find on them.

Overall, the weather had been pretty good today, but there were occasional gusting winds and downpours. In other words, typical Singapore weather for this time of year. If Steady Stare was going to be a viable option for the Singapore Police Force, its drone aircraft needed to be able to fly in less-than-ideal conditions.

A few more clicks and Jack found what he'd been hoping for. The Steady Stare video program was completely intuitive, but the training Dr. Singh had given him made it even easier. The Steady Stare aircraft had luckily been flying most of the day. The first screen he opened was a bird's-eye view of the entire city. He typed in the warehouse address, and the video image zoomed in to the western side of the city and with a few more clicks enlarged the warehouse and its grounds.

Jack suddenly realized that if the Steady Stare aircraft had been flying tonight it would've caught him on its cameras, too. Fortunately, that didn't happen. It was time to focus on the task at hand.

When Jack approached the warehouse yesterday it was heavily guarded. Tonight, the guards were gone and the contents had been removed. That had obviously occurred within thirty-six hours, give or take. Judging by the way Lian had insisted on taking them on the tour and taking them out to eat, it was now clear to him that she was keeping them occupied while the warehouse was being emptied.

He tapped on a few more keys and then hovered an arrow over the time scrubber, designating the calendar day, hours, minutes, and even seconds. It didn't take Jack long to find a semitruck pulling into the loading dock area. Jack decided he liked time travel.

A lot.

Because the truck was backed up to the loading dock

and the dock itself was covered, Jack couldn't make out what was being loaded into the semi. That was unfortunate, but not fatal. He pushed the scrubber forward in time until the truck pulled away. Jack then zoomed out several hundred feet, put a tracking reticle on the vehicle, then let the program run at 10x speed. He watched the truck traverse several streets and pull into another warehouse facility less than four miles away. Jack snapped a photo of the address with his phone.

Once again, it wasn't possible to see what was being unloaded from the truck. He pulled up the data on the warehouse ownership, though he suspected it was a shell company that would shield the identity of the real owner. He wanted to grab some faces for the facial-recognition software, but the two people walking around the truck both wore long-billed caps and had the OPSEC smarts to not look up. Even if he had grabbed a few faces and could get them to Gavin, Jack suspected they would've come up empty again if this was the same bunch who had secured the first warehouse facility.

All of that was bad luck. The good news was that whoever was moving this stuff around didn't simply load it onto a ship and send it on its way. But this warehouse, like the first, was butted up against the bay, and Jack suspected that a ship was en route to pick up the secretive cargo. How soon, he couldn't know. But sooner rather than later, no doubt, and whatever the shipment was, it was hot enough that the owners felt they had to move it just on the suspicion that Jack Ryan might dig further.

They didn't know how right they were.

Jack tracked the semi's journey out of that facility and back over to a rental yard across town. He snapped a photo of the image of the truck and the name and address of the rental yard with his phone, but he knew that neither would likely lead to anything of consequence. His target wasn't the truck; it was the new warehouse and whatever the hell had just been loaded into it.

Jack shut the Steady Stare program down, thinking about what his next move would be. He couldn't contact anyone by cell phone inside the building, including Gavin. He could call him on a Dalfan landline, but that call would be automatically logged and possibly recorded, and he didn't want to draw that much attention to himself, Gavin, or even Hendley Associates at this point, especially since he was now engaged in an illegal activity—several, technically.

Right now he didn't need Gavin, anyway. What he needed was a way to get over to that second warehouse. He couldn't use his cell-phone app to connect with another Uber ride—and if he used the landlines to call for a cab, well, who knows what that might trigger? He guessed that Lian's security team was probably still staking out his guesthouse, so using the company car Lian had loaned them wouldn't work unless he engaged in some fancy driving and shook them off his tail—but at night with little traffic and in the rain, with Lian's mandate to her team to never lose him again, he suspected that he wouldn't be able to pull it off short of a *Fast and*

*Furious* movie-trailer car chase. And even if he did, he'd only piss Lian off even more and sour his already strained relationship with her. His job overall was to smooth the merger transaction between two companies, not cause irreparable damage to that relationship. His suspicions about the contents of that warehouse were just that—suspicions. He didn't want to embarrass Gerry Hendley or Hendley Associates by going off on a snipe hunt that might not result in anything except screwing the pooch and ruining the merger.

Still . . . his instincts told him that checking out the warehouse was worth at least some risk. Stepping over to the window confirmed that the weather was still miserable, so walking or running the twenty-five miles or so to get there was out of the question. He needed a set of wheels. Fortunately, Feng had shown him where the keys were kept for the company delivery vans parked in the back. Technically, he would only be borrowing one of them, not stealing it.

Or at least that's what he'd tell the police after they arrested him.

**Y**ong sat at his desk, nude.

The storm blasted against the heavy plate glass of his twenty-fourth-story luxury condo, but his eyes were fixed on the same video images of the semitruck and warehouse that Jack was watching simultaneously.

"Ice?" Meili was nude, too, but in the kitchen, fixing drinks. She held a cube of ice aloft in a pair of silver tongs.

"No."

She muttered a curse to herself as she tossed the ice cube into the stainless-steel sink, then poured a couple ounces of Casa Noble Anejo, a fine sipping tequila, into two tulip-shaped Glencairn whiskey glasses and carried them into the living room.

"That's why you got out of bed? I was hoping you were looking for more porn, or maybe QVC."

"The alarm triggered." Yong lifted the glass to his lips and sipped, keeping his eyes on the screen. Unknown to Jack or Paul, wireless trackers were embedded in their

Dalfan security cards, keyed to an alert system on Yong's computers.

"I'm surprised you heard it. You were quite busy at the time."

"I'm a great multitasker." Yong threw back the rest of his tequila.

"More?"

"Of course." His eyes fixed on the heart-shaped mole over her lip, stirring a memory. Blood rushed to his manhood.

"What's Ryan up to?" She finished her glass.

Yong snorted; the blood retreated. "He's a nosy bastard. I've never known an auditor to be so pushy."

Meili stroked the back of Yong's neck as she watched the screen over his shoulder. "He's becoming quite a problem."

"He'll head to the warehouse tonight."

"In this weather? No way." Meili dragged her nails gently across his back.

"He's persistent."

"What do you intend to do about it?"

"Scare him off."

Meili stopped rubbing him. "We need to kill him."

Yong gazed at her. "Too risky. Besides, he won't find what he's looking for."

"No, he won't, but he'll just keep looking. You said yourself he's persistent. We need to get rid of him."

"We can't kill him. It will bring the cops in—or worse, the Americans."

"It won't be a problem if it looks like an accident. He's not supposed to be sneaking around in that warehouse,

right? A large crate could fall on him, or maybe he inter-
rupts a burglary in progress."

"It can't be traced back to me—or Lian."

"It won't."

"Let's do it my way first." Yong picked up his phone.

"There isn't much time." Meili picked up her phone.
"You call your men, I'll call the warehouse. If your plan
fails, mine won't. But one way or another, Jack Ryan will
be dealt with tonight."

The rain hammered on the metal roof of the garage as
Jack climbed into the white Nissan NV200 compact
cargo van plastered with a Dalfan-logo vehicle wrap. The
automatic garage door opened, and sheets of heavy silver
raindrops poured in front of the van's bright halogen
headlights. The storm was definitely getting worse.

The van smelled showroom-new. The odometer read
three hundred and forty-two kilometers. He logged in
his destination on Google Maps even though his cell signal was still jammed in this location, but he knew it
would pull up once he left the property.

He approached the automated gate and it swung
open. No guard was in the shack, but he was certain the
security cameras were logging license plates. With the
brim of his hat pulled over his eyes and his head tilted
down, he was confident that his face wouldn't be seen by
the cameras, allowing him the slimmest possibility of de-
nial if it came to that.

Jack pulled out onto Changi North Crescent and
headed for the PIE. It wasn't the fastest route, but he'd

done it enough times to feel comfortable taking it even if for some reason Google Maps or the onboard-vehicle GPS couldn't pull up his route.

He passed a silver Toyota minivan parked at the curb, facing in the opposite direction. He saw the driver's face when a bolt of lightning flashed across the Toyota's windshield as the big wipers cleared away the rain. Dark, scowling eyes beneath a thick unibrow tracked him as he passed. A Turk? Maybe. Hardly worth noting, except the Turk tracking him sat next to a blond man in his mid-thirties who was shouting into a cell phone.

His eyes also caught the bright black-and-white license plate bolted to the front. Easy to read, at least part of it. SAM 00 was all he caught. It reminded him of a dead friend, Sam Driscoll. It stuck in his brain.

But the mini movie scene in the front seat of the Toyota was over in a flash—literally—and Jack didn't think any more about it as he turned left onto Upper Changi Road North.

The AYE was mostly clear of traffic at this hour, but especially so in this weather. There were a few semi-trailers whizzing along, their big tires spraying plumes of water off the asphalt, but few cars. Jack couldn't make out the make or model of the vehicle several hundred yards behind him, but the halogen headlights had tracked with him for twenty kilometers now. Hard to believe it was a Dalfan surveillance team. Lian made it clear to her team he was never to shake them again. If that was a Dalfan vehicle following him, they'd make themselves known to him and keep close. More likely it was just a commuter coming home late from work in a storm.

Jack's high-profile van rocked violently as a sudden burst of gusting wind buffeted his vehicle. He wasn't interested in slowing down. A few kilometers farther, his spine tingled when the tires hydroplaned; he could almost feel the Nissan lifting off the pavement and skimming along on a thin sheet of water. A moment later he regained control easily enough and backed off his speed just a bit, only to have a big rig roar past him, spraying his windshield with even more water than the storm was throwing at him.

But Jack noticed that when he slowed down, so did the car behind him. *Isn't that what a tail would do?* he asked himself. Jack chuckled. *But so would a cautious commuter if he saw the idiot in front of him nearly lose control.*

Jack turned on the radio and hit the scan button. Most of the stations were in English. When he heard a melodious British voice announce "BBC World Service," he locked in the number.

"News from Asia," the female voice began. "More trouble in the South China Sea. Vietnam filed a formal protest earlier today with the United Nations after an incident involving the collision of a Chinese minesweeper and a Vietnamese fishing trawler near the disputed Spratly Islands. In an exclusive BBC Radio interview, the Vietnamese foreign minister complained of several recent encroachments by Chinese naval vessels in territorial waters claimed by Hanoi."

Jack heard more news: a meeting of ASEAN defense ministers, declining agricultural exports from Thailand,

and a new fifty-two-week high for both the Shanghai and Hong Kong stock indexes. But it was the weather forecast that had caught Jack's attention.

"The Australian Bureau of Meteorology in Perth is upgrading a tropical low in the Java Sea approximately one hundred and seventy-seven kilometers southeast of Singapore to a category-one tropical storm with gusting winds exceeding ninety kilometers per hour. Locally, expect strong gusting winds and heavy rainfall to continue for the next forty-eight hours with possible flood warnings for low-lying areas in Singapore, eastern Malaysia, Borneo, and Sumatra."

"That can't be good," he said out loud, grateful it wasn't hitting Singapore. He wondered how bad the storm would get. One hundred and sixty kilometers worked out to be about a hundred miles. Pretty far away. But fifty-five-mile-per-hour winds out there still meant a big-ass storm.

As if on cue, the car behind him flashed its turn signal and dove onto an exit ramp. Jack was practically alone on the road now. Fifteen minutes later he exited, turning onto Pioneer Road in the industrial district, heading for Tanjong Kling Road.

Jack followed the track on his Google Maps app along the tree-lined boulevard, where warehouses and industrial buildings stood neatly crowded behind cyclone fences. He'd slowed down to a crawl on the nearly empty street. The Nissan's furious windshield wipers slapped vainly against the sheets of rain pouring down, giving

Jack just momentary glimpses of open road between swipes, like the van itself was blinking. He couldn't read any of the street numbers on the buildings.

The warehouse location he was searching for should be just up ahead and on the right. He rolled down his window, hoping to be able to read the numbers on the next building coming up. The cool rain splashed over his face and neck as he held one hand above his eyes to shield them from the heavy drops pelting him. He needed to stop. He glanced back into his side-view mirror just to be sure there wasn't anyone behind him as he tapped the brakes, and that's when he saw—

*Oh, shit!*

The grille of an unlit semi tractor slammed into the rear of his van. Jack heard the sickening crunch of sheet metal and glass behind him and the shotgun blast of the airbag in front of him. The seat belt cinched across his chest like a hangman's noose as the polyester fist of the exploding airbag slammed his face, snapping his head against the headrest and crushing his body back into his seat.

And then things got interesting.

His ass lifted slightly into the air as it followed his strapped body when the entire van careened forward several feet at an oblique angle. His face punched the half-deflated airbag again when the vehicle smashed to a stop as it plowed into something immovable up front. What, he couldn't tell, because he was blinded by the airbag.

It all happened in about a second and a half, maybe less. It seemed like forever.

Dazed from the double blow to his head, he instinctively clawed at the deflating airbag to tear it away from his face, clearing his view just enough to see that his van was smashed against one of the majestic trees looming over the street. He turned in time to see the hulking, boxy shape of a big-rig tractor racing away. Its headlights were still off but, thankfully, not the light illuminating the license plate. His mind managed to capture the letters and numbers.

Just before he blacked out.

**48**

He woke to the sound of rain drumming on the roof, his eyes still tightly shut.

For a moment, Jack thought he was in a tin-roofed bungalow on a beach in Aruba, where he had once spent a week with a blonde who had laughing green eyes. He couldn't remember her name. Maybe he'd never known it.

But the splitting headache throbbing inside of his skull killed the dream and opened his eyes. The spattering raindrops sparkled in the lamplight against the spiderweb of the cracked windshield.

He woke fully now, and cursed, remembering what happened.

*What the hell time is it?* He glanced at his watch. He'd been out for about ten minutes, maybe more. As his mind cleared, the pain intensified. Mostly his headache, but also his face and neck, and his chest, still strapped tightly against the seat. He twisted around as best he could, expecting to see an ambulance or a police car, or at least a concerned civilian racing to his aid. He hurt like hell, on the verge of serious. He had no idea if he'd sustained internal injuries. But his momentary lapse of self-pity melted away. He couldn't be found here. Technically, he'd stolen the van. More important, he needed to stay out of the newspapers, and certainly the police blotters.

His first task was just to get out of the van. He was trapped by the belt, strapped so tightly he couldn't move his arms to hit the belt release. He pushed his legs against the floor panel as hard as he could, pressing his body deeper into the seat to give the locking mechanism the opportunity to release and slacken the belt. When it did, he reached over and freed himself from the seat belt, then pushed away the deflated airbag, dusty and crumpled on his lap.

Jack reached for the door latch and pushed, but nothing happened. He twisted around and unlocked the door, then tried again, launching against it with his sore shoulder. Nothing. It was jammed.

Of course.

Jack glanced through the smashed windshield. Still no cars in sight. Good. But it wouldn't be much longer until somebody came by and called it in. He grunted as he crawled out of his seat and over to the passenger side, finally managing to open the door and work his way out onto the street. He quickly hobbled over to the sidewalk and out of the light of the streetlamp. He surveyed the damage on himself first. No blood, no broken bones. He checked the van. The big truck had struck the van in the rear quarter panel on the passenger side. It was perfectly aimed to damage the van but allow the tractor to keep going. A hit-and-run accident? Or intentional?

Running with its lights off. Jack assumed it was intentional.

And that made it personal.

*Bastards.*

His throbbing head suddenly turned dizzy. He laid a hand on the van to catch himself as his legs began to buckle, but he willed himself to remain standing. A moment later his vision returned. *Must have stood up too quickly,* he told himself. *Or I'm in shock.*

And shock would kill him. So would a brain bleed or a dozen other injuries he might have sustained.

Jack grabbed his phone and started to dial the emergency operator but stopped. If he went to the hospital now he'd be there for hours, and whatever was in that warehouse would be gone by the time he got back. The other problem was that Rhodes said to keep a low profile. If he called this in, there would be hospital records to deal with and, worse, hard questions, probably from the police.

More important, he had a job to do.

He knew he was pushing his luck, but he needed to get inside that warehouse. He'd figure out his injury status later. As far as he could tell, he had all of his fingers and toes, and he could still make a fist.

One of the van's two rear doors was actually smashed open. Jack shoved it open further and checked the back. The cargo area was trashed, though still intact. Boxes of electrical components, spindles of colored wire, and thick paper-bound catalogs and technical manuals were heaped in a pile, having all been thrown from the metal shelving. He spotted a medical kit bolted to the wall and opened it, and found a box of Tylenol packets. He tore one open and tossed the pills into his mouth, chewing them into a bitter paste, his face souring as he swallowed. That would take the edge off, at least.

He crawled around in the pile further, searching for something else—exactly what, he wasn't sure.

Until he found them.

One was a toolbox. He rooted around in it. Mostly electrical stuff—needle-nose pliers, wire strippers, small screwdrivers. The heaviest tool he could find was a crescent wrench. Not exactly a weapon of choice, but it was a good hunk of cast steel. No telling who or what he might encounter. He pocketed it.

The other thing he grabbed was heavy but pliable. Probably a dumb idea, but his pounding headache wasn't going to let him solve any quadratic equations tonight. He decided to trust his instincts.

He extricated himself from the pile of electrical supplies and exited the van with a grunt. When he stood up, he saw the street number on the building in front of him. That meant the warehouse was two blocks farther up.

He arranged the items he'd pulled from the van on his person, then checked the street in both directions. He saw a pair of headlights a mile behind him, heading in his direction. Cop car? No flashing lights. But who knows? And if not this one, maybe the next.

If he was going to get in that warehouse, it was now or never.

He dashed across the street in a kind of a run-limp,

every muscle in his body screaming, his brain bobbling against his skull with every thudding step.

Jack smiled. It suddenly occurred to him that this easy, white-side vacation Gerry had sent him on just might wind up killing him.

Yong and Meili were dressed now and staring at the computer screen, watching Jack's red tracking dot advance toward the warehouse.

"I told you he was persistent," Yong said.

Meili was on her cell phone.

"He's on the way."

## 49

## FALLS CHURCH, VIRGINIA

Rhodes paced the floor of his fourth-floor office, ignoring the magnificent view.

Like his two defense-industry rivals Northrop Grumman and General Dynamics, Marin Aerospace was located in Fairfax County, Virginia. It wasn't a convenient location for manufacturing, and it didn't offer any particular economic or comparative advantages except for one: The small Virginia county in the northernmost reaches of the state sat just across the border from Washington, D.C.

As with every other major corporation in the United States, the most important business decisions Marin Aerospace made occurred in the halls of Congress. Access to legislators was more valuable than raw materials, cash, or credit. Legislative access—crony capitalism—was how Marin Aerospace acquired most of its government contracts, blunted potentially harmful regulations, tempered investigations into cost overruns, and otherwise kept the cash cow flowing with taxpayer-subsidized milk. Rhodes didn't like the way the game was played—most of his C-suite friends didn't, either—but he didn't invent the rules; he mastered them.

But today was a different kind of headache.

The kind that could get him killed.

Or worse.

He could wind up broke.

Rhodes had a lot of personal money riding on this operation. So would Zvezdev. But he wasn't a fool. He'd crossed Zvezdev once before. "All in the past. Time to make money!" he'd promised. But the wily Bulgarian was still a Slav, and Slavs had long memories—and even longer knives. He didn't dare cross him again.

Rhodes stared at the cell phone on his desk, willing it to ring. What was the delay? He was certain that Paul Brown would've already installed the USB drive he'd given him. Did he just forget to call?

*Idiot.*

Against his better judgment, Rhodes snatched up the phone and hit the only speed-dial number programmed into it.


**P**aul slept with his head in a puddle of his own drool on the kitchen table until his cell phone rang. He rubbed his face and pulled his glasses back on. He stared uneasily at the digital readout. He nearly knocked the empty whiskey bottle off the table as he picked up the phone.

"Weston?"

"What the hell's the delay?"

Paul winced. An old wound from a long time ago. The churlish, condescending Weston Rhodes he'd known in Sofia was suddenly on the other end of the line. He fumbled for his words, trying to gather his wits.

"Uh, the 'tea is brewing,' but I haven't had time—"

"Oh, forget the tea! We're not doing that now. Just tell me why you haven't installed that damn drive yet."

"The drive?"

"Yes! The goddamn drive I gave you!"

"Oh, yeah. Sure. Uh, there's a problem with Dalfan security—"

"A security problem? I sent you, Paul, because you're a problem solver."

"And I think I've solved it."

"Good!"

"But I still need time. It should be done within the next twelve hours."

"You only have twenty-four. You do understand that, right? Midnight, local. Your time, Paul. Not mine."

Paul thought of Carmen. He wanted to cry again, but didn't. "Yes, Senator. I understand. I'm doing the best I can."

"You're cutting it awfully close."

"I won't fail you."

There was silence on the other end.

"Senator?"

"Paul, I apologize for losing my temper. You just have no idea about the pressure I'm under. You know how unreasonable those bureaucrats at Langley can be. They're breathing down my neck."

"I understand. And trust me, it will be taken care of today."

"Without fail?"

"Without fail."

"I knew I could count on you. And thanks again, Paul. You're doing a helluva service for your country."

"Thank you."

"Oh, and be sure to tell Jack hello for me." Rhodes clicked off.

Paul shut his phone. Weston Rhodes was still a horse's ass, but it was his country that needed him now. Paul put a beefy hand to his throbbing head.

*My country might have to wait a few more minutes.*

Paul used his arms to lift his unsteady frame from the chair, heading for bed. He limped up the stairs, leaning heavily on the handrail until he reached the landing. He shuffled past Jack's bedroom. The lights were off, the door ajar. He pushed it open a little more. The bed was still made.

Paul frowned. He wondered if Jack was with Lian, having sex. They seemed close. But that wasn't good, at least from an auditing perspective.

# 50

## SINGAPORE

Jack approached the front of the north-facing warehouse. Two glass doors were locked and secured. A red flashing light told him they were alarmed. No one appeared to be inside, but he wasn't prepared to try to defeat an electronic alarm system. He decided to check out the rest of the steel building. Like the other warehouse and storage facility, the property butted up against the bay for loading onto a vessel and no doubt had rear doors for access.

Jack double-checked to make sure he wasn't being watched and stayed out of the sight lines of any security cameras he saw, pulling the bill of his Ravens ball cap over his eyes to further hide his identity. He made his way along the west side of the building, stopping at a steel door. It was padlocked. There wasn't a window to look into. He pressed forward.

The full moon was covered by high storm clouds. He passed as quietly as he could along the rest of the seventy feet of steel wall, guided by the dim light of a sodium lamp high overhead. At least the wall gave him shelter from the windblown rain coming out of the east. When he reached the back, he squatted low with a grimace and looked around the corner. Rain pelted the bill of his cap.

A square of light beamed out of an open loading-dock door halfway down the platform. There weren't any trucks or vehicles in the bays or any movement in or out of the open doorway.

But over the din of the pouring rain he heard voices. Talking, laughing.

In Chinese.

He approached the open bay, staying close to the shut loading-dock doors and careful not to bump into them. He knew they'd rattle if he did. When he reached the corner of the open bay door, he peered around the corner.

Three men, Chinese, sat at a folding card table, talking in normal voices and playing a game with plastic tiles. *Dominoes, maybe,* Jack told himself. More likely mahjongg—hugely popular in Asia.

One of them, the oldest—with short-cropped silver hair and broad, sloping shoulders—puffed on a thick cigar wedged in his square jaw. The air was clouded with blue smoke.

The table was located in front of a line of pallets, each stacked six feet high with boxes of DVD players wrapped in thick cellophane. One of the pallets had been torn open, and several of the boxes were stacked on the floor. Each box was big enough to hold several DVD players. One of them had been opened, and a unit removed from its packaging and tossed on the floor. Next to them, an electric lift table extended halfway up.

*What's going on here?* Jack rubbed his face, frustrated. It didn't make any sense. Had he gotten the address wrong? Or was this just a goat rope?

*Damn it.*

He decided to head back home to regroup. He'd turned to leave when he heard a shout.

"Hey! Hey!"

Jack saw Cigar Man smiling and waving him over, his face shrouded in tendrils of smoke. The other two men turned around. They were younger—one was in his thirties, the other about Jack's age. They smiled, too.

Cigar Man shouted something to Jack in Chinese, then turned back to the card table, studying the tiles in front of him. Probably something along the lines of *Join us in the game.*

Jack felt the weight of the crescent wrench tucked at his waist. He was glad he hadn't pulled it out like a weapon. If he turned and ran, these guys might call the cops, mistaking him for a thief. Better to come on in and play dumb.

Jack stepped out of the storm and into the warehouse, shaking off the rain from his jacket onto the concrete floor as one of the men shouted, *"Mah-jongg!"* Jack glanced up. The thirty-something guy punched his fists in the air in victory as the older man laughed and the younger one cursed.

Jack approached the table and saw the familiar tiles. He'd had a Taiwanese girlfriend in college who'd taught him the game—along with a few other things. The Cigar

Man blew another plume of smoke as he and the others swiftly turned the tiles facedown. Fond memories of midnight mah-jongg games in the dorm flooded his mind. He wasn't very good at it, but it was a lot of fun, especially when he was drinking PBRs. He'd played the game a hundred times if he played it once.

The three men laid their hands on the overturned tiles and mixed them up together, a communal act of security. The thirty-something shot Jack a quick glance and a faint smile. He wondered if he was the ace in the group.

Group?

*Mah-jongg takes four players—*

Jack spun right on his heel and ducked, sensing more than seeing the bat swing past his left ear. He didn't move fast enough. The heavy lumber smashed a glancing blow just below his shoulder, bouncing off his upper arm and crashing into the flimsy card table, scattering tiles in every direction. Cigar Man had already leaped to his feet and receded, while the two others pulled knives and jumped aside.

Jack pulled the wrench out of his belt as he spun on his heel, ignoring the bruising bat blow, and whipped the steel around in the long reach of his arm like he was throwing a Frisbee. The wrench broke the smaller man's neck just as he was lifting the bat for another strike. Jack stepped past the falling corpse and the bat clattering on the floor as he spun through the momentum of his swing.

Against the three other men he had almost no chance of winning, even though he had already dispatched their friend. His only chance was speed—and sheer audacity. In the time it took to spin and strike the bat man, the twenty-something was charging with a long blade, lunging forward like a fencer, driving the point of the knife straight into Jack's gut.

I t happened so fast Jack didn't have time for déjà vu—he just had time to lift the wrench above his head and smash it down on the man's confused face, caving in his skull right between the eyes. Blood gushed hot on Jack's hand as the sharp end of the extended wrench jaw sank into the bone.

Behind him, Jack heard heavy steps charging toward him. Without looking, he thrust his elbow back as hard as he could, aiming it shoulder high. His aim was perfect. The hardest bone in Jack's body cracked into the soft cartilage of the lunging man's nose. The Chinese man screamed as his body flung backward, feet high and flopping, like a man running full speed into a clothesline. His skull hit the concrete with a sickening thud.

Jack turned to face Cigar Man, smiling and puffing, his broad back against a pallet. He wrapped his thick fingers around the cigar stub, took one last puff, and flung it aside. In the same instant he reached behind his shirt and pulled out a razor-clawed karambit.

*Of course.*

Jack shuddered at the sight of it. Amador had shown him all too clearly what that blade was capable of in the hands of a man who knew how to use it. Cigar's confidence with the weapon was obvious.

Jack spun into his fighting stance, desperately trying to remember what Amador had taught him— *Stupid!* He told himself. *If it isn't in your muscle memory now, don't even try.* John Clark had taught him that in real close-quarters combat, there's no time for thinking—only instinct, drilled into him by hours and hours of practice. Jack had that in spades. He glanced at the karambit again, trying to shut his brain off.

*At least he has only one knife,* he thought.

Until Cigar Man pulled out another.

Fuck. Me.

He heard Amador's voice in his head. *When faced by a man who knows how to use two knives—RUN LIKE HELL!*

But Jack couldn't run.

He still had a job to do.

Cigar Man grinned, sensing an easy kill, even if the American was five inches taller. The man slid forward on his feet, gliding like a dancer.

Jack backed up, feeling the ground with his boots, hoping not to trip over one of the three bodies he'd put on the floor—

Too late.

Jack began to tumble backward on the corpse of the first man, and Cigar saw his chance, lowering his blades and charging.

But Jack saw his chance, too, as he regained his balance. He raised the wrench behind his ear and threw it as hard as he could. The heavy chunk of steel crashed into Cigar's chest. He *oomph*ed a blast of smoky air, stunned, dropping his knives. Before the blades hit the ground, Jack was on him, wrapping his arms around the man's throat. He didn't want to kill this one—he needed answers. But the old fighter wasn't finished. He blasted his two forearms up and between Jack's, breaking his grip. Then Cigar Man smashed his forehead forward, catching Jack on the chin.

The head butt felt like a gunshot against Jack's jaw, and white stars exploded in his eyes. In the hyper slo-mo of his adrenaline rush, Jack heard his wrench clatter on the concrete and even smelled the cigar stink on the man's breath.

Cigar Man's head butt missed its mark. Jack was staggered yet still in the fight.

The man lunged at him now, hands extended, reaching for Jack's throat. But Jack seized Cigar Man's wrists and dropped, pulling the man's hands against his chest and rolling onto his own back, shoving his boots into the man's crotch and thrusting his legs straight up, catapulting the man up and over until Jack let go. The weight of both their bodies and the centrifugal force launched the smaller man through the air, smashing him against the sharp steel corner of the electric lift table, snapping his spine.

Jack leaped to his feet. The first thing he did was check his body armor—the three-hundred-page Dalfan product catalog he had secured with duct tape inside his waistband. The blade that struck his gut had penetrated a good half inch. He thought about pulling out the paper armor but changed his mind.

The night wasn't over yet.

Jack checked Cigar Man's pulse, but his lifeless eyes were confirmation enough. Jack cursed. How could he find out who these jerkwads were?

He rifled through the pockets of all four men quickly,

keeping his head on a swivel and his ears sharp to make sure he wouldn't get ambushed again. The search yielded nothing, not even pocket litter. More proof they were pros.

Jack's only recourse was to snap photos of each of them with his iPhone, then grab fingerprints, using a military-grade phone app that Gavin had installed on every Campus smartphone. "Just in case," he'd said at the time.

Jack scanned the area again. Still safe. He knew pros wouldn't leave behind what he was looking for, but he needed to take an extra few minutes to check out what he could. He felt the pressure of the clock. No way these guys were working alone; their buddies could be just outside the door. Worse, the cops might show up. How would he explain four dead bodies?

Jack wasn't a sociopath, but he didn't feel bad about killing men who tried to kill him without provocation. That might not matter to the Singapore justice system, and he had little interest in finding out.

Jack picked the bloody crescent wrench up off the floor and wiped it on the shirt of the youngest killer, then pocketed it. No point in leaving evidence behind. He thought about trying to hide the bodies or even burning the place down to cover his tracks. He glanced up at the rafters and saw only two cameras pointing in his direction, both disabled. Yeah, they were pros, all right, and not any more interested in leaving evidence behind than he was.

"Thanks for the assist, assholes."

No point in adding arson and evidence tampering to any future charges. He told himself that, more than likely, whoever sent these guys were more interested in recovering their bodies than he was. Four dead men would lead to a lot of questions, some of which would lead back to their handlers.

Jack quickly inspected a couple DVD player boxes on the open pallet but didn't find anything other than DVD players. He could take the time to break into the front offices or make a more thorough inspection, but his gut told him he'd come up empty. It was safer and probably more useful to just get the hell out and back home, and send the photos and fingerprints to Gavin.

He checked the exit one last time to make sure he wasn't being followed, then crossed over to the east side of the building, opposite the way he came in, and put his crashed van a few hundred yards behind him as fast as he could with his run-limp before he activated his Uber app.

**51**

Jack spotted a nearly full dumpster on a construction site and hobbled over to it. He climbed up onto it and found what he was looking for—a rag and an empty cardboard box. He used the rag to wipe the blood off his hand and tossed the rag into the box, folded up the lid, and stuffed the box under a piece of gypsum board. Jack went to the other side of the dumpster and shoved the wrench into a length of PVC pipe, then stuck a piece of insulation in after it and buried it under some trash, along with the Dalfan catalog. In a perfect world he would have destroyed the evidence that could put him in jail for life—or worse—but he was out of time and his options were few.

He abandoned the dumpster and crossed the street, checking his Uber app. The blue dot rumbling toward him was scheduled to arrive in three minutes. He double-checked himself to make sure there wasn't any more blood on him or any other hint that he'd left four dead bodies in a warehouse just down the street. Bad enough that he looked like a half-drowned homeless man. No point in adding a serial-killer accent to the ensemble.

The bodily inventory reminded him that he'd been damn lucky tonight. Except for the sore arm where the bat had grazed him, he was relatively unscathed. Those hundreds of hours of backbreaking, muscle-cramping combat training drilled into him by Clark and Ding had kicked in as soon as he shut out the fear and the noise and let the fight happen. In fact, it was the combat training that allowed him to shut it all out.

Like Clark always said, the game is won on the practice field, before the game even starts.

The fight itself was savage and quick, like most fights are—not like in the movies, where the hero takes a dozen haymaker punches to the face and just keeps going. In real life, Rocky would've been in a coma after his big fight and never made it to the sequel, let alone another bout.

But there was still luck involved. All of his training and preparation couldn't overcome the million things that can go wrong in something as unstructured as close-quarters combat. A wild punch, a slippery patch of oil, a bat swung a second earlier. Anything and everything could have gone wrong. In real fights it usually did. But tonight it all went his way. Next time he might not be as lucky.

And sure as hell, there would be a next time. This was the life he chose. Duty, honor, country.

Come what may.

The Kia's windshield wipers couldn't keep up with the downpour. Daniel Lim, the Uber driver—a long-haired college junior studying logistics, he told Jack, with glasses as thick as the windshield—cursed the water-blurred red lights in the windshield. A traffic jam from hell.

"Stupid drivers! Just a little rain!" He pounded the horn.

The blaring horn shot through Jack like an electric shock. The Tylenol he'd chewed had taken some of the edge off his headache, but not all of it. He needed the kid to calm down.

"I heard on the radio last night a cyclone had formed in the Java Sea. Is that what's causing this?"

"Cyclone one, very low level. No worries for us! *Lah,*" Daniel said. "Just a big storm. Lots of rain."

"And the rain is causing all the traffic?"

"Maybe. More like nervous. If the storm gets too big, big problems. Lots of flooding." He pushed his glasses back up on his nose and hit the horn again, cursing.

Jack knew the Uber driver was paid only based on the destination, not time spent in the car like a regular taxi. It's one of the reasons the gig service was so popular.

"Look, Daniel. I know it's taking us a long time to get to my place. I'll pay you double for your trouble. So don't worry about anything, okay?"

The driver whipped around, a big smile on his thick lips. "Okay! Thanks! It helps a lot." He looked at Jack again. "You sure you okay?"

Jack could only imagine what he looked like, soaked to the bone, unshaven, and roughed up. He pointed at the windshield. "Better keep your eyes on the road."

"Yeah, you're right."

They crawled along for a few more minutes. Jack used the time to send Gavin an encrypted text message, along with photos and fingerprints of the men he'd just killed.

Up ahead, Jack saw police emergency lights flashing on the side of the road. The right lane was closed. Bright red flares burned. Between wiper blade swipes, Jack made out two cars crunched together. Traffic tried to merge left, including Daniel.

"Stupid drivers make a big wreck! *Lah*."

"Any chance that cyclone will reach Singapore?" Jack asked.

"Here? No way. A cyclone can't reach here. We're on the equator. There isn't a Coriolis effect. That's what makes the winds spin like a funnel. Typhoons and cyclones can't form below five degrees north or south latitude. Singapore is one-point-three-five latitude north. No problem."

"That's good to know."

Daniel rolled down his window and flapped an arm and cursed at a Lexus that wouldn't let him in. His face and his arm got soaking wet. The Lexus finally let him in. He merged over. He wiped his face with one hand.

"You know a lot about weather," Jack said, still trying to be friendly—and calm the kid down. But he did seem to know a lot for an Uber driver.

"I have a minor in meteorology. Fascinating subject."

"That's cool."

"Cool, sure. But no jobs in weather. That's why I study logistics."

The traffic stopped again. A Singapore policewoman blocked their lane while she waved a tow truck up. Daniel turned around, frowning.

"Vamei. I forgot about Vamei."

"What's 'Vamei'?"

"In 2001, Typhoon Vamei formed at one-point-four degrees latitude north. Came crashing into Singapore. Very bad."

"I thought you said cyclones couldn't form below five degrees north."

"They can't. But Vamei did! *Lah*."

Jack frowned.

"No worries! Java Sea is south, not north. No typhoons. You'll see. Just a little rain!"

"You're the meteorologist." It suddenly struck Jack that he hadn't stayed in touch with Paul. He was probably worried. He hit Paul's contact number.

"Hullo?"

"Paul, it's me, Jack. Sorry if I woke you."

"No problem. What time is it?"

"Late."

"Where are you?"

"On the way home. Don't wait up."

"Everything okay?"

Jack thought about telling him everything, but what would be the purpose? He'd just killed four men and, for all that blood, didn't find anything. And nearly getting killed in a stolen vehicle? All telling Paul everything would do is blow his cover with him—a clear and useless violation of his status with The Campus. So he lied.

"Yeah, everything's okay. We'll talk later." Jack hung up.

**B**y the time they slowed to a stop on the street behind Jack's guesthouse, the traffic had disappeared and the rain had let up quite a bit.

"See? No cyclone!" Daniel said, as Jack tapped on his Uber app, adding a tip that doubled Daniel's fare.

"Maybe you should be a meteorologist after all."

"No way. No jobs." Daniel checked the tip. "Hey, thanks for that. It helps a lot. School ain't cheap."

"My pleasure. Thanks for the ride."

"You need another ride, you send for me, okay?"

"A ride or a weather report, I'll be calling you."

Daniel beamed. "Okay!"

Jack hobbled toward the neighbor's backyard fence as Daniel sped away, his tires hissing on the wet asphalt.

**J**ack heard Paul before he saw him. His bedroom door was cracked open. Paul was snoring again. Jack shuffled down the hall just to make sure. Paul was on top of his bed, arms splayed wide, mouth agape, a rivulet of drool sliding down his cheek.

Jack shook his head, smiling, and headed for his

bedroom. He was wet, sore, and filthy. Time for a hot shower.

Except he was too damned tired.

He barely managed to strip off his wet clothes before crawling into bed. He passed out as soon as his throbbing head hit the pillow.

**52**

**P**aul didn't feel good.

In fact, he felt like hell. His head throbbed and his stomach was queasy. He'd been in bed when Jack called before. Now the alarm was screaming at him.

Feeling this bad, Paul thought he'd caught pneumonia. But he quickly realized it was the Bushmills that had put his head in a vise and his stomach on a merry-go-round.

He closed his eyes. The whirlies began again. He got dizzy in just a couple seconds and his knotted stomach turned from queasy to pre-projectile. He forced his eyes open and pushed himself up into a sitting position.

Better.

But still not good.

Tea. That would be good.

Coffee. Black coffee.

Better.

He scratched his ample gut and stood on his wobbly

legs, wiggled his feet into his slippers, and headed down-stairs for the kitchen.

He leaned heavily on the handrail as he made his way down the staircase, his mind a welter of confusion. Where had Jack been all night? At the warehouse? Or somewhere else? But this was just the latest thing. What about the other day when he came home from his night out with Lian Fairchild? He'd obviously been in some kind of a fight. Jack definitely carried himself like a guy who was used to that sort of thing, even if he never bragged about it.

Come to think of it, Jack looked like he'd been through it the day they met with Rhodes and got the assignment. He swore Jack had a black eye he was trying to cover up with makeup. Jack's excuse—that he'd been on vacation and fell on a hike—didn't smell right at the time, but Paul had shrugged it off.

Paul limped off the last stair riser and padded toward the kitchen. He'd never known a financial analyst to get into so much trouble or get injured so much in such a short amount of time. He was acting more like an opera-tor than an auditor.

Paul stopped in his tracks. A cold lump of ice spun in his gut, like the floor had suddenly fallen out from under his feet.

Was he being played?

Paul scratched his thinning, uncombed hair. Jack? An agent? If so, for whom?

He headed toward the cabinet with the coffee and filters.

If Jack was CIA, was he working for Rhodes? Rhodes

was working with Langley—technically, so was he, through Rhodes. So why wouldn't Rhodes have told him Jack was CIA?

He would have, unless Jack wasn't CIA. But then who was he working for? DIA? DOJ? FBI?

Paul scooped black Sumatran coffee into a filter and poured water into the coffeemaker.

No. Jack worked for Hendley Associates. He knew that for sure. He wasn't on the government payroll.

But then again, neither was he, and he was working for the CIA.

"Right?" Paul asked himself. "The CIA. That's what Rhodes said."

Unless Rhodes was lying.

And if Rhodes wasn't CIA, where did that leave him?

Paul shook his head to clear the confusion. Big mistake. He felt his brain rattle against his skull, exploding his headache.

Coffee, then shower, then think.

"In that order," he told himself, watching the steam rise from the wheezing coffeemaker.

"And then talk to Jack."

**P**aul was dressed and ready to go when Jack finally came downstairs, limping stiffly into the kitchen. Paul thought he saw a few more bruises on his face and hands.

"I've got hot coffee in a carafe," Paul said. "Or I can make tea."

"Just a cup of coffee. I need to hit the shower so we can get going."

Jack followed Paul into the kitchen. Paul poured him a cup of dark brewed coffee, black as motor oil but smooth as silk.

Jack looked pretty rough, Paul thought. Worse than he remembered. A swollen bruise had formed on the hand with the red knuckles. He looked like he'd spent the night bear wrestling.

"You okay?"

Jack shrugged. "Yeah, fine. Considering."

"Considering . . . what?"

Jack shook his head and rubbed his face. "Oh, crap. I forgot to tell you. I was in a hit-and-run accident last night."

*Forgot to tell me? That's a load of bull.* Paul swallowed his anger. "Where? When?"

"Across town. Checking out the warehouse we talked about—actually, a different one."

"You need to see a doctor."

"Nah. Just a couple of bruises. The airbag hit me hard after the truck rear-ended me, and I got knocked around pretty good. I guess I blacked out for a little bit."

Paul frowned with worry. "You really should get to a doctor."

"Not here." Jack took a sip of coffee. "Maybe when I get back."

"Is that why you have a black eye?"

"What?" Jack turned around and searched the counter. He found the shiny silver toaster and picked it up, examining his face with it like a mirror. It was a small black eye, in nearly the exact same place as the one he got when he slammed his head against the steel ladder in the North Sea. Was it the same bruise? Or a new one? Or did he make the old one worse again? He had no idea.

"Yeah, I guess so."

"Any idea who hit you?"

"No."

"Did you get a license-plate number?"

Jack lied. "No."

"I guess the Audi's totaled. Too bad. That TT was a sweet ride."

Jack shook his head. "I wasn't in the Audi."

"Oh?"

"I borrowed a van from Dalfan."

"Why?"

"Long story."

"We've got time."

"No, we don't. It's nearly ten o'clock. I need to grab a shower so we can get to work." Jack finished the rest of his coffee and dropped the cup in the stainless-steel sink.

Paul's eyes narrowed at the blow-off.

Jack turned around, scratching his stubbly beard. "Question for you."

"Shoot."

"That file you found, marked 'QC.' Did you download a copy?"

"No. Didn't think about it. Why?"

Jack's face soured. "Why not?"

"Just forgot. Why?"

"I'm not convinced there isn't a problem at Dalfan, and I'm afraid that file is all we have to prove it."

"Okay. We'll grab a copy when we get to the office."

Jack rubbed his aching neck. "Any Tylenol around here?"

"There's Advil in the third drawer on the left."

"Thanks." Jack yanked open the drawer, popped open the bottle, and tossed a couple pills into his mouth. He leaned over the sink and drank a few big gulps of water straight from the tap, then wiped his mouth with the back of his hand.

"You should see a doctor," Paul said.

"Heard you the first time, Mom."

Paul forced a smile. "I hear you."

"Heading for the shower." Jack shuffled achingly toward the stairs.

"You sure you're all right?"

Jack called over his shoulder, "Never better."

Paul stared after Jack, not at all sure he could trust him for anything anymore, especially the truth.

Jack stared at the billowing steam pouring out of the shower, his aching muscles begging to get in. But it suddenly occurred to him that he needed to contact Gavin with that plate number for the truck. Probably a dead end, but it needed to be checked anyway.

He ambled over to his dresser drawer and picked up his phone. He wasn't in the mood to deal with Gavin at the moment, so he opted for a text. It was late anyway.

Jack typed in the license-plate number as far as he could remember it, **SAM 00**. He started to hit send, but his sore thumb wavered. Was that the plate number?

No.

He wasn't sure where he got that from. The truck plate was six digits; he remembered that for sure. He saw the rear plate in his mind's eye again, racing away from the crash scene. Yeah. It began with an X. He was certain of that. And then he saw the rest.

He smiled to himself, happy his brain was returning to normal. He deleted **SAM 00** and typed in the correct plate number. He hit send and headed for the shower, hoping beyond hope that Gavin could find that truck.

P aul heard Jack's shower kick on when he sat down at the table with a cup of hot coffee and opened his laptop, checking for e-mails. He thought about working on his other Hendley Associates project, but he was too distracted at the moment. Too much going on, too much at stake.

And a headache that still wouldn't go away.

Rhodes's stinging rebuke still rang in his ears. He had until midnight tonight to capture the Dalfan encryption code, transfer it onto his CIA drive, then load the CIA drive onto the Dalfan desktop without anybody noticing, especially Bai. He also had to find a way to sneak the CIA drive past Dalfan security. There was plenty of time. He just needed the opportunity.

He hoped the CIA program didn't leave any traces behind. If it did, the Dalfan IT guys would be able to trace the upload directly to his drive—that was part of the security system, too. He couldn't plausibly deny that he'd done it by blaming someone else for stealing it and using it because it was biometrically coded to him and him alone with the thumbprint mechanism. He doubted Rhodes was setting him up. What good would it do him or the CIA to let him get blamed for the upload?

No, Rhodes wouldn't risk getting caught up in a scandal like that. He was, after all, a board member of Marin Aerospace. He risked losing everything if he was implicated in an illegal act of industrial espionage. Rhodes was also a vain and arrogant prick. If he got caught and implicated Rhodes, Langley would consider that a failure and would never call on his services again. Clearly, Rhodes was invested heavily in Paul's success. That probably explained his rude behavior last night. The man had every reason to worry. There was a lot at stake for him. And when there was a lot at stake, Rhodes did what every cornered rat did—he lashed out.

Paul took another sip of coffee. The image of Rhodes, angry and anxious, triggered the memory of the senator when they were both much younger men. A memory Paul seldom allowed to surface.

A memory too terrible to forget.

# 53

## JAKARTA, INDONESIA

She dashed toward the ten-story cylindrical building in the drenching downpour beneath her big black Nike golf umbrella. Her glasses steamed in the cool air. She was shrouded in a fashionably flowered purple hijab, the one immodesty the childless widow allowed herself. Beneath her rain gear and traditional clothing she cradled a small package wrapped in paper and twine. She had retrieved it from a post box just thirty minutes before. It came with instructions.

Sania Masood ignored the furtive glances of the men and Western-styled women entering and exiting the glass doors to the BMKG, the Indonesian Agency for Meteorology, Climatology, and Geophysics.

She wiped the steam from her glasses as she stood in the security line, careful to keep her gaze directed away from others, especially the shameless women. The line was longer than usual. *Of all mornings,* she told herself. The one morning she could not be late to work.

*Inshallah.*

When Sania neared the security desk, the uniformed guard recognized her instantly—they both attended the same mosque, just fifteen minutes south of here. She flashed a badge. The guard nodded slightly and with a nonchalant hand waved her around the magnetic metal detector so that she need not pass through it. This had been arranged.

Now all she had to do was get to the fourth floor.

## SINGAPORE

In the heavy rain and jammed traffic, it took Jack and Paul twice as long to make the short drive from their guesthouse to Dalfan HQ. The radio news reported that the big tropical storm in the Java Sea had stalled. Meteorologists had originally predicted it would head west, skirting far below Singapore but crashing into Jakarta. That stalled storm kept dumping rain on Singapore, however, and the streets were starting to flood, snarling traffic even further.

They arrived at Dalfan, Paul's limp worse than ever. Everybody was anxious and distracted by the storm. Jack and Paul were waved through security with a perfunctory check. Paul required a bathroom stop on the way to their offices. Bai wasn't in yet—that was a lucky break. Paul fell into his chair and jumped onto his desktop, Jack leaning over his shoulder. Paul entered his randomized passcode and logged in. For the next twenty minutes his chubby fingers sped across the keys, aided by the occasional mouse click. He opened file after file at blazing speed.

"You know your stuff," Jack said, checking around to see if they were being watched through their glass wall. So far, so good.

"Well, that's a great big chocolate banana."

"What?"

"The file is gone."

"The QC file you found before?"

"Yup. It's flat-out gone."

"You sure you're looking in the right place?"

Paul turned his head. They were practically nose to nose. "Seriously?"

"Maybe somebody moved it."

"More likely deleted it. I've already done a global search. It's gone."

"Couldn't it just have been renamed?"

"I did a search for files in the folder. Key words, you name it. Nothing."

Jack stood. "We need that file. It's the last shred of evidence we have." He paced around for a moment. "Wouldn't Dalfan have some sort of a backup system? To protect against data loss?"

"Yeah, sure. Good idea. Gimme a few minutes." Paul tapped keys furiously.

Jack decided to do some nosing around himself. He crossed over to his office and logged on to his computer and did some searching on his own. After twenty minutes, he gave up. He couldn't find anything. He returned to Paul's office.

Paul scratched his comb-over, frustrated. "I found the

backup system they use—it's hardware, located in this building, not cloud based. Near as I can tell, they keep the previous thirty days available on their backup drive, then probably download anything before that and put it in some kind of permanent storage somewhere. That file should've been in the thirty-day backup, but it's not. Somebody used a bot or some other automated sniffer to find every version of that file and destroy them all."

"Then we're screwed."

"Whoever built the file originally did it to keep track of the transactions. It's not likely they'd want to lose those records—otherwise, why keep them in the first place?"

"So whoever deleted those files made a hard copy before they deleted them?"

"That would be my guess. I can't tell you who or where, but at least there's the possibility—a remote one, I grant you—that you can someday recover the data."

About that moment, Bai came into view, beelining for Paul's office. Jack heard his phone ringing in his office next door. Only Yong or Lian had ever called him. Might be important.

"I'd better grab that." Jack dashed over to his desk phone.

Paul was grateful. He had clandestine work to do this morning, and he didn't want Jack snooping around while he did it. Unfortunately, Bai wasn't going to give him much room to maneuver, either. There was still more than twelve hours to pull this off, but suddenly that didn't seem like such a long time.

Bai shook his raincoat off and hung it up on the coat

rack next to Paul's, still dripping wet. "Good morning, Mr. Brown."

"Hello, Bai. How was your evening?"

"Not good." Bai dropped into his chair, exhausted. "Didn't sleep very well."

"The storm?"

"Yeah. And my mother. She's very worried. She thinks the storm will turn into a big typhoon that will come hit us."

"The weatherman doesn't think so."

"But she does. And she's a *wu*."

"A what?"

"A *wu*. Eh, maybe 'witch' in English. She tells fortunes, sees the future. For fun, mostly. But she's pretty good."

"You're serious?"

"Yes."

"And she sees a big storm coming?"

"Huge. She's very scared."

Paul smiled at the young man. "I think you're the one who's a little bit scared."

"I'm worried for my mom. My dad is dead. No brothers or sisters. So I look out for her."

Paul watched Jack hang up the phone, then head back to Paul's office.

"Everything okay?"

"That was Lian. She wants to see me."

"About what?"

"Turns out a Dalfan van was stolen and wrecked last night."

Paul feigned surprise. "Really?"

"Yeah, crazy, eh? There we were, you and I, watching

the local news together and then going to bed, and while we were sleeping, all of that happened."

Paul nodded his understanding of Jack's coded alibi. "Yeah, crazy."

"A stolen van?" Bai said. "I don't believe it. Cars don't get stolen in Singapore."

"Even Oz has its flying monkeys," Jack said.

Bai frowned. "Excuse me?"

"Never mind." He turned to Paul. "She's waiting for me on the third floor. I'll talk to her, then come back here so we can pick up where we left off. Okay?"

"Take your time. I've got plenty to do."

Jack nodded and headed for the elevators.

Now Paul had to deal with Bai.

But how?

**54**

Jack entered the third-floor office where Lian was located. She'd commandeered the space to meet with him privately, out of earshot.

"You wanted to see me?" Jack asked.

"Have a seat."

Jack took a seat. "You were saying something about a stolen van?"

"The Singapore police called earlier this morning. They found one of our vans smashed to pieces over in the warehouse district across town around two-thirty this morning."

"I'm sorry to hear that. Anybody hurt?"

"Not that I'm aware of." Lian's eyes narrowed, studying Jack's face. "You don't look so good yourself. How are you feeling this morning?"

Jack shrugged. "Didn't sleep well last night. The storm kept waking me up. Besides that, pretty good." Jack had taken the time to cover up his black eye again—thankfully, he hadn't taken the time to toss out the base makeup from his kit. He was fully shaved and showered, and his limp had mostly gone away. He was lucky she didn't ask him to take off his shirt. A wicked purple bruise painted his arm from the bottom of the shoulder down to his elbow, where the bat had hit and grazed him. It was sore to the touch, but nothing had been broken. Raising it over his head to wash his hair, though, had been a real treat.

"I hate to ask, but as head of security, I must: Did you steal our van last night?"

"No. Why would I? I have a company car at my disposal."

"Because you didn't want to be followed? To hide what you were doing?"

"I didn't do anything last night except watch the local news with Paul, then I went to bed. I was feeling a little under the weather."

"And he'll vouch for you?"

"Of course. Why wouldn't he?"

"Of course." Lian smiled. "Why wouldn't he?"

"What was in the van worth stealing?"

"It was one of our delivery vans. Electronic parts, wires, catalogs. The contents were worth maybe four or five thousand dollars, American."

"I'd think there would be more valuable things to steal around here."

"There are. That's what's so puzzling."

"And they took it all?"

Lian shrugged. "No. Actually, nothing valuable is missing, as far as we can tell."

"That doesn't make any sense."

"Unless they weren't stealing the van for the cargo inside."

"You mean, like, selling the van for parts?"

"Perhaps. But that doesn't make any sense, either. A Toyota Camry would be worth a lot more than that van. Why risk going to jail to part out a generic van?"

"Nothing else is missing from your property?"

"Not that I'm aware of."

"What did your security cameras show?"

"Isn't that an interesting question? I checked them first thing. Somehow, all of the security footage for the last twenty-four hours has been erased."

"That's weird."

"And on a hunch, I decided to take a look at the Steady Stare footage. Unfortunately, the drone wasn't up last night, due to the weather. But do you know what I found?"

"No."

"Twenty-four hours of video had been wiped away."

Jack frowned, genuinely confused. "How could that happen?"

"I was going to ask you the same thing."

Jack knew it wasn't him. But whoever had done it must have known that Jack had accessed that footage last night. He decided to take a chance. "You must have logs of whoever accessed that video yesterday."

Lian's eyes examined Jack's face, searching for a tell. "I don't suppose you can guess what I discovered?"

"That the logs have been scrubbed, too."

"Precisely."

"Someone's covering their tracks."

"Yes, they are." Lian sat forward. "I'll ask you again: Was it you?"

"No, I can guarantee you, it wasn't me."

She sat back, confused. "Then who?"

Good question. Apparently he had a guardian angel. Whoever had deleted the surveillance footage and log-in data probably disposed of the bodies at the warehouse, too, otherwise Lian would've mentioned it. Murder was rare in Singapore, and she would have heard about four dead foreign nationals from her police contacts. And if she thought that Jack really had stolen the van, she would've had him arrested already, or at least fired from the job. Since neither had happened, she must have had her doubts.

Or maybe she was saving that trump card for later.

Jack decided it was time to deflect and go on the offensive.

"I don't know if it's connected, but Paul and I were just looking for a file that has disappeared from the mainframe."

Lian frowned. "What kind of file?"

Jack had to be careful. He didn't want to tip his hand, and he didn't want to offend her. "Just one of the files we needed for our audit."

"That's rather vague."

"Agreed. But it's an interesting coincidence."

"Check the mainframe backups for copies."

*You thought of everything, didn't you?* Jack said to himself. "We did. All gone."

"Maybe it was never there to begin with."

"It was there, believe me."

"If it was so important, why didn't you download and copy it?"

Jack had been wondering the same thing. Why didn't Paul download it? It seemed an obvious thing to do, and Paul was a sharp guy. Did he really just forget, or was it intentional?

*Hell, maybe Paul's the one that deleted the file,* Jack realized.

"I guess we blew it. But I promise you I'm going to keep digging until I find it."

"Good, that's your job."

"Agreed." Jack stood to leave.

"I'll warn you once, Jack. If I catch you doing anything illegal, I'll have you arrested." She smiled. "Nothing personal."

"Yeah." Jack started to leave, then turned around. "You said that you were going to run those Aussie IDs past a friend of yours in the PD. What did you find?"

"Oh, yes. I forgot to tell you. Two of them have been released from hospital and deported. The third is still in hospital but scheduled to be released and deported tomorrow. All three have criminal records in Australia—mostly petty crimes, a few dropped assault charges—but no evidence of IC or military status."

"So we just got lucky and were jumped by the only three criminals in Singapore?"

"They were here illegally, too. Hooligans, the lot of them." She paused, then added, "Good riddance."

"Is 'Good riddance' for them or me?"

Lian smiled. "Good day, Mr. Ryan."

**55**

Paul turned to Bai. "Why don't you go use Jack's phone next door and call your mother, make sure she's okay, then go and get us a couple of hot coffees."

"I don't know."

"What?"

Bai shrugged. "C'mon, Mr. Brown. You know my job is to keep an eye on you."

"I've been a big threat, haven't I? Doing all kinds of crazy things."

Bai smiled. "No, not really."

"But this storm is a problem, isn't it?"

"Yeah. I'm worried about my mother."

"Then go call her on Jack's phone over there. Make sure she's okay. And if she is, why don't you run to the kitchen and fetch us a couple of hot coffees and something sweet? I won't leave here, I promise. Okay?"

Paul watched the wheels turning behind Bai's eyes. Finally he said, "Okay. Cream and sugar, right?"

"Plenty of both. Thanks."

Bai stepped over to Jack's office and dialed his mother as Paul logged on to his Dalfan desktop computer and opened his hard drive.

Paul watched Bai's animated gesturing through the glass as he spoke with his mother over the phone. An argument of some sort, Paul guessed. Bai was completely distracted by his conversation with his mother, so Paul used the opportunity to pull up the CIA file on his laptop.

As soon as Bai hung up the phone and headed for the break room, Paul pulled out his Dalfan USB drive from his desk and loaded it onto his laptop. The USB drive icon appeared on his screen. He glanced over his shoulder to make sure no one was watching. Thirty seconds later, a file labeled BigDaddyG appeared on his laptop.

Paul ejected the Dalfan USB and replaced it with his CIA drive, smuggled in his left shoe and fetched out in the bathroom earlier. He dragged BigDaddyG onto it.

According to Gavin, that was it. The CIA drive could now be loaded onto a Dalfan computer. All he had to do was install it into the Dalfan desktop computer and type in his passcode when prompted, and the mission would be complete—in thirty seconds or less.

Paul gripped the CIA drive between his thumb and index finger and pointed it at the USB port on the Dalfan computer. Just as the silver tongue of the USB drive was about to seat in the port, Paul stopped. He checked to make sure Bai was still gone, then opened his laptop back up. He pulled up the CIA file and opened it, drilling down into the sub files until he found the lines of code. He read them like a Talmudic scholar, his eyes raking over the numbers and letters, mumbling to himself as he read along.

And then he saw it. A familiar line, connected to another, and another.

"Holy schnikes," he whispered. "No way." He wished to God he could call Gavin and show him this. Incredible.

And incredibly dangerous.

"What the hell is that?" a voice said.

Paul glanced up, stunned by the voice. It was Yong, his face hard as flint. He pointed at the lines of code on Paul's screen.

"This?" Paul swallowed hard. Yong seemed capable of anything.

Yong's eyes narrowed. "Yes. *That*."

Paul slammed the laptop shut as Yong stepped closer, furious. Paul's mind raced for a convenient lie, but none came.

It was Yong's move now.

## JAKARTA, INDONESIA

Sania Masood sat at her workstation in her private office, curtains drawn, door closed. She studied the screen in front of her, but her mind was on the package in her drawer. It was nearly noon.

Her phone rang. She picked up.

"Deep Convection Analysis."

"Have you opened the package yet?"

Masood smiled. She recognized the man's voice. "The instructions said to wait until noon."

"Yes, I know. But please, do it now, while I'm on the phone."

"As you wish."

She put the call on speakerphone, opened her desk drawer and removed the package, then opened another drawer and pulled out a pair of scissors. She carefully cut the twine binding it and slid a thin fingernail underneath each perfectly placed piece of Scotch tape, lifting them in such a manner to not harm the contents inside. She then gently lifted the heavy box lid.

Her eyes widened.

The voice on the speakerphone asked, "Are you surprised?"

"Completely." Masood lifted the item out of the box.

Jane Austen's *Persuasion*. She opened the first pages. Published 1907, illustrated by Brock.

"I love it, Uncle. Thank you." She read the attached note. *Something to read tonight after your first day back at work.*

"It's my favorite Austen novel. I think you'll enjoy it."

"I'll start it on my lunch break, in the next few minutes."

"How does it feel to be back at work?"

"Don't you mean to ask, 'How is the pacemaker working?'"

He laughed. "Something like that. Are you okay?"

"I'm fine, Uncle. No problems, really."

An alarm blared on her monitor.

"Uncle, I'm sorry, I have to go." Without waiting, she hung up the phone.

The screen that Masood monitored featured a live

video feed from the Japanese geostationary satellite Himawari 8. Though owned and operated by the Japanese Meteorological Agency, the Himawari 8 fed images to the BMKG, the regional agency managing the Tropical Cyclone Warning Center. She was in charge of deep convection analysis, one of several optical and sensor operations provided by the sixteen-channel multispectral imager on board the solar-powered satellite.

She knew every monitor on her floor was alarming as well. Tropical Storm Ema was strengthening into Typhoon Ema—and charging north. Impossible. It had never happened before.

And it was heading straight for Singapore.

**56**

## SINGAPORE

Jack left Lian on the third floor, more determined than ever to find the missing QC file—and the person who tried to get him killed last night. He stabbed the elevator button, his mind racing. He needed Paul to work his forensic magic, maybe find a trace of when the file had been deleted—that would determine when it had been copied and downloaded to a hard drive. If they could figure that out, they might be able to get access to computer logs and find out which computer was used—unless those were deleted, too.

The elevator doors slid open and Jack stepped in, hitting the first-floor button, still trying to work the angles. If he knew which computer was used and at what time, he could figure out who was using it, but how, if the security-camera footage and computer logs had all been erased for the last twenty-four hours?

Whoever had covered Jack's tracks were really covering their own. But why? The only thing that made sense was that if Jack were hauled into the police department, they might start retracing his steps, and that would lead the police on a search for the culprits and the crime they had committed.

Jack pocketed the phone and got back to his main problem: How to find that file?

If Paul was right and the data had been saved, the easiest way to do that would be with a USB drive.

His Dalfan security brief indicated that the only people allowed to download data from the machines were Dalfan employees with Dalfan USB drives, each registered to just one individual. If Lian really wasn't responsible for the file disappearing, he might be able to convince her to pull every Dalfan USB and check for the file—or at least the trace of it, assuming that by now it had been transferred to somewhere else. If they could find the USB that had been used to copy it, they'd have their culprit. It was a long shot, but the only one he could think of.

The elevator door slid open and Jack headed for his office, nodding at the security receptionist at her desk, frantically typing away at her desktop. He waved his flash card and passed through the security door.

Jack saw that half of the workstations and offices were empty in the main work area. He bumped into several people who were gathering up their belongings and leaving. He supposed it was lunchtime.

Jack waved his security card over the reader to the last door, but he could already see through the glass walls that Paul wasn't in his office. He entered it anyway. He looked around. Didn't see Paul's coat or his laptop bag.

He turned around. Yong wasn't in his office, either, nor was Yong's junior spy, Bai.

Jack headed back through the first floor, now largely empty. He approached the security receptionist, who was pulling on her raincoat. Her computer was already shut down.

"Did I miss the memo?" Jack asked.

"You haven't heard? Typhoon Ema is on the way here. We've been told to go home and prepare."

"When will it get here?"

"Tomorrow. The news says it probably won't reach here, but the weather will get worse for sure." She grabbed her purse.

"I'm looking for Mr. Brown, my associate. Have you seen him?"

She pulled her hair into a ponytail and slipped a scrunchie over it. "He asked me to call him a cab. Said he wasn't feeling well."

"Did he say where he was going?"

"No, but I assumed he was going home." She pulled on a floppy rain hat. "Sorry, but I need to go. Anything else?"

"No, thanks. Be safe."

"You, too, Mr. Ryan. Find some high ground, and stay off the roads." She turned, then stopped herself. "And please tell Mr. Brown I hope he feels better soon."

"I will, thanks."

She bolted for the front door, her rubber rain shoes scuffing on the granite floor tiles.

Jack went back to his office and grabbed his stuff, too.

No point in going down with the ship—at least, not this one.

More important, he needed to find Paul.

In his office, Jack pulled on his coat and gathered his things. He noticed he was almost the last person on the floor. For a moment, he seriously considered rifling through Yong's office, maybe even Lian's and Dr. Fairchild's, too. If he had the run of the place, it would be the perfect time to nose around. But there were still security cameras working, and Lian's security team was probably still on the property, even if they weren't standing on the floor. And what would he find, anyway? Paul was the key.

Time to find Paul.

The traffic heading home was even worse than it had been coming in. Jack wondered if he would have been better off walking home. Or maybe swimming.

The security receptionist was right. The BBC report he was listening to said that Typhoon Ema was now a category 2 storm, heading north from the Java Sea toward Singapore, but at its current rate of speed wouldn't reach landfall until three a.m.

"However, a spokesman for the Indonesian Agency for Meteorology, Climatology, and Geophysics stated that computer models have proven wrong so far, and that it's equally likely the storm will resume its westward track. Dr. Paolo Pratesh of the University of Melbourne claims that global climate change is wreaking havoc with

ocean temperatures, causing the erratic behavior of
storms like Typhoon Ema, and called for an emergency
climate summit to address the crisis of manmade global
warming."

Jack snapped off the radio. Why did everything have
to be political? He pushed his irritation aside and con-
centrated on the traffic in front of him. The water level
in the street had certainly risen in the last few hours,
hitting the bottom rim of the tires on most of the cars
around him. Nothing to worry about, but he knew that
underpasses and other low-lying roadways would be
more difficult to navigate—maybe even impossible. But
no such hazard awaited him between here and the guesthouse. He was glad he was staying close by and not across
town, where his hotel had been booked.

Jack watched a low-flying passenger jet zoom across
his windshield, crabbing wickedly against a stiff cross-
wind, heading for nearby Changi Airport. He wondered
how soon until they closed down the airport and canceled all flights. The BBC newsreader said that wind
gusts of up to 125 kilometers per hour could be expected
by tomorrow morning—no way a plane could fly in that.
Judging by the way the trees were bending in the wind,
he was surprised they were flying now.

B y the time Jack finally made it to the guesthouse, the
driveway was covered with an inch of water. His
boots splashed as he dashed for the front door. He fumbled with his key but finally unlocked it and stepped into
the tiled hallway, where he shook off his raincoat and

hung it up. He thought about calling out to Paul, but if he was sick he might be asleep, and Jack didn't want to wake him. Paul seemed a little rough around the edges this morning; Jack assumed it was another hangover, but maybe he was wrong and Paul had picked up a bug.

Jack kicked off his soaking-wet boots before planting his feet on the carpet and heading upstairs, not quite jogging, but at least he wasn't limping. He was still stiff and sore as hell, though. When he got back downstairs to the kitchen he'd scarf down some more Advil.

He walked down the hall to Paul's room. The door was open. The bed was made and the room empty.

No Paul.

Jack sped back downstairs to the kitchen, calling out, "Hey, Paul! You around?" as he yanked open the drawer with the Advil. Jack tossed a couple tablets into his mouth and took another swig out of the kitchen faucet to wash them down.

"Paul?" Still no answer.

Where the hell was he?

**57**

Jack headed for the living room, searching for Paul. Maybe he was passed out on the couch.

Jack turned the corner and stopped in his tracks.

The glass coffee table, lamps, mirrors—all smashed. Pictures were knocked off the walls, sofa pillows scattered everywhere, chairs overturned.

It must have been one helluva fight.

"PAUL!"

Jack dashed through the living room and back into the kitchen, then out the back door and into the pouring rain toward the garage. He kept calling out Paul's name, but there wasn't any response.

Jack ran back into the kitchen, socks soaking wet, water dripping onto the floor from his jacket. He pulled out his cell phone. No texts from Paul, no e-mails, no voice mails, no missed calls.

Jack punched the speed dial for Paul. The phone rang. It went to voice mail.

"Paul, where the hell are you? Call me as soon as you get this. You all right, buddy? I'm worried." Jack hung up.

What to do? His phone rang.

"Paul?"

"Sorry, just me," Gavin said. "You want me to call back?"

"No, Gav. Sorry. What's up?"

"Those photos you sent? The fingerprints? Man, what have you got yourself into?"

"What did you find out?"

"Three of the guys came up zilch. I think I know why. The fourth I found—but it wasn't easy. In fact, it was a real bitch. I don't know how many DoD alarms I might have tripped getting it, either."

"If it wasn't easy for you, Gav, it would've been impossible for anybody else."

"That's nice of you to say, Jack. It's totally true, of course. But still nice."

Jack bit his tongue. "So, what did you find?"

"The one hit I got was for a character named Wang Kai, age fifty-one or thereabouts. He's a colonel in a PLA SOF unit, currently attached to Department Fifteen in the Ministry of State Security. His last known location was in Damascus as a so-called diplomatic liaison to the Assad regime."

"How in the hell were you able to hack into the PLA and MSS databases?"

"I wish I could, but I didn't. I just used my NSA back door to access the DoD mainframes. Turns out this Wang Kai guy attended a U.S. Army training program in 1998—an officer-exchange deal, back when we were trying to cozy up to the ChiComs. Anyway, the DIA guys were lifting fingerprints and DNA samples from cups, towels, silverware, and anywhere else they could get them from all of those visiting PLA comrades in the exchange programs. Photos, too. Of course, your guy was a lot younger then. He's a real badass. Or at least he was—until you wasted him."

"I didn't tell you I killed him."

"He looked deader than a doornail to me, and I doubt he would have voluntarily given you any of his fingerprints unless they were attached to a large-caliber bullet." Gavin chuckled. "Unless you're claiming you just found those four dead guys."

"You should've been a detective."

"It's not hard to guess that Wang's three friends were either PLA or MSS as well. They just weren't in any of our databases."

"Good work, Gavin. I appreciate it."

"Oh, there's more."

"Shoot."

"That license plate you sent me? On the truck?"

"A rental, stolen, or both."

"Why do I even bother."

"Because you care so deeply."

"Well, you asked for it."

"And I appreciate it. I just wanted to confirm what I suspected."

"So back to my other question, Jack. What have you gotten yourself into?"

"I'm handling it."

"Four dead Chinese spies can only lead to more live ones, and pretty pissed off. They're not exactly the forgiving types."

"Anything else you can tell me?"

"Maybe we should read Gerry in on this."

"You tell Gerry anything and I'll blood-eagle your ass."

"Nice *Vikings* reference, Jack."

"I try. And by the way, I'm not effing kidding."

Silence on Gavin's end. Finally, "Okay. I'll keep quiet—for now."

"One more favor. Can you ping Paul's phone?"

"Why? Did he lose it?"

"You ask too many questions."

"Gimme a second."

Jack heard keys tapping on the other end of the line.

"Found it."

"Where?"

"About fifteen feet behind you, and to your left."

Jack headed for the kitchen. Paul's phone was on the counter. The text display read **Hendley Associates**. Jack turned it off.

"Find it, Jack?"

"Yeah. Now help me find Paul."

## HENDLEY ASSOCIATES
## ALEXANDRIA, VIRGINIA

Gavin muted the Bluetooth device planted in his ear as he thumped across his office floor with his booted broken foot, checking the hallway to make sure no one had been listening. He shut his door.

He wasn't sure what he should tell Jack about Paul. Neither Paul nor Jack knew that he'd been working for both of them. In fact, Paul had demanded he not tell Jack about their working together in order to protect Jack. Isn't that why Paul had him send that capture software?

But now it was Paul who was in trouble. And maybe he was to blame.

"Gavin? You there?" Jack spoke in his earpiece.

Gavin unmuted. "Yeah, Jack. I'm here."

"Did you hear what I said? I need you to help me find Paul."

"Yeah, I heard you."

Jack was silent for a moment. "What aren't you telling me, Gavin?"

Gavin fell into his chair. "Paul and I were working on a project together."

"You mean apart from his work in Singapore?"

"Mmm, not exactly."

"What exactly?"

"Paul asked me to write him a piece of capture software."

"Capture software? To capture what?"

"He never said. But it was something on a USB. An encryption code."

"Why?"

"He didn't say."

"And you just wrote it for him? Hell, Gavin, if I'd known you had that much spare time, I could've found something interesting for you to do."

"Technically, I didn't write it. I mean, I jazzed it up a little, but the main code I got from somewhere else."

"So tell me why you got this for him again?"

"Paul told me he was worried that the woman you're having sex with is a Chinese spy."

## SINGAPORE

Jack stared at the phone, his face flushed with heat. "What the hell are you talking about? I'm not sleeping with anybody."

"Paul said you were sleeping with Lian Fairchild."

"That's complete bullshit."

"I've seen her picture, Jack. She's a looker."

"Shut your piehole, Gavin. I'm out here to do a job, not a girl. I'm telling you, there's nothing going on between us."

"Paul thought there was, and that maybe she was working for the ChiComs."

"Why didn't Paul tell me he thought she was working for the Chinese?"

"He thought you were sweet on her, and he wasn't sure she was a Red. He was looking for proof. At least, that's what he told me."

"And that's what the capture software was all about?"

"That's what he told me."

"And you believed him?"

"Why shouldn't I? Besides, he was just trying to protect you. So was I."

Jack's temperature dropped, his anger morphing into

regret. "Yeah, I guess so. And you're right, she's a looker. But no, I wasn't banging her, and I'm pretty sure she isn't a Chinese spy."

"But you had a run-in with at least four of them now. So Paul's instincts were right."

Jack glanced around at the destroyed living room. "Paul's instincts have gotten him into big trouble. Without his phone, there isn't any way to track him, is there?"

"No. Well, one."

"Tell me."

"Give me a minute. Hold on."

Jack heard the phone click. He wondered what Gavin was up to. Jack paced the living room floor, his eyes scanning for clues. He racked his brain. There was something needling him. He couldn't put his finger on it. Gavin was right. He had been dealing with some real characters the last few days. First the Aussies, then the Chinese—the guards at the first warehouse, and then the hit team at the second. Not to mention the truck that slammed into his van—who the hell were they? If he had to guess, the Chinese drove that, too. According to Lian, the Aussies were just street punks, not operators. But they might have been sent by somebody, including the Chinese.

Or were the Chinese working for somebody else?

Something about the white Australians was bugging him. Most of the Caucasians he'd bumped into in Singapore were tourists; a few were businessmen. Jack scratched his head. *But . . . wasn't there somebody else?*

Yeah. A blond guy, shouting into a phone. Where was he?

Jack shut his eyes tightly, trying to play the videotape

in his head. It was dark, then a flash of light. That's when he saw the blond shouting into a phone. That's right—a van. A Toyota van. And sitting next to him, the Turk with the bushy unibrow, staring back at Jack. The night Jack drove to the warehouse, he passed the Toyota van on the way there, parked in the opposite direction.

*Wait! The license plate. What was it?* Jack rewound the tape. The lightning flashed, snapping the fleeting image like a photo in his mind. He saw it clearly. White letters on a black plate. A partial. *SAM 00.*

The phone clicked on.

"Jack, it's Gerry Hendley on speakerphone."

*Oh, shit.*

**58**

"Hey, Gerry."

"Don't 'Hey, Gerry' me, Jack. What in the Sam Hill have you gotten yourself into?"

*Great question,* Jack said to himself. "You said to come down here and kick the tires. I guess the tires have been kicking back."

"What's this about Paul going missing?"

"Yeah, he's not here, and he doesn't have his phone."

"You think he's in trouble?"

Jack glanced down at the rubble. He lied. "Hard to say. But it's not like him to leave his phone and not tell me where he's going."

"Do you want me to dispatch Dom and Midas over to you to lend a hand?"

"No point to it. They're at least twenty-four hours away, and they can't do anything more than Gavin and I can. Besides, the airport is shutting down until the storm passes."

"We don't want to call the Singapore police if we can help it. Senator Rhodes wants us to stay off the radar if at all possible. But Paul's safety is more important than the mission."

"Agreed. I still think it's too early for that."

"I'm going to call Mary Pat Foley. She has resources near you."

Jack's jaw clenched. Gerry was spinning this thing up. The CIA chief of station was located in the U.S. embassy across town. Jack was certain they had their hands full with all of the Chinese activity in Singapore. He hated to pull them off their work if he could solve the problem himself. He also needed to prove to Gerry that he could handle it. He still remembered the stinging rebuke he received from Gerry after the Prague mission went tits-up. He already felt as if Gerry was trying to sideline him with this gig. Jack worried about his future with The Campus if Gerry thought he couldn't handle a white-side assignment, either.

"Give me an hour before you make that call, Gerry. I have an angle that Gavin and I can work. If it doesn't, we'll call in the cavalry for sure."

"You're the man in the field. It's your call. But whatever you do, find Paul."

"Yes, sir."

"I'll turn you back over to Gavin now. Keep me posted." Gerry's line clicked off.

"Gavin?" Jack asked.

"Yeah, Jack?"

"What the hell?"

Gavin quailed at the tone in Jack's voice. "Sorry. I was worried about Paul."

"What else did you tell him?"

"You mean, about the Chinese spies and all of that? Nothing. I just said Paul's gone missing."

"Ready to get back to work?"

"Shoot."

"It's a long shot. I've got another partial plate for you. A Toyota van. Probably a rental, but maybe not. The first three letters are S, A, M, and the first two numbers are zero, zero."

"Singapore plates use a three-letter, three-number combo. Shouldn't be too hard to find."

"Call me the minute you find something."

"Okay."

"Not Gerry. Not the Pope. Not the president of the San Diego Comic-Con. You call *me*. Understood?"

"Perfectly." Gavin rang off.

Jack pocketed his phone and headed for Paul's bedroom, hoping he might find a clue.


Jack walked through Paul's bedroom, looking for clues of any kind as to his whereabouts. He had no idea what he hoped to find.

Jack yanked open drawers and closet doors. Everything was neat and orderly, perfectly stacked and hung in place. No hidden devices or ransom notes or bloody towels or KGB badges.

*Crap.*

Then he remembered the incident with Paul in the bathroom and the USB drive after the SPF trashed their place. Despite Paul's assertion to the contrary, Jack had seen him pull the drive out of the shower curtain rod. He didn't really care why Paul had done that or why the drive was so important to him that he felt he had to hide it or that he had lied about it. Paul seemed harmless enough, and not doing anything he wasn't supposed to be doing.

Clearly, he was wrong.

Jack pulled the curtain rod down and removed both ends. He didn't see anything blocking either end, and he tipped the rod up high enough that the USB drive or anything else Paul may have been hiding in there would have fallen out.

His phone rang in his pocket. Jack tossed the curtain rod to the floor and answered his phone.

"That was fast, even for you, Gav."

"Don't thank me yet. It's a long shot, but I think I found the car. It's a local rental, signed out for two weeks to a V. Levski, with a corporate address in Sofia, Bulgaria."

"Bulgaria? That doesn't make any sense." Jack wondered if the Turk he saw with the blond man wasn't actually a Bulgarian.

"I'm texting you the GPS coordinates where the car is located."

"How did you find it?" Jack's phone dinged as the text arrived.

"The rental agency uses Swiss cheese for a firewall. It

wasn't a problem to hack into their GPS locator. I'm sorry, but that's all I've got. It's probably a wild-goose chase."

"It's a lead, Gav. Thanks. I'll be in touch."

Jack rang off and dashed down the stairs, praying it was more than a lead. He remembered Paul's phone and grabbed it off the kitchen counter. A message box indicated that Paul had missed three calls and a voice mail from Senator Rhodes. What the hell was that all about? He pocketed the phone, pulled on his soaking-wet boots, and dashed for the Audi TT parked in the driveway.

If the traffic was bad before, it was a pure hell now. Jack was surrounded by honking horns and red brake lights. Sheets of rain pummeled the Audi like a drummer on crack. His wiper blades couldn't keep up. The windshield blurred with water as fast as the wipers slapped it away.

It took Jack twenty minutes to move a hundred yards on the busy three-lane PIE expressway. He used the downtime to plot an alternative route over side streets to avoid the stampede of cars heading for higher ground. Fortunately, the destination wasn't too far away.

He took the first side street available and let the woman's voice on his map program guide him the rest of the way, almost due west of his guesthouse. On a regular traffic day the journey was no more than fifteen minutes.

Five minutes from his destination, Jack's phone rang. The caller ID read SEN. RHODES.

Strange.

He answered via the Audi's streaming wireless Bluetooth. "Senator Rhodes. What can I do for you?"

"Jack, I've been trying to reach Paul. Is he with you?"

*Yeah, I know. But why?* "No. I'm trying to find him myself. Is there a problem?" In the close quarters of the Audi's cabin, the pounding rain and squeegeeing wipers were deafening.

"I was just going to ask you the same thing. My God, it sounds like you're in a machine shop."

"Something like that."

"Paul was supposed to call me this evening. I've tried calling his phone, but he doesn't pick up. I'm worried about him."

"Why?"

"You may not be aware that Paul struggles with alcohol. He says it's under control, but that's what every drunk says."

Jack's jaw clenched. He resented Rhodes calling Paul a drunk, even though it was true. "You know it was his wedding anniversary yesterday."

"Oh, yes. Of course. I'd quite forgotten. Probably set him off. I need to speak to him immediately."

"I'll let him know when I find him." There was a long pause on the other end. "Anything else on your mind, Senator?"

Finally, "Jack, I'm concerned that Paul might be in some hot water."

"Why?"

"I can't read you in on that. Let's just say I asked him

to do me a favor. If he doesn't do this thing by midnight tonight, it's a problem."

"What kind of problem?"

"Just call me when you find him, will you? It's extremely urgent." Rhodes rang off.

Jack shook his head. *What the hell was that all about?*

**59**

Jack's phone rang again. "Gav, I'm a minute out."

"I know, I'm tracking you."

"How?"

"Your phone."

"Yeah, duh. What do you need?"

"Wanted to give you a heads-up. This isn't a goose chase after all. These Bulgarians or whoever they are really are after Paul."

"How do you know?"

"I'll patch you in." Gavin punched a few buttons on his end. Jack heard voices speaking in German over the Audi's car audio system.

"What am I listening to?"

"I hacked into the van's onboard Safety Connect, Toyota's version of OnStar. We're listening to them live."

"What are they saying?"

"They're supposed to go in and grab Paul in the next five minutes."

"You speak German?"

"I have streaming translation software. Ninety-two percent accurate. I think I'm hearing just two distinct voices."

Jack shut off his headlights as he made his final turn off Geylang Road and onto the narrow one-lane where the van's GPS signal was located. He was passing old two- and three-story buildings with crumbling colonial façades in fading pastel colors. The Geylang district was the seediest part of Singapore, but it was still a whole lot better than the nicer parts of some of the Third World shitholes he'd been to over the years.

"So where's Paul?"

"The transcript says the Pink Lily."

"Sounds like a whorehouse."

"According to an Ohio soccer mom on TripAdvisor, you're in Singapore's red-light district. Room three thirty-one. About five hundred yards ahead."

One of the German voices barked a command, followed by *thunk*ing sounds.

"What was that?" Jack asked.

"They're out of the vehicle, heading for Paul!"


Jack snapped the lights back on and gunned the Audi's 220-horsepower turbo. The all-wheel-drive Quattro transmission kept it from spinning out as the speedometer passed 100 kilometers per hour four seconds later. But the narrow street was crowded on both sides by parked cars. The Audi hit standing water and hydroplaned. Sparks exploded when his right side-view mirror sheared off. He jerked the wheel and the Audi's front bumper crashed into a green plastic dumpster left in the street, launching a shower of garbage onto the sidewalk.

Jack slammed on his brakes, screeching to a halt in a spray of water behind the Toyota van parked across from the "hotel"—a pale pink three-story building with PINK LILY on its sign. The street-front door was pushed open.

Jack charged out of the Audi and through the rain toward the door, his boots splashing in the puddles. He bounded onto the stairs, taking three at a time. He used the banisters to round the corners faster, and hit the third-floor landing winded but furious. A glance right down the hallway yielded nothing, but a glance left showed an open door, and there was the sound of crashing furniture.

Jack bolted for the open door. He arrived just as the unibrowed Bulgarian backhanded Paul across the face. The blond German turned in shock at Jack's appearance and reached inside his coat pocket, but Jack was faster with his fist, and he cracked the smaller man's jaw with a straight-armed punch, sending him to the floor, out cold.

The Bulgarian turned as Jack's blow landed on the German's jaw. He crashed hard into Jack, knocking him against the wall, smashing a cheap picture frame with a blue-armed Vishnu smiling behind the glass. The big Bulgarian grabbed Jack by the lapel with his left hand and cocked his right arm back, aiming the biggest fist Jack had ever seen at his face. The thick, hairy knuckles launched like a meat hammer at Jack's head, but Jack diverted the blow with a swipe of his left hand, sending the man's fist into the wall with a sickening crunch.

The man still had Jack's lapel bunched in his left fist, and his heavy right arm was pressed against Jack's face, pinning his head against the wall. Too tied up to throw a decent punch, Jack reached for his front pants pocket and pulled out his weapon of last resort, driving the tip of the stainless-steel Zebra pen deep into the soft tissue of the big man's lower jaw. The Bulgarian howled, clawing at the pen as he stumbled backward, his eyes wide with panic as Jack landed a kick to the side of his head, knocking him out.

"He's bleeding out," Paul said, rubbing the side of his reddened face.

Jack was still trying to catch his breath. He knelt close to the Bulgarian, careful not to put his knee in the pooling blood. "He's dead."

Jack pulled the pen out of the Bulgarian's jaw and wiped it off on the man's shirt. He saw Paul's disgusted look. "Can't leave evidence behind." He stood.

Paul took a step back into the small kitchen opening to the postage stamp–sized living room. "Who the hell are you, Jack?"

Jack frown-smiled. "You know who I am. I came here to find you." He fished around in his pocket and pulled out Paul's phone. Tossed it to him as a peace offering. "Thought you might need this."

"Who sent you?"

"Nobody sent me. Look, we need to get out of here."

Paul fiddled with his phone. He didn't look up. "What about him?"

Jack stepped over to the German, felt for a pulse. Couldn't find one. He wasn't completely surprised. It was a perfectly thrown punch, the momentum of his two-hundred-pound frame propelling his fist like a mortar round into the smaller man's jaw. A half-step shorter jab and the man would still be breathing.

"He's gone." Jack reached into the man's coat and pulled out a 9x18mm Makarov pistol. He showed it to Paul. "Soviet version of the Walther."

Paul glanced up from his phone, puzzled. He pocketed it. "Looks familiar. Can I see it?"

"You know how to handle one?"

"My dad was a cop." Paul took the small pistol in his beefy hands and cleared the chamber while Jack searched the Bulgarian, his back to Paul.

Jack's fingers gripped a pistol in the Bulgarian's shoulder holster. "Let's get out of here."

"Why did Rhodes send you, Jack?"

"I told you, no one sent me—"

The pain exploding in the back of Jack's skull cut his sentence short.

**60**

Jack blinked himself awake. His head throbbed, but his wrists burned like they were cut. It took him a moment to figure out they were tied behind his back. He was lying on his side, not far from the dead German.

Paul sat on a small threadbare couch across from him, the Makarov pointed at Jack's face.

"I'll ask you again, why did Rhodes send you?"

"Damn it, Paul! I told you he didn't."

"Then why were you talking to him on your phone ten minutes ago?"

"He called me, looking for you."

"That's my point."

Jack stretched his shoulders. "What did you tie my wrists with, piano wire?"

"Lamp cord. Last chance, Jack. Otherwise, I'm going to shoot you."

"Goddamn it, Paul, who are you?"

"That's what I asked you."

Jack winced against the hammer clobbering his brain. "Yeah, Rhodes called me, looking for you. But I was already on my way to find you before he called."

"Why?"

"You disappeared. I was worried about you."

"How did you find me?"

"I didn't. Gavin did."

"So Gavin's in on this, too?"

"In on what?"

Paul reached into his shirt pocket and pulled out Rhodes's USB drive. "This."

"What's that?"

"You tell me."

"I can't."

"You mean you won't."

"No. I can't, because I don't know what it is. Is that the one you had hidden in the shower curtain rod?"

"How did you know?"

"I caught you fooling with it after the police raid, remember?"

"Yeah, I guess so."

Jack winced again. "Can you at least cut me loose?"

"Not yet."

"Well, you better hurry. These assholes probably have friends, and they might be on their way over. We should get out of here."

"Maybe I'll leave and you can stay here and explain what you did to their friends."

"At least one of us would survive."

That caught Paul by surprise. "What did Rhodes tell you?"

"That he was worried about you, that he asked you to do him a favor, that if you didn't do that favor by midnight tonight, you would be in big trouble. That about cover it?"

"That's all?"

"That's all. He said he couldn't 'read' me into the rest of it."

"So you're not working with him, or for him?"

"Yes, of course I am, just like you, doing the Dalfan audit."

Paul snorted, pointing his gun at the two dead men. "You're no auditor."

"Technically, you're right. I'm a financial analyst."

"I never knew anybody in accounts receivable that could take out a couple of operators bare-handed. What are you, CIA?"

Jack shook his head. "No." Jack winced again. "C'mon, Paul, my arms are killing me."

"Just a second. If you're not CIA, what are you? FBI? DIA?"

"None of the above."

"Foreign service? Interpol?"

"Look, you're smart enough to know that if I'm with a sworn service I can't tell you. But Gerry will vouch for me."

"Gerry was working with Rhodes. I don't know if I can trust him."

"Gerry's good people. You know that. If Rhodes is pulling a scam, Gerry's not part of it." He looked into Paul's pale gray eyes. "And neither am I. If I was, my dad would kick my ass."

Paul chuckled. "He would, wouldn't he?"

Paul crossed over to the kitchen and pulled a knife out of the drawer. He cut Jack's bonds.

Jack sat up, rubbing his wrists. "Thanks."

"How's your head?"

"I'm gonna need a new one when we get back home." Jack touched it. Blood on his fingers. He stood up stiffly.

Paul's voice softened to a whisper. "I'm really sorry about that. It's just that I thought for sure you were coming to kill me."

Jack went to the kitchen, looking for a clean towel. "Because of that USB drive? What's on it? And what's the story on Rhodes?" He found one and pressed it against his scalp.

Paul sat back on the couch, the gun limp in his hand. "Last Monday when we got hooked into this thing and Gerry took you outside, Rhodes took me aside and said he was working with Langley, and that he had a special mission for me to carry out—loading his USB drive onto the Dalfan mainframe. But you saw how secure Dalfan was. It took me a few days to figure out a way to get around it, and I did. In fact, I was just about going to load it today when I decided to take a look at the code. I didn't like what I found."

"Which was?"

"Rhodes said it was just a piece of sniffing software that the CIA had written. He said they wanted to be sure that the Dalfan systems hadn't been compromised by Chinese malware before the merger with Marin Aerospace happened."

"Sounds plausible enough. Don't take this the wrong way, but why would Rhodes recruit you?"

Paul frowned. "We have a history. From way back."

"And he called in a favor."

"More like he stroked my ego, made me feel important again."

"Sounds like the Weston Rhodes I know."

Jack checked the towel. The bleeding had stopped. "Let's keep talking, but we should get out of here." They took two minutes to wipe off fingerprints and hide any other evidence of their presence before running for the Audi. Paul kept his gun and gave Jack the other one. They fell into the coupe soaking wet and sped away.

As Jack turned the first corner, Paul asked, "Should we call the American embassy?" He practically shouted over the pounding rain.

"And tell them what? You're involved in corporate espionage and I just killed two foreign nationals? They'd hand us over to the Singapore authorities as fast as they could. Besides, the storm has knocked out all the cell service."

"Oh, crap!"

"What?"

"My laptop. I left it back at the house. I need to get it."

"Why?"

"I copied Rhodes's software onto the hard drive. Not a good idea to leave that lying around. I've also got a lot of important work on there I wouldn't want to lose."

Jack smiled at the idea. "It's the last place they'd think we'd go."

"I hadn't thought of that, but you're right."

Jack made another turn, heading for the PIE. Traffic had cleared up considerably, but the rain was even heavier than before. The streets were flooding now. Jack couldn't go full speed even if he wanted to.

"So finish your story. You said you didn't like what you found on Rhodes's drive."

"I took a look at the code. I'm no expert, but I've read extensively on the subject of cybersecurity—kind of a hobby. I recognized a few lines. I don't know why they seemed familiar, but they did, so I Googled them when I got back to the guesthouse. I nearly wet myself when I discovered that it was a Stuxnet variant. Super-nasty stuff—the software that took down the Iranian centrifuges, remember?"

"Yeah. Why would the CIA want to load something like that into the Dalfan system?"

"I dug a little further into the software. Dalfan wasn't the target. It was pointed at the Hong Kong stock market."

"Hong Kong," Jack reflected as he pulled onto the Paya Lebar Flyover, heading for the PIE. The few cars that were on the road now were flashing their emergency lights. A wailing ambulance screamed past them in the opposite direction.

The trees on either side of the freeway were bent over by the fierce winds. Leaves flew like ash through the air, and branches skittered across the pavement. Jack fought the wheel to keep the car in line. A huge gust of wind buffeted the car, rocking it side to side.

"Wow! That was huge!" Paul said. "Where was I? Oh, yeah. Dalfan's security is air gapped, remember? They don't do Wi-Fi. But they're a registered stock on the Hong Kong exchange, so they're hardwired to the exchange's computers via fiber-optic cable. I think the program was designed to do to the Hong Kong exchange what Stuxnet did to those Iranian centrifuges."

"Why would the CIA want to crash the Hong Kong stock market?"

"They wouldn't. If the Hong Kong market crashes, then so does Shanghai's, then Tokyo's, then all of the markets in Europe, and the U.S. crashes right behind them. It would be a global economic catastrophe."

Jack whistled. "Doesn't sound like Langley, does it?"

"That's why I ran. Whoever wrote that software was a genius."

"Yeah, but it's the braniac who ordered it written that we're after. Any chance it could be Yong?"

"I don't think so. He and I had a run-in earlier, but he got a phone call that shot him out of the room like a scalded cat. Someone's pulling his string."

*Great. Another puzzle piece that didn't fit anywhere,* Jack thought. He glanced in his rearview mirror. No one following. He asked, "Why were you hiding in a whorehouse?"

"I told the taxi driver to take me to a cheap hotel. He thought I wanted to get lucky, I guess."

Jack grinned. "Holing up with a boom-boom girl until the shitstorm passes isn't the worst idea in the world."

Paul shot Jack an incredulous look. "I just wanted a place to hide until after midnight. Rhodes said that if I didn't get this thing installed by then, the software would self-destruct."

"Like *Mission: Impossible*?"

"Nothing that dramatic. A timer inside the program deletes a few lines of code and disables it."

"Why didn't you just destroy it?"

"It's evidence against Rhodes, and it's biometrically passcoded to my thumbprint. Without me, nobody can open it, not even Gavin. So I had to run, too."

"For what it's worth, your plan makes sense."

"And for the record, there wasn't any boom-boom girl."

Jack smiled. *Of course not.* "We'll grab your laptop and then we'll figure the rest of this out together."

"Thanks, Jack. I appreciate it. And I'm sorry I got us into this mess."

"I don't blame you. It's Rhodes I'm going to have a few choice words with."

Another gust of wind slammed into the car. For a second, Jack thought they'd been hit by another vehicle.

"What the hell's going on with this storm?" Jack punched the radio button.

". . . with gusting winds of one hundred and forty kilometers per hour. The storm is still tracking toward Singapore. Singapore authorities have issued an emergency alert, advising all citizens to stay indoors to avoid flying debris and downed power lines. Cell towers are down, affecting most cell service providers."

Jack snapped the radio off. "We need to get out of this weather."

"After we get my laptop, where do you want to go?"

"Somewhere where it doesn't rain."

**61**

Jack and Paul dashed for the front door of the guest-house, shielding their faces from the stinging rain and flying debris.

Once inside, Jack heard the sound of someone in the living room. He signaled for Paul to wait, then pulled the Makarov out of his waistband, holding it temple index.

He turned the corner, gun forward.

And found himself staring into the barrel of a SIG P229.

"What are you doing here?" Jack said.

"Drop your weapon," Lian said. Their pistol barrels were inches apart.

"Drop yours."

Tree branches knocked and scraped against the living room windows, rattled by the high winds.

"Where's Paul Brown?"

"I don't know," Jack said.

"Jack? You okay?" Paul's voice whispered behind the wall.

Lian grinned. She kept her eyes sighted down the barrel at Jack. "Are you okay, Mr. Brown?"

Paul stepped out from around the corner. "Yes, thank you."

"Can I trust Mr. Ryan?"

"He's a friend."

"But can I trust you?"

"Me? Of course."

Jack saw a flash in her eyes. She was calculating. She lifted her left hand from her pistol and raised the palm, then turned the pistol barrel toward the ceiling, signaling a stand-down.

Jack lowered his weapon and shoved it back into his waistband. "What are you doing here?"

"I was worried about the two of you," Lian said, holstering her weapon. "The storm is surging north. I tried calling both of you, but the cell towers must be down, so I drove over here." She gestured at the broken furniture. "And found all of this."

Jack had seen a silver Range Rover parked across the street but didn't think anything of it. The Dalfan company vehicles were all black. He turned to Paul. "You never did explain what happened here."

Paul shrugged. "When I figured out that I'd been played, I got mad." He shrugged. "Got drunk. Started smashing things. Kind of lost my mind."

"There goes the rental deposit," Jack said.

Paul toed a piece of broken pottery. "Stupid, I know. And then I called a taxi to find a place to hide."

"Why did you need to hide?" Lian asked.

Jack told her about the software on the USB drive and what it was apparently designed to do. She was stunned. He added, "Weston Rhodes is playing a dangerous game."

"My laptop," Paul said. "It's upstairs."

"Grab it," Jack said.

Paul headed for the staircase. The wind howled outside, amplified in the shaking tree branches.

"What dangerous game?" Lian asked.

"Don't know all the details, but there were some bad dudes coming after Paul, and they're tied to Rhodes somehow."

"That doesn't make any sense."

"I'd also like to talk to your brother."

"He and his girlfriend caught the last flight to Beijing before Changi closed."

"Let me guess. A business trip."

Lian's eyes narrowed. "What else would it be?"

"I'll deal with him later."

The glass in the living room window broke. They both turned to look. A tree branch must have—

*Oh, God.*

Two cylindrical grenades bounced on the floor. Jack and Lian turned and dove for the ground.

Too late.

The grenades exploded before their bodies hit the floor.

**62**

Jack rolled onto his back, blinded by the dark. A flash of lightning outside the smashed windows gave him a momentary glimpse of rain pouring into the living room. He sat up with effort, the fog clearing. He glanced over at Lian, still facedown.

Jack crawled over to her and checked her pulse. Alive. Another flash of lightning showed a trickle of blood coming out of her ear.

Jack rolled her over gently onto her back. She began to stir, then suddenly startled awake, her eyes wide with terror. She turned and stared at Jack, her face a welter of confusion.

"Flash-bangs. You're okay. Just take a second."

She blinked, then frowned. Jack knew the headache pounding inside her skull was as bad as his.

"What happened?" she finally managed, as Jack helped her to her feet.

"Couple of flash-bangs."

"How long were we out?"

Jack checked his watch. "About fifteen minutes."

"Where's Paul?"

"Wait here." Jack ran up the staircase, calling out Paul's name. He stumbled over a step in the dark but caught himself. Another lightning flash lit the hallway. Black shoe scuffs all along the walls. Jack ran for Paul's bedroom, still shouting his name. He dashed inside. The room was trashed.

Paul was gone.

L ian was in the kitchen, washing her face in the sink, when Jack ran back down. There wasn't much pressure in the line.

"He's not upstairs," Jack said, as he approached her.

"Not down here, either." She dried her face. "Those 'bad dudes' you were talking about must have followed you here."

"Or you," Jack said.

"He must have run away again, or they took him."

"I saw signs of a struggle upstairs. Paul put up some kind of a fight."

"My question is, why aren't we dead?" Lian said. "We were out cold. Two bullets in the head and we're not a problem anymore."

"I don't know, but I'm not complaining."

"Where do you think they took him?"

Jack checked his watch. "It's eleven twenty-seven. There's still time."

"For what?"

"We need to get back to Dalfan. They've taken Paul there."

"How do you know that?"

He grabbed her by the hand. "I'll explain on the way. Let's go!"

They took Lian's silver Range Rover. It had a better chance in the high water and it had all-wheel drive, too.

No one was on the streets now, which meant no traffic to slow them down, but Jack had to work the wheel hard to avoid the obstacles in the road—tree branches, garbage cans, sheet metal roofing, and abandoned vehicles. A couple times he had to jump the curb and run on the sidewalk to keep from hitting sparking power lines slithering in the street.

Jack took a chance on Lian and filled her in on the fight at the warehouse and then at the Pink Lily.

"You don't seem surprised," Jack said, taken aback by her nonchalance.

"It's not surprising, given the stakes involved. I'm just glad you're the one who survived."

"Six dead bodies will be hard to explain to the police."

"I think you're right about the four Chinese disappearing. They're probably fish food by now. So really it's only two you have to worry about."

"Gee, that makes me feel better."

"At least now I know you're the one who deleted all of my security files."

"No, I swear, it wasn't me."

"Then who?"

"Still working on that one."

"I still can't believe Rhodes wants to crash the world's stock markets."

"I don't think he does."

"But he gave Paul the software."

"Sure, but he didn't write it. That means someone else wrote it for him. So it's that coder I want to talk to—and the guy behind the coder. That's the asswipe who's behind all of this."

Lian powered on the radio. An emergency signal blared on every station, and an automated voice repeated: "SEEK HIGH GROUND NOW! STAY IN SHELTER! DO NOT DRIVE! AVOID LOW-LYING AREAS! HIGH-VOLTAGE LINES ARE DOWN! STAY INDOORS!"

Dead traffic lights swayed in the wind; streetlamps and building lights were all dead now.

Lian punched the radio off. "Only thirteen minutes to midnight. Drive faster!"

# 63

Deputy Ri stood in his cramped basement office, talking into the speakerphone on his desk. "Why hasn't it happened yet?" His expressionless face was beaded in sweat.

"The man I recruited failed," Zvezdev said over the phone. "I've taken matters into my own hands."

"There's no point in threatening you. You know what's at stake for both of us."

"There's still time."

Ri checked his watch. "Ten minutes."

"An eternity. We only need thirty seconds."

"Call me when it's done." Ri pushed a button with a trembling finger. Zvezdev was his last hope. The missions in Lisbon and Toronto had already failed.

Ri lit a Gitanes to calm his nerves. The chairman had sent him a carton yesterday. Choi Ha-guk was a reasonable man, unlike his crazed cousin, who murdered failed subordinates and their entire families with ravenous dogs, flamethrowers, or antiaircraft weapons. The chairman was a professional man. He understood that operations sometimes failed, no matter how well prepared and executed they were.

Ri rolled the burning Gitanes between his fingers, watching the twisting tendrils of smoke in the lamplight. He smiled.

Yes, Choi Ha-guk was reasonable.

If he failed, Ri would only face a simple firing squad.

He crushed the cigarette out in his ashtray and picked up the phone. The operator connected him with the RGB station chief at the DPRK embassy in Sofia, Bulgaria. The man heading up the unit was a cousin, loyal and efficient. He gave orders to stand ready and be prepared to move against Zvezdev within the next thirty minutes if needed.

Unlike Choi, Ri was not a reasonable man at all.

**64**

Jack killed the lights and slammed on the brakes. The Range Rover came to a splashing halt thirty yards from the Dalfan building, lit up like a Christmas tree in the middle of the blacked-out neighborhood. The Toyota van was parked on the sidewalk near the door.

"Emergency generator," Lian explained. "We need to keep the power on or else the security locks all fail. We also need the mainframe to keep running—a system crash would be fatal."

"Mainframe's on the fourth floor, right?"

"The control station is on the fourth, directly across from the emergency stairwell. It's the only place now where you can install a USB drive."

"That's where they'll have Paul."

Jack pointed through the flooded windshield. Between the momentary blink of wiper-blade swipes they could make out two men in the lobby.

"I can use my security pass to enter through an emergency exit in the back," Lian said. "I'll make my way—"

"No time."

Jack slammed the throttle into the floorboard. The Range Rover rocketed forward, leaping the curb. Jack used the parked Toyota van to cover his approach. Lian slapped the airbag switch, killing the safety devices.

The silver SUV came out of the night like a steel shadow. The two men in the lobby saw it at the last second and scattered as the front end smashed through the front glass doors.

Jack popped the brights back on and jerked the wheel hard left, tracking with one of the men running for cover. The left bumper caught him at the hip and slammed him against a concrete pillar, crushing his pelvis. He screamed.

Lian was out the door and firing her weapon, putting four rounds in the other man's chest as he raised his weapon to fire. He dropped like a rag doll, his pistol clattering to the floor. She turned in time to see Jack put a round in the head of the man crushed against the pillar, somehow pointing his weapon at Jack just before he ate one in the face.

There was no way to know if the men upstairs heard the racket downstairs, and at this point it didn't matter. They bolted up the emergency stairs two at a time, boots clanging on the metal stairs. Jack's heart raced with adrenaline, and a death-metal soundtrack crashed in his throbbing skull. They reached the fourth-floor landing and stopped at the emergency door. Jack pressed his ear against it.

Screaming.

Paul.

No way to know the tactical situation. Could be twenty guys. Could be two. Jack didn't care. His friend was in trouble.

Jack hand-signaled a plan—clear the room of tangos, assault the control room—then counted off with the nod of his head.

Three.

Two.

One.

*Go!*


Jack leaned hard against the locked emergency door so that when Lian swiped her security card it pushed open without a bang. He drove straight across the floor toward the glass-walled control station while Lian cut low and right, using the workstations for cover. Jack assumed if they were guarding the floor they'd expect someone to come in through the front and not the stairwell.

Jack was half right.

Two steps in, Jack saw a Caucasian man startle in front of him. He raised the pistol in his hand toward Jack. Too slow. Jack's gun was already up. He put a round through the man's throat. The lead passed clean through and smashed in a bloody spiderweb against the control-room glass, alerting a second killer standing next to a third man in a flat cap towering over Paul, blade in hand.

Two shots rang out on his right, one large-caliber and the other small, followed by the sound of tinkling glass.

Jack didn't have time to turn around and look—he was drawing a sight on the man charging out of the control room with a gun already pointing at him.

"LIAN!"

"CLEAR!"

Jack fired two rounds into the man's broad chest, spinning him like a top, but not before he got a round off. Jack swore his upper right arm got hit with a blacksmith's hammer. It turned him a quarter-step—and it saved his life.

The man with the blade standing over Paul had turned calmly and raised a small-caliber pistol in a confident, one-handed draw. Jack swore there was a smile beneath the man's thin pencil mustache when he fired. But the hit that turned Jack took him out of the path of the smiling man's bullet—a head shot. The slug *zoop*ed past Jack's ear like an angry hornet.

Jack returned fire. Two rounds shattered the man's forehead just beneath his flat cap as a third punched in just below his nose. The man flew backward, crashing into Paul, then tumbled to the ground.

Jack charged forward and kicked the dead man's pistol out of reach, then secured his own weapon. He saw Lian clearing the weapons and checking the pulses of the two others Jack had shot.

"Paul! Where are you hurt?" Jack instantly regretted the question. Paul's forearms were duct-taped to the chair, and the tips of the fingers of his left hand oozed blood.

"Jack, I'm sorry—"

"Where's the USB?"

"It's loaded!"

Jack glanced at the monitor behind Paul. EXECUTED flashed in red. The virus was launched.

Jack ripped apart the duct tape with his fingers as Paul burbled, red eyed and snotty. "He made me give him the passcode . . . I tried . . . I couldn't . . ."

"It's all right."

Lian dashed into the room. "All clear." She saw Paul's hand. She gasped. "I'll get the medical kit!" She ran back out of the room.

Jack checked his watch. Two minutes until midnight. Two minutes until the end of the world.

# 65

Jack freed Paul's other arm and tried to help him to his
feet, but the big man's knees buckled. Paul's good
hand gripped Jack's forearm like a vise to keep from falling. His hand strength surprised Jack, but he filed that
away as he helped Paul lie down on the floor.

Lian bolted back into the room with a medical kit on
her shoulder. She dropped down next to Paul and examined each of his wounded fingers. Even though she'd been
a cop for several years, the gruesome sight sickened her.

Jack saw the damage, too. The bastard with the pencil
mustache had pulled out Paul's fingernails. Jack felt
guilty as hell that he hadn't gotten there sooner.

"I'm sorry about all of this," Jack said.

Paul shook his head and moved his mouth, but nothing came out.

"I'm worried he might be going into shock," Lian
said, cleaning the wounds and stanching the blood.

Jack flipped the office chair over and raised Paul's

legs, setting them on the support strut about twelve inches off the floor, then pulled off his coat and laid it across Paul's heaving chest. Wind rattled the windows.

"Jack—"

"Buddy, just take it easy."

Paul's face beaded with sweat. "We've got to stop that virus."

"How? It's already loaded."

Paul pointed his good thumb weakly at his dead torturer. "Chuckles the Clown over there told me it wouldn't activate until Dalfan stock begins early trading at seven a.m. tomorrow. If we can call the CIO at the Hong Kong exchange before then, he can isolate it, clean it out—at least not activate it."

"Phones are down. The storm is beating the hell out of everybody and everything around here until ten a.m. tomorrow, according to the BBC."

"What about your embassy?" Lian asked, taping Paul's fingers. "We can try and drive there."

"Even if we reached it, and if anybody in authority is still there, they probably can't call out, either."

"The weather service said the storm was stalling," Lian said. "There are still flights out of Kuala Lumpur, north of here."

"Which means Malaysia cell phones and other services are probably still up." Jack knew there were a U.S. embassy and a CIA station located there. That's where he needed to go. "How long is the drive?"

"On a normal day? Three and a half hours, four with traffic."

Jack checked his watch. "There's just under seven

hours left." He glanced back out the window at the raging storm. "I have to try."

Paul saw the storm, too. "Of course we have to try."

"'We'? There's no 'we' here," Jack said. There was a slim chance of making it in weather like this. Maybe even less chance of surviving it.

Lian taped Paul's last finger. "You must stay here and rest. If you go into shock, you can die."

"Try and stop me, Ms. Fairchild." Paul started to rise.

Jack laid a hand on his chest. "I've got this."

Paul batted his hand away. "Forget that. You aren't the one that got played like a ten-cent kazoo. Besides, look at you."

Jack's upper-right shirtsleeve was bloody where he'd been hit.

"Let me see that," Lian said. She pulled a razor-sharp blade out of the medical kit and cut away Jack's shirtsleeve.

"Not too bad," she said. "Just a graze. Your skin is torn, but there isn't any muscle or bone damage. Does it hurt?"

Jack's adrenaline had worn off. "Feels like someone hit me with a branding iron."

"Give me a minute."

Lian swiftly cleaned and dressed Jack's wound. "Besides the antibiotics, I'm applying a topical analgesic. Hopefully that will help with the pain."

"It already does. Thanks."

"We'll have to keep an eye on it, but I don't think it will be a problem." She held up the cut-away sleeve. "Sorry about that."

Paul handed Jack his coat as he sat up with a grunt. "You'll need this."

"I wish you'd stay put," Jack said, as he helped Paul to his feet.

"I wish a lot of things, Jack." Paul examined his bandaged fingers. "And right now I wish I had a cup of tea."

"We don't have a vehicle," Lian said.

"Their van was out front. One of these guys must have the keys."

"I'm gonna find my pistol," Paul said, referring to the pistol Jack had given him earlier, as he reached into the coat pocket of his torturer. He found the pint-sized Makarov and a diplomatic passport—Bulgarian. It said the man's name was Petrov. Paul doubted it. He shoved it into his pants pocket anyway. He saw a smart leather satchel standing in the corner but didn't think to check it. He didn't know that after he had passed out from the pain, Wolz had made a call on a satellite phone to Zvezdev and, when he'd finished, put the sat phone back in the satchel.

Jack and Lian searched pockets, too. Jack traded his Makarov for the nine-mil Glock Lian's man had carried. He checked the mag. Thirteen rounds. Luckily, the man carried a second, fully loaded magazine with another fifteen rounds.

"Found them!" Lian shouted, holding the key ring high.

"Let's roll."

## 66

### SOFIA, BULGARIA

Worry was Zvezdev's best friend.

He hadn't survived KGB handlers, CSS purges, or criminal syndicate killers by being overly optimistic. He always assumed everybody at all times was trying to fuck him.

Because they usually were.

Which was why Zvezdev sat in his private office in his expansive estate, drumming his fingers on the gilded desk, worrying.

His call to Ri fifteen minutes ago was quite satisfying. Thanks to Wolz, the mission was complete. Zvezdev held no illusions about his relationship with the North Korean spymaster. If he had failed, Ri's agents would have already stormed into his house, killed his guards, and bundled him off to a safe house for some gruesome fate he didn't even want to contemplate.

Instead, Ri assured him that the second half of his enormous payment—in gold bullion, no less—would be deposited into a Cayman Islands bank vault within twenty-four hours, per their arrangement. Zvezdev confirmed by phone with his English banker that the transaction was pending. *All good.*

What worried Zvezdev was Wolz's earlier call, asking for permission to kill Jack Ryan, Jr., and Lian Fairchild. Zvezdev told him that killing Jack Ryan would only bring the wrath of his father, a capable and violent man. His orders from Ri were explicit: the mission was to be accomplished on time, and with no way to trace the crime to him. Zvezdev had done the best job he could to cover his tracks, and he assumed that the impending collapse of the world's stock markets would cause further confusion and delay for any investigators digging into the matter. But murdering the President's son would bring the full force and attention of the entire U.S. federal government into the case, and that was to be avoided. So Jack Ryan, Jr., lived.

And that's what worried him.

Zvezdev scratched his gray beard. Leave it to a worm like Rhodes to shield himself behind another man. It was actually a smart play to get Jack Ryan, Jr., involved in his scheme, Zvezdev admitted. But Jack Ryan, Jr., was a real pain in his ass now.

Wolz's listening devices planted inside the guesthouse revealed that not only did Brown know the real purpose of the USB but he had informed Ryan and Fairchild.

Zvezdev sighed. He should've let Wolz kill them both. That was a mistake. Brown was dead, at least. Besides his fee, Wolz insisted he be given free rein with the fat accountant. It was a small price to pay, as far as Zvezdev was concerned. He laughed.

"But a big price for Brown."

Of course, there was nothing that Ryan could do about the situation now. The virus was planted. All Ri had to do was wait for less than seven hours and his plan to collapse the world economy would be realized.

But Jack Ryan, Jr., would run his mouth. The line would be drawn back from the virus to Rhodes, and then to him, if Rhodes rolled over.

And he would.

Even if he killed Rhodes now, he was still in danger of being discovered. Ri wouldn't like that.

Now Zvezdev *really* worried.

Ryan and Fairchild had to die.

Zvezdev called Wolz again.

And again his sat phone didn't pick up.

Was the satellite service down because of the storm? No. Sat phones were designed for things like storms. If Wolz and his team weren't answering, it meant something was wrong.

And that something was Ryan. He was still alive. Had to be.

Did Ryan know about the seven a.m. launch?

No. How could he?

But what if he did?

Ryan would call for help. But he hadn't called the U.S. embassy or the CIA station in Singapore up until now; otherwise, they would be involved.

Perhaps Ryan couldn't make the call. And if he couldn't, what would he do?

*What would I do?*

*I'd drive to somewhere where I could get help.*

Zvezdev opened up his laptop and pulled up the storm tracker and latest weather report, then opened a second window and pulled up Google Maps.

Zvezdev swore bitterly.

He hadn't told Ri about the presence of Jack Ryan, Jr. The less Ri knew about the affair, the better. But now he had to know. It would be an awkward exchange. But necessary.

He picked up his phone and called Ri, worried that the American was about to cross into Malaysia and fuck them both hard.

Ri had to stop Jack Ryan.

Now.

## SINGAPORE

Lian explained that the shortest route from Dalfan headquarters to Kuala Lumpur was also the northern-most, and most likely to keep them out of trouble. They needed to take the Seletar Expressway (SLE) to the Bukit Timah Expressway (BKE) and cross the Johor causeway into Malaysia. Without GPS, Jack had no idea where to go, and Lian's knowledge of the roadway system was probably better anyway, so she drove. She told Paul she wouldn't let him come if he didn't agree to lie down in the back of the van and keep his feet elevated. He complied without protest.

It took them more than two hours to traverse the distance. They kept to the SLE as far as they could, dodging dead vehicles, downed trees, power lines, and finally a sinkhole, where they had to abandon the expressway for narrow side streets. On one occasion, Jack had to get out of the van to move an air-conditioning unit that had toppled into the road, and on another, he and Lian both needed to get out and push a stalled vehicle out of the way.

They got back on the SLE and finally arrived at the BKE junction, where a battery-powered road sign flashed that the Johor causeway was shut down.

"Now what?" Jack asked. "Swim?"

"In this weather? No. There's another crossing point west of here."

"How far?"

"At this rate, forty minutes."

An hour and forty-three minutes later they arrived at the Tuas Checkpoint, the gateway to the only other crossing point over the Johor River from Singapore to Malaysia. The Second Link causeway was almost a mile and a half long.

The only problem was that the Tuas Checkpoint—a customs facility—was shut down, according to the sign.

Even if it wasn't closed, they couldn't pass. The three lanes that fed into the checkpoint were completely jammed with hundreds of abandoned vehicles—some of them half turned around as panicked drivers foolishly tried to reverse direction in the one-way traffic.

Even the bus lane was jammed with abandoned vehicles. Everyone was gone, too—only vehicles remained. It reminded Jack of a giant painting he once saw at a county fair, *The Rapture*, only without the crashing airplanes and spirits flying into the sky.

"We're done," Paul said, sitting up. Rain slashed against the windows and thudded on the steel panels. The noise was deafening, and nearly maddening.

"Can you walk?" Jack asked.

Paul nodded. "Sure. Just don't ask me to run."

"What's the plan?" Lian asked.

Jack checked his watch. They had just under four hours to complete the journey and make contact with somebody who could stop the virus. "If the causeway was closed because of the storm, then all of this traffic got trapped. But there might still be a way over. Follow me."

Jack and Lian each supported Paul by the arms as they walked the hundred yards as fast as they could in the driving rain between the lanes of abandoned cars and trucks. They reached the sheltered concourse soaking wet but relieved to escape the ceaseless downpour. The open-air building looked like a giant airplane hangar without walls.

"Now what?" Lian asked. There were dozens of vehicles abandoned in here, too: the first ones prevented from crossing the causeway.

"Let's get to the head of the line." Jack pushed forward through the terminal, passing a small booth enclosed in one-way black glass. As the three of them scrambled by the door, a uniformed Immigration and Checkpoints Authority official bolted out of the tiny station. His blue shoulder boards bore silver sergeant's chevrons.

"What are you doing here? There's a big storm! Can't you see?"

"Where is everyone else, Sergeant?" Lian asked. Her

command voice caught the officer by surprise. Lian had passed through the Tuas Checkpoint many times. Normally, there was a small army of uniformed officers and civilian immigration officials to process the tens of thousands of people passing through here each day.

"Most went home to their families. Others are over in Terminal One. I stayed behind out here to keep an eye on things. Who are you?"

"We need to get to Kuala Lumpur, right now," Jack said.

"You're not going anywhere in this weather. The causeway is shut down until noon tomorrow. You can camp out in Terminal One with the other stranded motorists."

Jack's hands clenched. He hated the thought of clocking a cop just doing his duty. But too much was at stake, and they needed to get across the causeway.

Lian saw Jack's fists clenching, too.

She stepped between Jack and the ICA officer, flashing him her SPF reserve badge and explaining who she was.

The man examined her credentials closely, then shrugged. "You still can't cross the causeway. Too dangerous. The river is very high. Two cars were already thrown over the side earlier today." The sergeant waved his hands in the air to illustrate his point.

Lian stepped closer. "It's a national emergency. I'll take full responsibility."

"I can't."

Lian shoved her pistol in the man's face. "I'm sorry to have to do this."

The man's eyes got wide as eggs. "Don't shoot!"

"Just get back in your office and you'll be fine."

The man nodded furiously and backed into his booth, Jack and the others following him. Jack restrained him with ICA zip-cuffs while Lian kept the gun on the frightened officer. She apologized for the inconvenience, assuring him that what they were doing was necessary, and explained that tying him up was only a precaution against him calling ahead to stop them.

"We're not going to hurt you," Lian said.

"But there's one more thing we have to do," Jack said, towering over the man.

The officer looked like he was going to cry.


Jack headed for the far side of the checkpoint, following a line of abandoned cars queued up to cross but not allowed to because of the storm. He pushed the alarm button on the key fob. Lights flashed on a blue Honda Odyssey parked in front, right where the officer told him it would be. He felt bad taking the man's van, but they needed an accessible vehicle.

"There." Jack pointed, and killed the alarm.

The three of them made their way to the sergeant's vehicle and climbed in. Jack knew that modern cars were nearly impossible to hot-wire, despite what TV crime shows suggested.

This time Jack took the wheel. A wooden barrier blocked the Honda's forward movement. Its headlights pointed directly at the rising causeway and what he assumed in the dark was the Malaysian peninsula on the far end.

Jack cranked the engine over and the headlights lit up. Rain slashed through the high beams.

"Only a mile and half across, right?" Jack asked.

"Go as fast as you can. There won't be any cars out there. Should be clear," Lian said.

Jack nodded. "Like driving through a car wash."

"A really long car wash," Paul added. "A car wash that can kill you." He pointed forward. "How do we get around that barrier?"

Jack floored the gas and crashed through it.

**68**

The fuel-injected Honda accelerated briskly up the incline of the three-lane causeway, despite the fierce winds.

Jack wasn't sure how much water was on the road; even on the incline, it was pouring down the asphalt. Hydroplaning would be fatal on this road at high speeds, especially if they flipped off the bridge and into the river. He backed off to sixty kilometers per hour.

All Jack could see was the road in front of him and the sheets of rain blowing nearly sideways through the high beams. There weren't any lights on the Malaysian side. He didn't know whether that meant they'd lost power, too, or there just weren't any.

The rain sprayed against the side of the van like a fire hose. Jack fought the wheel as the cyclonic winds tried to shove the Odyssey across the three northbound lanes. A few minutes later he sensed more than saw when they crested the incline and began the descent toward the Malaysian border. He kept his speed steady.

The causeway flattened out. It was a straightaway shot to the other side, but they were closer to the raging Johor River than before, surging just below the barriers.

"Less than half a kilometer to go!" Lian shouted, smiling.

The van shuddered as it plowed through a puddle of standing water. For a second Jack felt as if the van was airborne—or maybe it was just his ass coming out of the seat. His guts tingled as if he were in free fall, but he corrected the steering, and the wheels found secure pavement again.

"Whoa!" Paul shouted from the backseat.

Jack saw that Lian still had one hand clutched on the "Oh, shit!" handle above her head and the other braced against his seat. She wasn't smiling now.

"Any cell signal yet?" Jack shouted back to Paul.

Paul stared at the phone in his hand. "Not yet."

Jack's eyes focused on the road in front of him. The high beams reflected in the heavy raindrops like a million tiny silver mirrors. It was distracting, almost blinding. He tapped the lights to low beam just in time to see the looming shape rocketing toward them over the rail.

Lian screamed as the wave smashed into the van like the fist of God, crashing on Jack's side and throwing the vehicle in the opposite direction, lifting the van off of its two right wheels. It slammed into the concrete barrier on the far side before it could tip all the way over.

Glass shattered and steel crunched when the Odyssey hit the barrier. The surging rush of water groaned against Jack's door. The glass near his face cracked but didn't break as water seeped in through the edges of the door. The van's engine stalled, but the headlights stayed on.

"Everybody okay?" Jack shouted as he twisted the ignition key and pumped the gas.

"All good," Paul said. "Storm surge."

Jack shot a glance at Lian. She nodded. "Fine."

Jack turned the key again. The engine wouldn't fire. "We're not going anywhere in this thing."

"What do we do?" Lian asked.

"Can't stay here. If another wave comes, it might push us over the side," Paul said.

"And we're running out of time," Jack said. He could see the end of the causeway up ahead. "Five, six hundred feet. We can do this."

The three exchanged glances. If another wave came when they were on foot, they were dead.

**69**

Let's go!" Jack pushed against his door, but it was wedged shut. He shouldered against it three times before it gave way. He jumped out and turned around to help Lian crawl over his seat to get out. Paul manhandled the sliding passenger door open, breaking the handle in the process.

For a moment the three of them faced east into the howling storm, hunched into the wind that was trying to knock them down. They held their hands up to protect their eyes from the stinging rain.

"Stay close to the rail," Jack said. "And let's haul ass!"

Lian and Jack draped Paul's arms around their shoulders, and the three of them managed a stuttering half jog. A hundred steps into their journey, Paul shouted, "Wait!"

They stopped in the lashing wind.

"What's wrong?" Jack asked.

Paul frantically patted himself down. "The drive! I don't think I have the drive!"

"Where did you leave it?" Lian asked.

"We've got to go!" Jack said. "We can't worry about it!" He grabbed Paul's arm, but Paul pulled away.

"I'm not leaving without that drive. It's the only evidence I have against Rhodes."

"Forget Rhodes."

"And whoever else is behind him," Paul added. He turned and started hobbling back toward the van.

Jack cursed to himself, then grabbed Paul by the jacket. "You and Lian keep going forward. I'll run back and take a look."

Paul frowned, conflicted. Finally he said, "Hurry." He draped an arm over Lian's shoulder, and the two of them paced their way toward the Malaysian border.

Jack lowered his head and ran full-tilt back toward the bright headlights of the dead Odyssey. He was crabbing against the wind, but he was making a lot better time than the other two.

Paul's sliding door was still open. Jack leaped in. The dome light still shone and the van's tan leather interior made it easy to see. He didn't see the USB, though. He jammed his hand between the seat cushions but didn't feel anything. He knelt down and checked the floor. His fingers bumped into a small flat object underneath the seat. The USB drive.

Relieved, Jack shoved it deep into his pants pocket, turned, and ran for the others.

Lian was strong but not invincible, and running under the weight of the obese American against the wind was wearing her out. They were less than two hundred feet from the shore when their pace slowed to a walk. She thought Jack would've caught up with them by now.

"Wait a second," she said. The two of them stopped and turned around, both gasping for breath.

Lian saw Jack's tall frame running toward them, silhouetted in the headlights of the van.

Saw the giant hand of the wave sweep across the barrier.

Watched him disappear.

Lian screamed and ran toward Jack.

The wave that hit him was smaller than the one that had smashed the van, but it was big enough to pick him up and slam him against the concrete barrier. By some miracle it hadn't lifted him higher, otherwise he would have been swept over the side.

By the time she reached him, the wave had disappeared. He lay on the asphalt, crushed against the concrete barrier, coughing up water and gasping for air. She dropped down beside him.

"Jack! Where are you hurt?"

"I think I broke my arm."

Jack caught his breath and cursed. He cradled his left forearm.

"Let me see that." She gently touched his forearm, examining the length of it. He winced violently.

"It's probably broken, but the break hasn't punctured the skin. Can you walk?"

Paul limped into the headlight beams, gasping for air. "I thought you were dead, Jack."

"You and me both. Let's get moving before the next one takes us all out."

Jack struggled to raise himself up, but he was badly shaken. Lian started to help, but Paul pushed her aside. Despite the searing pain in his left hand he grabbed Jack with both fists and lifted his heavy body to his unsteady feet.

Jack threw his good right arm around Paul's neck and the three of them hurried the best they could, Jack setting the pace, their eyes fixed on the safety of the far shore. Lian kept swiping the matted wet hair out of her face, and Paul's limp was more pronounced than ever. He was determined to stay at Jack's side and keep him from falling again, no matter the pain. Jack's injuries were his fault, and the guilt fired his limping steps.

Jack shuffled more than walked, pressing his broken left forearm against his chest, wincing with every step, praying that another wave wasn't looming in the dark, waiting to devour them.

# 70

## KUALA LUMPUR, MALAYSIA

The Reconnaissance General Bureau agents were rousted from their beds behind the crumbling walls of the DPRK embassy compound at twenty minutes after midnight by the RGB chief of station himself. The panic in his eyes underscored the urgency in his barked orders.

The station chief had only seven men in his command at the embassy. The task was straightforward enough: Find three spies who were in transit to Kuala Lumpur from southern Malaysia.

Photo IDs of the three were handed to the agents.

"Won't finding these three people on a peninsula inhabited by thirty million people prove difficult, sir?"

The chief parroted the explanation given to him. The three spies were almost certainly traveling by car, and two of the three spies were white. Moreover, no one was driving on the roads this time of the night, especially under current conditions. So, in fact, the assignment was not as difficult as it seemed.

"Agreed?"

"Agreed!"

The chief informed his men that he had received their deployment orders directly from Pyongyang. They were to split their forces between the only two crossing points, the eastern Johor causeway and the western Second Link. The mission was also specified:

Recover the USB drive.

Kill Brown.

Kill Fairchild.

"And most important, capture Jack Ryan!"

The four grim RGB men in the Kia Sorento with DPRK diplomatic license plates sped through the early-morning gloom and the drenching rains at high speed—far higher than caution warranted in the current conditions. The drive to the Second Link causeway across from Tuas Checkpoint at normal speeds would take almost three and a half hours. They needed to beat that time, and the late start didn't help.

Fortunately, the roads were clear at this time of the morning, and traffic warnings had urged Malaysians to avoid driving altogether until noon tomorrow, if possible.

The North Korean driver pushed the four-cylinder to its maximum, breaking far beyond the speed limit. The police wouldn't dare pull them over with their diplomatic plates—and no police were to be seen, anyway.

The edge of the unusual storm had reached Kuala Lumpur, but it was not nearly as destructive as it had been reported in Singapore and points south. Though the road conditions were dangerous, each man in the vehicle knew that death in a fiery car crash was preferable to what awaited them if they failed their mission.

## SOUTHERN MALAYSIA

Jack, Paul, and Lian finally reached the far side, safely away from the river but still pummeled by the ceaseless rain and wind. They stopped to catch their breath. No cars were around. Certainly no emergency vehicles. If anybody saw them make the crossing, they weren't doing anything to help them now.

"Now what?" Paul asked. "Keep walking?"

"What else can we do?" Jack said. He turned to Lian. "What time is it?" Not only had the wave broken his arm, it had busted his watch.

"Three twenty-eight. Three hours and thirty-two minutes to go." Lian shook her head. "We need to find a car, fast."

"You find the drive, Jack?" Paul asked.

"It's in my pocket."

"Sorry about that. I'm sorry about everything—"

"Just buy me a beer and we'll call it even, okay? In the meantime, we need to find some wheels."

"The Honda's lights are still on," Paul said. "Won't somebody come out and take a look?"

Jack shook his head. "Not in these conditions. Too dangerous. We can't wait around for them to show up. We're running out of clock."

"I know where we might find a car," Lian said.

# 71

Five minutes later, the drenched and weary threesome stood on the empty elevated expressway overlooking what appeared to be a used-car lot. The fenced property bordered on a two-lane road that ran east–west through a tunnel beneath the expressway.

A flash of lightning revealed more detail.

"Criminy. It's a pick-n-pull," Paul said.

"What?" Lian asked.

"A junkyard," Jack explained, as booming thunder echoed overhead.

Paul counted thirty cars in the yard, but they were all parted out. Some were stacked three and four high, wheels missing, engines gone. A large steel garage stood at the back of the lot.

"Well, at least there are plenty of cars to choose from," Jack said, grinning and grimacing at the same time.

Lian said, "Let's get out of the rain."

"Maybe there's a clunker down there that actually

runs," Paul said hopefully. He eyed the steep, grassy embankment. It wouldn't be easy for Jack to traverse it. Farther up, there was fencing along the expressway, which prevented a descent, and the embankment got even steeper, so this was as good as it was going to get.

Paul's eye caught sight of movement north, up on the expressway. He pointed. "Is that a car?"

Jack's eyes narrowed, trying to focus. Two miles away, a pair of headlights barreled toward them.

"They're flying," Jack said.

"An emergency vehicle?" Paul wondered.

"No emergency flashers? Not likely," Lian said.

"Then who?" Paul asked.

"Something's not right," Jack said.

A flash of lightning cracked overhead.

The vehicle's xenon high beams popped on, pointing right at them.

Lian shouted, "Run!"

A flash of lightning illumined the three figures standing on the expressway.

All four North Koreans saw them, but it was the section chief in the front seat who shouted and pointed at them.

The driver popped the xenon high beams on and stomped the accelerator to the floorboard. The two men in back drew their pistols and checked mags just as the Sorento hit a puddle and the SUV hydroplaned.

A collective *"Ah!"* rose from the three men not driving, but the driver was too busy concentrating. He avoided the natural inclination to tap the brakes; instead, he took his foot off the accelerator and pointed the steering wheel at a dry patch farther up.

The section chief shouted, "Faster!"

"I can't, sir! Too wet!"

The station chief cocked his pistol and held it to the driver's head. "FASTER!"

**72**

Paul tracked the Sorento's movement for a moment before turning his attention to the embankment. He put one foot down and planted it before easing Jack down into his position.

"I figure we've got a two-minute head start on those guys," Paul said.

"Lian, run ahead and scout that place out for us, will you?" Jack said through gritted teeth.

"Done." She bolted like a gazelle down the slick grassy hill, heading for the steel building. In a few moments her feet splashed in the flooded two-lane road running perpendicular beneath the expressway.

Paul cut a diagonal across the face of the embankment to lessen the angle, fighting to keep Jack upright. Jack slipped a few times in the descent, but Paul's sturdy grip kept the two of them on their feet.

Jack glanced up when he heard the chain-link fence

rattle in front of them. He barely made out Lian's figure dropping over the top of the fence and into the yard.

Paul and Jack had finally reached the bottom of the embankment when they heard brakes screeching hard above them.

"Let's haul ass," Jack said. The two of them picked up the pace to the sound of steel banging on steel, rattling the fence wire in front of them.

Three steps farther and they heard voices shouting in Korean above their heads. Paul instinctively turned a slight right, away from a direct line to the fencing, assuming the Koreans had guns and were taking aim—

Pistols cracked from on high, muffled by the sound of the rain. Extra-large splashes boiled up on either side of them—hail or bullets, Paul wasn't sure. More gunfire erupted, but this time in front of them as Lian took aim at the SUV high up on the embankment behind the fencing.

"Come on!" she shouted at Paul and Jack, as they ran the last hundred feet toward the open fence in a three-legged gait. Lian provided more covering fire.

Jack and Paul hobbled through. Jack's foot nearly stumbled on the big and rusted pipe fitter's wrench Lian had used to bust the chain.

Lian stood and watched the Koreans jump back into their SUV and rocket away, then ran in and shut the gate behind them and wrapped what was left of the chain around the gatepost. She pointed at the side entrance door to the steel garage.

Paul felt Jack's weight give under his arm; he was definitely losing steam. Jack needed rest, badly, and a doctor.

Ten yards away Paul spotted an electric golf cart parked next to a giant yellow forklift with huge front wheels—no doubt used to move and stack the junked cars.

They hobbled past the empty frame of an old Volkswagen Beetle before pushing through the doorway, and Lian slammed the door shut behind them.

"They're gone," Lian said, panting. She flicked on a flashlight she'd found on a workbench.

"What do you mean they're gone?" Jack asked.

Lian flashed the light around the open garage, checking it out as she spoke. "They just drove away."

"No way." Jack fell into a folding metal chair, exhausted, cradling his forearm with his good hand. "They're not leaving; they're moving."

Paul didn't like the sound of Jack's fading voice. In Lian's flashlight, Jack's skin looked ashen.

"What do we have here?" Lian approached a squatting shape under a heavy cloth in the middle of the neatly ordered garage. She yanked it off. "Wow."

It was a vintage motorcycle with a sidecar, painted olive drab. Lian read the logo on the teardrop gas tank. "Royal Enfield."

"That's an Indian bike," Jack said. "Guy must be a collector."

Lian flashed her light over it again. "It has keys, too."

"Moving where, Jack?" Paul asked.

"What?"

"Where are they moving to?" Paul repeated.

"They'll try and find a way down here, and finish the job."

Paul turned around and faced the door. "We passed a

traffic tunnel that runs underneath the expressway. If they can find that road, they can get down here."

"There's a turnaround three kilometers north on the expressway," Lian said. "The road out front of this building connects to it."

"That gives us four minutes, tops," Paul said.

Lian unscrewed the cap. "Plenty of petrol."

"If they get down here, we're all dead," Paul said.

"At least we have guns," Jack said.

"But we don't know how many more of them there are, and they might be getting reinforcements," Paul said.

Jack nodded toward the Royal Enfield. "Can you drive one of those?"

"I can," Lian said. She slung a leg over the motorcycle, turned on the gas, switched the key, and kicked it over. The small engine fired up instantly. She smiled. "There's room for all three of us."

Jack stood and limped over to the chain that opened the rolling back door of the building. He kicked away the latch that locked the door in place and started pulling on the chain as Lian rolled the bike toward the rear exit. He spoke to Paul over his shoulder.

"You and Lian hit the road out front and head due west. It's got to connect somewhere—"

"It does," Lian said. "About eight kilometers up the road it curves around north, and in another twenty it reconnects with the expressway." She looked at her watch. "We can't make it all the way to Kuala Lumpur in time, but maybe we can get within working cell-phone distance and make a call."

"That's the plan, then. I'll stay here and hold them—" Jack collapsed in mid-sentence. Paul caught him.

"Help me get him in the sidecar," Paul said.

Lian jumped off the bike and lifted Jack's feet as Paul cradled him by the upper torso. They wrestled Jack's heavy, limp frame into the sidecar and secured him.

"We need to get him to hospital now—and make that call." Lian jumped onto the saddle and scooted forward. "Get on behind me and let's go!"

Paul pointed at the motorcycle. "That's a lawnmower engine. Jack and I have over five hundred pounds between us. Those guys in the car will catch us and run us down on that thing."

"Paul—"

Paul checked the one mag he had in his Makarov. "You've got three minutes max now. Get going."

"Paul?" Lian's eyes finished the question.

Paul shoved his cell phone into Lian's pocket. "Gerry Hendley's direct number is on there. Call him the second you get a signal. Tell him to contact the CIO at the Hang Seng—or anybody else in charge. He'll make it happen—and then get Jack to a hospital. Now go!"

Lian grabbed Paul's jowly face and kissed him on the cheek, then gunned the engine and roared out of the garage.

Paul didn't watch her go. He hobbled to the front door, running through the plan in his mind. He knew exactly what he needed to do.

He also knew there wasn't enough time left to do it.

# 73

The North Korean driver made the hard right turn onto the narrow two-lane road and gunned the engine, pointing the front of the Sorento directly at the black hole of the traffic tunnel five hundred yards up ahead.

The four of them had already worked out a plan to assault the steel building. The driver would crash the SUV through the cyclone fence, then the four of them would egress and approach the building from four sides. Besides their pistols, they carried two shotguns, an assault rifle, and a dozen flash-bangs in the trunk—more than enough to get the job done.

The Sorento bounced on the uneven pavement as it rocketed toward the narrow one-way tunnel. The other tunnel for traffic in the opposite direction was clearly flooded, as was the other road. *No matter,* the driver thought. *I need only one.*

The SUV plowed full speed into the tunnel. In a

hundred yards he'd be through, then he'd have to angle the vehicle right toward the fence. He gripped the wheel tighter and pressed the accelerator—

The driver froze for just a moment as he tried to make out the hulking shape turning the corner at the far end of the tunnel. He slammed the brakes.

Too late.


**P**aul stomped the big forklift's throttle into the floor-board as soon as he made the turn into the tunnel. The turbo-charged Cummins diesel engine roared, launching the big high-capacity forklift straight into the narrow passage, its long steel forks high off the ground. Paul hoped he'd guessed the height right.

He had.

The left fork plowed through the Sorento's wind-shield, severing the driver's screaming face in half, just above the bridge of his nose. The section chief in the passenger seat ducked at the last second; the right fork harmlessly sheared the headrest off his seat but nearly speared the man behind him.

The forklift slammed into the SUV with a shuddering crash that rattled Paul's teeth and nearly snapped his neck as he gunned the motor again, powering up the lift and raising the Sorento by the roof until it smashed against the tunnel ceiling, pinning it there.

The three surviving Koreans shouted as they kicked open their doors and tumbled several feet onto the wet pavement below while Paul scrambled out of the left side of the cab. He pointed his Makarov forward and took aim at the section chief, sprawled on the pavement, his ankles broken, raising his weapon. But Paul fired first and put two rounds into the man's skull, killing him instantly.

The two surviving Koreans fired back. Bullets ricocheted off the tunnel walls and spanged against the forklift.

Something punched Paul in the ribs. He touched his side. His hand was bloody.

The agent behind the dead driver had dropped to his knees and was trying to pass unnoticed around the far side of the forklift. Paul saw the top of his head through the cab and fired through the glass but missed. He turned and ran around the back side of the forklift where the Korean had appeared, gun up. The Korean's weapon fired twice at close range, tearing into Paul's shoulder, shredding muscle and shattering bone. Paul's hand dropped the gun. But the pain turned to rage. He charged forward with a shout, thrusting his left hand into the Korean's throat, crushing his windpipe with his bandaged fingers and smashing his skull against the wall in a spray of blood.

Gunshots exploded from the back of the tunnel. Paul lifted the Korean and held him like a shield as he charged back into the tunnel toward the gunfire. Bullets thudded against the corpse as Paul lunged forward. But copper-jacketed rounds chopped into his shins like a fire ax until his legs collapsed beneath him. He tumbled to the asphalt with his shattered cargo.

Paul rolled over onto his back in time to see the gaping black muzzle of a pistol in his face, and the final, deafening flash—

The surviving Korean spat on Paul's corpse, then holstered his pistol. He pulled a kerchief from his pocket and wiped the bloody gore off his face. His ears rang from the gunfight, the sound magnified in the tunnel. He could hardly think. He walked to the edge of the tunnel and lit a cigarette to clear his head, staring at the empty road and the endless rain.

Now what?

No car, no cell signal, and the other two spies were nowhere to be seen. He'd failed the mission.

His life was over.

He turned around and stood over the corpse of the fat American, a single bullet hole in the center of his forehead. He flicked the cigarette away and knelt down close to the body, examining the face.

The Korean shook his head, haunted by the dead man's smile.

**74**

## FALLS CHURCH, VIRGINIA

**R**hodes shut the burner phone and tossed it onto his desk. Zvezdev hadn't picked up in two days. The fat bastard was hanging him out to dry.

Rhodes pulled the Kimber .380 from his wall safe and checked the magazine, then set it carefully on his desk next to the phone. He pulled out his legal passport and a counterfeit one he'd purchased a week ago, just in case the whole thing went sideways. *You don't have a plan until you have a plan to escape,* his father had taught him. Of course, that was in regard to fieldwork, but it was proving damn useful today.

It suddenly occurred to him that he wouldn't see his son grow up—at least, not for the next several years. But then again, his own father had been absent for most of his childhood, and he'd made out all right. Fatherhood, like most things in life, was overrated. The little nipper would be just fine.

His wife? Well, a pretty girl for sure, but just another

piece of ass. He was glad to be getting rid of her—for as little as she put out, she ran up a lot of bills. A twinge of guilt crept across his conscience. She'd have to file for bankruptcy, of course, and would undoubtedly lose the house. She might even have to get a job, poor thing. He couldn't pay child support, let alone alimony. His bank accounts were drained, his trust fund depleted, and all of the offshore money he'd invested in his bet against Dalfan stock was gone now.

And in an hour, he would be, too.

But then again, she was screwing her Pilates instructor. A smile crept across his face as he imagined her shock when she finally figured out that he had fled the country and left her holding the bag.

Rhodes startled as the library door swung open. He turned around.

"Jack? What are you doing here—my God, son. What happened to you?"

Jack Ryan, Jr., stepped up to Rhodes's desk, his battered face as grim as death. His left forearm was in a cast, and his hands were badly bruised and scraped.

"Surprised, Senator?"

"I thought you were in Singapore."

"I was. So was Paul."

Rhodes glanced over Jack's broad shoulder. "Where is he?"

"Dead."

Rhodes blanched. "Dead?"

"Don't play games, Wes. You called me and warned me he was in 'hot water,' remember?"

Rhodes had, in fact, forgotten that he'd called Jack in

a panic. *Stupid*. He took the measure of his merciless eyes. No point in lying to him now.

Rhodes fell into his chair behind his desk, and stared out of the wide bay window across the snow-covered lawn. "I really didn't mean for that to happen." Rhodes's imperious voice faded to a whisper.

"He took out three North Korean RGB agents single-handedly, saving my ass, and Lian's."

Rhodes sat up. "North Koreans?"

"You should know. You sent them."

Rhodes shook his head. "No. I didn't send anybody."

"At least one of us made it back."

"Thank God, Jack. I couldn't bear the thought—"

"Just tell me one thing. Why in the hell would you want to crash the world economy?"

Rhodes scowled in disbelief. "What are you talking about?"

"The USB drive?"

"It was a software program to crash Dalfan stock. I was using it to place a bet against it and cash in." The light turned on in Rhodes's eyes. "At least, that's what I was told."

"Bullshit. But even if you're not lying, you got Paul killed to turn a dirty buck."

"I swear I didn't mean to." Rhodes's face darkened. "Did Paul ever tell you how he and I knew each other?"

"No."

"Take a seat. I'd like to tell you."

"You don't have the time."

"Please. For Paul's sake. I want you to know the kind of man he was."

"Make it quick."

"Paul and I were together in Sofia, Bulgaria, back in the eighties. We both worked for the Company."

"I gathered as much."

"I was on the fast track—born and bred for it, right? Well, I was posted in Berlin until I got busted out of that assignment and demoted to Sofia—"

"Busted for what?"

"The ambassador's wife." Rhodes couldn't suppress a smile. "At his home. In flagrante delicto."

*Asshole,* Jack thought. "You need to finish this."

"So instead of getting fired outright, I was posted to Sofia—a nod to my father, who was still a man of some influence back then. I was warned that it was my one and only chance to redeem myself—a way to work my way back up from the minor leagues. Truth was, I was never really that good at field craft—especially at recruiting local talent—and I was under a lot of pressure to succeed. The one Bulgarian source I managed to develop was a man in the CSS—"

"Who?"

Rhodes read Jack's face again. A lie now was a risk, but burning Zvezdev would be even riskier. "Doesn't matter. Probably not his real name, anyway. Where was I? Oh, yes. So I worked out an arrangement with this contact. He was desperate for computer chips, which I provided, and I was desperate for intel, especially on KGB activities in the region, which he fed me at regular intervals. The only problem was that the intel was weak and not very interesting to Langley. My COS put a lot of pressure on me to up the ante or kiss my career good-bye."

"Where did you get them?"

"My official cover at the embassy was the U.S. and Foreign Commercial Service. I had access to department money, and I knew someone in Silicon Valley who supplied them to me through a shell company."

"And your COS approved of this?"

"He had no idea about it."

"Then you were breaking the law."

"Sure, but I didn't care. I was desperate."

"You were selling high tech to our enemies."

"Trading, not selling. And not all that high tech—CPUs for personal computers, mostly. It was a calculated risk. My Bulgarian contact couldn't get enough of them. Of course, it was actually the East Germans that wanted them, and the bastard I was giving them to was actually selling them to the Germans. Making a killing doing it, too. I didn't care. I just needed the intel he was giving me, and when my chief threatened to ship me back to the States and kill my career, I confronted my contact. Told him I knew he was selling those chips to Berlin for a profit, and that he'd be shot by his KGB handlers if they knew what he was up to. I told him if he didn't help me to pull off a really big score, I'd not only cut off his chip supply, I'd turn him in to Moscow."

"Where did Paul come into all of this?"

"About a week after I confronted my contact, I received a very late call. My Bulgarian friend was on the other end, very excited and scared at the same time. He promised me the biggest intelligence coup of my career—maybe anybody's. He said he had a high-level defector who wanted to come over. The only problem, it had to be done within the next two hours. And to come alone."

Jack frowned. "Sounds like a setup. Why did you believe him?"

"Because he was all about the shekels. He said it would cost me twenty thousand dollars. He knew I couldn't raise that amount of cash on such short notice, but we'd done business together, and he told me he trusted me to get it to him within the week. It sounded legit, so we set a place and time for the meet."

Jack checked his watch. "You've got about a minute, at most."

"For what?"

A look fell over Jack's face. It chilled Rhodes to the bone.

"So, where was I? Oh, yes. Paul. Truth is, I hardly knew him. I think we met once or twice at some interminable staff meeting. We were both with the Company, but he was just an accountant working in a shabby little office in the basement. Well, when I got the call that set the meet, I scrambled downstairs to the basement to grab keys for an old Lada we used for undercover work. The locker where the keys were kept was just outside Paul's office, and there he was, burning the midnight oil, and—"

Rhodes glanced out the window. Two black SUVs pulled up to the curb. Doors opened. Men and women in coats and armored vests marked FBI scrambled out. Rhodes stood, leaning on his desk, panic on his face.

"Jack—"

"What?"

"There must be a way."

"Afraid not."

Rhodes's eyes flitted to his desk for an instant. Jack followed his gaze. The Kimber .380 was only inches from Rhodes's manicured hands.

Jack slid his coat jacket back, revealing a pistol on his hip. "I'm begging you. Pick it up."

"I think not."

"Coward. Pick it up."

Rhodes took a step back from his desk, palms up. "I can't shoot you, Jack. I need you."

"Need me? What for?"

"You're my insurance. This whole affair—you're up to your eyeballs in it. So is your father. Defense contractors? Spies? North Koreans? Your father would never risk the scandal. It would ruin his administration. Call him. Call this whole thing off now, before it's too late."

Two FBI agents marched into the study. One of them held a sheaf of papers in one hand. "Senator Rhodes?"

"Jack? Trust me, this can all go away. Make the call."

Jack shook his head and smiled. "You really don't know my dad, do you? He called the attorney general himself."

"Then why are you here?"

"I was hoping I could save the taxpayers a few dollars."

"Weston Rhodes, this is a warrant for your arrest." The FBI agent tossed it on the desk as the other agent approached Rhodes with a pair of handcuffs. "You have the right to remain silent."

## 75

### SULLY, IOWA

Jack stood at the guest book in the foyer of the old Lutheran church, patting his pockets.

"Lose your pen?"

Jack turned around, surprised. "Yeah."

President Ryan handed Jack his own Zebra F-701 stainless. "Do I want to know how?"

Junior didn't say a word, but Senior recognized the look. Jack took the pen and signed his name on the register. He turned back around and held the pen out to his dad.

"Keep it, son. In case you need it."

"I saw Mary Pat inside. I didn't know you were coming."

"Security wouldn't let me tell you," Senior said, nodding at the two Secret Service agents standing behind him.

"It's usually a three-ring circus when you come to town. How'd you manage to keep this quiet?"

Senior smiled as he signed the register. "The press

plane was accidentally delayed a few hours by an unexpected mechanical inspection."

The first few notes of an old Hammond organ began to play in the sanctuary.

"It's time," Senior said.

The pastor concluded his brief homily and introduced President Ryan, seated in the front row, along with DNI Mary Pat Foley, CIA director Jay Canfield, Gerry Hendley, John Clark, and Jack Junior.

Junior recognized several other retired dignitaries from the IC community farther back in the chapel. He was surprised at their turnout. Was it just a courtesy to his dad?

The doors were closed and guarded inside and out by Secret Service agents as helicopter rotors beat the air above the small country church, keeping overwatch. The President's handlers weren't taking any chances after Mexico City.

President Ryan stepped forward. He paused briefly, laying a hand on the closed casket that stood in front of the altar before ascending the three short steps to the pulpit.

He glanced out over the small gathering of fifteen or so people, mostly gray-haired farmers and dairymen with their sturdy wives, all dressed in their Sunday best. They stared at the President, skeptical and surprised.

Junior felt underdressed in his short-sleeved shirt and tie, but with his arm in a cast and a sling, he couldn't manage a suit. His bruises had all turned to purple and yellow, and his scratches had scabbed over. He looked like he'd fallen through a hay baler. He wondered if these farmers thought so, too.

"It is my honor and privilege to mourn the loss and celebrate the life of Paul Brown with you today," the President began. "You all knew Paul better than I did, but I doubt that anyone here owes a greater personal debt of gratitude to him than me and my family, and I wanted to express that publicly." He turned toward the casket. "Thank you, Paul."

Senior gave the slightest nod to his son, who returned the same.

"Paul Brown was a brilliant, modest, hardworking man who rendered a quiet and selfless service to his country and his friends. Our nation was built on the shoulders of such men and women, and our greatness will be sustained by them as well.

"It may surprise some of you to know that I am not the first American President to praise the name of Paul Brown in a closed-door meeting among family, friends, and colleagues. In 1985, President Ronald Reagan awarded Paul Brown the Distinguished Intelligence Cross, the CIA's equivalent of the Medal of Honor. It is usually only awarded posthumously, but Paul Brown was not usual by any measure. Those that knew him tell me that he never spoke about the honor or the sacrifice that earned it. We only know about the events that transpired so many years ago thanks to the testimony of the only living witness, former Senator Weston Rhodes—"

Ryan glanced over at his son.

"—who unfortunately, owing to personal circumstances, couldn't be with us today. However, I think it's important for you, his family and friends, to better know the kind of man Paul Brown really was.

"Let me begin by reading the text of the speech Ronald Reagan gave when he awarded the DIC to Paul."

Senior removed a sheet of paper from his suit coat and laid it carefully on the pulpit, then put on a pair of reading glasses, perching them on his nose. He glanced up at the audience over the top of them. "I can't imitate the Gipper's voice, but I'm sure you all remember it well enough." He allowed himself a smile, looked back down at his notes, and began to read.

"'My fellow Americans . . .'"

## 76

### SOFIA, BULGARIA
### 1985

Rhodes dashed down the basement stairs straight to the security locker. He spun the tumbler lock until it clicked, then yanked the metal door open. The only keys hanging on the rack were for the old Lada, an underpowered four-cylinder with a slipping clutch and the sex appeal of an outhouse brick. But it was local and clean and his only option. The problem was that he hated driving a stick, and he needed to follow his paper map closely. Better if he had a driver.

Rhodes scratched his head, thinking about his limited options and the ticking clock, when his eye fell on the light shining out from beneath the door at the end of the hall. He hurried down that way. A name plate on the door read PAUL BROWN and FORENSIC ACCOUNTING. He didn't recognize the name. The door was ajar. He pushed it open wider.

The room was no bigger than a broom closet—in fact,

it used to be one, he recalled. A heavyset man sat hunched over a stack of ledger books, scratching notes on a yellow legal pad with one hand and squeezing a pair of hand grippers in the other.

"Excuse me, Paul," Rhodes began.

Paul startled and swiveled around in his banker's chair. "You caught me by surprise. No one's usually around this time of night except for the Marine guards."

Rhodes strode confidently into the room, his hand extended. "You're Paul Brown, aren't you? You probably don't remember me. I think we might have met at an embassy function a while ago. My name is Weston Rhodes."

Paul stood and took his hand, now even more startled that the famous spy, Weston Rhodes, knew his name. He nearly knocked over his steaming cup of tea. "Everybody knows you, Mr. Rhodes. It's an honor—"

Rhodes waved away the compliment. "Nonsense. We all have our parts to play, don't we? Speaking of which, I was wondering if you were terribly busy at the moment."

Paul turned around in his cramped little office, taking in the stacks of ledger books, notepads, cardboard boxes, a typewriter, a personal computer, a dot matrix printer, spreadsheets, and everything else he was using to conduct his current forensic investigation.

"Not really. What can I do for you?"

"Can you drive a stick shift?"

"Every Iowa farm boy does. Why?"

"I've got a little problem, and I need your help."

"Name it."

Rhodes talked their way through the few checkpoints they encountered on the way out of the city, doling out generous wads of paper lev to the Bulgarian policemen, resentful and bitter as always but who nonetheless waved them through as they pocketed the cash in their coats.

Paul sat stiffly in the broken-down driver's seat, his white-knuckled hands clutching the steering wheel like a life preserver, even after they cleared the city.

"You can relax now. This is the easy part," Rhodes said. He took a swig from a flask, then offered it to Paul.

"No, thanks. Never touch the stuff."

"Helps take the edge off," Rhodes said, taking another swig and capping the flask.

"You do this kind of thing all the time?"

"Oh, you know, 'When duty calls' and all of that."

"I think I like accounting better."

"I'd shoot myself if I had to sit in an office all day."

"It's not that bad. Numbers are interesting. They tell a story—"

"Yes, I'm sure they do. Let me check the map."

Paul tried to talk away his nervousness over the course of the next hour, but Rhodes wouldn't have any part of it. He lit a cigarette and filled the cramped cab with smoke. Paul kept waving his hand in front of his face and even rolled his window down in the chill night air, but Rhodes didn't give a damn and smoked one after the other.

The Lada wheezed and creaked over the two-lane asphalt, winding its way up the grade and into wooded farm country. Paul began to fidget. He'd forgotten to use the restroom before they left the embassy, and three cups of tea were battering against his tiny bladder.

"Slow down, I think we're close," Rhodes said, checking the map. "There, the next turn."

Paul slowed to a near stop and eased the sedan onto a rutted dirt road.

"Kill the lights."

"Okay."

They bounced along in first gear for another fifteen minutes, inching along through the ruts in the dark.

"Stop here," Rhodes said. "See it?"

Paul squinted through the filmy windshield. A quarter-mile away, a small rustic farmhouse stood in a clearing, a few lights burning in the windows. A black ZiL-117 was parked out front, the Soviet version of a luxury four-door sedan.

"That's Zvezdev." Rhodes checked his watch. "Excellent. We're ten minutes early." He checked all around them. "No one followed us here, and I don't see anyone around."

"That's good, right?"

"It's just supposed to be me and Zvezdev and the man we're picking up."

"What about me?"

"You're not supposed to be here. I was told to come alone." Rhodes grinned and patted Paul on the shoulder. "I don't always do what I'm told."

Paul nodded. "Where do you want me to park?"

Rhodes pointed away from the farmhouse. "Over there in that stand of trees. Keep your lights off."

Paul pulled in behind a couple thick pines and killed the engine as Rhodes reached into a coat pocket. He handed Paul a pistol.

"You know how to shoot one of these?"

"My dad was a cop." Paul weighed the 9x18mm Makarov in his hand as Rhodes checked the mag on his full-sized Beretta 92. "Why do I need it?"

"You probably don't." Rhodes snatched it back out of Paul's hand. "You'd probably just shoot yourself anyway." Rhodes pocketed the Makarov and reholstered his Beretta. "Just stay in the car and keep quiet until I return. It'll only be a few minutes. Understood?"

Paul nodded, still fidgety.

Rhodes frowned. "Are you all right?"

"I'm fine. I'll be here, ready to roll, when you get back."

Rhodes patted Paul on the shoulder again. "Good man." He carefully opened his door and closed it gently, avoiding making any noise.

Paul watched Rhodes pick his way through the trees and cut over to the road, then march up to the front door of the farmhouse. Rhodes knocked, and a man's shape appeared in the doorway. Paul couldn't hear anything from this far away, but everything must have been okay because he shook hands with the man and the two entered the farmhouse.

Paul rolled down his window. The car was stuffy and smelled like stale cigarette smoke. His bladder screamed. Paul looked around again. Nothing except the trees and the sound of the breeze in the pine needles.

He had to pee.

Paul carefully pulled on the handle and used both hands to open the door to keep it from squeaking, just the way Rhodes had done.

There was a tall bush on the other side of the car, open on one side, like a booth. He made his way over to it, unzipping his fly with each hurried step.

He stood in the middle of the man-sized bush and let go. A piss never felt so good. He directed his stream back and forth against the leaves to minimize the sound and to keep it from puddling. The splash made a little noise, but not much, like crunching leaves. It wasn't long before he was done and wagging himself dry.

But the leaves were still making noise.

Paul froze.

Feet were jogging through the forest, along with whispered, hurried voices.

He waited until the sounds faded before easing his way out of the bush and toward the farmhouse, then hid behind a tree.

Three men took up positions just outside the house. One faced out, his foot on a stump with an ax buried in it. The other two stepped carefully onto the porch, pistols out, hands on the door.

Paul's heart raced. Those had to be Zvezdev's men.

It was a trap.

Rhodes was a dead man.

**77**

Rhodes knocked on the farmhouse door. He was greeted by a smiling Zvezdev.

"Weston! You're early. Come in."

The two men shook hands and Rhodes stepped in. The door closed behind him.

A gun stuck in his ribs.

"What's this?" Rhodes asked, raising his hands.

Zvezdev patted him down with one gloved hand and pulled Rhodes's two guns out with his other, shoving both into his right coat pocket.

Rhodes surveyed the rustic living room. Rough-hewn boards, hand-woven carpets, homemade furniture. Simple, but large and comfortable. It would be considered primitive in any Western country, but by Bulgarian standards it was better than most.

"Guns make me nervous. Or should I say other people's guns." Zvezdev holstered his pistol and smiled again.

Rhodes lowered his hands. "You had me worried there for a moment."

"Then how about a *rakia* to calm your nerves?" Zvezdev crossed over to a weathered sideboard, the only factory-made piece in the room. He poured two glasses.

"Don't mind if I do. Nice place. Yours?"

"Recently acquired." He handed a glass to Rhodes.

"ZiL still running well?"

"I'd rather have a Buick, but what can you do? *Nazdráve.*"

"*Nazdráve.*"

They tossed down their brandies. Zvezdev poured two more.

"So where is the fellow?" Rhodes took more brandy from the Bulgarian.

"In the kitchen. You'll meet him in a moment. Good doing business with you, Weston. *Nazdráve.*"

"*Nazdráve.*"

They drank again.

"Let's get to it, shall we?" Rhodes said. "Clock's ticking."

"Of course. Follow me. Oh, wait. I almost forgot." Zvezdev reached into his left coat pocket and produced the Makarov and handed it to him. "You'll need this."

The kitchen was attached to the living room, separated by two green woolen Army blankets that served as a room divider. Zvezdev pushed through the blankets, Rhodes followed.

Inside the kitchen was a wood-burning stove, a small refrigerator, cupboards, and a table and chairs.

And a corpse.

The body lay sprawled on the wooden floor, face-down, the head matted with blood.

"Is that my defector?" Rhodes asked. His eyes drifted to the table: a stack of money, a bag of coke.

"Yes. A filthy Roma, but a good smuggler."

"What happened?"

"Earlier this evening, I followed him here. Discovered him taking the money you gave him for the drugs he brought you. I came in just as you shot him, but you turned your gun on me, and I had to shoot. At least, that will be the official story in my report."

Rhodes felt the blood drain out of his face. "What's the problem we're having here, Tervel? I thought we had an understanding."

Zvezdev raised his pistol and pointed it at Rhodes's face. "We did, until you threatened me."

"I just needed one big score, I told you that."

"Sure, 'one big score,' and then there would be an-other and then another, always with the threat hanging over my head. I know how it works, Weston. I use the same technique myself." He nodded at the corpse. "He was a problem, too. Two birds? Is that what you say? And when I tell my bosses, they will be pleased. Maybe even give me a medal."

A man's scream broke outside the farmhouse. Zvezdev turned toward the living room. Rhodes raised his Makarov and pulled the trigger.

*Click.*

Empty. Rhodes's heart sank.

Zvezdev had switched guns on him.

Gunshots rang out as the front door crashed open. They couldn't see what was happening.

Zvezdev pivoted toward Rhodes, his pistol held high, as more shots rang out from the living room.

Rhodes recoiled from the gunfire, slamming his back against the kitchen wall. The butt of the Bulgarian's gun cracked into Rhodes's head, knocking him senseless.

Zvezdev grabbed Rhodes by the collar and retreated to the back of the kitchen as the body of one of his men crashed through the blankets and spilled onto the floor, an ax buried in his spine—followed by Paul, blood spattered and crazed, a gun in his fist.

Zvezdev lifted his pistol to shoot, but Rhodes had recovered enough to push the Bulgarian's arm down as he fired. Paul grunted as blood erupted from his knee.

Paul grabbed at his wound with one hand as he went down, but he lifted his pistol with his other, taking aim at Zvezdev, now cowering behind Rhodes. He held a fistful of Rhodes's hair in one hand and jammed his pistol into the back of Rhodes's neck.

"Weston! Tell him to put the gun down!" Zvezdev shouted from behind Weston's back. "We can work this out!"

Rhodes's hands were up, his face a grimace of pain and fear.

"Paul! He's right. Take it easy. We can work this out."

Paul's aim didn't waver. "Let him go."

"Drop your gun first," Zvezdev shouted.

"Let him go," Paul repeated.

"Okay. Okay. I'll let him go. Don't shoot. All friendly, yes?"

Zvezdev released his grip on Rhodes and lowered the pistol.

Paul saw Rhodes relax.

Zvezdev shoved Rhodes forward, took aim—

Paul's weapon fired.

# 78

The rifles fired a third time. The seven CIA Honor Guardsmen lowered their weapons and stood at ceremonial rest.

Jack Junior stood solemnly, his eyes glued to the casket as it lowered into the ground. It should've been him being put into the cold earth today, not Paul. He felt grateful, and ashamed.

The funeral ended. President Ryan shook hands and offered condolences to the friends and family in attendance, ignoring his chief of staff's silent reminders. They were supposed to be wheels-up in forty-five minutes for the flight to Beijing, and they were more than an hour away from the airport. Ryan shot him a look that finally drove Arnie off. *First things first.*

Jack Junior approached a distinguished silver-haired gentleman chatting with John Clark. He offered his hand. "Captain Miller, good to see you again. I just wish it wasn't under these circumstances."

The airline pilot smiled. "I understand, on both counts."

"How do you two know each other?" Clark asked.

"I could ask you the same thing," Jack said.

"David and I go back a long way, don't we?"

"When dinosaurs ruled the earth."

The two old vets shared a chuckle, and obviously an unspoken bond.

"And you both knew Paul," Jack said.

"All of us old-timers knew Paul Brown," Miller said. He glanced back at the grave. "It's a shame more people won't."

Jack shook Miller's hand again. "Take care."

"Same to you."

Jack drifted over to the other gravestones, weathered but well maintained. A lot of Browns. Paul was laid to rest next to Carmen, but he was surrounded by five generations of family. A long history in one place. Jack felt a hand on his shoulder.

"How's that busted wing coming along?"

Gerry's voice was unmistakable. Jack turned around and lifted his cast. "You know, this thing would make a pretty good weapon."

"I bet. And how are you doing, son?"

Jack shrugged. "Can't shake the feeling I let Paul down."

Gerry shook his head. "You were out of commission. Paul stood up when it counted." He nodded back toward the grave. "He's with Carmen now. He would tell you everything is as it should be. The two of you did a helluva job. Thanks to you, the world economy is still humming along, and the world never knew about it. That's a good day's work, as far as I'm concerned."

"Paul was the one who figured it out while I was running around chasing my own tail. Speaking of which, any news on Yong Fairchild?"

"Probably in China for the foreseeable future. The Dalfan deal with Marin Aerospace is dead in the water. Dalfan stock took a hit because of that, but not too bad, and the Singapore authorities are combing over their databases and records to see what Yong might have stolen. It's a mess, but not a catastrophe, thanks to your tail chasing."

"Thanks."

"I just got off the line with the AG. No charges will be filed against you by the Singapore authorities for anything you did over there."

"You read my after-action report. That's hard to believe."

"Dr. Fairchild is an influential man, and Lian made you out to be quite the hero. The government of Singapore is officially 'grateful for your service.'"

Jack shrugged. "I'll take it."

Gerry pulled him closer. "And the thirty million dollars of emergency aid we're sending them for the cleanup effort didn't hurt any, either."

Jack rolled his eyes. "Seriously?"

"They need the help after that typhoon, believe me." Gerry turned serious. "I also wanted you to hear this from me. Rhodes cut a deal with the FBI."

"What?"

"It's the way the world works, son. You bait the hook with the little fish in order to land the big fish. That software on Rhodes's USB drive was dangerous stuff. Our people are sure it was written by the North Koreans, but Rhodes never dealt with them, only a middleman by the name of Zvezdev. We need to roll up Zvezdev if we're going to nail Choi's hide to the wall. So it's going to be fifteen years at a Club Fed for the ex-senator, seven with good behavior."

Jack shook his head, disgusted. "Can I at least get in on the action?"

"I'm afraid not. Mary Pat is running the Zvezdev operation. But I'm certain we'll have some black-side work coming up soon—if you're up for it."

Jack grinned. "Are you kidding? A black-side op sounds great. After a white-side gig like Singapore, I could use the rest."

# 79

Zvezdev had purchased the modest stone-and-red-tiled home because it was on the Adriatic Coast and he loved the sunset, and also because it was near his favorite beach bar. Or at least that's what the real estate agent said in her interview with the SOA, Croatia's intelligence service.

The American team leader was on sat comms waiting for orders from DNI Foley. The seven men under his command—three Croatians, four Americans—wore tactical gear and NVGs. The team leader assured her that four hours of surveillance found no evidence of either guards or kinetic defenses.

"Place looks empty," he reported.

Bad intel, or bad luck, Foley offered. She gave the word to go.

The breaching team went first, the others followed.

They cleared each room. Nobody was there, least of all Zvezdev.

The NVGs came off and someone popped the lights on. The team leader ordered a thorough check of the house, and to bag any evidence they found. They'd all been briefed. Zvezdev was tied to a North Korean operation, and they needed to shut it down.

One of the Croatians opened the refrigerator, half looking for a cold water—or a beer. Instead, he found something else.

"What the fuck is that?" the Croatian asked the man standing next to him.

An American named Suh took the chilled jar from his hand. "Looks like *kimchi*."

"What's that?"

"Korean food. Fermented cabbage, onions, chilis—you name it." Suh unscrewed the jar and sniffed it. "Smells funny."

He held the jar closer to his face. Examined it closely. His eyes narrowed.

"Oh, hell no."

The team leader broke into his comms. "Say again?"

Suh rescrewed the cap.

"I think we found Zvezdev."

**Tom Clancy** was the author of more than eighteen #1 *New York Times* bestselling novels. His first effort, *The Hunt for Red October*, sold briskly as a result of rave reviews, then catapulted onto the bestseller list after President Reagan pronounced it "the perfect yarn." Clancy was the undisputed master at blending exceptional realism and authenticity, intricate plotting, and razor-sharp suspense. He died in October 2013. Visit tomclancy.com and facebook.com/tomclancyauthor.

**Mike Maden** grew up working in the canneries, feed mills, and slaughterhouses of California's San Joaquin Valley. A lifelong fascination with history and warfare ultimately led to a Ph.D. in political science, focused on conflict and technology in international relations. Like millions of others, he first became a Tom Clancy fan after reading *The Hunt for Red October*; he began his published fiction career in the same techno-thriller genre with *Drone* and continued with the sequels *Blue Warrior*, *Drone Command*, and *Drone Threat*. Maden is honored to be "joining The Campus" as a writer in Tom Clancy's Jack Ryan, Jr., series. Visit mikemaden.com, facebook.com/mikemadenauthor, and twitter.com/MikeMadenAuthor.